Vita Maglia

A novel by Brit Malorie

Hi Amelia,

Thanks and please enjoy it!

B. Malorie

April 19, 2014

This book is dedicated to the greatest man in my life,

my Dad.

I love you more than all the words I've ever written.

Chapter 1

He had to find the boy before nightfall. The island was no place for an old man, but once dark fell, things could get a hell of a lot worse for someone like him. Hale Brecker quivered as seawater trickled down the back of his neck. Pain flared up in the cinched skin of his bound wrists. A swell smashed into the side of the boat and tossed him into younger bodies. The boat's hold was full of runaway teens and twenty-somethings, but the blindfolds only added to their excited chatter. An island so secret no one could know the route or coordinates. Brecker whispered fiercely to himself: "Find the boy and get off the island, find the boy . . . wait." He kept forgetting. Zander was no longer the boy he remembered, but a defiant young man, running as far as possible from his father's scientific research.

Brecker picked up bits and pieces from the excited chatter around him: how the island of Kadera was like no place in the world, without law or boundaries, something supernatural. South of the Cook Islands, the land was not claimed by any country. As far as Brecker could tell, whoever controlled it remained invisible. And for young people looking to escape, whether from police, predators, or furious parents, Kadera was pure freedom. But at what cost?

There were voices above him and the heavy thud of ropes landing on the upper deck. After the workers unbound everyone and removed the blindfolds, Brecker massaged feeling back into his arms and legs. He tried to remember all of his careful planning, but would any of it matter? The dock crew had taken everyone's cell phones away, so he was completely on his own. He'd have to go by instinct to even find the young man, something he didn't have much of. Brecker wasn't a spy or ex-military, just a simple doctor. To tell the truth, he looked like he'd gotten lost on a garden tour in Florida. He ran his hands quickly through his hair, wishing he'd dyed out some of the gray or added makeup to cover the sagging lines in his skin. His khaki bag rested tight against his lower torso. It was loaded with a few official-looking documents and cash sewn into the sides. How much would it take to lure Zander home?

A flag rippled above the dock. Its background was a deep purple with traces of blood-red. Seven concentric circles rose up on it, creating a hypnotic effect. As the kids swarmed the docks, a strange blending occurred: Australian, Italian, American, Thai, all swiftly converted to Kaderian, an alien species with its own language. Maybe that's why Brecker felt caught in a dream. One kid had a line of piercings from the tip of his chin down to his chest. Smoke rings of plum and passion fruit floated up from miniature cigarettes. Sunscreen and alcohol fumes mixed in with the fruit, making Brecker queasy. Girls with doe-soft eyes bumped along, sucking on pacifiers with patches of denim stuck strategically over their bare bodies. Another kid had a ghoulish tattoo of a brain printed on his bare skull and blood ink trickling down his shoulders from the blackened bullet holes. Glances flickered at Brecker and away, so quick he might have imagined them. He chuckled at his own paranoia. Why would anyone care about him?

He'd long ago lost patience for the wild places of the young, but his friend Jason would have loved exploring Kadera. Jason Grace had done quite a bit of traveling after his wife died, bringing trinkets back home to his young son, Zander. About five years ago, Brecker had noticed his friend had become obsessed with a recent project. Jason had finally confessed that he'd made a tremendous discovery, something that would change the world. Brecker had responded by laughing so hard his sides ached. But he wasn't laughing now. In fact, he'd been made head of the discovery since Jason died three months ago. A discovery that would bridge the gaps between science and the paranormal, the human brain and the soul. But a pivotal piece lay on this island. Zander might be stubborn and selfish, but he was also needed to continue his father's research. Leaving him to rot in this godforsaken place was not an option.

Herds of bodies smacked into him, hooting and shoving. Brecker scanned the top of the crowd for that familiar head of copper strands. He really should have left this up to his security team, but he wanted to give Zander a choice, not force him home with guerrilla warfare tactics. Brecker bent over and caught his breath, the hills spiking ache through his knees. He looked out over the island. Forested mountains touched the clouds in the aquamarine sky. Cliffs devoured by ferns and vines, a jungle thrusting up from sand and stone. The ocean shone in gradients of blue-green glass. The land was crescent-shaped, with several lagoons jutting in from the ocean. A mountain range provided the boundary between the eastern and western halves. The western half lay concealed beneath a thick growth of tropical canopy. A single tree rose above the canopy. He headed into the eastern rim of the island and met white sand beaches dotted with huts and tiny hostels. His skin stuck to his linen shirt, with pools of sweat collecting under his arms and trailing down his shorts.

The path opened into a large square of activity. A powerful drumbeat coursed up through the ground. Brecker sighed—he didn't see Zander anywhere. Hours seemed to fly by and he only grew more lost. He kept meaning to ask someone, but that damn drumbeat burrowed into his neck and made him lightheaded. The smells changed rapidly, from rank pools of body odor to fresh sea-life to the never-ending smoke. Fingertips scraped the back of his neck and he flinched. Brecker turned quickly but couldn't catch who was doing it. There was so much touch here: stroking of hair and skin, licking of earlobes and chins. He closed his eyes and colors flashed against his lids. Dark pink and vivid spring green mixed with shades of cinnamon. The smells climbed up into his head and he wanted more. He wanted to bury himself in the stench of the sea and bodies and fruit, like he could go crazy.

He passed a man and a woman spreading paint over each other's skin. The woman cooed, letting the man massage the dark into her flesh. He lit a flame and bent down, the tiny light flickering at the woman's heel, then drew it up along her side. Brecker moved to stop them, then watched, paralyzed as the fire swirled in great rings around her body.

"It tingles," the woman crooned, raising her hands in the sun. The flames fanned out in the breeze.

A whisper near his earlobe. "Don't look too long."

"Won't they get hurt?" he asked the air, his voice dreamy. The couple hugged and the fire jumped in great swells between them. Piercing yells turned into moans. The flames dissolved, leaving an iridescent glow on the skin. No one else seemed concerned. Brecker shook himself out of his daze, then spied the small can of black paint the couple had used. He pocketed it.

He caught the gaze of another woman from across the crowd. She was older like him, with deep lines creasing her eyes and mouth. She seemed disturbed over something. Sunlight hit her hand, making Brecker wince. The shine of a photograph? Her fingers clutched and smoothed the photo out as her voice climbed above the din. The crowd quieted and watched her morosely. "Where is she?" Her unwashed hair swayed around her face as she shouted. "My daughter, Sara. Help me find her. Where is she? What did you do to her?" Her voice rose and she punched out at several kids who turned from her. She made it to Brecker and her hand formed a hook, scraping down his side. She fell to her knees and he tried to help her up.

The air rippled around his face, a rush of heat and dampness. The strangest feeling passed through him. Everyone drew back, yet there was a morbid curiosity in the crowd's gaze. Out of the silence came scraping sounds. The woman let out a painful moan and pulled at her blouse. Brecker closed his eyes for just a second, the briefest moment. Her voice was so loud and the sun so bright. Then it happened. Tiny slices appeared on her lips and chin. They curved down her neck, the slashes rising across her chest. Her cheekbones bloomed in red smears. Impossible. Flesh cutting on its own? Her eyes bulged and she choked, her body whipping around as crimson rings encircled her throat. She clawed at the invisible, at the breathless air. Her movements slowed, her arms folded, then her legs collapsed. Brecker watched as men approached her from both sides and lifted her up. This must be a dream. That's why his mind reached for her, but his hands remained weighted at his sides. Then she was gone. A breeze flowed through and shivered the downy hair on his forearms. The daze lifted and the chatter rose up again. Everyone drifted away.

The thing that he couldn't quite wrap his head around, the thing that had to be imagined . . . the edge of black along the cuts. Dark blossoms that grew with the blood, that looked so damn familiar. And the sound of each cut. Like something gnawing on the flesh. But there was nothing there. He saw nothing. It couldn't be . . . it had to be. . . .

Brecker hugged himself, a sudden desire to crumple like she did, to be very small and far from this tragic place. What was happening here? He kept seeing her face, the sheer helplessness in it. He paused, willing his heartrate to go down. He was overreacting. The attack on the woman had to be an illusion, something to entertain the kids.

He looked at the sky, a bit stunned. He could have sworn the sun was right above him, about noon and now it seemed more western, like it had moved forward alarmingly fast. Dusk was coming. He should have a few more hours, yet his body wouldn't stop trembling. What would arrive on Kadera without the sun? A year ago he would've laughed at himself, a befuddled old man afraid of the dark. He'd traded ideas of God and Satan for a foundation of science and medicine. But now he knew better. His faith had slowly returned, not because of his Catholic boyhood, but because of what Jason Grace had found. The discovery. What it meant for every person . . . alive and dead. . . .

A girl crossed his path. She couldn't have been older than sixteen, her hair a mass of blond tangles streaked with rust color. A choker stretched tight across her neck, a series of triangular black shells. Each shell's surface lay etched with white strands, like spiderwebs flung over ebony. Her tongue made a clicking noise.

Maybe she could help him. He started to pull out Zander's photograph, but her fingertips caught his wrist, leaving indents of heat. Brecker closed his eyes and felt a stirring, a flash of a cottage, someone grabbing the back of her neck, cutting the blond hair. And a name. Cye.

"I know who you're looking for. Come," she whispered. He hesitated. How could she know? She must be wrong, but perhaps she could take him further into the island.

The girl spun in a circle twice and pointed to herself. "Cye."

Strips of cloth were slung over her shoulders and around her hips, any bare skin awash in freckles. Her feet were sheathed in shoes of sand. Cye stayed three feet ahead, gracefully weaving in and out of the crowd, hips rising and falling with the drums. The dark shells could be found everywhere—on clothing, in jewelry, even scattered on the beach.

"Come," she ordered. She led him further underneath the tropical canopy. Brecker held his head as he swayed with nausea. Why was it so hard to concentrate? Dammit. He really needed to gauge his location, but the canopy only let in slivers of light.

Finally, they came to a wall of solid vines. Cye lifted the plants and he climbed through. A lagoon lay before them, enclosed on three sides by cliffs carved from volcanic rock. Scores of black and white birds floated on the turquoise water. A waterfall cascaded down the far side, the fine mist coating Brecker's face and neck. Teens were cliff-diving nude, holding their noses closed and screaming. Cye's head flicked around slyly, looking for what? Brecker realized she was much more aware than she appeared, with brief snatches of lucidity in the blank eyes. She never looked at the bag he carried. Balancing on her bare toes, she slid down a rock incline to the cavernous space behind the waterfall. Everything was soaked and very dark back there. The water thundered in his ears. He had to go by her facial expressions and fast hand movements for direction.

Brecker glanced longingly at the eastern side. The docks seemed very far away and he had no idea of where they were going. Why was he doing this? He paused a moment. Yes, he was doing this for the research, but as vital as that was, Zander's life was more so. The boy couldn't lose his life here, like that woman, that screaming woman. . . .

Cye slipped her hand behind a human-sized boulder. She slid onto her belly and tucked her head underneath. Her wire-thin body slipped through quickly and Brecker found himself alone. He felt behind the rock and couldn't see anything. There was nothing there, just slime and rough edges.

"I can't fit," Brecker shouted. His hand found a space behind the large rock. It appeared impossible; he would get stuck almost immediately. A significant drop, perhaps to a tunnel? There had to be another way.

"Trust." A single word echoed from the space. As strange as it sounded, he believed the girl. It was that lone touch, a memory passed between strangers. The barest edge of a survival bond. Brecker wrapped the strap of his bag around his ankle, took a deep breath and crawled inside headfirst. A loud whoosh of air escaped his throat. Wet sand piled into his shirt as he squirmed through, compacting his ribs into his lungs. He crawled towards the specks of light.

He popped out of the tunnel, struggling. He felt himself lifted up; the girl was curiously strong.

"It's a city," he said, bewildered. So this was what the canopy and the mountains hid from view. There were several dome-shaped buildings molded from translucent green glass. They were blanketed in vines and tropical flowers like they'd sprung straight out of the earth. A tributary split the city in half and poured through the rockwall, forming the waterfall Brecker had climbed behind. The saltwater ran crystal clear:

streaks of magenta and indigo propelled across the surface as tropical fish searched for food. Sand lizards in speckled brown and olive-green jumped near his sandals.

Men and women carried supplies by canoe down the tributary. Laboratory equipment was tied securely to one canoe, while another held four liter glass jugs. The people carefully unloaded the supplies onto carts and rolled them into one of the buildings. Paths of white crystal crunched under his feet. They all walked barefoot, their skin sinking into the spiky surface. What was going on here? Some kind of scientific commune paradise? Brecker ran his hand through his hair. He was desperate to enter one of those domes but stopped himself. There was hostility in the air, a protectiveness.

The people here were still young but more alert somehow. In fact, they seemed too cautious. Shifty. The slightest breeze ran through the city and all the exposed limbs quivered in violent spasms, as if whatever made the kids alert also increased their sensitivity. Their eyelids fluttered in ecstasy at the prickly rush. Hence, there were barely any clothes: the women were in beaded skirts and bikinis, the men bare-chested in surfshorts. Octagonal wooden tables sat covered in split mangoes, darkly skinned coconuts, papayas, and green bananas. Mixed in with the fruit were tall amber bottles full of liquid. Brecker grabbed one and grimaced at the smell. It overpowered him, repugnant, like a mixture of strong herbs and kerosene. He was about to replace it on the table when his fingertips buzzed. Then they buzzed again, spasming, yearning for the liquid. He had to forcibly remove his hand.

A haze filled the sky, like smoke clearing out. It gave the air a shimmery quality, like he was breathing in cloud. Brecker braced himself against the rock. He inhaled full breaths but only grew dizzy. He could understand why some of the kids stayed near the ground. If the air had a slight inebriating effect outside, the city was unbearable. A metal sign lay on the ground, bent and corroded, with the name "Marae" in white paint.

Cye appeared to be looking for someone. She stopped and closed her eyes, her hands outstretched, sniffing the air. Brecker waited, perplexed. "I should tell you who I need to find . . ." he trailed off.

She moved again, her hands drawn close, fluttering against her chest like an injured bird.

There was something else. Brecker kept seeing broken legs, missing eyes and fingers, even reddish burns on the side of faces. What was happening to these people? His throat thickened, adrenaline kick-starting his heart. It was as if the island were a predator that had injected him with some kind of venom. Now it only waited for him to weaken before the kill. He couldn't think, he couldn't strategize against it. His nose and mouth grew numb. He needed to find Zander and get the hell out of here. Cye touched someone, a body crumpled in a low-lying hammock between two palm trees. "Honey," she cooed. She took a melon lying on the ground and scooped out the center, then slid the pale green slivers into his mouth. Liquid dripped off her fingers and she slowly licked the trails of juice along his face. The body stirred.

Brecker came closer. "You have the wrong person."

That couldn't be Zander. Skin stretched over his ribs like wax, eerily pale. He looked emaciated, nearly comatose. The doctor pushed Cye aside and felt along the boy's neck for a pulse. It was very faint. Anger rolled through Brecker so much that his hands shook with it. What had these people done to the boy? He wanted to protect, to cradle and heal. He had to get Zander out of here.

Brecker pulled him roughly out of the hammock and carried him through the crowd. People turned to watch them. Fear numbed his legs and spine, but he kept moving. Something was horribly wrong here. He had to get Zander back to the tourist area, safe and secure in real civilization. Safe. Secure. Brecker counted backward in his head, an old trick from his emergency room residency. But the numbers kept spinning.

He just wanted to lie down and make the dizziness go away. His chest felt compacted with sharp pains, a heart attack?

Where was the girl? Cye had disappeared. The tunnel. His eyes searched but only found a solid stretch of rock wall. Damn mirage effect. How was he going to get Zander to the other side? There had to be a real entrance. Did everyone just burrow through like moles? He scraped at the rock feebly. Someone had to help him. They must understand how sick Zander was. Brecker needed to drop him, to rest. His muscles kept shaking and his vision faded. Everything swam around him.

The realization came. He had to slow down his thoughts to comprehend.

Silence. All the muttering, the chatter, the laughter had stopped. A dozen men and women surrounded him. A new cunning seeped through the dazed looks. It was too late.

He backed up until he hit the rocks. The crowd surged. Zander fell out of his arms and Brecker was buried under pummeling fists and hard knees. Harsh coughs racked his body. He turned over; the wavy vision of a fist above him. It landed in his solar plexus and pain seared his chest. He curled into a tight ball as feet slammed into him. Shrieks and screams and cheers roared. Oh God, it felt like he was dying.

Brecker moaned, bracing himself to sit up. Fingers dug into his shoulders and shoved him down, grinding his face into the white crystals, cutting deep grooves in his skin. Female laughter bubbled up on his left. Every breath sent a fresh burst of pain up his sides. A hand pulled him up by his hair and slammed his head against the rock. Everything went black.

Chapter 2

A lone howl rang through his blood, reverberating from his head to his feet. It cut off short, like a wolf in pain. There were wolves in Colorado, but he couldn't be home yet. He had to get Zander first. A hand lifted him up by the back of his head so he sat upright. A man stared down at him. Light reflected off metal. There was metal on the man's face. Brecker tried to process this when the man waved a hand and silenced the barbarians. That brat Cye hovered next to him, Brecker's bag clutched in her greedy paws.

Why was it so dark? He realized it was near dusk. Dusk and the last boat had sailed—there was no way out of this nightmare.

"Do you like him?" Cye murmured.

"Hush, dove." The man had green eyes, vivid with hints of gray. His hair was dark brown and slightly curled. A flash of light glanced off his chin again. A metallic plate along his jaw? Brecker's eyes widened. The guy was built like a tree, over six feet tall with great swaths of muscle around his torso and arms. There was a keen awareness in his eyes, a probing quality, as if deciding the most entertaining place to cut or punch or rip.

The man knelt down near Brecker and spoke slowly. "My name is Lynch Katlan and this is my island. You were caught stealing one of my bodies."

"These are real people, not your damn prisoners," Brecker shouted back, then grimaced as a ferocious pain crawled up his side. A fractured rib? It felt like razors floated inside his skull. There was wetness in his hair, possibly blood? A concussion? To reduce his panic, he began short, paced breaths. He had the strangest sensation of being outside his body. Cold fear trickled down his neck, a fear of the madness that must rattle inside this man's mind. Could he really lose his life here? He shut his eyes, trying to remain upright. What if he didn't return to Colorado?

Lynch leaned in close. There was a scent in the air, something like . . . Brecker searched for it. A breeze of peppermint?

"What do you do for your life?" the man asked.

Brecker paused. What an odd question. He couldn't think to lie. "I'm a physician and a scientist."

Lynch nodded. "Then you must appreciate my work here."

"Yes." The word was out before Brecker knew he'd said it. What did the guy mean? Marae, the scientific supplies? All these sick people, the missing limbs?

The crowd went silent, anticipation rubbing against itself. Lynch stood and pulled a square of cloth out of his pocket. He worked the fabric over every inch of skin on his hands, quick yet methodical. His gaze returned to the door of the closest building.

"You disrupted me," he said quietly to Cye. "This work takes precision, concentration."

She bit her lip, meek again. "But he was trying to steal Z—"

He hushed her, then pulled out a fresh cloth from his pocket. He repeated the process on his hands.

Pain shot up Brecker's ribs. He winced and shifted over an inch.

Lynch's head snapped around. He watched the doctor's side.

"I'm sure you can appreciate my dilemma," he said. "Discipline is the heart of any great system, but it's essential with unstable minds like these."

"Of course, lawlessness is vital as well." Lynch chuckled and motioned to the eastern side of the island. "The perfect lure. It pulls in so many bodies." He drew out the last word, as if tasting it.

It wasn't the sight of the man's face that scared Brecker; in fact, he was quite handsome, deceptively angelic. It was something in the eyes. Eyes that wouldn't stop flickering to Brecker's wounded side. Lynch grinned. "I wish we could get some privacy. I have these tools. . . ." He twisted his hand in the air. "Well, I believe you're a man who can appreciate a unique design."

His palm slid along the back of Brecker's neck. The doctor's insides heaved as he spoke. "You're not going to get away with this. Whatever you're doing to these poor kids."

The edges of Lynch's eyes crinkled for a second, in disappointment? He pulled his hand away and let out a guttural laugh. His back and neck muscles relaxed. "I'm not sure what you mean. Kadera is paradise. Nothing more. Nothing less."

"Fine, kick me out then." Brecker stayed still, his head in agony, his vision blurred. *Don't look away. Don't look down or away.*

Lynch made a harsh clicking noise with his tongue and turned. Brecker sighed. The inquisition was over and he was no threat, a mosquito of a man. A reasonable man who lived among reasonable people. Insanity was something to read about in manuals, not bargain with in the jungle. Furious shouts erupted from the barbarians surrounding them.

"Come on," Cye growled, her hands trembling.

"Not yet, dove. The crowd needs their show." Lynch did a half-turn and issued his command: "Burn him in Kyre."

Screams took over and fists struck the air. Two men came up and grabbed Brecker's arms. Lynch and Cye went inside one of the domed buildings. The men dragged him and the crowd followed with chants. Brecker's feet kept catching on the sand as he kicked and struggled. His mind refused to accept what was happening. How could a gang of thugs just do this? Only yards away, tourists were laughing and joking and eating spiced fish.

They dragged Brecker down an isolated stretch of beach to a small pile of wood. He searched the faces of the two men, trying to comprehend that they were actually going to let him burn. One of the guys was heavyset with a double chin and a bald head. He moved slowly, twitching ever so often. The other was much smaller, wire-thin like Cye, probably about her age. Sunglasses covered his eyes and his black hair stood up in clumps. Stubble painted his face and his skin was surprisingly pale.

"Hey, Pete? Is this enough?" The heavier one asked, but the smaller guy watched Brecker intensely. Shades of crimson and tangerine painted the horizon. Sunset was coming.

"Nah, Alex, the guy won't burn on that little pile. Let's really build it up. Lynch has to see it from his beach."

"He said it's not supposed to get that big," Alex whined.

"Trust me. It'll be awesome." Pete added thick planks of rotting wood to the pile.

Alex let out a happy giggle and gathered branches from farther down the beach. When he was out of earshot, Brecker crawled over to Pete. The crowd milled around, eager yet distracted.

"Please, you have to—"

The kid put a finger up to his lips and shook his head.

Brecker sat quiet. Was this some kind of trick? After Cye, he couldn't believe anyone here. Besides, his money was gone and the last boat had left.

Alex came back and they layered the gray, worn planks into a pile. They forced Brecker onto the pile and tied wide ropes around his mid-section. Pete pulled a metal flask out of his pocket and shook liquid onto the wood. Brecker expected whiffs of lighter fluid, but instead met something citrus and sour.

He shivered as he watched the eager faces in the crowd. He'd never actually seen human beings so devoid of empathy, worse than animals. He couldn't appeal to any of them.

Pete took out a lighter and flicked it open. Every eye grew wide and watched the tiny flame.

"You want to see him BURN?" Pete shouted and the people screamed back. The kid lit one of the soaked branches. Brecker stared up at the sky. It still wouldn't sink in. He thought the hardest part of this trip would be convincing the boy to come home. That should have been the hardest part . . . Zander. He'd probably die in this place as well and no one back home would know what happened. Sorrow filled his heart as the flame flushed the wood in slow motion. It appeared to leak out with the glow that had been on the couple's skin. The glow blew out into the dusk, creating a plasmic radiance. It zipped up the branches, spreading over the pile in a matter of seconds. There was this strange tingling that started at his legs. This wasn't so bad. Perhaps it would be over soon.

As amazing as the Kyre was, Kadera's sunset was that much more. Streaks of fuchsia and marigold climbed over the horizon. The flames pooled with the sky's blaze, spurring them higher. The sunset bent back to the billowing fire, the colors streaming in circles. Shapes of animals and birds flickered in the tapestry, designing stories in the air. Smells of kelp and brine inflamed Brecker's nose and mouth. He could no longer trust his own mind, the Kyre annihilating the edges of his perception. The flames swallowed him whole, a heat so vicious it chilled him to the spine. It felt like the smoke burrowed under his skin, gathering itself only to split him open and spill out onto the sand.

The sunset breathed and pulsed like a giant heart. He couldn't close his eyes as something inside him strained to connect with the radiance. As he realized he was about to die, Brecker's mind seized in wonder. "What is this place?" he murmured, the words evaporating on his lips.

A whisper near his earlobe: "Can you see it? The extra fire. . . ."

"Yes," he sputtered, the smoke filling his lungs for the last time.

Brit Malorie

Chapter 3

Sand poured into his mouth and piled high onto his chest. Brecker sputtered, his throat retching and rejecting it with plenty of saliva, his muscles convulsing. The blaze still ran hot against his eyelids. He saw the crowd and skittered backward—they'd come for him again. But every person stood hypnotized by the magic interplay between sunset and flame. This Kyre was definitely much bigger than Lynch must have intended. It effectively neutralized the crowd, turning them into entranced zombies. Brecker felt along his arms and clothes. How was he still here?

Pete helped him up and they climbed up the sidepath, heading for a grove of palm trees.

"What is that stuff?"

Pete shrugged. "Kyre? Kadera fire. No one really knows."

"What were the chemicals in your flask?"

He chuckled. "It's not the chemicals."

Brecker stopped suddenly, his throat and skin still hot. "It's some kind of drug, isn't it? The food's laced, the drinking water. Whatever's in those amber bottles."

"You'll never believe me."

Brecker wished his heart would stop racing. There was this overwhelming sense of urgency, like every second could be the end. The images from the Kyre popped through his brain like a psychedelic.

Pete interrupted his thoughts. "Do you have any money on you? More than what Cye took in that bag?" Brecker hesitated. So that's what this was about. The kid's hands wouldn't stop shaking. He couldn't get whatever drug he craved, hard as that was to believe in this place.

"I can get money in the Cook Islands," Brecker replied. "I'll wire for as much as you need. But the last boat's already left."

"There's another one that comes through a couple of times a month. For special deliveries." He pointed down to the beach. "I've unloaded it a few times, so I know the layout and the crew." Pete looked back, hesitant. "I had a feeling you might be my ticket out. I came here with Zander almost a year ago. I'm sick of it. I'm sick of the endless work, the beach, the idiots."

He refocused on Brecker. "The boat docks on Lynch's private beach. It's dangerous, but not as dangerous as staying the night. The crowd won't be distracted long. Once Lynch finds out you're gone, he'll search the entire island."

"What about Zander?"

Pete stopped, his jaw tense. "Are you kidding? Listen to me carefully, old man. They. Will. Kill. You." His hands caressed the tattoo around his neck. "A protective order was put on Zander a couple of days ago. Something's about to happen. I wouldn't be surprised if he disappeared any minute."

"That's why it has to be now."

The kid shook his head. "Zander's important. Nobody knows why, he doesn't even know. But he's not allowed to leave. Ever. You have to save yourself."

Brecker paused. His veins flooded with adrenaline, the need to escape, retreat. Maybe he should just come back later with his security team or international police and raid the island. Or simply abandon Zander to his choices. The kid had been desperate to get away from Colorado and his father's research. Brecker shook himself. No. No matter how angry he was, no matter how stupid the boy, Zander couldn't stay in this brutal place. The doctor wasn't sure what was going on here, but the child whose broken legs and sprained arms he'd healed would no longer be a part of it.

"No. I can't leave without him."

Pete gazed at him, stupefied. "He means that much?"

"He could mean everything." Brecker felt dizzy. They were running out of time.

Pete murmured absently, "Zander's not supposed to be that sick. Why did he take so much Seed? That amount would kill anyone a dozen times over."

"Sick." Brecker paused, thinking. "What happens when someone needs a hospital, like a medical emergency? Would he be let off the island then?"

"For drugs? We take care of that here."

"If he got burned badly. Third degree. He had too much of the fire. You said it yourself, people are drawn towards it." Brecker ran his fingers over the can of black paint in his pocket. It should be enough if he added something else.

"Tough sell. I've only seen that once, when one of the guys got his arm ripped open."

Pete looked uncomfortable, his eyes moving everywhere. What if he changed his mind and decided betraying Lynch wasn't worth the risk? But there was something else in his eyes, too, a wanderlust that Brecker had caught in Zander a few times. When it was time to move on, these kids would move mountains out of the way.

Brecker's voice grew solemn. "There were dead bodies, weren't there? Mixed in with the unconscious ones."

Pete groaned and shifted away from him then. "Yeah, the doses can be tough to control. Dehydration, infection. There are separate boats for, well, when we sort everyone out."

Brecker didn't want to think about what this kid was saying. "They use bodybags, right? Can you grab one of those and Zander and meet me back here? I have to go back down to the Kyre."

"I don't know, man." Pete's hands shook.

Brecker grabbed his shoulder and steadied him.

The kid nodded. That instant trust again between strangers. "Be careful. The crowd will be coming out of the daze soon," he said.

Brecker slipped down the path. He moved on pure adrenaline, his senses hyperalert. He watched the Kyre from behind some large trees. Some watchers were shaking their heads, standing up and moving away. Others stayed slack-jawed, as if on a powerful high.

When Pete and Alex had built the larger Kyre, he'd seen some of the charred remains from old ones in small piles. Brecker crawled to one of those piles and scooped up the ash into his pockets. His eyes watered; the ashes smelled overwhelmingly of the same chemical in Pete's flask. He crawled as fast as he could back to the path, noisily crashing over broken branches and dodging rocks.

Brecker waited in the spot a few moments, studying the isolated stretch of beach. There were no lights in the houses down there, but Lynch could be in the basement or returning from somewhere—

He heard steps and darted behind some palm trees. What if Pete had been caught? A group of young people passed him, laughing and chatting. Brecker sat frozen, trembling. He'd been so stupid, thinking this was all innocent partying. He wondered if he could somehow make it back to civilization, to the warm tropical drinks and laughter of the tourist area. Those docks seemed very close.

But they'd find him before dawn. They'd never let him on a boat, especially now that he'd escaped and defied that monster, Lynch. And the most important thing: they'd never let Zander go. What could they want with the boy? Unless they knew what he was. If they knew the importance of his father's discovery and Zander's role in it, but that was impossible. The research was protected under the best security, layers of it. Zander didn't even know what it was, so he couldn't have told them. Something itched in Brecker's mind, something familiar about that sunset.

Noises. Brecker lowered himself again, then sighed in relief. Pete hiked up the path, holding a filled bodybag over his shoulder. They found a hidden spot and he set Zander down on the ground. Brecker quickly checked his vitals. The breathing was very shallow, his pulse faint.

"Zander, it's me. You know, your family doctor." The term sounded bizarre in these surroundings. "I'm going to take you home."

Brecker pulled out the can of black paint and dumped the waxy substance over Zander's bare chest and shoulders, up to his neck. He mixed in the ash from the old Kyre pit, letting the black stiffen like tar on Zander's skin, hoping it would pass as burnt flesh in the dark. It smelled chemical, distinctly like Kyre, a blend of too sweet and medicinal.

"Wait. It needs something else." Pete pulled out a knife. He made a small cut on his forearm and held the wound over Zander's chest. Drops of blood sprinkled down onto the paint and ash. Brecker closed his eyes and swayed. The ash and blood and chemical crawled up his spine and clawed into his nose and throat. He wanted to ask Pete why his mouth watered with the smells and his nose tingled with color. And why he could see his own pain, a charcoal black edged in ruddy orange.

Pete zipped the bodybag so only Zander's head showed. He picked him up and they headed down to Lynch's beach.

"The special effects on this island. I have to know."

Pete winked. "You should blame it on the drugs."

"What do you mean?"

"Just," he hesitated. "I've been everywhere, believe me."

Brecker did believe him. His voice had weary age in it, a hardness. The kid sighed. "But I've never been to a place like this. The people aren't special or anything. It's Kadera. The island's special."

The doctor did wonder though. There must be something more. The heavy breathing, the Kyre, that sunset. As if the air were infused with some aerosol psychedelic. The pain in his ribcage dulled to a broader ache through his chest. "But why do people come here? Stay here?" he asked.

"Nowhere to go, man. Everybody's got a reason."

Guided only by moonlight, they traveled slowly. Brecker moved overhanging branches away from Pete's head. They made it down to Lynch's beach, staying close to the cliff wall. Brecker felt his way, his palms grated on the rock, every footstep placed carefully so he wouldn't trip.

Pete stopped about one hundred feet from the dock. Waves lapped lazily onto the sand. Men moved in single file off the boat, carrying boxes up. Another man stood close to the boat. Brecker could see what looked like a large beachhouse about fifty feet on the other side of the dock. His heart trembled—no lights were on. Could they be that fortunate? Perhaps Lynch had already gone down to the other beach and found the Kyre simmering down.

Pete motioned to the water. "Get in. You'll have to swim out to a small ladder on the starboard side. I'll help you up after the boat starts moving."

"What about all those men?"

"They'll stay here. The boat goes back empty for more supplies, so they only need a few guys to run it. We'll have to figure out how to get you off in Rarotonga."

Brecker wanted to ask more questions, but Pete gestured for him to enter the water. Most of the men were now inside the warehouse and the boat's motor started up.

He slid into the warm water. He took a deep breath and stayed under the surface as long as he could, taking shallow, baby strokes. He couldn't extend completely because of the pain in his skull and across his side, but the water reduced the sting. He gently broke the surface to breathe. Pete carried Zander across the beach and up the long dock. His head bent at a submissive angle, as if he were just a drone carrying out an order.

"What's going on?" the dockman barked out.

Pete shifted Zander's weight. "Hey, Chuck. Lynch said to take this guy to that hospital in Rarotonga."

"What happened to him?"

"Whadya think? Fucking idiot jumped right in the Kyre. Just boom. Right there."

"So?" Chuck shrugged.

"So look at him."

Chuck peered down, studying the face. "That's not, ah shit."

Pete nodded. "Yeah, it's him. Get there as fast as possible."

"He looks really bad." The dockman reached out. Brecker's heart seized. The guy would realize it was paint and ash.

Pete pulled Zander away from the outstretched hand. "Don't touch him! Have to avoid infection. Let's just get out of here."

Pete started to move past him, but Chuck grabbed his shoulder. Brecker shivered in the water. Slime brushed past his torso and something wound up his leg. He reached down and was rewarded with a swift bite.

"How do I know Lynch approved this? No one gets on the boat."

Pete's eyes flickered to the boat, but he shook off Chuck's grip. He let out a hoarse laugh. "I don't have time for this bullshit. I'm just there, man, chilling next to the Kyre with a Hypna, watching the ladies dance when this guy goes batty and jumps in. I mean, smell the dude. Can't hear him *breathe*. Yeah, he's far gone and I'm wasting nightlight, but when Lynch gives an order, gotta go."

Chuck's eyes strayed to the beachhouse. His leg jittered on the wooden deck.

Pete turned and edged in close, his voice low but furious. "You know what? I'm gonna head up to Lynch's place and let him know Zander Grace is dead because of your lazy ass. It's great you knew about the protective order, but, hey, just let the kid die fifty feet from the beachhouse. Go ahead. Look, he's right there. Go up and say hi." A single light blinked on in the house, shadows flickering through it. Brecker shut his eyes and let out a silent prayer, something he hadn't done since his schooldays at St. Mary's. If that man was there, please don't let him look outside and wonder what held up the boat or who argued on the dock. Let him be distracted just this once, just for one minute.

Chuck peered close to Zander and stood still. The light went out and that seemed to make up his mind. "Alright, okay. I don't, I don't want to bother him. Grace does look bad. Get on and we'll try to speed it up."

Pete let out an irritated chuckle and followed the other man up onto the ship. Brecker felt the ladder rattle as the boat pulled away from the dock. He pressed his face into the wood, thanking whoever was out there for Pete and his smartass hoodlum rhetoric. The dark of the water felt thicker somehow, beckoning. *Just slip in.* His eyes migrated to the house.

***

The door opened and a figure walked outside in bare feet, crushing the sand. He paused a few inches from the water, a lit cigarette between his fingers, the moonlight pooling in the slick metal on his face. He stared at the boat, his head motionless, catching a series of anomalies and tossing them in his mind, daring them to build into something tangible. A motor left too long running, pieces of a heated conversation, and a strange ripple pattern in the water, possibly caused by an obstruction along the starboard side. His palm warmed a cell phone; he opened it and pressed a number. A burst of smoke erupted from his mouth and nostrils. He watched it linger on the moon as a brief halo, then shut the phone mid-ring and slipped it into his pocket.

Chapter 4

Light crept in through the open window and rested on the man, causing him to shift and stir. He lay curled asleep in a narrow armchair, his neck crooked at a painful angle. The room looked like it belonged in a hospital rather than a house. Monitors let out short beeps and screens cast blue lights on the walls. A twin bed lay in the center of the room. An IV trailed out from it like an umbilical cord.

The body in the bed let out a small whimper, and his eyelids fluttered against heavy sleep. Hair partially hid the heart-shaped face. The prominent chin and large cheekbones resembled a classic teen heartthrob, looking much younger and naïve than his twenty-five years. A nurse entered the room and changed out the IV. She bit her lip as she tapped the older man's shoulder.

"I think you can spend tonight in your room, Dr. Brecker. His vitals are nice and steady. He should be awake in a few hours."

Brecker nodded, wincing as he brought his head up. He'd kept watch the last two nights, still suspicious of the rapid improvement in Zander's condition. The nurse handed him the latest lab results.

"Thank you, Caroline," he said absently, scanning the figures.

He worried about the boy's heart. After a childhood accident, Zander had been left with a murmur and a thick bluish ridge of scar tissue on his chest. God knew how much damage these new drugs had accomplished. He scanned the beeping monitors: heartrate, blood pressure, body temperature. The drug that Pete had mentioned: Seed. It appeared the body grew very chilled as this drug left it. Brecker had never seen it before, a derivative of morphine. It acted as a sedative in certain brain regions while stimulating others. He imagined it would be a thrilling high, like one could soar through the sky, with a steep landing, leaving the user wanting more. It looked like Zander would survive, but the drug wouldn't leave his brain for another three weeks, which meant insomnia, severe mood changes, headaches, nausea. Detox.

Standing beside him now, Brecker felt hope. He'd never seen drug concentrations so high. Really the boy should have died, yet there seemed to be no permanent damage. The nurse was right: Zander could wake at any moment. A new fear entered the physician. He knew the Grace temper well. Rather than be grateful for a life restored, Zander would be furious at his capture. A love of freedom flowed through the boy, and Brecker would have to be careful, even devious in deepening his snare here.

Over the last few days, the doctor replayed the events at Kadera, shifting angles, praying that he hadn't let information out, anything that would lead Lynch and his gang back to Colorado. He'd slipped off the boat at the Cook Islands and met Pete at the hospital, trading money for Zander's frail, shivering body. Pete had waved goodbye, jaunting down the street, kicking coconuts out of his path. Brecker's last view of the sarcastic teen had been spikes of black hair and that tattoo stretched long on the back of his neck, with no idea of the value in his choice to save two lives. He could only hope the kid knew how to disappear into thin air.

At the hospital, Brecker had managed to inject Zander with a shot of Naloxone, a drug that reduced opiate levels in the blood. Taking the first plane from Rarotonga to Auckland, he'd seen men searching the airstrip moments before they took off. That's where their trail ended, and that Lynch monster could drive himself insane searching for their scent. Luckily, Brecker knew how to cover his tracks well. Fake passports for Zander and himself. The wire source for Pete's money was re-routed many times and finally blocked. He'd borrowed the cell phone of a fellow tourist on the street in Rarotonga and made a call. He' left an innocent message coded for his security team as to the location and time to pick them up. A plane had picked them up right as they landed on the airstrip in Auckland with no flight plan or crew log. Once he was home, Brecker had tried contacting the authorities in surrounding countries, but it was like hitting a granite wall. They either thought he was making the place up or reassured him the island was just innocent fun for young people.

The doctor now stood in a bedroom at Grace House, a mansion tucked away in the White River National Forest, just outside the town of Redstone in central Colorado. It served as the Graces' family home for the last few decades. Now it also housed the Pensare, pronounced *Pen-sa-ray*, the team of scientists Jason had slowly built up over the last five years. As the Pensare's new leader, Brecker's decision to bring Zander home had not been popular. After Jason's death, they'd discussed all the viable candidates to carry on the experiments, and Zander was the absolute last resort. Everyone was well aware that the boy would be the hardest to convince, the most dedicated to his own selfish needs. He was immature and held a deep jealousy against the research for taking his father away. Yet Brecker believed, as Jason did, that Zander was the natural choice, with a sharp intelligence and a physics background, all combined with courage and curiosity. A hero hidden under layers of resentment and adolescent rebellion.

The nurse propped the door open and exited the room. A cane flashed in the doorway, then lightly scraped the floor. A man came in and stood next to Brecker. Tendrils of white hair lay combed over the bald head. His cardigan hung too large on his bent back.

"Good morning," Isaac whispered. The oldest member of the Pensare at seventy-five, Isaac Rosen had been Jason's mentor in graduate school. A physicist and researcher for decades, he and Brecker had been the first ones let in on the discovery.

"He should wake soon. We have to make some decisions."

"If Zander can survive that level of drugs, he should be able to make it through what we'll ask of him."

"I'm more worried about him staying long enough to find out," Brecker sighed.

A black man in his early forties entered behind Isaac, his long fingers tapping away at his phone. The overhead light reflected on his bald head. At 6'4" he stood taller than the other two men. His small eyes darted behind glasses, hypnotized by the backlit screen. A goatee covered his mouth and chin.

"Did you get the data back from the brain scans?" Brecker asked.

Gage Madison nodded. A recent addition to the Pensare, his expertise in neurology was already proving valuable. "Not as much damage as I'd expect, in fact, pretty minor. I'm sure the Grace genes came into play." A thread of bitterness traced his voice.

All three men were silent as they watched the slumbering body in the bed. Once upon a time, there were patients, clinical trials, labs, academic papers. There was no time for any of that now. Everything revolved around Jason's discovery.

"Let's say Zander does wake up. How do we go about this? Do we just tell him the way Jason told each of us?" Isaac asked.

"His first instinct will be to run, like a caged animal. Especially when he finds out why he's been brought back," Brecker said. "No one tells him anything. Let him recover, physically and mentally. We need to build his trust as much as we can. And his curiosity."

"We won't be able to hold him back for long," Isaac replied.

"If he finds out too soon, we'll lose him," Brecker said adamantly.

Gage interjected. "I still think we should bring in the other travelers."

Brecker groaned. He was sick of this damn argument. "We've tried. They're busy with their own lives."

Gage took off his glasses and looked up at the ceiling. Brecker felt his frustration growing. Why couldn't the man just let it go?

"Zander could destroy everything. The research is fragile, vulnerable," Gage said. "I'll say it until we all go deaf. An addict is the worst possible option. He should stabilize in rehab first."

"And I'll repeat myself again." Brecker's tone turned icy. "You heard the word addict and gave up. I know him better than anyone here, dammit. He's our best chance. Zander only has to travel once and he'll dedicate his life—"

"You're too close to him to be objective," Gage interrupted.

"He's here now." Isaac banged his cane loudly on the floor. "As you're both well aware, we don't have much time. We have to go with what we have. We'll tell Zander the risks and rewards and let him make his own choice. I can't believe you found him and made it out of there, Hale."

Brecker hesitated. He didn't want to say they were all safe yet. Who knew what information Zander let slip on Kadera? Lynch could be on his way to Colorado right now. But they were not without their own defenses. Grace House and the Pensare were protected by a security team, all ex-military based out of Colorado Springs. Even if that man showed up here, it gave Brecker some comfort to think of the firefight he'd have to walk through.

"So, it's agreed? No one breathes a word until he's ready. Let's tell the others," Isaac said. All three men nodded.

Brecker left the room and walked farther down the hallway on the upper floor, surveying the magnificent great room below. He'd visited Grace House frequently over the last few decades as the family's doctor, especially since his medical practice was based in Denver. The mansion had three levels: an upper level, a main floor, and a basement. The hallway he walked down now was actually a balcony that hovered above the vaulted great room of the main floor. Immense pane windows were filled with juniper-pinyon trees, giving the illusion of a treehouse. Broad skylights cut across the ceiling, pouring morning light over the exotic plants clustered on both sides of the entrance. The Grace House seal was inlaid in the hardwood floor, the initials GH carved in a natural stone medallion. Past the seal, there was an elevator that moved between all three floors. Staircases curved around the left and right sides of the elevator.

Underneath each staircase was an entrance to the back areas: the library, the kitchen and dining room, another conference room, and more bedrooms. There was an overall feeling of space and light, yet the house also branched into intimate nooks and secluded rooms. The basement contained a full laboratory with ventilation and offices for the Pensare members. Outside, the driveway curved around a natural pond with wild birds and amphibians. Native Colorado wildflowers and shrubs guarded the entrance to Grace House, the steps leading up to massive oak doors five inches thick that stood tall under a stone archway. The back of the house opened into a lanai and a sunroom with even more plants. Four bungalow cottages sat nestled behind the mansion, along with the garage and a helicopter pad.

Brecker made it to the end of the hall and crossed his arms behind his back. He loved the view from this particular window. Acres of Colorado forest rolled out before him, sheer granite cliffs in the distance. Jason had kept this house because it was very secluded, buried deep in the wilderness and surrounded by security measures. Because of what Grace House had to protect.

What he'd told Lynch was true: Brecker was a physician and a scientist. Not a natural leader. Grace House had been drenched in grief since Jason's death. He could see it on every person's face, but they had to move on. The Pensare needed someone greater than Brecker, a catalyst to bring the group together again.

Now that the boy's life appeared to be saved, Brecker's mind grappled with the next challenge: how to keep him at Grace House long enough to believe. When Zander first woke, he'd be very weak. The Circle could help with his healing. Hadley might be willing to do a few favors. Brecker chuckled. Only for extra allowance, of course. They'd have to work together to spur the young man's curiosity. Although that drive was dead, it could be reawakened, especially as his mind was freed from years of drugs.

He privately wondered if Gage was right, if he'd made a colossal mistake. The unintentional release of this discovery to the world would be catastrophic, the greatest moral upheaval in human history. Brecker traced an exaggerated "M" in the condensation on the window, curled around the edges. A genetic mutation. An accidental lightning strike. That's all it took for science to break through the Veil, to enter where it was never meant to. His hands trembled, streaking the condensation.

Brecker had the strangest thought. If he were truly brave, he'd scatter the travelers and scientists and destroy the Recipe, all the notebooks and lab results. Wipe all knowledge of it from the face of the earth. The world was never meant to know and science would end up going too far. Tinkering with Pandora's box.

Where had the idea come from? As soon as it came, Brecker fought it. He didn't have the strength to let the discovery go. He smeared the letter on the glass, the chill seeping into his fingertips. One day far in the future, he may regret not doing what he should have.

Brit Malorie

Chapter 5

A silky texture met his lips. It smelled like lavender, followed by the sharp sting of soap. His mouth parted, expecting a fine mist of saltwater. It should be here. His muscles prickled as they woke from a long sleep. He waited for the cloud to drift on, to let the sun bake his earlobe, to flash over his lids in shades of coral and deep red.

Zander Grace opened his eyes. He could make out the ceiling cracks above, dark branches from all the years of his life. His bedroom. Metallica posters still hung on the walls. School trophies from math club and track were stacked on the small bookcase along with textbooks and loose papers. A cedar dresser and nightstand rested next to his bed. An armchair in paisley fabric sat next to a window with gauzy white curtains. Smells of Colorado pine and dank scum from the pond out front. He tried to laugh, then winced at the thick pain in his skull. Was he still on Kadera, dreaming of his room? Or was Kadera the dream? He didn't understand. Two years and he was home again.

He tried to brace himself up, but his muscles went rigid. He teetered a moment, then slammed back down on the mattress. His hands formed claws and ripped down the sheets. He needed drugs. Seed. There was no Seed here. Dry heaves wracked his throat. He couldn't lift his arms, his legs. What the hell was he doing back here? It had to be his father controlling him again, always shoving him where he didn't want to go. The information circled out of reach. His mind wouldn't let it in . . . something Brecker had written in an email, something about Dad. He hugged himself, crying out in short yelps. It felt like a burning vise constricted him. Flames dove into his muscle tissue and organs, shredding him in half.

His bedroom door cracked a couple of inches. He heard Brecker's voice outside: "The Pensare . . . Maglia . . . don't tell him . . . addiction."

An older nurse in lilac scrubs peeked inside and gave a short knock. Zander watched her through wavy lines as his eyes watered.

"Finally, our little hero's awake. I suppose you don't remember much of me."

He bent over and almost toppled out of bed. The woman caught him and held him upright.

"Breathe, just breathe. Melodramatic boy, that hasn't changed," she tsked. A wet cloth moved over his face and left a trail of coolness. He shoved himself against the mattress, taking in more air with each gasp.

"Oh, God, the pain. The pain, Nora!" he yelled. Her face smeared before his eyes and black spots traveled over it.

"Here, sweetie, drink. Drink," she ordered. Water dribbled down his chin from the cup. She moved his head onto her shoulder, then delivered a swift kiss to his forehead. Zander buried his nose in the scratchy fabric of her scrubs. Nostalgia. The tangy smell of the unscented Jergen's lotion she used, the moist feel of her hands. Nora had been Brecker's assistant, then she took over the caregiving role for the household when Zander's mother died. Gray laced the black bun woven tightly at the base of her head. Her eyes had a business-like efficiency, though he could always make her laugh.

The water traveled down his throat and deeper into his chest. After a few minutes, he relaxed. Nora released him and he sunk his head down into the pillow. "How long have I been out?" he croaked.

"A few days or so. I've never seen anyone so sick, dear, not even your wonderful father near the end. God bless him." Her eyes grew sad.

Brecker's message. The realization felt far away. "Dad?" he asked. His hands trembled.

Nora clasped them between her palms. "No worries about the shakes, dear. I don't know what kind of heathen drugs they had you on, but you'll have the shakes and vision problems for a bit. Dr. Brecker was so lucky to find you." She smiled wistfully.

"As far as your father, well, he just didn't wake up one morning." Her bottom lip quivered. "He traveled every day there at the end, filling up those notebooks as fast as he could. It was a shock to all of us, you know." She rubbed Zander's arms. It unnerved him to have another person touch his skin.

"What happened? Does anyone know?"

"No one's really sure. Like I said, he was traveling to Maglia every goshdarn day there for a while. His poor heart couldn't take the strain."

"Maglia? I don't remember—"

Nora's hand flew up to her mouth. "Oh, stupid, stupid me. Dr. Brecker warned me not to go into all that. No worries, dear, he'll have a nice long chat with you. Your handsome head'll be chock full of that stuff."

"Okay." Zander's handsome head already pounded. She bustled around him too fast, everything in blurred images. "Stop a second, wait."

He let out the saddest groan, then turned his mouth into a deep pout. "Nora, my head really hurts. The pain's unbearable. I'm sure you have something—"

"Like aspirin?" she asked, a slight purr to her voice.

Zander coughed. "A little stronger than aspirin. Just for now, for the pain. Aches, chills." His voice sounded as sweet and pathetic as possible. "You guys can't take me off everything, right? Please? Just this one time?"

Nora gave him a wink. "You know, I may have something. Hold on a bit." She stood up and walked to the door.

"Oh hello, Dr. Brecker." She scooted past him.

Zander groaned again, this time for real.

"The prodigal son." Brecker pulled out a stethoscope and pressed it against Zander's chest. "Heartbeat is weak, but it'll do. How are you feeling?"

"Like a corpse revived," he replied. "If this isn't a dream, I'd love an explanation."

"It's as real as it gets. Not sure dreams have detox symptoms," Brecker chuckled.

"How did I get off Kadera? And why? How did you know I was there? What day is it?"

Brecker sat down on the end of the bed and patted Zander's feet under the covers. He ticked off his fingers. "Let's see. Today is the last day of May. Early summer. You're a twenty-five-year-old white male, half-alive and half-dead near Redstone, Colorado. Oh, and there are six new ducklings in the pond outside."

Zander resisted his smile. "And?"

"Your last email was from the Cook Islands. When it became obvious you weren't coming back, I tracked you." He shook his head. "I'll let you know the nightmare I went through later. For now, you're welcome."

Zander shrugged his bony shoulders. "Why did you take me? You knew I didn't want to come home." He winced a little, hating how heartless he sounded. But it had taken so much strength to leave Grace House, to run as far as he could. Now it was for nothing. He gulped out of the water glass, but his mouth stayed bone-dry. A sickly smell wafted up from his skin and doubled his nausea. Brecker just watched him, probably happy he was suffering.

"Listen, I'll be honest with you. The plan," the doctor let out a loud sigh, "was to ask you to come home on your own. But things changed fast."

"Okay."

"You were unconscious. You were dying. I had to get you out of that toxic place."

Zander started to interrupt but stopped himself. He knew how Kadera looked from the outside. Especially to someone like Brecker. Seed was the kind of drug where it was tough to tell the living from the dead from the dying.

"And that monster Lynch?" Brecker asked. "How is it possible for such a man to run free?"

"What are you talking about? Lynch is my friend, they're all my friends," he insisted. "That was my real home you just took me from."

Brecker stared at him, obviously stunned. "That man almost killed me, Zander. His orders were to light me on fire in front of a crowd."

Zander waved him off. "That's just what he does. It's all fake, just entertainment for the tourists."

Brecker ran his fingers through his hair, a familiar gesture when he was stressed. "Zander, you can tell me it was just fun on that island, but the level of drug in your system, I mean, help me to understand. Why did you take so much? You came close to ending everything."

An uncomfortable silence descended and Zander looked away. When had he last seen Dad? Had it really been two years ago? His face, his voice . . . Zander shook his head. He couldn't do this now. *He couldn't.*

"We'll let you rest, but there's also a decision—" Brecker stopped. He looked like he wanted to take back that word.

"What?" Zander murmured. He wanted to be left alone.

"Why don't you rest—"

"Just tell me."

"A stipulation of Jason's will was that four months be devoted to the Pensare's use. That means you stay at Grace House and participate fully in the research."

"What? The research? That damn fantasy's still going on?" His voice was hoarse.

The door opened and Nora came in. Zander's eyes widened with expectation. She set down a wooden tray on the bed in front of him.

"Dammit, Nora, you know I didn't mean this."

Garlic emanated from the buttered sourdough. Layers of Muenster, Swiss, and cheddar dripped over the sides. Tomato soup bubbled in a ceramic bowl on the side, with dollops of sour cream and scattered basil. Finished off with a glass of cold milk.

"Your favorite." The nurse looked quite pleased with herself.

He looked to Brecker, but the man just laughed, a deep rumble that bounced off the walls. "I'm afraid that's the only drug you'll find here."

Zander rolled his eyes. He remembered a bottle of codeine from his college days, stashed in one of the bathrooms in the basement. He wasn't an addict, despite their suspicious looks. He was simply averse to detoxing. Try putting Brecker and Nora through that and they'd be on his side quick.

"He needs a haircut," Nora clucked. She licked her finger and pushed scraggly bits of hair out of his eyes. Zander batted her away. His normally auburn hair was a greasy dark. His ribs also protruded, which probably wasn't a good sign. There was also the problem of his skin—it wrinkled and hung off him like a very old man.

Brecker smiled. "Why don't you take a few days? Just relax, enjoy being home. We can talk about the research later."

Zander yelled up at the ceiling. He was trapped. Brecker knew he couldn't get back to Kadera without money. Nothing had changed—Grace House just had a different crackpot leader. What if they wanted to transplant a chicken heart in him or something?

A wounded look crossed Brecker's face. He motioned to Nora and they left. Zander stared at the food. The nausea subsided and an intense hunger followed. He ate slowly, his teeth sensitive on the crisp bread. The soup went down better, funneling into a pocket of warmth below.

Alright, he needed to assess. He'd sleep for a while, get his strength back. Wash this stench off his skin. Explore a bit, figure out the Pensare's great secret. He searched his brain and came up with nothing. Yes, his memory was shot, but he never did figure out what Dad had been up to. The man had been fanatically secretive.

How could this fantasy still be going on? What could serve as such a powerful obsession for so many years? Brecker didn't care about him enough to simply save his life. There had to be something important at stake, something substantial. The Pensare was already in control of the Grace millions, so it wasn't money. What could be so valuable these old men refused to let it go?

Brit Malorie

Chapter 6

In the volcanic tunnels beneath the island's surface, Lynch Katlan had his own room, a stark place where his tools were kept clean, very clean, and secure. The walls were a lovely beige tone with stain-resistant paint. He cleaned the room himself in the afterglow of his work. It was toughest to get the splatter off the ceiling, but he had a ladder now.

Despite running such a large operation, Lynch made few mistakes. But he remembered the error that cost him Zander Grace. *Remembered* was the wrong word. He grew very near obsession, analyzing his distraction from every angle. Yes, his work had been interrupted, but he should have listened to Cye. A single name. Who had the old man been caught stealing? He groaned. The morning's ball of pain was already gathered at the base of his skull. And there was only one way to spell relief.

The kid lay on a long plastic table, his ankles strapped at the top, his arms strapped down beside his anemic torso. "So, Pete, I guess you didn't run far enough. Costa Rica?" he asked. "So little faith in the reach of my organization."

"Yeah." That damn arrogance wouldn't leave the kid's voice. "Listen, Lynch, you're pissed, I get it. But really, one wasted guy? You have hundreds out there. Why's he so important?"

Lynch paused. Why wasn't the kid more afraid? He'd noticed an irritating sheen of invincibility around these newer ones, like their thick skulls couldn't quite believe it could happen to them. He'd have to cure that.

There were footsteps above them, bodies rustling in the new morning. He walked over to a stereo system and selected one of the newer playlists. He closed his eyes, lingering on the first few notes, the crescendos. A melody of voices surged from speakers mounted in the ceiling.

"Gospel music?" Pete asked.

"Yes. A live recording. Can you hear it?"

"Hear what?"

"The passion. The intolerable hope that God will enjoy it."

He tightened the strap around the kid's body, then injected a syringe full of green liquid into his vein. Just a little lubricant to open up the mind. The table jumped and jarred for a few minutes before the shakes subsided. Lynch slipped his right hand under Pete's neck. Using the island's special properties, you could pick up sensations and emotions through the skin. The tourists here would sit in long chains, and if the person at the front felt a cool breeze, the sensation rippled through the rest of the chain. It was fun until someone in the line got stuck in a cycle of depression. Then you had a whole group of sobbing or hysterical kids.

Of course, the ability to collect actual images and sort through them took much more skill. Lynch pressed his palm into Pete's neck and found the usual. Sex, partying, drinking Hypnas, then repeating the same damn things in Costa Rica with the money the doctor had given him. These kids never did anything of use. Lynch searched for information Zander might have confided in Pete. Where he came from, anything from his childhood. All he got were two very stoned kids, laughing all the time, swimming, sleeping during the day.

He should've read the doctor. He remembered placing his hand on the old man's neck, then pulling back. Why did he pull back? Lynch snapped his fingers. Yes. It was the fear. The fear in the doctor's eyes saved the man. If Lynch had seen any strength in those eyes, he would have read the man and realized his true motivation. Then the doctor would be dead and Zander would still be here. Disturbing how the eyes deceived. Lynch chuckled.

"You want to know why Zander Grace was not just another wasted kid on my beach. That's fair, Pete. You should know why you're about to go through what you are."

He moved to the end of the table next to the kid's feet, then removed the shoes and socks. He took out a pocketknife, one quite dear to his heart. It was small, but had an edge so sharp it cut through flesh like melted butter. He tapped on the big toe. "One. I don't like my bodies stolen, alive or dead." He moved to the next toe and tapped again. "Two. Zander knows a hell of a lot about what we do here. You better pray we find him. Three. He's an essential piece in Kadera's grand plan." Lynch spun the knife in a small circle. "Hence the protective order. In fact, you picked the absolute worst person to help off this island. Now that's irony."

Lynch picked up three white towels from the cabinet and laid them in perfect rows beneath the kid's head. He wrapped his left hand in a glove coated in blunt metal spikes. "I've figured out why you're not afraid, Pete. Maybe you think we're still friends. Maybe you think I'm still a nice guy."

Kneeling down, he held one side of the kid's face still and plunged the metal fist into the other side. A crack sounded loudly in the room. Pete's eyes bulged as he struggled for air. A red circle oozed outward on the towel. Blood and saliva and snot collecting in one tidy place.

The kid's eyes became glassy. His jaw slackened and spit trailed from his mouth. A tiny drop fell on Lynch's skin. He shuddered, then forced himself to stay still. He pulled out his cloth and wiped it, then again. Again. "Pain is necessary, of course, but what's the point of learning your lesson if you're too out of it? That's one of the key concepts in my experiments. The right combination of torment and clarity."

He injected a small amount of clear fluid directly into the neck. After a few minutes, the kid seemed to wake up a little bit. Lynch leaned over him.

"What happened to you?" Pete asked.

"You mean this?" He touched the metal on his chin. "Bit of a yawn actually."

"No, I mean you. What made you like this?"

Lynch paused, startled by the question. He thought for a moment.

"A perfect childhood," he said, with reverence. He twitched his finger to match the gospel music, then moved it in a circle and up to the ceiling, as if guiding the voices to heaven.

He slipped a miniature candy cane in his mouth. The peppermint flavor seeped over his tongue as he crunched the harmless shards. He pulled out a medium-sized metal box, his fingers tracing along the edges. This toolbox was specially commissioned to his exact standards. It was unlike anything else in the world.

"What the—oh my God." The kid rattled around on the table.

Lynch let out a low chuckle. "I see my toolbox is already Kadera legend."

"You don't have to use that. I told you everything. Some kind of doctor, I think a doctor, I mean a medicine-type doctor." His words were tumbling fast now, a new urgency pulling all sense from his mind. Lynch paused, savoring.

"He knew Zander from before. He was going to. . . ." The kid searched for more, something more to save himself. ". . . to New Zealand."

"The guy covered his real location well. Too well for a simple doctor. There's something you're not remembering." Lynch wiggled his finger.

"He bribed the dockmen. Ask them! Please, Lynch, man, don't do this."

"Ah, correct again. The docks are a problem. For the importance of the work we do here, you'd think we'd have better protection. Losing this and that. Left and right. But you try running a place full of junkies and thieves." Lynch pulled a corkscrew-looking object out of the metal box, something he affectionately called the Driver. Pete's eyes grew wide.

"Don't worry, it's been sanitized," Lynch reassured him. The goal was not to simply inflict pain. Hell, you could use tools found around the house for that. No, Lynch believed there was one place that could truly rip the mind from the body, the body from the soul.

He pulled away Pete's shirt and palpitated the organs, the ridge of muscle. Now, he had a theory about the spot. . . .

"Wait! Shit, I just remembered. I thought I imagined it, but I think it's real," Pete screamed out. Lynch grimaced. He should wear earplugs, but then he'd miss out on the subtle noises of anguish, the symphony that most of his kind ignored. He traced the Driver along the edge of the kid's side. Perhaps it was the point where the stomach met the pancreas.

"There was this card mixed up with the money, a business card. I don't think the doctor guy realized it was there. Like, um, he'd dropped the card in his pocket and the money was in there."

"And this card said?"

"Let me remember, let me remember. I tossed it. I know, I know." Pete's eyes squeezed shut.

"I have a great memory. Do you know what it's like to have a great memory among so many shitty, drugged-out brains, Pete? It means an enormous amount of power—"

"Like that movie! By Kubrick, the girl and the old guy?"

"*Lolita?* One of my favorites."

"Perfect. Yeah." Pete's face relaxed and his breathing steadied for the first time all morning. Something inside Lynch clicked. This was it. This was the moment he lived for.

"That's what the business card said?"

"It was a nightclub. Miami."

"The Lolita in Miami, Florida. Sounds enjoyable."

"Yeah," Pete murmured.

"So that's it, huh?"

"Yeah. Did it help? You know, enough?"

"Maybe. Let's play a bit more and see what else we can find."

Pete choked up again. "I won't tell anyone what we do here, I promise. Please, Lynch!" The boy's mind could be starting to separate. But there were still hours to go.

"Shush now. Stop embarrassing yourself. Like I tell my other guests, because of your sacrifice, we're making strides in the science of confession." Another chuckle grated from Lynch's throat.

He could almost taste the salt in the tears streaming down the kid's face. Better than any meal in Paris or Prague. Almost better than the bodies flowing in rhythm above him, his control deepening over them every single day. He began to whistle. The melody calmed his nerves and allowed Lynch to really enjoy his work.

"Honestly, what kind of punishment is death? The release of death is the same as letting you go back to the putrid muck of your life. You've been helpful, Pete, so I'll tell you—no, *show* you a secret. One friend to another. It's really the in-between, the space between life and death. Therein lays the sweet spot. The place where the party never ends."

Chapter 7

When Zander woke again, he expected Cye to be snuggled against his chest, sand to be gritting his crevices, and laughing off yet another bizarre dream from home. Instead, he startled to see the clock's electric blue letters against the black. 5:00 a.m. A distant bird song came in through the open window. Nora had left him a pair of clean sweats. He fumbled his worthless limbs into the clothes and struggled out of bed. A wheelchair sat in the corner of the room; Zander crawled over to it and lifted himself up. He felt impossibly drained—so exhausted it was difficult to believe he'd ever be normal again. Yet he also wanted to explore a little. Rolling out into the hallway, he peered around the corner. Everyone was asleep.

The last time he saw her, Grace House lay covered in rustic Victorian decoration—layers of gray paint, stiff velvet drapes, and beaded lampshades. And many, many paintings of dogs. Spaniels, terriers, even the occasional bulldog. His grandparents had purchased the house when its previous owners had died quite mysteriously, his grandmother eager to contact them through séance. Zander rolled his eyes. The wrought-iron antiques and floral wallpaper had been particularly strange next to the dead animals mounted to the walls, victories from his grandfather's hunting expeditions in the Colorado wilderness.

But it looked like Dad had modernized Grace House over the last two years. Most of the crusty shag carpeting had been replaced by hardwoods—cherry, mahogany, and pine laid down in unique spiral and cross-cut patterns. All of the gothic and hunting memorabilia has been removed; bright new colors and impressionist art decorated the walls. Modern sculptures composed from natural rock and wood hung from the ceiling. Dad had left the stained-glass windows that were built with the house back in the late 1800s.

Zander rolled quickly to the elevator. He had to find that bottle of codeine before someone woke up. The itch not only throbbed now; it unleashed earthquakes of its own. The elevator clanged as it arrived upstairs, opening its doors with a loud ding. He cursed and looked around. After descending to the basement, he stopped in the hallway. To the right was the old bathroom with the loose board, but his gaze traveled to the left. The offices were down there and there might be information. The pills could wait.

Rolling down to the Pensare offices, Zander had to admit he was impressed by all the new expansion down here. He flipped on the light in the lab to find brand-new lab instrumentation on every bench, plus extra unopened boxes collecting dust in the corners. A second conference room had been added and another lab area full of electronic monitoring equipment he'd never seen before. He let out a loud groan. Brecker had him trapped here with nothing, yet the Pensare were busy spending money like it poured from the mountaintop.

The farthest office had everything arranged in tidy piles; a physician's black bag sat on the edge of the desk. Zander flicked on the lamp. Charts and instrument lists. An extensive security log. Twenty different security measures had been set up around Grace House: overlaying alarm systems; round-the-clock security teams monitoring the grounds and the house. Complicated algorithms protected the computer system, along with monitored internet and cell phones. A reinforced safe, five feet thick of steel. Probably where all of the significant data and his father's notebooks were kept.

Zander shook his head. It was all so ridiculous. The Pensare acted like they were protecting the greatest discovery on earth. Dad's paranoia had been intense, too, though Zander had gotten used to it over the years. Jason Grace had made his son use false names all his life, including when he went away to college. He was to use only cash, fake addresses, nothing said about his past. Zander's habit of guarding his identity grew so strong that he even took different names while traveling and when he came to

Kadera. Zander sighed. He'd always made sure never to get too close to anyone.

He sat back in frustration. Was there anything here he could actually decipher? He'd pulled a master's in Physics from the University of Colorado by age twenty-three, but he couldn't understand raw data and statistics without a reference. He noticed a manila folder tucked away under the file cabinet.

The folder held a series of black and white photographs. They looked like highly detailed X-rays, but he'd never seen anything like them. One looked like a tree, with ghost-white branches pouring out of a center pole of light. A second photo zoomed in on the branches, revealing how they crisscrossed and spun around each other in a mesh pattern. A third photo zoomed in on the center pole: a helix structure floating around a layered core. Markings on the last photo showed chemical symbols for magnesium, phosphorus, and iron.

Zander suddenly laughed out loud, and the sound echoed harshly in the isolated room. Whatever these photos were, it was nothing he nor anyone else in the real world had ever heard of. After replacing everything back into the doctor's neat piles, he noticed something behind the door. His photograph lay tacked to the middle of the wall with words scribbled underneath it. "Zander Grace. Physics background. Resentful of Jason. Arrogant. Risk-taking." He shook his head. To his left was a large photograph of his cousin Calvin. Two years older and enraptured with the Catholic Church, he'd been sent to the Vatican for special study in the priesthood. Words were also scribbled underneath his photo: "Calvin Grace. Italy until October. Calm. Contemplative. Highly mechanical."

So the Pensare's little experiment must have a genetic component. He and Calvin were the last of the Grace lineage. And there must be a time constraint; otherwise, the Pensare would just wait another six months for the "contemplative" choice. They wouldn't have even bothered with Zander.

Then he turned to the last photograph. It was the profile of a young woman and looked like it had been taken from a distance. A breeze must have whipped up her ebony hair; it floated above her shoulders. She clutched a bag close to her chest. There was anxiety in her gaze, like she knew she was being watched. The words underneath said: "Bryn Sansa. Wants her own life." He stared at the photograph, taking in her delicate Japanese features, the perfect oval of her face, her lips pressed together in worry. She was incredibly beautiful, but it was her eyes that held him, the fierceness there. He wondered what her life could be. Why did she cling to it so badly?

Zander rolled back down the hallway, then stopped outside the next room. His father's study. He could tell by the shadows that the Pensare had preserved it, right down to the smell of Jason's old-fashioned clove aftershave.

After losing his mom, Zander's five-year-old brain tried to understand, to fit the loss into his tiny world. He remembered scratchy glimpses of her funeral. His dad's hands, so many lines in them, calloused from tinkering in the lab. When he was upset, Zander still pictured those hands. The only person left. He'd search for the clove scent every day for months afterward, only to be pushed away. Go play with your cousin. Go play in the woods. Just go somewhere else. Then Dad was gone, too, traveling endlessly, burying himself in the research. And Zander built a safe place for his heart that no one could enter—not Nora, not Brecker, not Cye. Not anyone he'd met since.

The day he graduated college, Dad had put his arm around him. "It's time, Zander. I want you to join the Pensare. I've kept the discovery hidden all these years until you were ready. Now you can fulfill your destiny."

He realized two things in that moment. His father had never loved him like he did the discovery. And Zander hated it with a passion he'd never held for anything else. He ran away that very night. He would never see Dad again.

Zander almost tipped out of the chair as dizziness overcame him. He couldn't breathe. Acid leached at the back of his throat. The craving pulled him under; his mind couldn't break through it. He sat frozen for minutes, struggling to remain conscious. The pills.

Taking in short gasps, he rolled quickly to the bathroom. He spied the loose floorboard, a hiding spot he'd found early in his college days. The wheelchair barely fit inside the door. The burn flowed through his legs and up into his arms, then deep into the muscle, an ache so loud he couldn't see straight. The floorboard creaked as he bent down and pressed on one end to lift up the other.

"There you are," he whispered. Slipping a pill into his palm, he slid the bottle back into its hiding place.

"What are you doing?" a female voice called out behind him. He swiveled his torso around. A kid stood there. She looked eight or nine. She had large eyes with pale green irises and a button nose. Her dark blond hair was wispy and cut to her rounded chin. She held a giant cat— literally, a giant. It was covered in dense black fur, with tufts of smoke-colored pieces mixed in. The cat had to weigh thirty pounds and looked more like a raccoon.

"I'm ten, actually. I know I look younger. And he's only sixteen pounds," she said, her tone confident. Her fingers combed through his fur.

"Only sixteen pounds?" Zander replied. "Hard to believe. You're going to have to let me out."

She stepped back out to the hallway. He reversed the wheelchair, exited the bathroom, and spun around to face her.

"You're Zander Grace, aren't you? The Pensare talks about you a lot." Her face scrunched up, like he was a puzzle she might solve.

"Yep, that's me. What do they say?"

"Mean things. All true. Gotta decide if you're the hero or the villain." She nodded, as if this made sense. Striped leggings ran up her twig legs and a black T-shirt was knotted low around her waist.

"Where did you straggle in from?" he asked. He rolled the pill between his fingers, then imagined the bitter taste swirling in his mouth.

"Oh, I live here. I'm Hadley Porter. And this is Bumbles. Please don't mention his weight again. He's sensitive about it." She dropped the cat, but instead of scampering off, he collapsed on the carpet and stretched to maximum length, his belly lolling to one side. His tiny head and honey-colored eyes rotated upward.

"He looks like—"

"—a were-cat," she sighed. "I know. Half-werewolf, half-cat."

Zander felt perplexed. His face must be an easy read. "Are your parents here? Are we running a daycare now?"

"No, my parents didn't want me anymore." Hadley shrugged. "So the Pensare adopted me."

"Nice and weird. Isn't it lonely living here? Don't you want kids to hang out with?"

"No, I'm very advanced for my age." She tilted her chin up, defiant.

Zander chuckled. "You know, they say that to all the little weirdo's to make them feel better."

Hadley ignored him. "Plus, I frighten other kids and they're mean."

"Right," he said slowly. "Listen, I need to get back upstairs."

"Okay. We'll hang out later."

Zander nodded. What a bizarre little girl, like someone much older and someone much younger were twisting around in that brain of hers.

Hadley stood there for a moment with a peaceful grin, then abruptly walked into the bathroom and shut the door. Zander paused, listening. He didn't think she'd seen him—Wait, wait, the sound of the board being moved. Shit! Struggling to the door, he pushed it open. Launching his weak body forward, he slammed his hand on the toilet. His knees hit the floor with a loud bang and he winced. The white discs hovered briefly underwater before flushing away. Weeks of bliss zoomed goodbye.

"What the hell? What the hell are you doing? You stupid brat!" The blood pounded through his face. Dammit. That bottle was his last shot. And the girl had that grin on her face still. It took all his willpower not to slap it off her.

"You don't need those. You think you do, but your brain is sooooo sick of them," she said, eager to share this illumination, as if he gave a damn.

"How did you know? How did you see me? I'm going to kill you." A coughing fit interrupted him, his knees digging into the wooden slats, his lungs burning.

"No, you won't. You barely have enough strength to roll that chair." She giggled.

She helped him onto the wheelchair. He backed into the hallway and turned. "I can see why your parents got rid of you," he said, his voice spiteful.

"They were scared. But you shouldn't be. We're going to be friends."

"That's reassuring. Trust me, you'll pay for that someday. I don't care if you are a kid."

"Eww . . . I'm shaking. No, wait. That'll be you in a few hours."

He groaned and rolled away from her. He wanted his last pill and sleep and oblivion. Hadley ran around and blocked him.

"What now?" he grumbled. "Please hold still and let me run you over."

She held out five of the white discs in her sweaty palm. Zander reached, but she dodged him and sprinted back towards the bathroom.

"Give those to me," he ordered. Only five pills, but maybe if he spaced them out.

"These are stupid. I have something way better," she said. Zander felt a strange numbness travel down his arms and hands. He should just take the pill he'd managed to save, but greed blinded him. Five more were right there. If he could just get to her, he'd force them out of her grubby little fist.

Hadley bent down and set one on the carpet, then she patted her knees like he was a dog. "Here, boy, come on. Come and get it."

Dammit, he was disgusted with himself. Scavenging pills off the ground. He knew he wasn't an addict, not even close. But the pill was just lying there. It didn't belong on the floor. Really it was a hazard.

"What if your cat waddles by? He might eat that and die," Zander called out.

"Bumbles won't do that. He's smarter than you." Hadley backed away three feet and set another pill down. He gave a dramatic sigh and scooped up each one. Where was she going? It was all storage back here. He played her game until they came to a large room at the end of the hallway. Zander rolled inside. The room had been turned into some kind of yoga palace. Flexible silicone mats covered the floor; the walls were coated in an evergreen paint with white trim. A mirror covered the eastern-most wall.

Hadley strutted around in a circle. He felt a kick in his back as the chair tipped forward; he fell on the floor with a loud smack. She moved the chair to a corner.

"Alright, where are we?" he asked.

"Just a room, booger. Try to relax."

A soft light washed in from windows carved out of the basement corners. Zander froze. There were voices out in the hallway and they were headed inside.

Chapter 8

Two women and a toddler walked into the room. "Well, hello there. You must be Zander." The first woman sat down by his side. Native American, she was petite and adorable with waist-length black hair and tanned skin. The toddler plopped down in her lap, a miniature version of her with cropped black hair and chubby cheeks. Her pink pajamas had Dora the Explorer patches. "I'm Raleigh Bryant. This is my daughter, Asha." The toddler stood up and ran behind her mother, then peered out shyly at Zander.

"Say hello to the nice man, Asha." Raleigh prodded her.

"Hello," the girl said, sticking her fingers in her mouth.

"Such a lovely aura," a voice sounded from behind him.

"It's not so hot now," Hadley interjected. "Barf."

The other woman shushed Hadley with a kiss on the top of her head. "I'm Kalista, but everyone calls me Liz." She sat down across from Zander. She had lots of muscle and a little roundness, her skin a rich coffee dark. Her hair was bound in long braids and knotted into a thick bun. The braids were stained on the edges with red, like henna dye. Tiny black spots freckled her face. She wore a shimmery robe of royal purple with slippers to match. Her voice had a deep bass to it, melodic with raspiness, like she'd smoked for a few years.

The four of them formed a broad circle on the mats. Asha scooted on her butt until she was in the center. She kept a wary toddler eye on Zander.

"I'm so happy you've come home, Zander. I think you'll be essential to the research," Raleigh said brightly. Zander was a bit mesmerized by the mauve color of her lips. He wished he'd cleaned up a bit.

"What, um, what do you all do here?" he asked.

"We call ourselves the Circle—" Liz started to explain, but Hadley held up a hand.

"Dr. Brecker wants to take things slowly," she said, her voice stern.

Liz batted her hand down. "Oh, nonsense. The sooner the boy knows what he's getting into, the better for all of us. Nowhere else to go, right, honey?" She winked at him.

"I do have places to go, actually. Just a little cash flow problem at the moment," Zander grimaced. "Plus, this is my house."

"Your home," Liz corrected him. "And we're also your home now. So you might as well get comfortable."

Zander nodded. He was actually pretty uncomfortable. He'd always assumed the Pensare was made up of hard scientists—biologists, chemists, physicists like Dad and himself. But he had a terrible feeling that he was about to be enlightened.

Liz grasped his hands. She massaged his palms, digging her thumbs deep into the tissue. Zander wanted to cry out at the prickling sensation. His neck, shoulders, and head relaxed.

"Now, we're going to do some meditation exercises, then Hadley's going to pass some energy through you. And it'll go so much better if you relax and accept and leave the questions for later. Nod your head yes," she said. Zander nodded viciously, his eyes watering from the tingling torture on his hands.

"It'll help you heal," Hadley added as she took one of his hands.

"Excellent. First is breathing. Everyone do as I do," Liz said. They all breathed in deep, so long that Zander thought his lungs would burst. Then they let it out in short, hard drives. Asha sat in the center of the circle with her tiny legs crossed, ultra serious. He found it hard to believe that a two-year-old could meditate, but maybe Raleigh wasn't a typical mom.

After they finished, Zander actually felt pretty great, a little buzzed actually. "Why do I feel so good?"

Hadley laughed. "Oh, I passed Secondo positive through you. Nice, huh? You have a very clear signal. I could find you with my eyes closed."

"What?"

"Psychic joke, Z-dog. Try to keep up."

"Psychic? Secondo positive?"

Liz explained. "Hadley and I are psychic. Raleigh's our holistic teacher. We're the spiritualist team of the Pensare. We call ourselves the Circle."

Zander watched her face carefully, looking for a little smile that would betray the joke, but there was nothing. The woman was absolutely serious. He burst out laughing. A hurt look crossed Hadley's face. The women waited patiently for him to stop, their faces serene. He finally did stop but only to ease the sharp pain in his ribs.

"I don't know much about psychics, only that they like money," he hinted.

Liz smiled. "Yes, much like scientists. Do I act psychic? What is one supposed to look like?"

He raised his eyebrows and motioned to her purple robe.

She wiggled a finger at him. "Honey, this is my bathrobe. My brain's a bit different, but I'm not a sorceress."

Raleigh rolled her eyes. "Okay, you two. Zander, we should start. The Circle works with a form of energy called miran. Miran is emotional energy. It's partially transferred through the senses: touch, obviously; the sound of someone's voice; smells that seem familiar. Now everyone has a receptor in their brain for this energy, but it's more sensitive for some people versus others. And it can grow with use. People we call empathic, like therapists, nurses, teachers, etc."

"The human body is a deep reservoir of miran. Stress and depression can result in physical symptoms of body aches, pain, and sores. Miran is stored in objects as well, like a wedding ring or a child's blankey." Raleigh paused. "I'll use an extreme example—the phenomenon of tears appearing on statues of Mary. Enormous amounts of miran in the form of religious belief are poured into these statues and finally, the stone reflects that energy through a physical change."

"Also, Elvis on the potato chip." Zander nodded.

Raleigh's eyes narrowed. Her voice held an edge, like he was a child that needed discipline. "Please focus, Zander. There are seven levels of miran: Prima, Secondo, Terzo, Quarto, Quinto, Sesto, and Settimo. The levels are exponential, so rising from Prima to Secondo is much easier than rising from Quarto to Quinto."

"Prima is the lowest energy level and the simplest transfer—for example, if someone smiles at you on the subway and you feel a tad chipper for the next hour. Terzo would be like a great conversation with a friend. Sesto is reserved for very deep love, like a long-lasting marriage or the parent-child bond."

"What about Settimo, the highest level?" Zander asked.

Raleigh sounded irritated. "We're not able to measure Settimo yet. Naturally, there's a negative version for every level too, so fourteen in all. Prima negative would be, um, a curse perhaps, or name-calling. Terzo would be a nasty fight or anxiety at work. Sesto is quite grave—severe depression, fear."

"And Settimo would be a great evil, like the devil?"

She raised her eyebrows. "Yeah, sure. Like I said, we can't measure it."

An uncomfortable moment passed. "You know, I need to take her up for breakfast," Raleigh murmured, picking up Asha. Zander's stomach growled. He started to crawl over to his chair.

Liz stopped him. "Honey, please stay a bit. Hadley and I want to go through some exercises with you."

Hadley prepared herself. Her small ribcage puffed and deflated rapidly as she went through exercises with her eyes closed. "We need to begin your training with ascension and descension. Eventually, you'll learn how to control the fourteen levels. Seven up, seven down."

"Got it. Like a gear shift." Zander's head swarmed with questions, but he'd reserve them for Brecker.

Hadley sat on the side of them and positioned her palm against the bare skin on his back.

"Tell me what color you see," Liz said.

"Um, a pale yellow, like a cream, I guess." The color flickered across his closed eyelids.

"That's Prima positive. Now, moving on to Secondo positive." Zander felt pressure and warmth from Hadley's palm. The color became a butter yellow, then a heavy gold. "Now Terzo." The color flashed to a sunburnt orange. The feeling grew. He felt wonderful, intense, like there was a ladder with different rungs and he was climbing it slowly, settling into each layer.

"Quarto." The orange moved into a rich brick red, flooding his vision. He ascended, almost floating. Powerful, like he was back on Seed. His breaths seemed impossibly deep, the air thick and rolling through his lungs.

"Quinto." The red turned a deep purple, royal. He was soaring now. The energy carried him to new heights. Liz and Hadley inhaled together. Zander's eyelids fluttered.

"Focus, Hadley dear. Press onward," Liz reminded. Beads of sweat traveled down Zander's back from Hadley's palm. She pressed it hard enough to bruise, murmuring something.

"Sesto." The deep purple grew into a vibrant blue, like the center of a flame, the tallest throne looking down. He wished he could stay in this place. Hope inflated his chest like a balloon.

"Now, back off slowly," Liz whispered. Zander fell down through the colors.

"Okay, now we'll descend. This will be very unpleasant, sugar, but you must feel it for yourself. Hadley dear, roll the negative." The banal cream color shifted into a light gray. Not so bad.

"That's Prima negative." The light gray shifted through darker shades of gray. Secondo's a flint gray, Terzo was steel, Quarto a cavernous charcoal. At first, the worry developed into a light sadness, then he descended into anxiety, panic. Fear. The gray climbed along his spine to his limbs, reaching for the air in his lungs. His muscles shivered. Hadley's palm sent ice shards into his skull.

"Quinto negative," Liz quietly announced. The panic sunk into depression. Zander cramped into a place of nothing, so small. Subterranean. No air.

"Sesto negative." The gray swirled into bottomless dark. He drowned in the inky blackness. Wetness fell down his cheeks. Death cradled him. There was no way out.

"Ease him out slowly," Liz murmured. Hadley refocused and drew him up through the shades of gray.

Liz cupped his chin. "Open your eyes, Zander love." He shivered, clinging to the peaceful cream color of Prima positive, then met her gaze. His head wobbled—no strength left in his neck or limbs. She pressed her lips to his wrist. He immediately felt better.

"Why would anyone want to descend?" he asked.

Hadley scooted back against the wall, her head hung down, recovering, taking in short breaths. Liz sighed. "Sometimes you have to use negative miran to pull others out of the dark. We haven't done that in a while. It's not easy for her."

Zander nodded. It was all too much. He had no idea his father had supported all this. He felt overwhelmed by belief, choked off from reason and fact.

Liz continued, "Your aura's strong. The Circle will link onto it easily."

"What is an aura exactly? A scientific definition, not the New Age scam one."

Liz laughed. "Oh baby, I love a skeptic. Raleigh mentioned the human body carries the deepest reservoirs of miran. This supplies the tremendous power of human touch. We use our bodies for some of the deepest connections we have—not just sexual, but hugging, holding, carrying another person's heart. The miran reservoir in the body emits a signal that we call the aura. It's developed through your genes and your environment all the years of your life, so it's completely unique. By the way, you have a rich aura, Zander love, but it has a feature I've never seen before."

"Oh yeah?"

She nodded. "You have a great spot of brittle red."

"Brittle red?" he asked. Hadley joined them, her cheeks still blushed from the exertion.

Zander had to admit he felt amazing, the best he'd felt in a very long time. Not a drug high, but more of a clean, endorphin rush. The heat flowed from the base of his head down into his muscle tissue, giving him an energetic glow. He felt like oxygen surged from his lungs to the furthest reaches of his body.

"The Circle will use your aura to track you and keep you safe," Liz said.

"Track me where? To this Maglia place Nora mentioned? Is it dangerous?"

Liz winked, her supple dark skin reflective in the light. Zander found himself liking her despite his frustration. "Oh sugar, you'll find out soon enough."

Brit Malorie

Chapter 9

The light gushed under his eyelids with traitorous violet. The craving for nicotine surged in his blood. Lynch rose from his bed and walked to the window, his bare feet careful to avoid Cye. Her body spooned the sleeping dogs on the floor, her face buried in a panting neck. He had to get out of here. The noise throbbed in his head, a rush of heartbeats, canine and woman. The dogs smelled much better.

The ocean vapor hugged him as he stepped outside. Sun split open the Kaderian sky. Sand the color of bone rippled in great sheets before him. The speckled fin of a humpback whale surfaced, then flattened on the water with a rolling smack. Strips of banyon trees floated above and hooked into the roof. Brine smells of kelp and bird excrement combined with the scent of empty Hypna bottles scattered on the beach. Waves reached hungrily for the trails of lust from the night before. Lynch absorbed it all, digesting the island in deep breaths. He tapped a cigarette out of the pack, enjoying the catch of paper against paper. Lighting the tip, he paused, tasting the seconds of the first inhale.

A rickety bamboo table and chairs were set up on the verandah. Cye set down an espresso coffee for him and pineapple juice for herself, then held out her hands. He inspected them, then allowed her to cut slices off the bread. Lynch bit into a piece, tasting the coconut, creamed banana, pawpaw, and nuts. He soaked the bread with tangy kaffir lime syrup. Cye brought out another plate: steamed taro leaves and smoked marlin strips. Lynch mixed the two—the bitter of the taro resting in his jaw, spiked by the salt of the fish.

The mountains cut across the sky like black teeth. The island's volcano had lain dormant for five hundred years, the last eruption creating pockets of lava and underground tubes that gushed with water. Cye sat her little rump down on the sand and dug her toes in, resting her chin on oblong knees. Lynch raised his arms and hooked his fingers on the rafters, the breeze creeping up his ribs and fluttering over his bare chest, his jeans loose around his waist. It was more than love. Kadera.

A figure appeared on the horizon and glided towards the beachhouse, holding a green nylon bag. He scowled at Cye, his mouth a dark slash. She kissed the tips of her fingers at him. Looking deceptively like a Greek fishing boat captain, Damaris murmured hello. He stood about five feet four inches tall with a petite build, his hair slicked back in a ponytail. His generous nose hooked halfway down, and his black eyes could be warm and gentle up to the moment he made the first cut. The man tapped his foot on the sand and Lynch followed him.

The island's main resource was tourism, specifically the money they gleaned from these rich kids. The kids thought they wanted anarchy, so that's the illusion Lynch gave them. Kadera had to have the right blend of violence, sex, and rumor. Too normal and the kids got bored. Too hardcore and they got scared, running home to their mommies and daddies in Europe and the U.S. They came here to hear their own hearts race, to relish the euphoria, the mysticism, the sensual release. Then they returned to their cozy hotels or campsites for the night.

"Such a serious poet these days," Damaris said. "I imagine it's the Grace kid?"

"We tracked the doctor to Auckland, but the trail dead-ends there. I don't understand. It's like they disappeared into thin air."

Damaris chuckled.

Lynch wished he could see the humor in it. Normally, he watched the public kills, but he'd been distracted that night, working on a project that he'd planned for several weeks. It was almost morning before he learned the doctor and Zander were gone. And that traitor Pete. No flight records, no witnesses, not a soul. It made Lynch deeply suspicious. What kind of money bought a disappearance like that? He and his crew had used their contacts all over the world, but there was no trace of Zander Grace, not even a damn birth certificate. How was that possible?

They came upon a mass of nesting birds on one of the shoals. Birds from all over the world migrated to Kadera and stayed through the wet season. Damaris opened the bag and tossed a handful of birdseed. The birds swarmed them. Indian mynah, kakerori. A patch of ebony swiftlets chattered. The vibrant colors of the fruit doves stood out, smears of fuchsia and lime green.

"I've spoken with the other heads. You're to stay in Miami until you have Grace."

Lynch nodded. He'd expected this. He'd never met the heads of the Pulsae, the gang that ran Kadera and other exotic places like her around the world.

Damaris's tone remained neutral. "How could you let him escape? We had him. Hell, he came to us." He cursed under his breath. "There's been talk about taking away some of your projects."

Lynch's breathing quickened. He'd expected this, too, but his stomach still rolled and he felt dizzy.

Damaris gave a deep sigh. "But I'm indulgent. At least until Miami is done."

"Understood," he replied, relaxing. It was always difficult to leave Kadera, but the idea of setting a trap made him feel better. It would have to be special, one that Zander would struggle and claw against only to mire himself in deeper. Things must be put right. Lynch's gut tingled just thinking of all the details to get into place.

Damaris handed him a miniature candy cane. The peppermint flamed up Lynch's tongue and spiked down his throat.

They climbed up a swell in the beach. Damaris scattered seed across the open space and let out a low whistle. Edges appeared in the air, boundaries barely defined by the granules. Lynch spread his hands over the invisible surface and found a hairline crack. He filled his mouth with the peppermint flavor from the cane, then blew gently into the opening.

The edges separated and Lynch quickly ducked his head inside, then his body. Damaris followed. To any observer, they simply disappeared.

They climbed for several minutes up a steep incline. Lynch curled his bare toes into the rock to keep from sliding. The yellowed limestone shone on the water. His head felt tipsy from the stale air in the damp cavern. Amber fluid seeped from the crevices. They climbed upward, finally reaching a metal door. They entered one of the green glass buildings.

"It won't stay the same," Lynch murmured. Marae. Organic odors of packed earth and moldy plantlife emanated from crates stacked against the walls of the dome. Small amounts of natural light penetrated the glass, bathing everyone in an eerie greenish hue like they were all corpses. Every day they received more sophisticated equipment from Japan for optics, odors, tactile. To sense what could not be.

Damaris still refused him any information about Marae. Lynch could only guess at fragments, dropped pieces of conversation, bizarre cargo. The great rituals that had worked for hundreds of years on this island weren't so effective anymore and no one knew why. Something had changed almost twenty years ago—a small action that had multiplied and they'd suffered since that day. And strangely, he sensed it had to do with Zander.

Men brought out a glass cube that stood about five feet tall. Opaque crystals coated the inner surface of the glass along the boundary. Damaris flipped a switch at the cube's corner and a small fan started. The new breezes tossed up the pale crystalline powder in the bottom of the cube. The powder shimmered in the green light as it dispersed.

"The glass is lead-acrylic, several layers of it. It protects against the gamma radiation," Damaris called out to Lynch. "The powder is Cesium-137." The crystals began to glow. Lynch realized they were scintillation crystals, most likely anthracene. They showed luminescence when exposed to ionizing radiation.

"Look," Damaris wiped his finger on the glass. The space inside the cube grew darker. As Lynch watched, the air swirled into black then went deeper. Great rivers of ebony spun before them, rolling, ticking against the glass. He tried to pinpoint exactly what it was. He swore that the damn thing kept changing. Vapor turned to liquid droplets, then into a sheet of charcoal. First the black flowed, then stopped as it hovered near his skin. It appeared to reach for him. The cube vibrated and Lynch wondered if the sides would break. Damaris pressed his face against it, careless of the radiation.

"It's heaven," he whispered.

"What—" Lynch started to ask, but then the black diminished to gray swirls. Then it all disappeared completely.

"Why?" he asked. The entire experience had lasted for about ten seconds.

Damaris looked crushed. "It heals itself too quick." Lynch realized that was all he would get out of the man. These agonizingly tiny clues were all he was allowed—at least until he could capture Zander and bring him back here.

They exited the tunnels and walked back to his beachhouse. A group of kids were hanging out on the sand, smoking Seed and frying up fish. Lynch grimaced. The little shits were getting bolder. Visitors might gawk and stare, but usually no one dared come near his house out of a great fear, supported by rumor about his rule on the island. He wondered if this new arrogance might stem from an emerging ringleader, a giant Tongan named Palefu. The man had amassed quite a bit of power on Kadera over the last few months. Unfortunately, the problem would have to wait until he got back from Miami.

Near the group of kids, a dog limped on the sand, starved and slovenly, her canary-colored fur matted and drenched in some kind of oily fluid. She must have slipped off one of the ships. The dog barked, probably craving the group's fish guts strewn out on the sand. A cracked-out kid with glassy eyes and broken teeth stood up and kicked sand at the animal. When that didn't scare her off, he grabbed the dog by her neck and dragged her to the water line, laughing.

"Hey, watch! We're gonna cook up wet dog!" he screamed at his friends. The other kids ignored him and passed around a pipe, billows of white smoke clouding their bored faces. The dog backed up on her hindlegs, her head darting from side to side. He struck the animal, then dragged her deeper into the water. She let out piercing yelps, her hindleg twisted at a wrong angle.

"Excuse me," Lynch said dryly.

Damaris made a short clicking sound with his tongue. "Fine. Be quick."

The dog jerked her legs and attempted to paddle, her head bobbing up for air. The kid didn't notice Lynch until a fist came up and splintered his nose and cheekbones. Long trails of blood and saliva plopped down in long strings. A large rock rose conveniently out of the water. Lynch palmed the kid's skull and slammed it down with an explosive crack. The other kids stared at him slack-jawed, like he was a monster that rose out of the ocean. A sudden growl erupted from his throat and they scattered over the beach. He dragged the body up onto the sand, then rinsed his hands off quickly in the seawater.

He paused and a tongue lapped at his fingertips. Lynch rubbed behind the dog's ears. He felt along her coat, opened the mouth, checked the teeth. A ravenous hunger crawled up his ribs and pain throbbed in his left ankle. He let the dog slurp the fish entrails, then he lifted her up, heading to the beachhouse.

Damaris stepped in beside him, his face amused. "Yet another pet. You're getting quite a collection."

His smile dropped. "But it's time for a trade." He nodded up to the porch. Cye gave them a sullen look, her body draped lazily over the wood.

The wind whipped up her dress and she made no effort to conceal herself.

"You have yours, why can't I have mine?" Lynch asked.

"Mine are under control. She's a distraction for you. And she might overhear something."

Lynch wanted to ask what that would be, since they told him nothing. Instead, he said, "She's important. She holds clues about Zander. She was very close to him here."

"Fine, keep her for now. But if you lose Grace again, she's gone."

Lynch's muscles went rigid. He didn't understand his attachment to Cye, this idea of caring about a person. Had Zander's feelings for the girl left a lingering residue on him?

He studied her, a mixture of brunt, hard angles in her face and body. While Zander was busy drugging himself into a coma, Lynch had groomed the young girl, telling her she was important, charming her. Then he used small tests to dominate her and increasing violence to keep her controlled. He'd taught her how to use Kaderian skills: brushing up against strangers in the crowd to gain information, predicting the stillness before a creature attack, blending into the chains to gather memories. She brought him victims, betrayed her friends. It had been Cye who had mentioned Zander's real name to him, which she had fleshed out during her and Zander's love-making. Secretive as he was, the kid couldn't hold back the information during his weaker moments. Lynch hadn't thought much of it until he mentioned it to Damaris. The man had grown pale and demanded an immediate protective order. Unfortunately, the girl wasn't properly trained then; she had picked up Zander's name, but nothing else. The little bastard remained a mystery.

Lynch brought the dog around to the outside shower. He washed her gently, getting as much oil and dirt out as he could. He grabbed a knife from inside the house, then knelt down and cut away the knots in her fur. She licked her swollen leg and his hand. *They are like us.* He closed his eyes, remembering Petal's rules. *No children, no animals. You are like me and they are like us. But others, men and women, they deserve it. They always deserve it.*

He killed someone in front of Cye as a test once, and the silly girl had been so ridiculous as to beg for the man's life. Too much humanity left in her. He had hoped she could be like Petal—a companion—but no one was like him. Even Damaris was different. He viewed killing as merely functional, with no inherent love for it.

His time in Kadera had revived memories of that special summer he turned fifteen, a time upon which his entire life pivoted. His aunt had come to stay with him and his mother Miela in their small town on the outskirts of Ohio. He was already different from other boys by then, consoling his strange desires in the woods, burying rabbits and squirrels in the fields nearby. His aunt had lit a fire under those desires, teaching him how to lure, how to capture, and about the euphoria of giving pain. He shook a little, missing her. Even psychopaths longed to be understood, to be wrapped in their own nebulous shades of love.

Lynch brought the dog in and let her join the pile of other dogs that snoozed on billowy mats. He spent hours unlocking his mind, releasing Petal's musky scent, the mass of black curls swarming her back, forming a V. Her mouth taunting, always on the brink of disappearing, of abandoning him. Petal was a powerful force here because she lay inside him, and whatever lay inside rose to the surface in a place like Kadera. A shudder moved down his back. Especially what happened to her at the end of that special summer.

An ending that carved the endless tunnels in his mind, tunnels that he drenched in blood but never filled.

Chapter 10

After meditation, Hadley brought him back up to his room and he slept. Zander's mind returned to sunlight floating on water. *Shimmers of aquamarine and emerald drew him closer. Flecks of salt dried on his skin. He pulled the smoke of Seed deep into his lungs. The tunnel glistened before him, black piled on black, a doorway carved into the rock side. His toes dipped into something wet that flowed out from beneath the door, warm and thicker than water. He heard whistling, a lovely melody that didn't match the dark and the wetness and the powerful smells that spun him around, causing him to lose direction. The whistling grew louder. A sudden scream sent tremors through his body. His legs moved on their own—he had to get away. His body slammed down on the rock. Hands grabbed him—*

Zander startled himself awake. His room. This was his room. His heart thudded as he gulped water out of a glass from his nightstand. Where had that dream come from? During his year on the island, he'd spent a lot of time with Pete and Cye at Lynch's beachhouse, relaxing and eating great food. He'd been helping to purify Seed and transform the drug from a yellow, salt-like substance into a billowy white powder for the more elite clientele. There were lots of rumors about hidden tunnels beneath Kadera; he must have stumbled into one somehow, only to get caught and shoved back outside. He simply couldn't remember.

Did his friends ever wonder what had happened to him? Certainly not. They still had swaying hammocks and the beach, the fruit wine and the honey-drenched pork rolls at the beachhouse. Would he ever see any of them again? Would he ever have that sense of freedom again in his life? The nostalgia came over Zander in waves so strong he lay motionless.

He looked on the nightstand and under the covers. Hadley must have swiped all the pills again; they were almost certainly flushed away. After he bathed and dressed, Nora taught him some muscle exercises and brought the remains of breakfast up from the kitchen. Zander was surprised at his intense hunger: he wolfed down the pancakes, sausage, hashbrowns and orange juice, then asked for seconds. Obviously pleased, Nora came back with several plates full. He ate everything and let out a hard belch.

"Your color's looking a mite better. And I'm happy your appetite matches that of a healthy twenty-five-year-old man, as far as I can tell."

"So, Nora, unless I dreamed it, I met a very strange little girl this morning. Just how many people are staying here?" Zander asked.

"Ah, yes, Hadley Porter. The research is very intensive, so most of the Pensare members live here. I also have a small staff that comes in during the week—a couple of maids, a groundskeeper. Extra nurses come in for the doctor's experiments. Speak of the devil."

Brecker knocked gently on the door and stuck his head inside. "Good afternoon. Are you feeling up to meeting some people?" He entered the room followed by three other men. "You remember Isaac Rosen, your father's advisor in graduate school?"

The man gave him a frail hug, then tapped his knee with his fingertips. "Good to have you back, son."

"Hi, Isaac," Zander replied warmly. He remembered all the strange treats Isaac brought him from overseas when he was a kid: fish oil sweets and seaweed jerky. The guy was in his mid-seventies and the closest thing Zander had to a grandfather.

"And this is Gage Madison, a neurologist who recently joined us from Johns Hopkins. Great work from someone so young." Brecker motioned to an attractive black man with a shaved head and a thick goatee surrounding his mouth. The man gave Zander a somber nod and didn't reach out for a handshake.

"Isaac and Gage comprise the scientific team of the Pensare, along with myself," Brecker said, a note of pride in his voice.

"Oh, good. I wondered if there were any scientists left at Grace House. I had a fantastic session with the spiritualists this morning," Zander said. The clues piled up, frustratingly out of reach. A doctor, a neurologist, and a physicist. Together what did they make? What kind of experiments required a neurologist? He silently made a list: physics, genetics, brain chemistry. And psychics?

Brecker ignored him and motioned to the third man, dressed in black with a large security vest. "I'd like to introduce you to the head of our GUT security team, Trey Marshal. GUT is all ex-military personnel. They're supposed to stay in plainclothes so as not to attract attention in town." Brecker frowned. The man was clean-shaven with a square jaw and a buzzed haircut.

God, his hand almost crushed Zander's. Men patrolling around Grace House? The guy had a row of nice little weapons clamped around his security vest, including a rather large gun strapped to his side.

"You'll have orientation with GUT in a few hours," Brecker said.

"Why?" asked Zander.

Trey answered him. "You need to know where you're allowed and which areas are restricted. Also message relays, passwords, emergency protocols, the design of the security systems. We'll go over all of it. Pretty essential if you want to get around the place."

"Are you kidding? This is my goddamn house—"

"We'll see you in the main entrance at 1600 sharp." Trey cut him off and strode out the door.

"What crawled up that guy's—"

"As you can see, things have changed a bit since you left," Brecker interrupted. "Security is vital."

"What's so important you have to protect it with ex-military?" he asked.

Brecker responded with another one of his obnoxious smiles. Zander shoved his hands into his pockets to avoid choking him.

"Gentlemen, we have a lot to discuss," he said. Zander tried to stand up to join them, but Brecker patted his knee.

"Oh, no. Not you. Relax, Zander. Sleep, eat, do your exercises. Whether you need them or not." The doctor gave him a little wave and left. Isaac and Gage followed him out.

"Wait a minute," he called out. He wanted to ask about all this psychic crap, but Brecker shut the door. He sat down on the floor and stretched for a few minutes, yet nothing relieved the searing ache in his muscles. As damaged as his body was, his mind was truly awakening. He wasn't sure what the spiritualists did to him this morning, but for the first time in a while, he could think clearly. Amid the detox symptoms and the grief and the confusion, an intense curiosity rose up. He had to find out what was going on.

Just then he heard a small commotion outside. He braced himself against the doorway and managed to stumble out to the hallway. Brecker's words floated up from the great room below. Zander leaned over the balcony and caught a glimpse of black hair and slim hands gesturing frantically. It was her. The girl from the photograph in Brecker's office. Two security men stood near the front entrance, passively watching.

"Please stay a little longer. We can show you more evidence."

"I can't stay, Dr. Brecker. But I am worried about him. His body's deteriorating so quickly," she said.

"His mind is still vibrant. He wants to see you quite badly, Bryn. You just have to travel."

She hesitated, then shook her head. "I know you don't understand, but I can't." Her hand trembled by her side, then clenched tightly. "I won't watch him suffer. I won't help you."

Bryn stepped away from him and Brecker called out, "You'll regret it the rest of your life."

"It's my choice," she replied. She started to walk forward, then abruptly spun around and pointed a finger at him. "What you're doing here, you shouldn't be."

The doctor looked flabbergasted. The security guys filed around her, one on each side, yet she had the fiercest look of them all. Her delicate body glided through the air with grace. Her dark eyes traveled upward and locked onto Zander's. She tore her gaze away only when the front doors closed behind her.

He stumbled as fast as he could to the window at the end of the hallway. She climbed into a large SUV. One of the security guys moved into the driver's seat, and the truck headed down the driveway. Zander rested his upper torso on the balcony railing. His entire body went weak with tingling sensations and his heart wouldn't stop fluttering. He wanted to know everything about her.

He glanced around. The hallway and the great room below were both clear. His legs shook, but he braced himself up on the railing. He needed to ask Brecker about her. Who had she been so concerned about? Why did she refuse to participate in the research? He made it to the basement and heard voices in the conference room. He gently slid down to the floor and peeked in through the cracked door.

Gage fiddled with a projector at one end of the room. Shelves lined the walls, holding textbooks, journals, scattered jars, and specimens. The sour smell of preservative lingered. Isaac reclined in a leather armchair, writing slowly on a notepad, his cane lying against the armrest. Brecker paced and muttered to himself, his hands gesturing excitedly.

"Got it," Gage said triumphantly.

Zander held his breath. A three-dimensional image of a giant brain filled the open space. It was as tall as a man and the sections were lit in a rainbow of colors. Gage looped a tiny sensor on the back of his hand. The image rotated with his fist.

"Alright, let's remove the neocortex, then the medulla," Gage murmured. He pulled his hand back and parts of the brain floated away from the main structure.

"The claustrum," Brecker interrupted. "Zoom in on it." Gage concentrated, targeting the different layers until a gray, sheet-like piece rippled in mid-air, the edges curved in like wings.

The doctor whistled. "Zander's claustrum is even bigger than Jason's. It spans the length of his brain, with three times more surface area than a normal human's. I'm surprised it fits in his skull."

"Along with his massive ego," Gage snickered. Zander frowned.

"You know, the function of the claustrum is to take separate senses and unify them into a single stream of consciousness. Take a rose, for example. You see the crimson, smell the fragrance, touch the velvet of the petals—the whole experience unified," Isaac said, almost to himself.

"Yes, for normal humans. For our people, it's the Maglian sensor. It lets them see, hear, smell the Maglian layer," Brecker said, his eyes wide.

"Our people?" Zander whispered just outside the door. He shut his mouth quickly.

"I don't think there's any doubt, gentlemen. This is the link," Isaac said.

Zander felt a deep chill. He dug his fingers into the plush carpet, swaying. Whatever they'd done to him during meditation, it was wearing off. The ache clamored in his head. He should really get back upstairs.

"The claustrum is also the key to psychic ability," Brecker asked.

"Yes. The gift is definitely genetic with Hadley, doubly concentrated from both her grandmothers. With Liz, it appears to come from her accident as a child. Brain trauma caused her claustrum to send out more connections to other parts of her brain in order to stabilize itself. Extremely rare, even among psychics," Gage responded.

"Let's go over the aural body scan," Brecker said. Gage clicked on the laptop and a three-dimensional image of a body appeared. Gage swirled his hand upward a couple of times. Shades of blush and tangerine appeared at the edges of the figure, then grew into vivid colors. His arms were soaked in butter gold, his legs and lower torso in a royal blue. The colors spun and separated over the length of the body. Gage rotated the figure in the air. Zander gasped. A tint of blood appeared over the heart. A great spot of brittle red. The exact shades he'd seen in his mind during meditation, right down to the sunburnt orange of Terzo positive. How was that possible?

Zander felt a poke in his shoulder blade. Hadley stood next to him, hands on her hips. She pointed at him and motioned up the stairs.

Brecker frowned. "If Zander's claustrum is that big, I wonder if it'll take less voltage to fade him. We'll have to ramp up the shock to his brain slowly."

"What the hell?" Zander cried out. "You're going to electrocute my brain?"

Brecker groaned. "Dammit, Zander. How much did you hear?"

"Not nearly enough," he grumbled.

"Hadley, you were supposed to keep an eye on him."

The girl shrugged. "I fell asleep. Sneaky."

"Get him back upstairs, please."

"No." Zander stood up and braced himself in the doorway. "This is the great and wondrous research that my father spent a huge chunk of my life on. I'd love to hear why it's made up of junk science. Tell me or I'm gone."

Brecker raised his eyebrows and passed a look with Isaac. The older man motioned to him. "Go on."

He sighed. "Alright, well, do you remember how Jason used to study psychic phenomena? He used to say—"

"Oh yeah, I remember. How someday we'll see witchcraft and the occult and clairvoyance as new realms of hard science. Once we understand the metaphysical connections between us."

"Suffice it to say, this research is about those connections. That's why Jason made these choices for the Pensare: a mix of hard and soft scientists, aiding, supporting each other. I promise you, Zander, your father's discovery is revolutionary. For all mankind."

"That's a pretty big promise, Brecker."

"If it wasn't for Jason, scientists wouldn't have broken this boundary for another hundred years. But due to a few lucky accidents and the Grace genes, we're pioneers in this field. Yourself included."

"Geez, that makes it better. Just fry me up," Zander said.

"Extra crispy," Hadley inserted. She chuckled, but her face turned to concern as Zander teetered. She raised a hand to his back, but he dodged her. No more energy crap.

"I can't believe this. I can't believe you people want me to stop taking drugs," Zander shouted, pointing to himself.

"It would help if you could," Gage replied heatedly.

"Alright, enough," Isaac said. "I'm tired of this pointless fighting. Just go through the simulation with him. Hopefully, he'll give us a chance."

Zander wobbled into the room. A large jar sat on a shelf above his head. It looked like a piece of tissue floating in liquid. Holding the wall, he edged towards it.

"What the—" He read the plaque resting at the base of the jar. "Claustrum. By donation of Dr. Jason Grace." His father's brain. The room spun away from him. His fingernails dug into the paint and his legs went slack.

They'd taken a piece of his father's brain. They'd torn him apart. The Pensare had no limits, no morals. His fists locked. He could barely see, couldn't breathe through the rage. Adrenaline pounded through his blood. How could Brecker do this? Didn't the man believe in anything? Zander felt himself let go. Brecker shouted for him to stop. Hadley moved her hands over her eyes, her bottom lip trembling. His fist came out and the breaking sound of glass echoed in the room. The pain was unbearable. He felt drenched, the chemical smell filling his nose and mouth. He collapsed on the floor and lifted his hand, blood running down the sides. Shouts surrounded him as he passed out.

***

Brecker quickly checked his vitals. What a damn mess. Gage helped him carry Zander upstairs.

Nora was inside Zander's room making his bed. Her mouth dropped open in surprise as they set him down. "What happened? All this blood?"

"Get my bag," Brecker ordered. He examined Zander's hand. "Thank God, it looks like superficial cuts, nothing that requires surgery. The last thing we need is more delay."

"You're kidding, right? What's it going to take, Brecker?" Gage's voice rose in pitch. "We're depending on a dead man's choices. There are more reliable travelers. Mature, safer ones. Why do you protect him? He's going to destroy this research."

He shoved the doctor's hand away from Zander's. "Stop coddling him and listen to me."

"I have to stop the bleeding—"

"You know what I see?" Gage shouted. "A spoiled kid who's never had to sacrifice anything. Zander's in the middle of the greatest breakthrough in history and all he does is whine and fight us. And smash things."

"He's grieving."

"He's a child. We need a traveler with . . . I don't know. Reverence."

"Shock, denial, sorrow. All natural reactions."

Gage pointed to himself. "No, what I'm doing now is a natural reaction. What he just did? Shattering a jar with an incredibly valuable specimen inside? That's out-of-control drug addiction."

Brecker grew quiet. Nora entered the room with his bag and a bowl of warm water.

"Come on. Let's hear more excuses," Gage said.

The doctor shook his head. He held Zander's hand tenderly and let the liquid wash out the cuts. "Someday you'll understand. This is the only hero possible for Maglia. One who travels through the light and the dark."

Chapter 11

The night before he was to leave for Miami, Lynch took his evening bath. First, he used the outside shower, rinsing off the day's filth of sea-life, sand, birdshit, and all the little smears and specks from island living. He drew an exact proportion of hot and cold water into the porcelain clawfoot tub for the perfect temperature: two minutes of hot, then three minutes of cold, then two minutes of hot and so on. He undressed, sighing deeply as the water slid over the great sheets of muscle in his torso. No scent, just pure water and few minerals. He used an exact order of soaps: first the cleanser with mild abrasives, then an exfoliating soap, then a medicated soap for disinfection. He finished with transparent glycerin soap with a special oil blend for moisture. The best moment was when the dirty water flowed down the drain, far away from his skin. Then a final wash with clean water.

Sometimes the tension became unbearable—his need to kill versus his need to be clean. He had to admit the spray of human fluids was one of the most irritating consequences of his habit, but he'd narrowed it down. Now it only took a dozen or so projects a year, about one for every full moon, to satisfy him. His nightly bath resolved some of his stress, his habit resolved the rest.

The night air dried him as he stared at his naked reflection in the full-length mirror. He had a hole in the front of his jawbone from an incident in Pakistan a few years back, but the chin implant looked attractive enough. It was the size of a half-dollar and looked like a new-age piercing of shiny metal. His only other flaw was a large scar he'd received as a child—hard ridges and gnarls of tissue on the back of his neck. A gift from his mother. The scar was actually vital protection here, shielding him against intrusive readings on Kadera. Hair the color of cocoa, slightly curled at the ends so it nicely framed his face. Deep-set eyes, prominent nose, thin lips. Emerald eyes with a ring of steel gray at the outer edge that appeared to glow when the light hit them right.

He looked like such a good person, a decent one. Intensely handsome, almost angelic. Broad chest tapered to his waist, which curved down to long, powerful legs. Kadera helped him see what he needed to be in order to lure them. *I am like you. I am what you search for.* The ability to charm, to be likable. People wanted to trust. They wanted to believe their own eyes.

A new weapon lay on the side table: a silver claw measuring about eight inches in length. One end was honed to a razor-fine edge, the other end a ring that slid over his middle finger. He placed the claw on his hand and brought it up to the mirror, studying the grip, the reach of it. Cye called out that dinner was ready, then paused in the doorway. Her eyes drank in the naked turns of his body.

Her fingertips slid along his lower back and he winced. This would always be a problem. He'd seen it in the girl's eyes early on, but could not give her what she longed for. Any normal desire for women had been extinguished inside him at age fifteen. Besides, he could never lose control like that. What if a woman actually *read* him during sex? The idea disturbed him so deeply he became nauseous.

Her hand trailed on his skin and rage shook him. She knew never to touch him—*never*—but the stupid girl kept hoping. Lynch bent her over the side table and drew the claw up her thigh, against skin so pale it shined in the moonlight. He scraped the flesh, longing to flay the lean muscle open, to watch it redden and wither. She cried out and the claw clattered on the floor. He bent her arm back farther and she let out a choked sob. His blood sang, loving her pain, drinking in the anguish. He bit her earlobe as his hands moved up to her neck.

"Is this what you want? To die? Stupid, stupid, stupid." His hands wouldn't obey him, they wouldn't leave her neck. Colors flashed in his eyes as he saw what she saw. The lack of air built pressure in his lungs and the euphoria made him float. He hated her for taking him to the edge, then denying his release. He had to stop himself though. She was valuable. Lynch did the only technique that could bring him back. He thought of Petal, her teeth scraping her tongue, lulling him into a trance, explaining the rules. Her hands touching his face, the musky scent of sandalwood. He released Cye and moved outside. Minutes went by as the night air caressed his bare skin and carried away the heat and euphoria.

He came back inside, entered the bedroom and slipped on clean shorts. Cye sniffled, her face still puffy and red. The lovely sting of antiseptic hit his nose as he entered the dining room; she'd already swabbed the scratch on her leg. He sat at the wide bamboo table and sipped a special wine made in Rarotonga, steeped in banana, passion fruit, and mango. He placed a fillet of mahi mahi on his plate, then added spoonfuls of pawpaw salsa on top. She'd made some of his favorite— steaming hot pork rolls with gravy and applesauce. Island food became a staple for him during the years he'd spent in Thailand and Vietnam, but he still had uncontrollable cravings for his mother's Hungarian cooking. On those nights, no matter the temperature, he'd stay in the kitchen and make gulyásleves, a goulash soup with pork, flavored with onion, caraway, and paprika. Also pork sausage with garlic, the onions fried to brown in lard and mixed with lots of tomatoes and green pepper. And Cye would complain, holding her pert nose and avoiding the beachhouse for two days.

As the rich food filled him, so did a special warmth. Now was the time to sweeten her to him. He thanked her for the delicious food and complimented her beauty. He took her hand and kissed her fingertips. Suspicion and fear fell away as her pinched face gradually relaxed. She tilted her head, wishing to obey.

"Dove," he murmured, his fingers stroking her neck. "I want you to remember Zander."

She shifted away, pouting. "I've shown you everything I remember." Lynch willed himself to be patient. The damn girl still felt like Zander was hers and resisted giving him up.

"Listen to me. Zander cared about you. He fought off other men for you. Why? How did you exploit him?"

Cye winced. "It wasn't like that. He was nice to me. He protected me here."

"You were vulnerable for him." Lynch studied her, trying to see what a normal man would see. A young girl, naïve, fragile. She needed shielding from the world, her thin arms shuddering in the breeze. He chuckled. Could it be that simple? Could Zander see himself as a hero, charging into battle, rewarded with the princess? Lynch thought of the business card Pete had mentioned. The doctor must have explored other places in his search for Zander. He probably visited this nightclub right before he'd come to the island, since the card lay forgotten in his pocket and a man usually brings little clothing for travel. If he'd visited this nightclub in his search, he must have had reason to believe Zander was there. A reason. . . .

Lynch examined Cye, his thumb pressing on the indent of her upper lip, her small eyes craving any speck of praise. He wondered if the reason could be a girl like her, soft in all the right places. And if this girl might hold Zander's heart. Satisfaction rose in him. A plan was forming.

Chapter 12

"So I'm curious to know more about psychics," Zander said. Hadley curled her head into her arm as she scribbled figures on her math homework. Her room lay buried somewhere under piles of dirty clothes, dishes, and crumpled-up papers. Her books teetered in stacks as tall as the ceiling. Why didn't Nora make her clean up this mess? When Zander was growing up, the woman had terrorized him by walking into his room any time she pleased. She even caught him with girls a couple of times.

Embarrassed about his blow-up, he'd avoided everyone except Hadley and Nora for the last two weeks. He also joined the GUT security team twice a day at their training center in Glenwood Springs. He could feel strength returning to his muscles and his mind had grown much clearer. Although he'd never admit it to Hadley, meditation was the best part of his recovery. It calmed his nerves and set off powerful endorphin rushes. He still had immense cravings for Seed, but he found that if he went to meditation or for a run, the cravings would subside.

"What do you want to know?" Hadley murmured. She pushed her homework away with a grunt and her cheeks swelled up into a fish face.

"All of it." He laughed. Brecker still refused to give up any details about the research, only babbling on about how Zander still needed to heal. The man was only buying time though. He must know that once Zander found out what they were doing, he'd tear apart all their mystical evidence. The Grace money should be going into real research that could help real people, like nanotechnology, cancer treatments, vaccines—not wasted on fantasies and fake science.

"Well, do you know what the winning lottery numbers are going to be?"

"Nope. I can't tell the future or anything. But if I'm near someone, or touching something that was important to them, I get strong feelings about them and the stuff going on in their lives. Pictures in my head, smells, tastes." She rolled her eyes. "Drama."

"And the Pensare team figures out how you do this?"

"Yep. But it's much more than that," she replied as she turned back to her homework with a little smile.

"Didn't you read my mind when we first met?" he teased her.

"Well, I'm supposed to build a shield around every person here." She groaned. "Gotta respect privacy, let people keep all their weirdo thoughts to themselves. You know, so I don't get a God complex, ultimate power, take over the world, blah, blah, blah." Her hands waved in protest.

"Might be important."

"Yep. You should know your face is so obvious. There's not a shield thick enough really—"

"Alright, well, can you try? My thoughts'll traumatize a ten-year-old," Zander grumbled. "I wish someone would tell me what's going on."

"You're not ready yet. You'll just reject it and run away again."

He laughed. She sounded so certain, like a psychotherapist or an evangelical Christian.

Hadley strutted over to a wooden box in the corner. She tossed off the pile of books on top of it, letting them land on the floor with a thud. Radiohead played softly from her stereo. He was amazed that she listened to the same kind of music he did—Radiohead, Muse, Rise Against. Shouldn't tween girls be caught up in boy bands and Taylor Swift?

"I help the police department in Glenwood Springs sometimes—well, just one of the cops who's a little more open-minded. Psychic work is still frowned upon." Her face concentrating, she dug through the box.

"I can't imagine why," Zander smirked.

"Here we go." She pulled out a worn slip—shimmery, white silk with shell buttons. A tag was attached to one strap with an evidence number. "This belongs to a girl who went missing a few weeks ago. Her name is

Jen. I try to spend a few minutes a day with each item, see if any new information comes out."

She pulled out a denim jacket along with the slip. "This jacket is her boyfriend's, Jeremy. It helps if I concentrate on a relationship in the person's life. I can usually pull more details that way."

"Do the images scare you?"

"Sometimes. I always sit with Bumbles and he absorbs a lot of the stuff I can't handle." The cat was perched on the edge of Hadley's bed.

"Hard to believe he absorbs anything but food," Zander said, raising his eyebrows.

"Yep. Dogs, cats, horses. That's why when you're upset, they immediately make you feel better. Just stroking their fur absorbs negative miran. They're like. . . ." Her eyes went up to the ceiling. "Oh, I don't know. Giant sponges." She laughed as her fingers rippled the cat's coat. The line of black hair along his spine stood out in a faux mohawk. Irritated, Bumbles escaped but not before Hadley planted a kiss on his head.

"Sounds like a lot of work and time." Zander perked up. Clue here, clue there.

"Yeah, plus the search is so draining," she said, throwing her hands up wildly.

"Can I watch you do a reading?"

"Nada. It might get messy. Snot could leak out of my nose," Hadley replied, letting out a little shiver of tween embarrassment.

Zander shook his head. She really believed this stuff. He checked his watch. "How about if I catch up with you in a couple of hours? I have a workout session with GUT. Although I think they're tired of me," he whispered.

"I can see why. You're the biggest dork I've ever met. Sick of you." She made a giant S with her hands and pointed at him.

"Just bring your little girlfriends in for a sleepover. They'll get crushes on me and then you'll be the cool one."

She turned away and he almost missed the wobble in her chin. "Can you grab Bumbles? I want to wash my hands so I don't get anything false."

"Hadders . . ." he trailed off as she shuffled to the bathroom. Now that he thought about it, he never found her chatting on the phone or on the computers downstairs. She was always stretched out on the floor with her head in a book, Bumbles snoozing by her side. Zander went downstairs and searched the main floor. He finally found the cat in the kitchen, staring up at the fridge.

When he got back to the room, Hadley was on her bed with a tape recorder resting near her feet and the slip draped across her knees. Her hands moved across the silky fabric, alternately stretching and crumpling it up. Bumbles seemed to know his job. The cat launched onto the bed and crawled up under her arm, propping up her elbow. Zander closed the door quietly.

A couple of hours later, he returned from his workout and came in through the side entrance. He found Nora in the kitchen, the tingly scent of frying bell peppers and onions in the air. He scooped a few slices out of her wok and she smacked his hand with the spatula. Zander shook his fingers out and gave her a pitiful look, then managed to steal a soft flour tortilla from her other side.

"Not until dinner," she insisted.

"You know, all I do is eat, sleep, and work out. Sympathy would be nice."

"Take a break then. Cook. Wash dishes. Do laundry," Nora replied sweetly. He rolled his eyes. "Hadley's looking for you."

"I'll do her a favor and grab a shower first." His skin was saturated in dried sweat. Trey had really kicked his ass this time, and all he really wanted was steam, Nora's fajitas, and the deepest sleep before tomorrow's session. He was heading up the stairs when Hadley appeared at the top, her arms crossed.

"What are you doing?" she cried out. "I've been waiting forever. We need to go right now."

"Why?"

"Everyone else is busy and GUT won't take me alone. They think a kid needs a chaperone. Jerks," she scoffed. She headed down the stairs to meet him.

"I don't have time to change? Shower? Are you going to tell me why?"

She pushed him down the stairs and out the front door. "Let's go."

"Wait, I thought it was a missing girl? Shouldn't you talk to the police about it first?"

"They won't believe me," she replied, her voice tense. They got into one of the SUVs and she told the driver the address.

"Does Dr. Brecker know where you're going?" the driver asked.

"Yeah, he doesn't care. Hurry!" Hadley said. The driver radioed to him anyway, got the okay and they left.

"What did you see?" Zander asked.

"Someone's going to get hurt," she whispered. The driver studied them in the rearview. Zander sat back. He didn't believe any of this stuff, but she obviously did. Most children were fueled with drama, but this little girl took it to the next level. Then again, maybe she just had an overactive imagination and a gift for reading facial expressions.

"Why are we going so slow?" Her legs jittered and stomped the truck floor. The driver kept glancing in their direction. Zander wasn't sure how much the GUT personnel knew about what went on at Grace House. Perhaps they were paid to keep their minds and mouths shut. The SUV drove into Carbondale, the closest real town. Hadley swung her legs out and kicked the back of the driver's seat. Her body kept wiggling—she looked like she might pop out of her skin.

Her face crinkled up. "Do you think I'm weird?"

"Yeah, but it's alright. Most people are." He pointed to himself. "I'm the worst. A recovering addict? Like a giant toad with pus-filled warts. You're much cooler. In fact, I'm lucky you hang out with me."

Hadley giggled. "You do smell after a workout. And you should really shave more often."

"See what I mean? Lazy and smelly."

"Yep. Thanks for reminding me. Wait, we're here. That's it, that's it," Hadley squealed, opening the door before the driver came to a stop. Zander grabbed his bag and chased after her. For having such little legs, she was quick. He followed her up to a red brick house, 345 Wharton Street.

Hadley rang the doorbell. "I should tell you something. Jen's been missing for a couple of weeks. This is her boyfriend Jeremy's house. He lives with his parents—"

A woman opened the door. She looked stressed beyond belief, her skin pale with gray rings under her eyes. "Can I help you with something?"

"My name is Hadley. I'm working on Jen's case, but I need to talk to you about Jeremy. He's in trouble."

"Working on Jen's case? With the police? But you're a child." Heavy worry lines surrounded the woman's deep-set eyes. Her dark hair stretched back tight from her face.

"We don't have time to talk. Jeremy needs help fast." Hadley darted under the woman's arm and disappeared down the main hallway.

"Where's she going? What are you people doing here?"

Zander didn't know what to do except walk into the living room. The tall ceiling made the room appear bigger than it really was. A stack of "Missing" fliers sat on the coffee table with a girl's picture on it. Family portraits lined the wall. The smell of spaghetti sauce drifted in from the kitchen.

He stood awkwardly, not sure what to say. "I'm really sorry about this. Hadley's a dramatic kid. Very special. Is that the right word?"

"Are you her father?" the woman asked.

Zander chuckled. "Ah, no, I'm too young to be her father. Just a friend. Although we do live together . . ." he trailed off. This was not going well. Hadley came back with an older man marching behind her, his hand clamped on her shoulder. He had dark brown hair with gray at the temples. His face was deeply lined, too, but he acted like he was used to being in charge.

"What's going on, Joan? Do you know this little girl?"

"I've never met these two in my life."

"You have to help Jeremy. Right now!" Hadley yelled.

"He's in his room, Frank," Joan said, wringing her hands. Zander guessed she did that a lot.

"I talked to him about an hour ago. He seemed fine."

"But he's not. He's hurting himself." Hadley started to cry.

Frank knelt down and gripped her shoulders. "You have to stop this. Our family has been through a real nightmare these last two weeks. I don't know who set you up to this, but it's cruel." His hands tightened and he shook her a little.

"Hey, there's no need for that." Zander pulled him off.

"Well, if you can't control her—"

"Nobody's controlling anyone. We can solve this right now. Go check on your son," Zander bristled. "Prove her wrong."

"She's a kid. How can she know anything about him?" Joan asked.

Zander hesitated. The woman was right; it was impossible. Either this was Hadley's version of a prank, or perhaps therapy wasn't out of the question.

He looked down at Hadley. "How's he hurting? Can you tell?"

She sniffed, her nose runny. "He's like you. Doing drugs. A lot. Too much at once."

"Well, that answers it." Frank raised his hands. "My son's never done drugs in his life."

Zander almost laughed despite the tense situation. He'd heard that one a few times. "Has Jeremy been under suspicion in his girlfriend's disappearance?"

"Well, yes, but it's all a mix-up."

"So he could be depressed? And maybe hiding it?" Zander kept his voice steady. Raise the questions. Come on, come on.

The man stared at him, doubt clouding his gaze. He ran down the hall.

Hadley squeezed his hand and Zander knelt down next to her.

"He's almost gone," she whispered, her eyes softening under the tears.

"You did everything you could. You're very brave," Zander murmured. He pulled an extra towel out of his bag and gently patted her face. "Next time let's work on your opening technique, okay?" She nodded, her blond hair stuck to her cheeks in clumps.

Frank ran back, his voice breathless. "His door's locked and he won't answer."

Hadley's chin wobbled and Zander gave her a brief hug. "You stay out here. No matter what."

He motioned for Frank to follow him. "You got a screwdriver?"

"Yeah." The man looked in the hallway cupboard then handed one to him. Zander was 99.9% sure she'd be wrong. She had to be. This Jeremy kid would be perfectly fine, just spacing out to music or playing video games. Then they could go back to Grace House like nothing had ever happened. He unscrewed the handle. It popped off and he opened the door. There was no possible way Hadley could know.

He flipped on the light. Dammit. The kid was stretched across his bed, incredibly pale, a pair of cut nylons wrapped tight around his upper arm. The syringe lay near a scribbled note.

"Call 911." Frank shouted down the hall. He checked Jeremy's pulse while Zander examined the syringe. He knew what the kid was feeling at this moment, the sensation of flying. Release from all the pain and guilt over the last few weeks. His eyes were rolled back in his head and his chest didn't rise.

"I can't feel a pulse, I can't feel it, I can't feel it," Frank shrieked, cradling his son's head.

Zander reached out and tucked his fingers under the boy's neck. "It's faint, but it's there." As he watched the man's grief, he was suddenly grateful Brecker had been the one to find him on that island.

The paramedics arrived within minutes. Zander glanced at the note. The kid did feel guilty about his girlfriend and figured this was the only way out.

He and Hadley climbed back into the security truck. He brimmed with questions, but the little girl just stared forward. Her head gently tilted until it rested on his shoulder, then sank down into his side. Her eyes closed after a few minutes and her breathing deepened. Zander didn't understand what just happened, but he knew two things for sure. He was damn glad he'd gone with her. And he wanted to know more.

It was late by the time they got back to Grace House. He carried Hadley up to her room and laid her down in the bed. She buried her face in the pillow, wheezing with light snores. Zander took the elevator down to the basement. He kept going over everything the little girl had said. Could she have figured out any of that information on her own? Did a cop tell her? Even if she'd been told by someone, how did she know the exact time? Then there was her overwhelming heartbreak, her certainty. Somehow Hadley knew this kid was dying. How was that possible?

Zander walked out of the elevator and made his way down the corridor to the one light shining at the far end. It had been two weeks since his journey to Brecker's office in his wheelchair. Something had changed though. He was ready.

Brecker sat in his office, looking over diagrams, the lamplight casting shadows on his skin. He looked up, his glasses teetering on the end of his nose. Books surrounded him with titles like *The Mind-Body Connection, Psychic Therapies,* and *The Medicinal Power of Prayer.*

"Hello. You two make it back alright?"

"Barely," Zander replied.

Brecker smiled. His hand shifted over an inch, strategically covering his notes. Zander had a sudden flash of his father doing the same whenever a person walked into his study.

"Did you know that she could do that?" Zander asked.

"Hadley's adventures. Good thing you're around—you can watch out for her."

"She saved a life."

"Ah," the doctor murmured. "A good day then."

"You don't seem disturbed by that idea."

"By what idea?"

"That a child can know the things she does."

Brecker closed his notebook and took off his glasses. "Of course, I'm not disturbed by it, Zander. What you just witnessed . . . it's everything." His voice softened. "Everything we've built over the last two years, everything your father sacrificed for. What he gave his life for."

Zander's shoulders slumped. "I want to know why. Or how. Or anything."

Brecker looked away. "I don't—"

"Listen, I know why you've held back from me. I'm the worst skeptic and I'm not promising that will change. But I want to understand the science of Hadley. How she can know what she does? 'Cause from where I'm standing, it's impossible."

"The very edge of impossible, actually. My favorite place. Perhaps it's time to tip over the side." Brecker nodded. "Meet me in the training room tomorrow morning."

94

Chapter 13

Lynch sat far in the back of the auditorium. He withdrew a bottle of aspirin from his pocket, opened it, popped four in his mouth and swallowed them dry. Miami sweltered in mid-June, an alien landscape that felt impossibly dense, like a truck kept dumping pounds of air over his head and skin. He missed home. The Lolita was more like an opera hall than a nightclub, quite grand with eight floors and over thirty rooms. Outdoor piazzas were located on either side along with two pools and several saunas. He'd paid the club's owner, an Indian multi-millionaire, ten grand just to have full access to the place over the next few weekends, including the dancer's warm-up.

Why did the club hold a special place in Zander's heart? It could be the obvious amount of drugs filtering through the place, but there was nothing unique there. If his weak spot was of the female variety, then the club's fifty dancers were a good place to start. Yes, it was a burlesque club with plenty of skin and lace, but all of these women were trained in modern dance. They wore elaborate costumes and practiced their choreography several hours each day. The main stage was over five thousand square feet and held several performances on weekend nights.

It was late in the evening and hip-hop nonsense poured from the overhead speakers. Lynch sat silent, studying the dancers as they practiced. Mario and Drex reclined next to him, chatting absently. They had been on his crew for two years now. Lynch didn't feel he demanded much as an employer. He wanted individuals who were clean, observant, and thorough. They must be able to follow orders. They must be respectful and Lynch-fearing. And once in a while, they might be exposed to a smidge of violence. He smiled. The other men he'd brought were busy scouting Miami for any sign of Zander. Lynch refused to believe the kid had only come here once or twice. This place had to be worth something to him.

Lynch decided to head backstage for a closer look. One did not experience such heavenly anatomy every day. He strolled through the halls and peeked inside the dressing rooms, doing a quick survey of each face. Mostly blondes, some brunettes. Too loud, too shrill, too dumb. Too muscular, too thin. A couple of the girls were small like Cye and he looked a bit longer at these ones, but no. They didn't have that touch of vulnerability in the eyes. He sighed. It paid to be thorough, but he could be on the wrong track completely. Perhaps the doctor came here for his own lust, an older man with younger tastes. Lynch shook his head. Although his interaction with the doctor had only lasted minutes, the man seemed far too rigid for that.

So how did the doctor know to look here? This place was most likely a favorite of Zander's, or perhaps he'd lived in Miami at one time. But he was not from here. Lynch made a habit of studying people in great detail, and he had the distinct impression from his voice and manner that Zander came from the western states. He had that cowboy attitude, a love of privacy and open spaces and independence. Life as slow as a glacier.

Lynch exited the back area and came out by the side of the stage. He leaned against the wall and allowed himself to relax. All the exquisite bodies in motion. Hips and thighs flung over shoulders, feet twisting in great circles. Broad hands catching waists, only to let fly again. His eyes focused on one set of extended limbs that tapered beautifully. Thick waves of black hair tied up, strands loose. Her torso spun tightly, creating its own gravity and repelling the air. Instead of an abrupt stop, the dancer slowed ever so gently and fell into her partner's arms, her legs sliding outward with grace.

Her back had a particularly elegant look—petite shoulders angling down to a tight waist before sweeping out to slightly rounded hips. This girl was long and slender with a lovely assortment of curves. He tried to imagine her scent. Something that zipped the nose, like almond or citrus. Clean. She turned away from him, stretched, her arm encircling her head.

The choreographer called out for her to resume her position. And when Lynch saw her face, he knew. She had touches of Japanese in her look, with large eyes and slender cheekbones. A perfect dimple lay in the center of her chin, giving her a sweet vulnerability that made her look younger. Her mouth hardened when her feet wouldn't land properly.

That was it. The soul in those fluttering dark eyes. And the quiver in her chin when she got mad at herself. The perfect blend. That's the one Zander wanted. Either he was already dating her, or he wanted to desperately. Unfortunately, the girl was also perceptive. Her hand stroked the back of her neck, an anxious gesture. Her eyes flashed towards Lynch and her forehead crinkled with a look of suspicion. When she turned again, he crept back down the auditorium. He pointed her out to Mario and Drex, then motioned for them to follow him out.

The three men exited the auditorium and headed down the hallway. Lynch pushed down his nausea. Damn withdrawal. Dizziness, difficulty breathing. It was tough to concentrate. He felt outside himself, a hangover that wouldn't let up, no matter how much aspirin he took. He needed Kadera. But not when he was so close to his prize.

A woman stood near the building's exit. She spotted them, finished her conversation and closed her phone. Dressed in a short leather skirt, high heels and a slinky tubetop, she leaned against the doorway and gave Lynch a pout. Her top magically shifted so the lace rim of her bra flashed. He motioned for the other men to leave. Drex grinned and gave a low whistle.

"Hey honey, you're gorgeous," she said, tapping her tongue against her teeth. Lynch wondered if that was supposed to be erotic. He smiled and touched her obscenely bright red frizz of hair. Hmm, maybe it could work somehow, at night. He wanted it to work very badly. His hand slid over the back of her neck. The smell of vodka permeated.

Her tongue rimmed her lips. "You want to party tonight, sugar?"

Lynch slid his hand an inch to the side, then to the other side. Dammit. All he could feel was the warmth of her skin. How irritating to be like other people.

He looked full into her eyes. She stared at him with adoration, obviously pleased at the attention. She lowered her voice seductively. "Do I turn you on, sugar?"

He leaned in until his lips were right at her ear. "No. But you could."

"How's that?"

He whispered all the things he would do to her, all the lovely little details. He grew titillated just hearing them out loud. The woman may have caught a few of the words: "Muscle flayed open . . . bone splinters . . . blood splashing . . . punctured sternum . . . diced kidney." Her eyes grew wide and her mouth fell open.

Lynch squeezed her jaw hard. The soft flesh of her earlobe tantalized him. He wanted to shred it between his teeth. "Does that turn you on?"

She just blinked at him.

He groaned and touched his forehead, the headache already pulsing in his temples. "I apologize. I know we're both excited, but we'll have to save this for another night."

She nodded, her mouth still open.

"Good." He left her and exited the building. Drex and Mario were waiting outside. "Alright, back to the dancer. I want her name, I want to know everything about her. Where she lives, where she comes from, her family." Lynch held up one finger. "Be very discreet. She can't know. I don't want her warning him."

The men followed him around to the front of the club. He half-turned and looked up at the white marble of a statue—a naked female, her arms outstretched to the sky, courageous, emboldened. "You know, I'd really like to meet Zander's girl. Schedule a private dance for me."

Chapter 14

The morning after his talk with Brecker, Zander entered the new training room in the basement. Two enormous orbs stood on foot-high platforms. Each orb was composed of giant black hoops that overlapped and crossed each other. Wide nozzles lined each hoop's inner surface. A pair of goggles and gloves rested next to the platform.

Gage was dressed in his usual tie and suit, helping Brecker set up equipment. The doctor looked up at Zander and smiled. "Good morning. I think we're about ready to go."

Zander nodded to Gage. The man avoided his gaze. "Have you ever experienced a virtual reality ride?" he asked, his voice already tense.

"No."

"This is a pretty archaic system compared to most, but it does the job visually. Your dad and I spent quite a bit of time making it as accurate as possible. He logged hundreds of hours in here for training."

This was archaic? Zander marveled at the orbs, each big enough to fit a man inside. He ran his fingers along the edges of a hoop, then pulled back sharply. Gas poured out of the nozzles all at once, slipping over his skin. The goggles and gloves rose up to the center of the orb and stayed there, pressed by gas flow on all sides.

Brecker caught his eye and nodded. "Yes, that's where the user is suspended. It allows you to move freely; you can somersault, do cartwheels, anything."

He sat down on a small cot next to one of the orbs and motioned for Zander to sit on the other one. "Go ahead and strip."

Zander raised his eyebrows. He took off everything except his boxer shorts, then crawled through a side panel to the center of the orb. The goggles fit snugly over his eyes so no outside light penetrated. He slid the gloves on, then jerked back as a blue screen flashed across his vision. A timer icon appeared in the corner.

"Stay absolutely still. A red laser is passing over your body now, scanning a digital image of you into the system," Gage called out. The timer reached zero and there was a rushing sound in Zander's ears, like water moving past him. His skin was coated in cool breezes.

His body levitated, inch by inch, until his weight went slack. He floated in mid-air, the sensation hypnotic. Pulses of warm and cool rippled over his skin. The tiny amount of hair on his chest swayed. He stretched to his fullest length and laughed as he performed a quick somersault.

"I'm glad you like it, since this is where you'll spend most of the next few weeks," Brecker said. The blue screen in Zander's glasses turned black again, then abruptly white. Not a solid white, but a translucent haze. He moved his hands out in front and they appeared in his line of vision. The haze lifted, revealing a world of glass and rock. On closer look, some surfaces were mirror-like, others rose up as towering sheets of granite and obsidian. It actually looked a bit like wild Colorado if it were all rock and cliffs. There were no trees or cars or people. He touched the side of a boulder; blue and green minerals glittered in the rock. He peered inside a nearby cavern. Giant crystal stalactites arched downward from its ceiling. Crimson smoke poured out of the granite outcroppings. Dust whirlwinds floated off in the distance. Zander studied his hands, then down at the loose clothing over his body. Virtual reality was definitely the future.

A digital image of Brecker came into view. "Okay, let's stay here a moment."

"Why are we going through this elaborate setup? Not that I don't enjoy it, but why can't you just tell me what the discovery is?"

"I'm a pragmatist. Out of all of the Pensare members, I was probably the most skeptical of Jason's discovery. I found the simulator really helped my mind to grasp it. I think you'll work the same way. Maybe if you spend enough time in here, you'll gain the courage to go on your first trip."

"I'm going somewhere?"

"I hope so. To a place where few have been, but where every heart lingers," Brecker replied.

"Okay. Didn't figure you for a Hallmark man." Zander did a cartwheel on the cloud cover, then climbed up the side of the nearest cliff. He was so light he could almost bounce up. Once on top, he bolted across the surface. "I can't believe this. It's so freeing, so . . . whoa. Whoa!" A steep drop-off came up too fast. He stumbled and reached out to brace himself. Rewarded with a fistful of vapor, he hit the bottom of the hundred-foot drop with a thud. His back twisted and he panicked.

Brecker laughed. "Come back. We need to continue our conversation."

Zander felt tingling in his arms and legs, but not in pain. The gentle breeze still drifted over his skin from the orb. Feeling very stupid, he stood up. "I thought I was hurt."

"You expected the fall to hurt, so it did." Brecker walked over to him and helped him up. "Cooler than drugs?"

"Obviously, you've never taken drugs," he chuckled. "Still pretty cool."

The older man's face grew serious. "Jason's discovery is so pivotal to mankind, Zander, it's beyond belief. I think it might help if I started in real-life terms. Have you ever met someone and felt like you've known her forever, like fate pulled you to each other?" he smirked. "Or at least how it's depicted in the movies?"

"I've heard of it, of course. Soulmates, true love, best friends, all that."

Brecker nodded. "Take your father and our thirty-year friendship. A random meeting on a train, right? He happened to be reading my article when I stepped aboard. One glance. But what drew my gaze? Why did he chose that seat, pick up that article to read at that exact moment?"

Zander shrugged. "Pure chance."

"What if instead of pure chance, we were really drawn together like a pair of weak magnets?" he asked. "Have you ever felt anything beyond your senses, beyond your own mind that you couldn't explain?"

"I don't think so." Zander felt a sudden tingling at the back of his neck. He brushed off his skin.

"I'm sure like most scientists, you don't believe in psychics or ghosts. But what if we could explain those, too?"

Brecker raised his hands wide. "Right now, science assumes all psychics are fake. Ghosts are vivid only in the imagination. Biology declares soulmates and love at first sight to be simple animal instincts, lodged deep in the brain. Our senses take in information and filter it down to our conscious mind. But is that it? Neurons processing facial structure, nervous tics, a flash of eye movement. This person is good, this person bad. Protect yourself. Fall in love."

"Of course. What else could it be?" Zander replied. He shifted his weight uncomfortably. Where was the man going with this?

Brecker exhaled a deep breath. "Vita Maglia."

Zander groaned. That name again. "Alright, so I guess I'll ask the million dollar question: What is Vita Maglia?"

"Vita Maglia, or 'life mesh' in Italian, is what we consider the fifth dimension. As you know, on earth we have three spatial dimensions: length, width, depth. Then there's the temporal dimension of time. Maglia is one more layer, but it's an emotional layer. Some might call it a spiritual dimension."

"Maglia's all around us, a layer underneath everything we do, see, touch. She's invisible, but she's there. When we pass a current through a special part of your brain, your normal senses go away. So you won't see the normal world anymore; you'll only see what's underneath it, the Maglian layer. You'll walk around, splash in the nitrogen pools. Spy the exotic creatures."

As if on cue, the strangest-looking bug Zander had ever seen flew up in front of his face. He squealed loudly, darting away from the awful thing. It had no eyes, just hundreds of small tentacles reaching out, possibly to suck out his brain. Its tail whipped around, almost colliding with his hand. It chased him a moment, then disappeared up into the atmosphere.

Brecker laughed and waited for him to settle down.

He motioned to the rock surrounding them. "The Maglian layer should look like a faded version of the earth we see everyday. Just rock, dirt, dust, water vapor." He held up a finger. "It does look like that, but the chemical bonds are different, so instead of water, there are nitrogen pools and great lakes of ozone. The cliffs and mountains are the same that you see normally, but the edges glitter in shades of turquoise and magenta. There are also giant crystal formations, smoke geysers, and great caverns of glass and metal."

Zander laughed. "I feel like I just walked into a Tolkien scene. So what's the point of this dimension? You mentioned something about emotions?"

"Everything evolved in Maglia in order to care for the strands. Hold on," Brecker said. "Gage, zoom us in."

Zander steadied himself as the simulation moved underneath him. They came close to colliding with one of the cliffs.

They arrived next to a curling tentacle hanging from the sky. "A human strand," Brecker motioned proudly. It looked like a vine, about twenty feet in length. When Zander looked closer, he discovered the core was made up of many smaller filaments wound together. Tiny specks of mineral floated around the core in a helix pattern, flashing in a rainbow of hues like lavender, russet, spring green.

"Each strand is a mixture of gases and metals. It has positive and negative energy centers," Brecker paused and took another deep breath.

He knows I'm never gonna believe this, Zander thought.

"Each strand is a human soul. When life begins, a strand is flung out and it grows during a person's life. At death, the strand is cut and pulled into Afterlife."

"Throughout her life, a strand makes connections with other strands. These tangles represent our relationships, our families, our great loves. It's that feeling of knowing someone truly, deeply." He tapped his chest. "I know it's a bit shocking—"

"This is just . . . it's really impossible, Brecker," Zander replied. "Emotions are just synapses firing in the brain, neurotransmitters across channels. If there's a soul, it's definitely located in the human brain."

"That idea is effectively medieval now," Brecker said. He motioned for Zander to step forward, then pointed up. The strand twinkled before them. It looked like a long vine with small tendrils growing out of it. The top of it stretched up higher and higher until. . . .

Zander had to remind himself to breathe. Above him, what looked like millions of these vines crisscrossed each other in a huge network. Bursts of light skittered across them, making the web glittery. There were shady stretches too, some pitch black, others a steel gray. The mesh seemed to go on forever.

One moment the strands flashed metallic, then luminescent, then a gunmetal sheen. They remained still, then appeared to pulsate, reaching for each other, tangling. There were billions above him, cross-linked in a giant web.

"The mesh. Our connections, our relationships," Brecker murmured.

Zander shook himself. "I don't know what to tell you, Brecker. Nice fantasy you've built here, but I need solid proof."

"I know it sounds like complete science fiction—"

"You've got that right," Zander scoffed.

"—but so did television, lasers, and atomic bombs before the twentieth century. I hate to get poetical, but throughout mankind's history, we've searched for true love, soulmates, the occult, even angels and demons. That search was always beyond the realm of science. Until now."

"You're telling me this is a person's soul?" Zander asked. The strand's minerals flickered in the shifting light. He had a deep desire to brush the floating specks with his fingertip.

"If we were to fade through the Veil into the real Maglia, then yes, it would be."

"The Veil?"

"Remember that Maglia exists as a layer over our physical world. In between Maglia and us is a shield of protection called the Veil. It blocks us from interfering with our own souls and keeps the Maglian creatures inside their dimension. Believe me, this protection is essential to everyone involved. You wouldn't know it by looking at the simulation, but there's tremendous danger in Maglia."

"The Veil's meant to keep out physical bodies and it does. But consciousness is a different matter. It's extremely rare, but some minds can pass through the Veil. We call them travelers."

"My father?"

"Yes. And perhaps yourself."

Realization dawned in Zander. "So that's what you meant by taking a trip."

"Yes. Let's start from the beginning. When Jason was ten years old, he was struck by lightning. Not only did the strike not kill him, he experienced Maglia for about thirty seconds. When he woke up, he convinced himself that it was a dream, but the vision stuck with him. He carried a piece of copper, a substance known to attract lightning, for years after that, but he wasn't struck again until—"

"Yeah, I know. When I was five. My parents and I were at a picnic. When the storm hit, Mom wanted to leave, but of course, Dad had to be right there. And look what it cost us." As if agreeing, Zander's heart skipped a beat. The blue scar throbbed on his chest.

Brecker frowned. "Alright, well, Jason traveled to Maglia for the second time. After losing Cecilia and almost you, he decided to experiment with energy sources until he could simulate a lightning strike. About five years ago, Jason took his first artificial trip to Maglia. He kept detailed records of all his observations."

"All under the radar, of course."

"Believe me, Zander, this is all under the radar. Everyone here has signed iron-clad confidentiality agreements. No information about Maglia can get out before the Pensare decides it's the right time. It would cause mass chaos."

Zander sighed. The nut jobs might love it.

"Our time's almost gone. One last thing I should mention though. Look up."

He stared up at the mesh. It really was strikingly detailed for a simulation. Small gas bugs buzzed and crawled along the strands. Lights shimmered and danced in a range of colors. But there were also the deepest spirals of ebony and gray.

"When you travel, you'll meet the creatures that inhabit Maglia, which evolved specifically to care for the strands. Just like on our side, there's infinite variety. The bug-looking creatures, gliders, are just the beginning. There's also a kind of beneficial bacteria called nesso. And the carnivorous plants called pianta. The two most important species we've encountered are the Lusha and the Vipera. The Lusha are the points of light you see moving above."

Zander did see them, the flickering patches that appeared and disappeared at random. As he looked closer, he realized they just moved very fast. A point of light that was alive?

"The dark patches you see above are the Vipera. They're the shadows that balance the Lusha. These two forces affect the flow of positive and negative charges on individual strands and in the greater mesh. We believe," Brecker hesitated again.

Here comes another zinger, Zander thought.

"These two species are better known as angels and demons."

"As in the Bible?" Zander groaned. "You know, I was actually curious there for about a minute, but that's too far out."

Brecker laughed. "That was the tipping point, huh?" He pointed up at the mesh. "When you fade into Maglia, they'll appear in their true form, as light and shadow, but they can morph into anything they want. To the actual people at home, they appear as anything they need to be. An angel with a sword, a beloved grandmother. The person's greatest fear, monsters."

No kidding, Zander thought. His brain felt numb, like it was trying to process great amounts of information at once. His gaze naturally traveled up to the mesh. Sparks of light shot across the web, submerged under patches of dark, then broke free. "Monsters, huh? Why are the Vipera built like that?"

"They evolved that way. Vipera rip apart the strands in order to feed on the metals and gases interwoven in the core. As they feed, they release negative energy in the form of depression, anxiety, rage."

"What about the Lusha creatures, the angels?"

"It's the opposite. They help the strands thrive and increase our relationships. They pour positive energy into the mesh and heal wounded strands with pulses of light," Brecker replied. "Let's get out of here. Gage?"

The cloud vapor suddenly rose up around Zander, blocking him in. His vision went to black, then blue. He was gently lowered to the bottom of the orb. He pulled off his goggles and looked around, disoriented and insanely thirsty. Gage helped him onto a cot and handed him a bottle of water. Brecker got dressed next to him.

"What now?" Zander asked.

"Well, you have to give us the chance," Brecker said, his voice irritatingly tinged with hope. "The other travelers are not available and there's not much time." He stared off for a moment, then squeezed Zander's shoulder. "Don't think of that now. We'll go through training first, then you can decide if you want to travel."

Zander's thoughts returned to the other travelers Brecker mentioned, specifically Bryn Sansa. Did she believe in all this? Strangely, it made him feel better to think she did. He didn't understand why, but his nights were filled with dreams of holding her tightly, her face tucked into his neck, her lips fluttering on his skin. She needed him and he just kept falling into those dark eyes. He'd wake up, his heart shuddering with intense love like nothing he'd ever felt.

He caught himself wondering where she was, what she was doing. Who she was loving. If this fantasy could somehow bring her closer, he was willing to try it out.

Chapter 15

There was a Catholic church in Glenwood Springs named St. Sebastian. Two stories high and built of timber from the surrounding woods, the church's main attraction was the heavy gold cross that hung over the entrance. Five diamond-shaped windows of brightly stained glass caught the rising sun on the church's eastern side. Despite the glamorous exterior, the church was humble inside, with oak pews leading to a wooden altar and a lectern where services were conducted. A prayer room was accessible from the outside so devout Catholics could pray as needed. Twin bell towers rang on the morning of every Sabbath, a sound that lifted the hearts of men to the divine God who created and redeemed souls.

The church hosted three priests, 245 parishioners and a single garden fenced in by wrought iron. The rectory's vegetables were supplied by this garden: drooping Roma tomatoes, shiny bell peppers, and golden oblong squash.

"Now, these are fairy trumpets." He drew the branch forward and pulled off one of the flowers. Hadley took it and rolled the coral tube between her fingertips.

"They're just the right size for a fairy to walk by and toot on one," she said.

"The trumpet shape is perfect. Insect bodies are coated in pollen as they access the nectar. Then they spread the pollen to other trumpets. Just look at that design." He looked up at the low sun in the sky. Thank goodness she came in the early morning hours to help, before the heat could bear down on the bald crown of his head.

"Father Seth, look. The ants are fighting over something," she gasped. "It's a caterpillar. They're hurting him." Red legs swarmed the rotund body, its stripes shuddering grotesquely. Hadley reached to save it, but Seth caught her hand. The body stilled and the ants grew into a mountain, drenching the poor creature.

"Ants need food, too, my dear. They don't get Nora's blueberry muffins for breakfast."

"I hate it," Hadley said, her voice tender. She turned to another patch of flowers. "Oh, a dragonfly."

Its wings reflected the pink shimmer of the hedgehog cactus below it, the elongated body a bright sapphire blue. "You know," Seth said, "some believe that God started diluted in the single-celled organisms, then He grew more concentrated into bugs, fish, reptiles—"

"—and dinosaurs, I know. And giant insects. So cool," Hadley murmured.

"Yes, then mammals, like cats, dogs, monkeys," Seth said gently. "Pooling, becoming ever more concentrated. And do you know where most of God ended up?"

"Uh, people?"

"Yes. Others believe that God breathed the divine in man alone. Have you been reading the book I gave you?" he asked.

"The one about bugs? I love it," Hadley said, trying to ease the dragonfly onto her finger. It escaped to the far side of the shrub.

"That one, too, but I meant the Bible stories."

"Oh, yeah. They're okay. Except," Hadley stopped.

"What is it?"

"Do you think God likes people?"

"Do you?"

She shook her head. "He's a really mean dad."

"Sometimes. Maybe He's a little sad like you were, watching the ants hurt the caterpillar."

"No." Hadley looked up at the sky. "He could stop it but He doesn't."

"If He stopped the fighting, how would we all learn and grow?"

She stood quiet. Seth could hardly hear what she said next. "He could've stopped what happened to my brother and He didn't."

It took him a moment to realize what she meant. Hadley rarely talked about losing her older brother, Adam. In fact, Seth wondered how much she remembered. He'd spoken to her parents when she'd first arrived at Grace House, but the Porters were mired in their own grief and unsure how to handle hers.

"I think God takes away a lot of brothers," he said.

She looked up at him. "You really miss your brother, huh?"

"Every single day." His voice cracked a little.

"You know, Zander misses Dr. Grace as much as you do, even though he pretends he's okay." She blew breath upward, fluttering her bangs out of her eyes. "When are you going to visit him?"

Seth pointed to another caterpillar, lumbering among the purple petals of the columbine flowers at their feet. Hadley blew softly, rippling its bright yellow fuzz.

"I don't know. We didn't get along when he was growing up. Not much room in my nephew's head for faith," he said, smiling. Seth was a member of the Pensare, yet he resided at St. Sebastian. He took confession, studied scripture, and when his health allowed, delivered sermons. Here he could forget the hard decisions about Maglia or Zander or the Grace legacy.

But that's precisely why the Lord had given him this challenge, a sacred obligation that would affect more souls than he could ever save by himself. "Do you get along with Zander?" he asked.

"Yeah." Her voice descended to a whisper, like the young man stood a few feet away. "But he's kinda full of himself. Don't tell him I said that."

"Full of himself? Most children are."

Her laughter bubbled up. "Zander's *supposed* to be a grown-up."

Seth winked. "Oh, that's right." They moved down the pathway to the next row of flowers.

Hadley cocked her head to the side. "He's just been waiting for Maglia. She makes me pretty grown-up."

"Definitely." Seth wished that were true for his nephew. Jason had always let Zander go wild, absolutely no discipline, and now they'd all pay the price. Rebellion, drugs, deserting them for that hedonistic island. Seth had been as vehement as Gage against bringing Zander back. Either the kid would simply run away again, delaying the research by months, or he'd be a danger, disrupting the delicate forces in Maglia, perhaps altering the dimension or eliminating access for other travelers.

They walked through the garden. Seth pointed at weeds and Hadley dug them up, shoving the offensive plants in her gardening tote, the extra-small gloves loose on her hands. He had to remind her to slow down; it was difficult to stand too long on his legs. Lasting trauma from his one disastrous trip, but it'd been worth it.

He winced at the arthritic ache. Hadley stopped him and took his hands in hers. Warmth traveled up his palm. "You should let the Circle help," she said, her voice stern.

He jerked away, then grimaced as the pain flooded back. "So you've told me. You three should do an infomercial."

"Huh?"

"Nevermind," he chuckled. He took two aspirin every morning and left it for God to decide the rest of his day. Seth tried to appreciate the Circle, but there was still this reluctance inside him. He understood their role in Maglia, but he could never accept psychics and meditatives as true healers. That's why Hadley needed to be shown a spiritual alternative.

He picked a rose, studying the hint of cream color in the petals. He imagined the molecules of chlorophyll catching sunlight, millions of genes inside a microscopic cell, replicating itself and building proteins. An invisible orchestra. Seth brought the fragrant creation to his nose and breathed. Perfection. Every atom fitted through evolution. So why was man so flawed? Was it the burden of reason? Or perhaps it was the lingering animal instinct. He appreciated science as a tool for understanding God's design in the world. It was the scientists that alarmed him. No reverence meant no boundaries.

He murmured to himself. "Maglia. They'll destroy her."

"What did you say?" Hadley called out.

"Oh, nothing. What do you have there?"

"There are holes." She inspected his tomato plants. "You should protect them better."

"Yes, parasites. My soft heart will be the end of my garden," he said. "Can you strip off those dead leaves there? Why don't you take these copper mallows home to Nora?" He picked a few of the vivid orange flowers, the centers a sparkling gold. A breeze traveled over the path. He closed his eyes and leaned back, letting the air move under his glasses and over the last few wisps of gray hair. The sun warmed the deep grooves in his face and his anxiety lifted. The Lord had seen fit to place Seth inside this discovery. He'd provide guidance for all the moral decisions to come.

Seth had been retained as a permanent deacon in the church during his marriage. After his wife abandoned him and their young son, he'd been granted an annulment. Years later, he'd finally been given permission to become a full priest, the proudest day of his life.

After pruning, he and Hadley made their way up to the garden's entrance at the side of the church. His son, Calvin, had helped him build this garden before leaving for his studies at the Vatican. The main path from the church branched onto six sidepaths, with each path leading to dense rows of flowers and vegetables. A brilliant tinkerer, Calvin had also built an irrigation system. Seth turned a single spout at the entrance and watched water gush down the carefully laid routes, finally trickling into the last rows.

Seth sighed. He couldn't help thinking that if his son were home now, the Pensare could avoid this whole Zander mess. Calvin had always been a quiet, soft-natured boy, full of study and temperance. He'd give wisdom and understanding to the traveler's role, a true soldier of God, fighting alongside the Lusha angels. Pride surged in Seth's heart, climbing upward like the sun above him.

But in order to keep Maglia safe until Calvin's return, Seth had to keep an eye on Grace House. This meant making peace with his nephew.

***

That afternoon, one of the GUT trucks dropped Seth off in front of Grace House. He went to his room on the main floor and put away his suitcase. He prayed for a few minutes, the rosary beads clicking softly. It was time.

He took the elevator upstairs. Knocking, he let himself into his nephew's room. Zander sat on the floor next to his bookcase. Sun from the window reflected off the copper pipe in his hand, projecting a triangle of light on the boy's face. Seth recognized the pipe from that day twenty years ago, when he'd visited Jason and his five-year-old son in the hospital and identified Cecilia's body in the morgue.

Zander looked up at him, surprise on his face. "Hadley told me you'd aged but . . ." he trailed off.

"I know. My one trip didn't go so well." Seth hobbled in and set his cane against the wall. "I should have trusted the Circle more, I suppose."

Zander nodded and turned back to the pipe. "I was just, I don't know. Remembering, I guess." His face softened. He seemed completely different than the angry young man Seth remembered.

"I didn't think you recalled anything about that day."

"Stuff's been coming back, dredged up by the detox." Zander felt the hard ridge of bluish tissue running down his chest. "Flashes of the picnic, the storm rolling in. Dad holding this." He set the pipe on top of the bookcase and sat down on the edge of the bed.

"Yes. Jason found it at an antique shop shortly after his first trip. Copper attracts lightning." Seth joined him and patted his shoulder. He saw the little boy again, immature, defiant, but perhaps he could change.

"I should warn you, Zander. There's simply nothing like Maglia. You'll crave her, be thrilled by her, live for her, like—" He stopped short, not wanting to say the word.

"Like a drug. I know. You and Gage believe I'm the worst person the Pensare could've chosen. You're probably right." Zander wiped his cheeks with his shirt sleeve.

Seth felt embarrassed. He lacked confidence in the boy, but suddenly he wanted to hope. Perhaps he could help guide his nephew to maturity, a chance he never had with Jason. His brother was the most pig-headed of scientists, and most of their early lives were spent in screaming matches over science versus religion. Like most men, Jason hadn't understood the power of his own discovery. Maglia was the validation of God's creation—everything Seth had dedicated his life to.

He looked over the boy's handsome face, stricken with grief. Perhaps Seth could give him a warmer view of the Church. It could contribute so much. He'd been discussing the possibilities with Brecker, a lapsed Catholic. Seth's back and neck muscles tensed. In fact, the research should really lie in more responsible hands—

Zander interrupted his thoughts. "Do you remember my mother?"

"Cecilia was a wonderful woman. You three were a real family, something I never thought my brother would have. When he was with her, Jason was as close to normal as he ever would be. She had dark curls like mahogany. Highly intelligent, warm. Of course, you have her eyes, that dark, almost violet blue." Seth shrugged. He'd been caught up in his own rocky marriage around that time. He wondered now if he could have made an impact on the boy back then, channeling him into a more positive direction like Calvin.

"I loved her laugh, how it bubbled up out of nowhere. And she'd rock me to sleep at night. Even after she thought I was asleep, she'd sing me another lullaby."

"Jason spent the rest of his life trying to make up for her sacrifice. He had to prove Maglia was worth the price," Seth replied.

"You know, I remember Maglia in my dreams," Zander said. "I realized it soon after the simulation. A world where a little kid can float up like a feather and all around him is light and shadow and clouds."

He took a deep breath. "The thing is, Uncle Seth, I keep telling myself it's all lies. That he was wrong to give up everything for it. To lose Mom. To lose himself. Just the delusions of a crazy man. But I can't get away from the dreams." Zander braced his head between his hands. "How can Maglia be a lie if I remember her?"

Chapter 16

Over the next three weeks, Zander marveled at how short a time it took to become a new person. Through meditation with the Circle every morning, he learned how to ascend and descend through the miran levels on his own. He studied neurology with a reluctant Gage to determine how his mind faded through the Veil and how it interacted with the Maglian layer. He enjoyed flirting with Raleigh as they discussed legends about the human soul and researched potential methods of traveling, including séances, shaman healers, and even psychedelics. All of his free time was spent in the simulator, which happened to be the best video game in the world.

Standing tall at six feet two inches, his twice-daily sessions with GUT gave him inches of lean muscle around his mid-section and broadened his shoulders. Along with his strength training and running, the security team trained him in kickboxing and jiu-jitsu techniques. The summer sun brought out strands of gold and red in his auburn hair. Nora kept it trimmed so it gently curled around his face, just barely out of his eyes. He insisted on keeping his sideburns a little long, despite her protests.

He loved the evenings he spent in the library with Isaac Rosen poring over physics textbooks and Dad's old journals. The library smelled of dusty books and spices like cinnamon, nutmeg, and pumpkin, as if Nora kept her Christmas potpourri on full blast all year round. Watercolor paintings of the White River National Park were spaced evenly on the burgundy and tan walls. Small tables and chairs stood in clusters. The lights were turned down low next to the blue shimmers of the gas fireplace. Nora stood in the doorway and Isaac waved her over.

She brought two large mugs of Isaac's tea, a thick mixture with ginger and honey. It was an old family recipe passed down to Isaac from his mother for chilled mornings in Poland. Zander remembered how he grimaced when trying it as a child. The elderly man blew on it, the air quivering the white bristles in his mustache.

Zander sank down in the soft leather armchair. He loved grilling his father's old friend. "So, if you haven't seen any of it yourself, how do you know Jason and Seth aren't making it all up?" he said, teasingly.

"Brecker didn't tell you about our mini-fades?" Isaac chuckled. "With enough energy and the special Recipe that Jason concocted, anyone's mind can fade through the Veil and experience Maglia for about thirty seconds. I've done it, Gage has, Brecker. But we mere mortals can't survive longer than that. Our hearts and brains shut down. You and your relatives not only survive it, you can travel for several hours, even days inside the Maglian layer. But you'll still have trauma. We're still not sure why traveling ages the body faster. That's why we're excited to have a young traveler."

"The Recipe?" Zander asked.

"Yes, after many years of experimentation, Jason found just the right mix of chemicals for the fading process. With the Recipe and your enlarged claustrum, you won't need huge surges of energy. Just a gentle current passed through the brain." Isaac cleared his throat. "We use deep brain stimulation by implanting a brain pacemaker just behind the clavicle bone. Wires travel under the skin, from the pacemaker up into the brain where they insert directly into the claustrum. Sounds gruesome, but it's actually pretty routine by now. Very effective treatment for Parkinson's, epilepsy, maybe even Alzheimer's."

Zander nodded. Gage was performing his DBS procedure tomorrow. Hopefully, the man didn't decide to give him a lobotomy. His first trip to Maglia would be in three days and he was very nervous. So nervous he found himself asking the same questions over and over to relieve his stress. "So Dad's body stayed here?"

"Yes, in our travel room. To everyone else he remained asleep, but his mind was in Maglia."

"But I'll have a body there?"

"Not a real one. Your mind forms a body out of the air molecules in Maglia."

"Automatically?"

"Yes, your mind needs something to cling to, so it immediately forms a body to house it, using your own memories and nervous system," Isaac replied.

"I don't know. Sounds like a couple of movies I've seen. Pretty damn sci-fi." Zander laughed.

"You laugh, but physics works differently in the Maglian layer. The mind can move much faster, over great distances. Your body is made out of air. With enough mental control, you could change into different forms."

Isaac paused, his eyes dreamy. "With the right skill level, Maglia may be limitless."

"You're telling me I can be a superhero?" Zander raised his eyebrows.

"Yes," Isaac replied, distracted. He took a sip of tea and winced. "Seventy-five years old and I can't save myself from a burned tongue."

"Is that why Maglia looks like it does? Metallic rock and crystal and granite?"

"Yes. The dimension is built from the same atoms as ours—carbon, nitrogen, lead, etc. But due to her new physics, those atoms form different structures than in the home layer. So you get crystal cliffs, metallic ledges, and new plant combinations. And the container for the human soul? Not a body with arms and legs, not that exquisite computer we call a brain, but," Isaac winked, "a strand. A coil that conducts energy, but not just any kind of energy. Strands conduct miran. Emotional energy surging all over the world, between every human being. The power of evolution."

"Tell me about Hadley and Liz again," Zander asked, his leg starting to jitter. Of course, it was natural to feel nervous, but he still hated it in himself. He should be stronger than this. Three days. He closed his eyes and imagined Isaac as a soothing grandfather, telling him fantastical stories of a place he'd never have to go.

Isaac continued. "Okay, let's simplify it down. Imagine a giant network of wires. The wires crisscross and connect with each other. Now imagine some of those wires are special. They're able to pull energy from another wire. Energy that contains information—what food he likes, where he was born, the color of his eyes, how he feels about his life. But with billions of wires, it's very hard to find just the right one. That's why psychic visions are very random. It's like finding a needle in a haystack. Obviously, a psychic's strength and training make an enormous difference."

"Hadley."

Isaac nodded. "Hadley's a talented psychic. But more importantly, she's a concentrated power source. Think of her as one of those natural hot-water springs, but instead of water, she spouts miran. I went with your father when he found the girl and she's the real reason for many of his breakthroughs." He tapped the arm of his chair.

"We'll have to go again tomorrow, my boy. As you can see," Isaac's hand rose, trembling, "I have to take my medication and retire for the evening."

Zander took the elderly man's arm. They left the library and walked down the main hallway towards Isaac's bedroom.

He shook his head. "I still can't really believe it."

"You will," Isaac murmured softly. "Then you can never go back to your days of innocence." He let out a creepy old man chuckle.

He pointed through the open entrance to the dining room as they passed it. "Did I ever tell you I saw a ghost right there? A heavy-set fellow with a beard and a foul mouth."

Zander smiled. "I used to see them sometimes as a kid. I never left my room at night."

"Yes, Grace House was built in the late 1800s, I believe. You know, when a person dies," Isaac said, "his strand is cut at the source."

He made a scissoring motion with his fingers. "Cut."

"And it falls into Afterlife," Zander finished the thought. His back shivered. "The great vortex called the Calamata. It whirls underneath the mesh and catches the broken strands."

Isaac patted his back. "Correct. At death, a person's strand is cut and it's supposed to fall into the Calamata and pass into Afterlife. That is the normal process." He sighed deeply. "Unfortunately, not all of them make it. Sometimes cut strands become trapped," he lowered his voice, "among the live ones."

Zander's mouth dropped open. "Ghosts."

"Yes. When a strand is cut, it whips around quickly. Sometimes it's caught in a nearby bundle of living strands. It becomes so intertwined that even the tremendous gravity of death cannot tear it away." His voice turned sad. "It haunts the living souls until a traveler or a Lusha can release it."

He made it to his bedroom door then turned. "You know, Zander, even if you only heal a few souls in your lifetime, it makes a difference. Over the years and decades, as the research gets stronger, we can set up healing stations all over the world. There may be a way to heal a strand without traveling, or perhaps some healers can reside permanently in the Maglian layer and help the Lusha. Maglia's a wonderful obligation, a tremendous gift. We can cross a frontier that science and medicine have not been able to touch."

Isaac closed his bedroom door. Zander stood there thinking for a few minutes. Ever since he was a child, he'd always been skeptical of what others told him. Something he'd inherited from the Grace line perhaps. That's why he was so willing to take his first trip, despite his anxiety and fears. He had to see Maglia for himself. Discovery of the science behind the human soul? And not just individual souls, but all the mysterious connections between them?

He cocked his head to the side, listening. He swore he heard a beeping sound, like a machine in a hospital. It seemed to be coming from the very last bedroom. He went through this hallway many times a day, yet he'd never noticed that sound before. Zander poked his head into the room. The first thing he saw was a ventilator.

An Asian man lay in a bed, his skin sallow. Remnants of a beard appeared on his square jawline and tiny grey hairs covered his head. An IV was inserted in his arm from a hanging bag, and the beep was coming from a heart monitor.

"Oh, honey, what are you doing in here?" a voice said behind him. A hand pressed into his back.

"Who is this guy? What happened to him?" he asked.

Liz tied up her robe and sat down on the edge of the bed. Her braids flowed loose over her shoulders with beads woven through them. The tingle of baby powder filled Zander's nose. "His name is Elder Sansa and he's one of your father's dearest friends. His body's in a coma, but his mind resides permanently in the Maglian layer. He can't come home."

Recognition dawned in Zander. "Sansa? He's related to Bryn? This was the man she was talking about?"

"Yes, Elder is her father. Now you know why she can travel. The Sansa genes are like the resilient Grace genes, hardy and fast healing. Both families also have enlarged claustrums."

Zander sputtered, hopelessly confused. "I don't understand. How can he be her father? He looks nearly eighty years old. And like he hasn't been out of bed in months."

"Ten years, to be exact. It's complicated."

Alarm bells filled his head. "Liz, you have to tell me what happened. Did this happen when he traveled? Did the Pensare make him like this?"

"Oh, sweetheart, no, no. Let's see, about ten years ago, Elder Sansa was on a research trip, studying jellyfish off the coast of his native Japan. He has a severe heart condition, but he was taking medication for it, so we're not sure how he lost consciousness. He was submerged in the shallow water until some sunbathers found him and got him to a hospital. His brain didn't get enough oxygen, which left him in a deep coma. Somehow his mind crossed into Maglia and became trapped there." Liz touched his hand. "Jason met him on one of his earlier trips. He got permission from Elder's wife for his body to be transferred to Grace House."

"This is Bryn's dad," Zander whispered. "She hates that we're keeping him alive?"

Liz nodded. "She wants her father to be at peace. She has the impression that he's suffering because his body has aged so badly, but she's wrong. Hadley and I talk with him in the Maglian layer. He misses people, but he's happy there with his experiments. He'll be your mentor when you take your first trip."

"Why doesn't Bryn want to travel? Why does she hate the research?"

"I'm not sure, sweetheart. I don't know her well, but I can already tell Bryn's very special. She's also quite private, but I imagine her reason is similar to yours. Freedom, her own life." Liz waved her hand irreverently, as if dismissing young person silliness.

"Okay, okay." Zander dug his fingers into his temples. "Elder's mind is stuck there," he muttered to himself. Jason died so early, only fifty-five years old. Seth was fifty-two, but his body was so traumatized he looked seventy. And now this? "No, no, no," he whispered. Was this the price of the research? A crippling old age and early death? Risk of a coma?

"Wait." He held up a hand, quite rudely, in Liz's face. "Just wait. The Pensare didn't put these side effects in the brochure."

"Elder is a pivotal part of our research. He and Jason discovered how to heal human souls, to relieve depression, anxiety, pain."

"That's great, that's just great. But you guys can't revive him?" Zander felt dizzy, his face flushed. One little accident and he'd be stuck over there, his body a vegetable here.

Liz smiled gently. "Be patient. You'll understand when you travel."

"No!" Zander slammed his hand against the wall. "I want to know right now. You weren't going to tell me about this guy? Am I going to look like him in five fucking years?" He motioned to the stricken body and shouted again. "Am I?"

A pained look crossed Liz's face. "Love, we don't know. We've never had a young traveler. You might age faster, or you might not. And yes, you can die there, or you can die here. The Pensare never lied to you. Maglia's dangerous, but the research is worth it."

"Oh really? You don't have to go there."

Liz stood up. Her eyes flashed and her voice grew thick. "Now stop that. Young man, you have no idea of the trauma I've been through, or Raleigh, or the kind of evil Hadley's seen. The Circle will be with you every moment, helping you, protecting you. Taking the brunt of the pain from the dark things. Most can't say that in their own lives here."

Zander glared as hard as he could at the woman, but her eyes were narrowed. They were at a standstill.

Liz finally gave a deep sigh. "Alright, I realize the unknown is a frustrating place for you scientists. Always gotta conquer it, shove it into marked containers and move onto the next." She reached out and brushed his hair from his eyes, then cupped his chin in a firm grip. "But you know, most of the time you'll have to linger in the unknown a good while. Let's make peace with it while you're here." Her voice wavered and Zander could see the deepest sorrow in her eyes. He believed her. But his temper was on fire and he wouldn't back down. He did have a choice, dammit. He didn't owe the Pensare anything.

"Give me your hand. Maybe this'll do some good."

He drew back, wanting to stay angry.

Her mouth hardened. "Now, child, you know it's best. Don't fight it." She took his right hand and placed two fingers in his palm. "Close them heavenly blues, Zander love."

"I want you to know I'm not going to forget about this." He took a deep breath and closed his eyes. His hand grew warm and the anxiety drained out of him. He pictured charcoal gray tendrils rising to the surface of his skin and releasing out through his palm. Gentle warmth flowed in. His heart calmed, embraced it. His eyelids fluttered open. He saw his anger from a distance now and wondered what really caused it.

"Now, you let that cradle you as long as it does. And come back if you need more." He watched her lips move, hypnotized. The beads in her hair clicked together, a distant sound. Taking his arm, Liz walked him back up to his room and left him lying on his bed, staring at the ceiling in the dark.

Brit Malorie

Chapter 17

Lynch sat alone in one of the private rooms on the sixth floor. Each room had a balcony with a view that extended over Miami, the lights sparkling for miles. A cool breeze floated in from the ocean and reminded him of home. The room was full of cream and sand shades with a few splashes of color—a vase of roses, some pottery in the corner, a painting on the far wall. Electric candles were the only light source. Lynch studied the flesh-colored jaw adhesive in the mirror. He'd had it fashioned here actually. Couldn't have the girl giving his description to Zander. The adhesive molded against the metal on his jawline and gave him a very normal look. He sank into the velvet plush of the chair. He'd enjoyed several dances in Asia—of course, those were for a different purpose. This was strictly art appreciation. He'd almost snickered when the club's owner had warned him against touching the girl.

Almost a month in and he still had to give a full report to Damaris each evening of his progress. Lynch drummed his fingers on the armrest and hummed. Zander Grace. Why, oh why was this dumb bastard so important? His men had found out that the girl's father died when she was thirteen, and she'd run away from home at sixteen. Her mother was trailer trash and nowhere to be found. She'd finished her high school diploma a few years later, then bounced around different dance schools until she ended up here. A couple of serious boyfriends, but nothing on the radar now. They'd monitored her for the last week and found that the girl lived and breathed dancing. She went from her apartment to the club and back, met with girlfriends occasionally, but so far no men. No one to miss her.

The door opened and the girl stepped in. She smiled, but there was tension in it. He'd been told initially that Bryn Sansa did not do private dances, but somehow the club's owner had convinced her. She dimmed the electric candles.

"Please stay where you are," she said quietly. He heard rustling behind him as she disrobed. Music started from the corner, a blend of cello and piano. Fingers glided over his back. He wore a simple black shirt and jeans, yet wished fervently that he wore nothing. She moved in front of him. A corset enclosed her upper body with lace ridges supporting the lovely swell of her cleavage. The corset flared out to a short skirt.

Her body was incredible, but her movements made him hold his breath. It took years of practice to gain that fluidity. The girl made love to the air and spurned the floor. He wondered what moved through her mind as she performed. She focused far more on the dance than on acting provocatively for the client. Lynch respected that. He felt an immense urge to see her on Kadera, the island spinning her on cushions of sky. There was soul in her motion, the candle's point of light lost in her dark eyes. A tremendous sadness. This woman had a secret, something she cradled inside herself, something that influenced her entire life.

Unfortunately, that secret might be buried so deep it would take a visit to his table to extract it. Lynch wasn't sure he wanted that for her. It felt like it would be the desecration of a temple. He chuckled and shook his head. Who was he kidding? When the time came, he wouldn't hesitate. Bryn finished with a long spin, her back arched, the ball of her foot gliding on the carpet. She bowed to him and gave a triumphant smile. Stepping behind his chair, she slipped on her robe, then moved to the doorway. He grasped her arm and she recoiled.

"Just a moment, dear. Has my money allowed time for conversation?" he asked sweetly.

She hesitated, her eyes flitting to the doorway. She turned to him.

"Your name is Bryn, correct?" He held her hand. "You're the best dancer I've ever seen. Tell me a little about yourself."

"What do you want to know?" Her voice was surprisingly deep, a little husky. Her chin rose, stubborn, with that adorable little indent in the center.

"What do you do here? Anyone special in your life? A husband? A boyfriend?"

"I'm the lead dancer in a couple of productions, but I work mostly on choreography. I've been dancing about ten years, I guess." She shrugged. "No one special."

"Well, you dancers have to give us men hope. But you can tell me the truth. You're very beautiful, almost ethereal. I refuse to believe you're alone."

Her mouth hardened. "Believe it. I have to go. I have a performance."

Lynch frowned. Was she always this defiant? Time for a different tactic. She tried to pull her hand away, but he held it and stood up. He slid his palm along her hip. There it was. A tremor of fear as her eyes searched for the door. She backed up against the wall.

"I apologize for my possessive streak, but you will not leave. We're going to have a pleasant conversation. I simply want to know about the men in your life. It'll make me feel better. Current boyfriends, ex-boyfriends, eager clients."

"You know, I do have a boyfriend. The security guy, just outside," she hinted, her bottom lip trembling.

"I don't think so. And don't worry, security's been paid off. I like privacy for my dates. You know," he jerked her head back and sniffed along her face, "you're a very clean person. You have no idea how I love that in a woman." He longed to cut that defiant streak out of her.

Bryn fumbled against the wall. Her hand slipped down into a hidden panel there and a gun slid into her palm. He slammed her body backward. Her finger slipped and the trigger went off. The noise deafened as the shot ricocheted off something hard and tore into the painting on the wall.

Lynch took in a deep breath and snatched the weapon from her. He emptied the bullets and tossed it into the far corner. This was why he hated guns. Too unpredictable.

"You flinched at the last moment. Why? What was the last thought in your head?" he demanded. "Did you think you were about to kill someone normal?" He touched a long scratch on his cheek and found the hole in the flesh adhesive. There was a tiny dent in the metal implant where the bullet grazed.

The gunshot had caused a commotion outside. Well, there went that strategy. The girl ran out and he let her go for now. Hopefully, she was frightened enough that her hero would come. What a delicious new ingredient in his plan to torment Zander. And when he brought them both to Kadera, oh, the fun they'd all have.

Chapter 18

"After the initial shock, we'll continue to run electricity through your brain to hold your place in Maglia," Brecker said. Zander was laying on a hospital bed in the travel room. He shivered and tried to focus on the doctor, who inserted a large needle into the IV. The liquid was a deep purple with hints of crimson, swirling in great rings into his IV fluid.

"What's that?" his voice quivered.

"It's the combination of chemicals Jason found that works best for traveling. We call it the Recipe. You know all this, Zander, you've been studying for weeks now. Just relax."

"Remind me," he pleaded.

Brecker sighed. "The Recipe will lower activity in other parts of your brain while overloading your claustrum. Your normal senses will go away and the senses that interact with the Maglian layer will dominate. So instead of seeing and hearing the normal world, you'll see and hear the layer underneath it."

Liz stood on Zander's other side with her eyes closed, murmuring and gesturing in the air. Nora seemed fascinated yet irritated as she tried to work around the beautiful psychic.

"And the Circle pulls me back home, right?" Zander blinked rapidly. A tear ran down the side of his face into the pillow. If this was a mistake, it'd be the worst of his life.

"Yes, when it's time to return, we'll do the reverse: ramp down the current to your claustrum. And your normal senses will come back and then you'll wake up. At least, that's how it worked with Jason's trips."

"What's Liz doing?"

"Uh, I think she's calling in some protection," Brecker said, his tone distracted as he fiddled with the IV.

"I'm asking for a blessing from the Archlusha," Liz replied. She let out short bursts of breath and held herself still. Then her lips touched his forehead. A trail of amber from her skin floated down, piercing the antiseptic smell of the travel room. "Safe journey, Zander love. Rest in the cradle of the Circle."

Then she left. Chills crawled down his spine and panic pooled in his gut. This wasn't going to work; there would be an accident and he'd be a vegetable. He'd die painfully. "Brecker, listen. I don't want to do this. Let's call in the others. Maybe I can help train so it'll go faster for them."

The doctor squeezed his hand. Zander looked into his eyes under the small glasses. He'd never noticed how light green his irises were, the rims speckled with brown. There was reassurance there, an understanding of the fear. "It'll be okay, I promise. Try to meditate."

Zander started his breathing exercises, inhaling and exhaling in rhythm.

"Here." Brecker placed a soft caramel in his mouth. "Can you taste that?"

Zander nodded.

"Good. When the taste goes away, let me know."

Brecker said something to Nora; he mentioned the word Circle. His mouth moved with no sound.

Something was wrong. The color was leaking out of Brecker. The brown hair in his beard, the ruddy peach of his skin faded. Zander's hand gripped the cotton blanket underneath him. The blanket's sunshine yellow color paled to white and the soft cotton felt like paper. The antiseptic smell of the room was gone. The sugar swirled on his tongue. *Wait.* Zander worked his mouth, struggling for the flavor. He caught Brecker's gaze and shook his head. The tears came faster now. What if they couldn't bring him back? He'd be stuck like Elder. He didn't want to do this, he wanted to stop—

The color receded until only the bare outline of Brecker's clothes was left, sketched in gray lines. Zander turned his head. Nora smeared past him in sketch form. The machines, the charts on the walls disappeared.

Silence, then a trickling sound in his head. The lines faded. Zander focused on the movement of air in and out of his lungs.

He was dying. It was all impossible from the beginning. He tried to quiet the swell of panic in his heart. Tints of color seeped into the wall. The colors from meditation, the purple and blue and brick red. They grew into splashes, walking past him, leaning over him.

The air disappeared from his lungs, his throat. The weight of his limbs, his head, everything was gone. The colors shimmered too vibrant. There was too much light. He had to stop the light from coming in, but he couldn't raise his hands.

"Zander." A voice murmured next to his head. "Zander Grace. Welcome to Vita Maglia."

His vision cleared and he could suddenly see so far, but also distinctly, like a telephoto lens. The Japanese man before him looked completely different than the ancient body in the bedroom. He looked young, about forty years old, dressed in a simple tunic and pants, his feet bare. Small, curious eyes met his, but they held warmth. He had a broad nose, a beard, and black hair that hung down to his shoulders.

"My name is Elder Sansa."

Zander stood up, hesitant, weak. His body felt insubstantial, like he could be swept away by a breeze. He looked down and saw that he was dressed in the same clothes as the older man. "How did I get these?"

Elder smiled. "By looking at mine."

Zander nodded. He hadn't realized the mental projection would work so quickly. "I feel so light. Like I'm made of air."

"You are." Elder motioned down to his own body. Zander's razor-sharp vision could see a rippling effect in the older man's image. He held up his own hand. It shimmered as the air particles pooled and flowed together.

"You'll get used to it. Believe me, I've had many years." Elder waved his hand quickly, leaving a trail of air particles that scattered. "Soon your body at home will feel like the stranger."

"I really feel like I could simply float off." Zander wondered if his feet would plunge right through the cloud surface. Instead they recoiled gently with each step.

"I'm still at Grace House?" The mansion towered above him as a collection of gray lines. There were no people, only moving figures of Maglian color.

"Yes. See that?" Elder pointed to a streak of russet orange crawling near Zander. It glimmered with hints of tawny and nutmeg. The barest edge of a whisker reflected in the sunlight.

"Is that Bumbles? His aura?" Zander laughed and reached for the cat, but the splotch of color loped off. Then all the colors faded, along with the gray outline of Grace House.

"What happened?"

"The last of the fading process. In order to move around, they have to pass quite a bit of current through your claustrum. Which means you won't see anything but the strands. No cars, no houses. No people." Elder's voice grew sad.

"Let's give you a real look at the place." He motioned for Zander to follow him, then handed him a small metallic box. "Slide this into your pocket there. It's called a calix. It's a small device that produces positively charged molecules. It's not much, but it gives some protection."

"I can't believe it's real. I can't believe all this Maglian crap is actually real," Zander said. It felt like he was floating in the simulator, but the cool breeze moved through his entire body, under his skin, in between his organs. He gingerly stepped on the gas surface, brushing haze out of his path with his bare feet.

"This could be the surface of the moon," he said. "If it were covered in life and light." Maglia stretched before him—a rock world with cliffs in metallic shades and luminescent white boulders the size of buildings. Massive crystal formations sparkled in dizzying shades of turquoise and jade greens. They walked past lakes of nitrogen with gas billowing on top. Creatures similar to bugs buzzed by his head, searching with a dozen eyes, lifting their tentacles to land next to long stretches of indigo plants and rose-colored grass. Twinkling lights skittered over the landscape. They passed a crater on its side. Black steam poured out of it and swirled over them. Zander brought up his hand. The black mixed with his particles, giving his skin a sooty look.

"Am I in Oz?" he laughed. "There's so much here. I never want to leave."

"Don't say that. It might come true." Elder pointed to himself. "Oh, and here's a clue. Look up."

Zander found one of the low-hanging strands, then followed it up to where it clustered with dozens of other strands. His eyes continued upward to where the cluster joined millions of glowing vines, spreading as far as he could see. Enormous couldn't begin to explain it. Pulsing with brilliance and color, they twisted and weaved over each other. Light beams moved along the web followed by pockets of shadow.

He knelt down and swept away vapor. The ground beneath him appeared to be sand, but it felt spongy and yielded to his feet. He scooped up the granules, shifting them in the light. The largest ones rested on his palm, but particles still dropped through his hand, misting below. He had a grainy feeling after, like the grit had trickled through his brain.

"You must remember that you're made of air. It's tempting to achieve bigger, bolder things with this lightness—higher jumps, faster runs. But you're also quite vulnerable. We take our skin for granted at home." As if to demonstrate, Elder's hand brushed his. Tingling started in Zander's core, then branched out, rippling over his form. Flashes of busy streets, children playing, small bowls of rice and fish. Elder pulled away and the tingling retreated.

"Our minds just touched," Zander murmured. "It's real. Maglia really exists. A layer beneath us." He could never go back to how he'd been before. His father had been right this entire time. A flicker of guilt rose up and spread quickly through his form. He immediately fought it, suppressed it until it went away. He shoved it into the same place as his grief, to be dealt with later.

"I didn't believe him. But how could I have known?" he murmured. "It feels like a fairytale, even now."

A burst of light fluttered close to them and appeared to whisper to Elder. Zander tilted his head and the spark changed with the angle, scattering lavender rays of sunlight. The man nodded and whispered back.

"What was that?" Zander asked.

"Well, I guess they're normally thought of as angels, but they're called Lusha."

"That's one of the Lusha? They talk to you?"

Elder shrugged. "All the time. And this isn't just any old Lusha." He grinned and motioned to the light. "Don't be rude, say hello."

The spark moved over to Zander. He was about to say that he didn't feel anything when thoughts surfaced in his mind. *Griffin help Zander Jason son.*

"Griffin and I have relied on each other for ten years, like an old married couple," Elder said, affection edging out his voice.

"So to the strands, they appear as angels? Like Nora's figurines?"

Elder laughed. "They appear as whatever the person needs to see. Sometimes it's a winged angel in blinding glory, sometimes it's a loved one, sometimes just the light they are."

The strands looked like very long vines hanging down from the clusters above. One particular strand hung in solitude. Elder leaned in with a coy smile on his face. "Do you hear that?" Zander listened close to the strand. It sounded like water lapping on rocks.

"It's the sound of her faith, ebbing and flowing like a tide into her heart. What do you smell?" Elder asked.

Zander shivered. "It feels like a biting wind, cold. Tinges of strong mint, the kind that knocks you back a step. What is it?"

"It's her loneliness," Elder said quietly. He studied the coil before them. "Alright, let's stay a moment. We don't have time to heal her, but you can at least experience a strand. Go ahead, brush it with your fingertip."

As Zander probed deeper into the strand, ripples of chill spiraled outward. A gnawing worry that cut to the bone. Images flashed through his mind, blended in the colors of miran energy. Her children grown and gone away, her husband dead. Friends distant. Every minute spent with strangers on a screen. Memories dimmed, life grayed in. What was left? Nothing of interest.

Elder called him back. Zander found it difficult to pull away from the sad woman. "I just want to infuse her with some positive. Can't we do that?"

"She won't accept high doses of positive or any help from the Lusha. A soul grows so mired inside its own despair that it refuses light."

"What do we do then?" Zander asked, disgruntled. This didn't seem much like healing, more like commiserating.

"You experience the strands around her. Find one or two that are already well-connected in the mesh."

Zander brightened. "We give her some friends? Bring a little pop back into her life?"

"Someday, when we have more time. I know it's hard to just leave her, but we have so much to see for your first trip."

They walked a little farther. There were these creatures that Zander had to keep stepping over. Giant warts covered their heads with fringe waving on the sides of their gelatinous bodies. The colored organs and tubes were visible inside them. One creature stopped and swiveled its head around. Zander picked the thing up but dropped it quickly. "Hey! It bit through my finger. Kind of."

"It thought you were another snorkler. The creatures here defend themselves," Elder chuckled.

Zander briefly wondered what would happen if he stepped on the thing? Would the gas parts dissipate? Explode on him? The snorkler shimmied away on the cloud cover.

Strands hung around them in thick clusters. Zander zoomed in on a specific pair—a slender strand wrapped around the length of a much thicker one. He pointed them out to Elder.

"That's a child and mother. See how the child's strand is wisp-thin? Like trees, strands grow wider and longer with age."

"What's that growing on them?" Zander asked. Tiny flowers had sprouted on the intertwined strands. The petals were a deep indigo with spots of blush and yellow.

"Those are the nitore, some of the flowers here," Elder said. A tinkling sound rippled through Zander. He closed his eyes and leaned into it, drinking in the melody.

"Nitore sing lullabies to the strands and provide many of the chemicals that help them grow into large bundles. Think of the magnetism in a big family—sitting around tables, laughing and enjoying each other, generating warmth. There's also the nesso—good bacteria that's invisible," Elder explained.

The strands seemed attracted to each other; they swayed close and connected tendrils, even with strangers. The people up in the home layer probably felt odd things, sudden impulses and emotions, without any idea where they came from.

Zander drew his hand towards the mother's strand just as a transparent, spider-looking thing skittered down the length of it. It rubbed its forelegs together and placed a drop of glassy liquid along a rift in the coil.

"What's that?"

"They're called gliders. They live on the strands and eat the nesso bacteria. They also seal up tiny cracks in the coil and add layers of protection against harmful insects and bacteria."

Fear swept through Zander's heart, a trembling chill that flooded his body. An ebony vapor encircled the strand a few feet above them. The creature solidified into a dark ribbon with a pearl luster; he hadn't realized they would be so lovely and enticing. The ribbon coated the coil and it dimmed, losing its sparkle while the Vipera fed. An icy sound traveled to him, like dozens of tiny, sharp teeth clicking. Shrill cries erupted as it skittered down the strand towards them. Zander covered his ears, then realized the sound kept coming. The cries multiplied into screams, rushing into his mind.

Griffin swept in between them and blocked the creature. The ribbon crawled back, repelled by the sudden positive charge. The new light reflected off the glossy blackness and gave it the strangest effect—a set of ravens about to peck, then the light shifted into a pair of faces with an ax, then a windowpane drenched in thunderstorm and splashes of blood.

"What am I seeing?" he asked Elder.

"Vipera collect memories from older strands, then they use those memories to arouse curiosity in new strands. It takes much less effort if a person lets them inside."

"Let's go," he said to Elder. "Quickly." He resisted the urge to look back, despite his attraction. The Vipera appeared much too simple. Supposedly, they were just animals that fed on the strands. But he detected a sinister intelligence underneath. They could adapt, manipulate, seduce. Build their power.

"How much do you know about these creatures?" he asked the older man as they walked.

Elder sighed. "Honestly, I only get bits and pieces from Griffin. The Lusha are not sure what to make of us. No human is supposed to have access to this ecosystem."

"Yet here we are," Zander said. "Maybe we can shift the balance a little."

"It's a serious responsibility," Elder replied harshly. "It's essential that you follow Maglian law. You start breaking it, you could change Maglia and have a profound effect on all the souls of the world."

Zander turned from him and studied the mesh above. Of course there should be some limitations. But how could he truly help people if he was blocked every time by these invisible laws? No wonder Elder hadn't made a lot of progress over the last ten years here.

He turned back to Elder and nodded reassuringly. He'd only change things if there could be a real benefit.

A strange stirring vibrated through Zander's form and a whisper. He stopped, listening. "I hear something, but I can't make it out."

The older man's eyes searched him, his mouth twisted. "Zander, there are other creatures that evolved here. Every ecosystem has mutations. They are worse than the Vipera."

The whispers grew louder. Zander could make out his name, fragments of words, echoes of their conversation. The whispering pulsated. His eyelids fluttered; he could barely keep them open.

"It sounds like a name . . . I don't know."

"Adriel." The older man turned away from him then, a look of severe pain on his face. "This isn't anything human. Listen to me. You have to stay away—" Elder braced suddenly. A force rippled through his form and his back bent in a deep arch. Zander reached to catch him and his fingers scraped the man. An endless tide of fear. A gunmetal gray pool of it. And a thinness. Elder's strand was so thin in places it could break. Zander felt pulled by an immense gravity and powerful winds. The Calamata. The man could die at any moment.

He closed his eyes and called for Griffin. The point of light skidded over and blinked in between them. One last chuckle and the whispering faded.

"What the hell was that?" he demanded.

Elder managed to right himself, still gasping. "Please, Zander, there are monsters here. Just, don't speak to anyone, especially in human form. No matter how normal they appear."

He was flabbergasted. "Does the Circle know about this?"

"Yes, but the Circle can't help you. These creatures look like you, but they lie and sabotage," Elder said. Griffin circled and spread warm light down the man's neck.

Zander lowered his voice. "Can you feel it, too? Your strand thinning?" Elder looked away.

"I don't understand. You're only what, fifty?" he gasped and brought his hand to his chest. "Is this what happened to Dad?"

Elder paused. "No one knows what happened, not even the Circle. He was alone here, studying the Woods when his form collapsed and he died at home."

He took a deep breath. "Your strand will also thin, Zander, the more you come here. You'll see it in increased aging and possibly an early death."

Elder's form kept rippling. He bent down, his face wretched in pain, never quite catching his breath despite Griffin's help.

Zander shuddered. Why did he think he could do this? Become a great healer and help the research? Have his life really mean something? When every trip meant he'd turn out like this.

"I know it's sobering," Elder murmured, "but you should know the consequences. Maglia's been my home for the last ten years. I love her dearly, but there's one regret. We don't know each other—"

"It's okay. What can I do?"

"It's my daughter, Bryn. I need you to give her a message. Maglian laws prevent travelers from interfering with familiar strands, but Griffin is allowed to send me images from her life. She's in danger. She's been threatened—" he stopped, coughing.

Zander nodded. He listened to Elder's message carefully.

"You can't tell me who's threatening her?"

Elder shook his head. "Griffin doesn't give me much, I'm afraid. If you can place her under the protection of Grace House, I'll be forever grateful. I must warn you that Brynsie's very stubborn. She's still young and can be cruel."

Zander laughed, trying to lighten the mood. "Believe me, cruel words from a woman I've had. I'll try my best, but she probably won't want my help. Bryn sounds pretty fierce."

"You should go now. Griffin has to help me heal and I don't want you to see—" Elder trailed off. "If you go back to the clearing where you first woke up, you just have to lie down and the Circle will guide your mind up into the home layer. Please remember what I said. There's much to fear in Maglia. The creatures here are curious about us, and they'll use travelers to their advantage."

"We're valuable," Zander said slowly. "Why?"

Elder's eyes flitted away. "I'm not sure why, but they'll use any trick they can. You must protect yourself."

Zander headed back to the clearing where Grace House had faded. He forced his anxiety down and kept an eye out for Vipera. Was Bryn truly in danger? Who could be threatening her? His hopes rose. If he offered her protection, perhaps she'd feel okay about living at Grace House to be near her father and to learn more about the research.

The first thing he saw upon waking was Brecker's triumphant grin. He tried to lift up his arm and couldn't. It felt like pounds of mud were piled high on his chest.

"Just sit for a few minutes. Don't try to get up," the doctor said. "Everything go okay?"

"Yeah, yeah." Zander stared at the blanket, his eyes adjusting. The cotton was a sweet sunshine yellow again. Nora buzzed around him, removing his IV and massaging his muscles. He pictured Seth's cane, the lines crisscrossing the hollow face. Dad in the cemetery. The way Elder collapsed on the cloud surface, his deep fear and sorrow.

"It's Elder, isn't it?" Brecker asked, quietly. He laid a warm cloth on Zander's forehead. Water trickled by his ear.

"It's way worse than you guys think. He won't last more than a few months."

Brecker nodded. "We should do as much training as we can. Since you tolerated it well, we'll send you back in tomorrow—"

Zander's shoulders flinched, his stomach very queasy. "The way Elder looks. My father's death. Seth's aging. That's what'll happen to me if I keep traveling?"

"Tough to say," Brecker replied, his tone distracted.

"Can I get a few days off? Relax a little?"

"Of course. You've worked very hard the last few weeks." Brecker turned away and fiddled with the equipment.

Zander lay quiet. Now that he knew Maglia was real, could he really sacrifice everything for her? He needed time away from Grace House to think about his life and what he really wanted. Elder's daughter might have some answers. Maybe she already knew the risks and that's why she refused to travel.

The next day, GUT drove Zander to the airport. Hadley told him where Bryn worked. A nightclub in Miami called the Lolita.

Brit Malorie

Chapter 19

Massive rings carved from white marble surrounded the Lolita's entrance. Twenty-foot metallic gold doors were surrounded by giant aquarium spheres, the water full of rare shark species and glistening tropical fish. A trio of multi-tiered fountains sent geysers thirty feet into the air. Gargoyles perched on the east and west towers, with each tower overlooking a circular pool surrounded by orchid gardens. Multi-colored lights sparkled on the hundreds of guests in tuxedos and ballgowns, many in full costume. Zander waited in line for an hour, feeling very plain in his white collared shirt and thin black tie. A drop of sweat trickled down his back and landed at the base of his spine. The humidity here coated everyone in a glossy sheen like they were mannequins.

His ears hurt from the loud music, and he closed his eyes against the strobe lights, his senses still raw from the trip. A woman stood behind him in line, her bright pink hair reeking of harsh dyes and a boyfriend's musk. Zander buried his nose in his sleeve. A couple leaned on the railing of the balcony above him. They laughed and the man spun her a couple of times, then slid his arm across her bare back. Skin resting on skin. He licked her ear and she tipped her chin upward as giggles seized her body. Zander closed his eyes. He could hear it through the Veil. The swish of their strands as they crossed, tendrils reaching and folding in great knots. He took a deep breath, then realized the sound was just the fabric of the woman's skirt catching against itself.

He perked up—there was something in the air, an eerie stillness. A cough came from the adjoining street. His eyes searched but found nothing in the darkness. "Hey, I need to speak to Bryn Sansa," he said. The bouncer crossed his arms. Thick rolls of muscle rippled against the tight cotton of his T-shirt.

"You don't talk to the dancers, Romeo. But you're in luck cause she's up next. Better get a seat now."

"Alright." Zander started to move forward, but the bouncer put out his hand. He pointed to a guy sorting through piles of cash. "Entry fee: $100."

He followed a long line of couples beneath a grand archway. A nest of glass elevators stood in the center of the great room. Serpentine hallways branched off, possibly into the private rooms available for guests. Zander wanted to explore, but everyone seemed to be in a hurry. He entered the main theater and came across several rows of mahogany chairs with blue satin cushions. The frescoed ceiling was lit by a chandelier on the left, a square portrait of Jesus watching your sins on the right. The stage was shielded from early eyes by majestic velvet curtains. Electric candles lit up the sides. The auditorium rapidly filled with visitors in everything from fetish leather to clerical robes to lingerie. If this was some kind of nightclub, it was like nothing he'd ever seen. He wasn't sure whether to expect topless dancers or a play about Victorian morality.

One chair sat empty in the center of the front row. Zander moved quickly and grabbed it. He smoothed out the wrinkles in his shirt, his stomach nervous. He kept feeling like he was being watched, but that was impossible since he was the simplest dressed guy in this place.

"Have you seen this show before?" he asked the person next to him, a compact man dressed in a three-piece suit of gray velvet, complete with a violet tie. His hair was slicked back, his mustache pencil thin. Zander loosened his own tie a little.

The man responded by doing a tiny twirl in the air with his fingertips. "Mmm . . . you're looking for a summary, perhaps? Quite impossible. It must be seen to be believed." Zander chuckled, thinking about the last time he'd heard the word impossible.

"My name's Otto." A thick Czech accent sliced the man's words and his fingernails were oddly elongated.

"But, come on. A hundred dollars?"

The man looked at him like he was an idiot. He gestured to the crowd. "Most of these people would spend much more for a glimpse of Bryn Sansa."

Lights dimmed and the chatter stopped. A bass drum crept upwards in volume until it pounded in his ears. Five barefoot ninjas in black lined up on stage, their faces masked. In a combination of martial arts and dance, they kicked, punched, and jabbed the air. The center ninja was catapulted upward by the other dancers, her slim body twisting and spinning. She landed and crouched at the very front of the stage, only two feet from Zander. The other dancers broke open her costume to reveal a dark red kimono that flowed to her knees. Then they pulled apart their own costumes, revealing black kimonos. The silk reflected bright lines from the electric candles.

Slender swords lay on the stage and each dancer picked up one. They cut the air, barely missing each other. The center woman in the red kimono was surrounded by the others. They caressed her body as they unraveled strips of silk from each side of her dress. She paused, her body a perfect S-shape, her bare skin showing through with only red string holding the dress together. The other dancers flung her to the front of the stage again, then pulled her back. They removed her mask and she turned away, hiding her face. Her black hair was bundled with silk ties. She jerked as each dancer sliced through a tie, letting her hair fall in waves down her back. Zander grinned. He wasn't sure what it all meant, but he liked it.

She turned suddenly and his breath stopped. Fierceness hardened her mouth and candlelight glanced off her slim cheekbones. Her lips were brushed into a scarlet pout, her eyes black.

"That's her," Otto nudged him excitedly.

"I know," Zander whispered. His chest hurt suddenly, the air expanding it too fast. He figured it was a heart attack and didn't try to breathe.

The other dancers unmasked and moved in unison behind her. Bryn's body melted into the music, her arms and legs a blur, fueled by the drumbeats. The dancers picked her up and carried her around the stage. The kimono wrapped her like a second skin, hugging the narrow waist and lifting the curve of her hips. The bare skin flashed from her sides as she twirled. The dancers tossed her in the air and she landed at the front of the stage. She rewarded the crowd with a coy smile, her hair floating up like a dark cloud around her face, a red ribbon tied in an elaborate bow on her right wrist. Clapping erupted. All five dancers strutted off the stage and mingled. Bryn sauntered among the guests, flirting, evading fingertips.

He could only breathe in short gasps, his chest impossibly tight. His hands kept shaking. What the hell was happening? Suddenly, she was there. Bryn's palm slid up his shirt and jerked his tie against his throat. The red on her lips glowed like blood, like she'd devoured something. He touched her bare skin and a buzz moved through his fingertips. She bit the side of his hand, then dragged her mouth over his palm. Her foot curled into his thigh, her toes digging into the muscle. Zander choked out a single word. "Stay." She shook her head and moved on. The space increased between them, dammit. He willed her to look back. Bryn stopped and turned. There it was. That look in her eyes, like she wanted him so badly. Shivers flooded his chest.

She rushed him. Zander grunted as her knees plowed into his lap. Her hands gripped his hair and rocked his head back, her mouth urgent and hot and melting into his. He pressed forward, tasting the warm kiss. His fingers got caught in her hair; she smelled like vanilla. Bryn broke the kiss, her face stunned.

"Why?" she murmured, the heat of her breath tingling his bottom lip. Zander lay paralyzed in the seat. His heart felt like it could pound right out of his chest. She left him and merged with the other dancers on stage, a confused smile pasted on her face. They encircled their arms and bowed. The lights dimmed and the crowd roared.

Zander couldn't stop trembling. "How, how?" he sputtered. He could spend the rest of his life chasing what just happened.

"You little dog," Otto chuckled. "You didn't say that you knew her."

"I don't."

"Well then, you certainly received the VIP treatment. You two were drawn to each other, like, like," Otto twirled his hand in the air, searching for the word.

"Magnets," Zander said, his voice cracking. Heat rose to the surface of his skin. He wanted to barter and beg, steal and caress. There had to be a trace of her. He untucked his shirt and rubbed his face into it. Otto grinned. Men probably did that all the time here.

"I've watched Bryn Sansa many times, but you brought out something very special in that lady. I've never seen her kiss a spectator. Not very professional." The man studied him as if Zander could be exploited.

"How?" He swallowed, feeling strangely drunk. He tried to imprint all her details on his brain: the vanilla scent, the silk of her hair, the curl of her foot into his thigh. He imagined pulling her into his arms and simply loving her. The realization left him stunned. This was what he'd been longing for. Why he'd been so obsessed for the last month. Bryn didn't feel like a stranger. He closed his eyes, letting his soul ache, feeling his strand reach for hers.

"How do I talk to her? Something, I have something important to tell her," he asked.

Otto laughed. It sounded like a donkey braying. "Every man in this room has something important to say to Miss Sansa. By the way, you're wearing lipstick." He chuckled as Zander wiped his mouth off with his sleeve. "Unfortunately, our flower is done for tonight. If you have a few thousand handy, you can request a private audience."

Zander choked a little. He knew it, there was something about this place. "Wait, you're telling me Bryn's a, she's a. . . ." He didn't want to say it out loud.

Otto's eyes widened in recognition. "Oh no, I apologize. Her body cannot be bought, only her company, her conversation, a dabble of flirtation. A brief moment when you're the only man in her eyes." The guy's leg jumped a little, his fingers massaging the gray velvet of his suit. "Americans tend to believe places like the Lolita are designed for a seedier purpose, but it's really about delaying desire." He lifted a finger as if giving a lesson. "The exquisite tension between virtue and vice. One pays *not* to be satisfied."

Zander nodded like he understood, but his thoughts never left Bryn. The smudge of red on her bottom lip. Her eyes looking back, wanting him.

Otto inspected the crowd. "Packed tonight. Must be hundreds of people on all eight levels. I've heard rumors about an elaborate ventilation system here at the Lolita. Perhaps one large enough to hold a dancer's slim body? It makes sense, I suppose. The dancers need a slick exit if a dodgy situation arises."

"Did you ever hear where the entry point might be?" Zander asked quietly, his eyes searching Otto's. "I won't hurt her. I just have to deliver a message from someone she loves."

The other man quieted and something passed between them—a small but instant trust between strangers. "Follow me."

Otto got up and led Zander back through the main thoroughfare, then he disappeared around the corner. Zander was about to follow when he caught a hardened gaze from someone across the room. The man had a long torso and a goatee. His brown hair was cropped close to his scalp. His eyes floated to a crowd of loud people. Then his gaze returned, staring openly at Zander. He checked his watch. Zander had that prickly feeling again in his gut. He needed to find Bryn and get her out of here.

"Come on," Otto whispered. They dodged couples and threesomes. Some groups drunkenly stumbled with laughter; others remained quiet and subdued, blending into the walls. Women in lingerie and corsets flirted with patrons—their laughter tinkled off the glass chandeliers.

They went up the stairs to the third floor. Otto turned another corner, then another, then he finally slipped into a utility closet. A mop and a broom stood in the corner, with window cleaning fluid and paper towel packs stored neatly on a shelf.

"Have you done this before?" Zander asked, not really wanting the answer.

"Of course not." The other man winked. "Then again, if one can't afford to play, a glimpse is good enough. I'd join you, but I'm getting too old for espionage." He let out a low chuckle, then climbed the shelf and felt along the ceiling.

"Found it," he whispered. His now usefully long nails popped off one of the panels. He climbed back down and motioned to Zander. "Follow it as long as you don't die from claustrophobia."

"How do I find her?"

"Each exit point has a vent. Peer into each and see if she's there." Otto licked his lips. Zander hurried before the guy changed his mind about joining him. He pulled himself up into the ventilation system. Otto snapped the plate back into place behind him. Zander's torso was lean but still got squeezed at certain places. He stopped at each vent. There were plenty of shrill giggles, inebriated slurs, loud music, but no Bryn.

What was he going to say if he did find her? Could he really expect her to come back with him? Maybe Elder's message would spark curiosity in his daughter. Maybe she'd be magically driven to follow Zander across the country. Yeah, right. He let out a harsh laugh, his palms slipping on the metal surface. His sweat left grime and streaks. He stopped, his heart fluttering. He could see through the slits in the last vent.

Candlelight lit the side of Bryn's face. She tied her robe, white satin that flowed along her arms and brushed her knees. After rinsing her face, she patted her skin with a towel. The scent of vanilla spread through the air as she dabbed lotion in her palm. She sat down on a chair and propped up her left foot.

She paused and pulled something out of her robe, a necklace. There was a silver ring on the end of it, bent and oblong and very worn. Bryn murmured to the ring and pressed it to her lips. Starting at her ankle, she massaged the lotion into the tendons, then along the side to the arch and the ball of her foot, spreading her toes. Her hair was clipped back, but pieces floated down around her face. Zander felt hypnotized, drawn to this private moment.

Gathering his courage, he knocked on the vent. She looked up, startled. With some effort, he lifted out the metal slat and slid through. He hung on the edge, then fell to the floor, toppling to his side on the carpet. Wincing, he stood up with his back to her. Zander turned—and met a sleek gun pointed at his head.

Chapter 20

"Get out." Her gaze was very cold, her voice menacing.

"Hold on, hold on. I'm not here to hurt you." Zander backed away. The gun was the size of her palm, silver-plated with a black grip. There was sweat on the grip, her finger sliding on the trigger. What if it went off by accident? Or on purpose.

"I'm not here to hurt you either," she replied. "But I will."

"There was no other way to see you. I need to deliver a message," he said. "I'm sure you don't remember me, but my name's Zander Grace. I need to talk to you about your dad and Grace House."

Her eyes studied him as if trying to gauge his threat level. She put down the gun but kept it tight in her grip, holding it against the length of her bare thigh. "Wait, you were out there, in the front row." Pink flushed her cheeks. "Sorry about the kiss. I don't know why I did that. We're not supposed to—" Bryn stopped. She bit her lip, then moved to the back wall of the dressing room. Opening a hidden panel, she slid the gun inside and closed it. Her eyes still viewed Zander warily as she pulled her robe tight, the satin spooning over her lovely curves.

He was stunned for a moment—the husky voice didn't match her delicate look. In fact, she had a toughness to her. He scanned the room. Three candles provided the only light, casting round shadows on the walls. Clean and simple. No pictures hung up, no clutter. A sweet scent filled the air—fresh lilies in a vase on a table beside the door. Her shoes and costumes glittered in the closet. On the farthest wall, two French doors were open and a breeze floated in from the balcony.

She looked older than twenty-three, maturity etched around her eyes and mouth. Her large eyes were round with dark brown irises. There was a tiny indent on her chin. The dance kept flashing in his mind. Her ghost still embraced him, the softness of her lips, her hair as silk strands against his skin.

The words fumbled out of his mouth. "Your dad said you were in danger."

Bryn looked away. *She knows what I'm talking about,* he thought. "Has anyone threatened you? Given you strange vibes lately?"

Her mouth hardened. "Just you." She studied him. "You're trying to trick me into going back to Grace House."

Nerves flooded him. The air felt sparked somehow, dense with static. He wanted to touch her, make sure she was real, run his fingers through the cold weight of her hair. Was his voice high and shrieky, like a nervous kid? Why had Elder wanted him to do this? He sounded nuts.

Bryn laughed. "Brecker's damn persistent, I'll give him that. Maglia is special, but I can't be a part of the research. No matter how many attractive men he sends," she hinted.

"But Elder said—"

"Let me guess. You can't tell me how I'm in danger, or from whom? But you want me to fly away with you, a stranger?" She sighed. "Listen, I have a great life here. Tell Brecker his strategy didn't work. I can't just abandon everything." She turned from him and began sorting through her costumes in the closet.

The irony was not lost on Zander that only a month ago he sounded just like her. He sat back on his heels against the wall. He wanted that powerful connection he'd felt during the dance, but there was only distance now. The magnetism must be a part of her act.

He stood back up. "I'm sorry I bothered you. I'll leave now, no need to call security." He turned and went to the door.

"I don't understand," she called out, surprise in her voice. "I thought you had a message."

"You don't care."

"Listen." She came up close to him and her little finger slid around his. Zander's stomach dropped a little, all tingly nerves. "It's a tough situation, but it's not your fault. Elder Sansa was a man I barely knew. He loved science and he loved traveling—in fact, he loved anything that wasn't hanging around a kid and her crazy mother. His coma just gave him a better excuse to be gone." Her voice wavered.

There was a commotion outside in the hallway. Those prickles again in his gut. What if that man had really been watching him? A new tension filled his shoulders and chest. Something felt wrong. "Can we talk somewhere else, please? This place isn't safe for you anymore."

She smirked. "You're going to save me?"

"Please. Come to Grace House with me tonight."

Bryn raised her eyebrows. "Ok, I'm curious. How are you going to convince me?"

"I'm only asking for one night."

She gave him a sly smile.

"I mean," he fumbled, "you should hear my side. Brecker's never been to Maglia; he can't describe it like I can."

Her smile deepened and her hand slid into his. "I guess I could learn more."

He paused. What else could he say to convince her? "Plus your dad really wants to see you."

Her smile dropped and her lower lip trembled. "Okay, I can't take any more of this. You have to go."

She brushed past him and opened the door. A bouncer spotted them and started a quick waddle down the hallway.

Zander was stunned. Why did she react that way? "I wish you could see," he murmured, his throat dry. It was hard to speak with her so close up. Those eyes. Warm brown, with flecks of amber. They made him delirious. He wanted to show her Maglia desperately, to make her understand. Her father wasn't gone. "I know there's nothing I could say, but if you came with me. . . ."

He cupped the side of her face. Bryn took a shallow breath and hugged herself. "Okay, the message. When you were a kid, he brought you back an oyster from Japan. You carried the pearl everywhere. When you lost it, you wouldn't stop crying, and Elder told you that pearls don't matter." He paused, trying to think. "Wait, why don't they matter?" The bouncer was almost to them. "Because you're made of the same stuff as stars. Just wait—"

An arm crossed his neck from behind. He choked, the man lifting him off the ground a few inches. "Sorry, Miss Sansa, guy snuck right in," the bouncer said. "We've been looking for you, buddy. Your people are outside."

Zander let himself be taken. He'd failed. The guard dragged him down the expanse of hallway. The thick metal of the exit door clanged. The guard finally got the door open and pulled Zander through to the stairwell. Bryn stood outside her dressing room, gently wiping her eyes with her sleeve. He stared through the rapidly closing door, willing her to look at him again, just one more chance. Her gaze caught his and his chest filled with hope. Then the door banged shut.

Chapter 21

When Zander conveniently strolled into the Lolita and within Lynch's grasp, the man was sitting in the club owner's office with his legs crossed and palms together. The owner sat across from him, a smallish Indian man engulfed by an obscenely large desk. He dressed conservatively enough in a purple silk shirt and black velvet pants, finished off with black and silver cowboy boots. An ivory cowboy hat lay on the desk. His petite hands tapped on the oak of the desk. The tapping created a very dense sound. Obnoxious.

"I can't help you anymore, Mr. Katlan. I can't have you threatening my best dancer. I can't have your men harassing my guests. I think your time with us is done." His lips puckered. He seemed quite desperate to be in charge. The rowdy scent of Old Spice collided with the flowery lotion wafting up from his hands.

Lynch studied him. The man probably wanted another fee, which Lynch was not going to pay.

"I will call the police," the man stated, his voice wavering.

"Oh, I'm sure you will. Make yourself feel a little bigger," Lynch chuckled. He was about to tell this man exactly what he would do when they were interrupted by a knock at the door. Drex came in and whispered in his ear.

Lynch exhaled. Could it be? Were the gods that kind? He told Drex to wait for him outside. The man left and shut the door behind him.

Lynch grinned and stood up. He moved to Mr. Tambe's side and sat on the desk. He gripped the man's neck tightly, then pinched his earlobe. Even the man's cries were pitiful. "Mr. Tambe, my mood has improved recently, so you won't be maimed," his voice went deeper, "or gutted," his voice went deeper, "or killed tonight."

The man's head twisted down and he whimpered. Lynch continued. "Now let me tell you something vital. If any of those three things occurred, all of your money, those stacks of hundreds that you probably rub your crotch on at night, would mean nothing. Let me repeat. Nothing. Nod for me."

The man's face turned slightly purple, blending in with his shirt. He nodded, his eyes watering. Lynch loosened his grip slightly, just enough to let the man breathe. Blood spots appeared on his gloves from the man's earlobe. The owner's hand reached underneath the desk. Lynch swayed Mr. Tambe's entire body away from it so his fingers feebly scratched at the wood. "No, no, I don't think so. I've had my fill of guns from your assertive women."

He leaned in. "Give me tonight. I will take what I need, *everything I need,* and you will not see me nor any of my men for the rest of your life. Sound like a good deal? Nod for me."

The man nodded again, his breathing labored.

"Now, I need your mind very clear for this. Is there anything you're not telling me about Miss Sansa? Any more hidden panels? Does she have a secret knowledge of kung-fu?"

Mr. Tambe shook his head ferociously and strings of saliva floated out of his open mouth. Lynch groaned and wiped his gloves on the man's purple silk shirt. There was a slight hesitation in the man's eyes. He cared for his dancers, and he was hiding something that may protect them. Lynch didn't like it, but he was constrained for time. The mouse had scurried in, sniffing for his cheese, and it was time to release the trap. His men had checked Bryn Sansa's dressing room while she was out, and there didn't appear to be anything besides the gun panel.

Lynch paused, assessing. A few minutes of torture could save a lifetime of regret. But he really wanted to get to that mouse.

"Show me to your camera room." He held up a finger. "Not the boring one with your security feeds and your bouncers sitting around eating stale pizza. Your real camera room. The one with the most scrumptious views."

Mr. Tambe nodded, looking very ill. Lynch allowed him to stand up and the two men walked out. Drex joined them and they walked down a series of hallways, then down into the service elevator. They entered the 3,500-square-foot garage, then they passed the security center filled with camera views of the hallways and entrances and main areas. Mr. Tambe led them to a non-descript door next to the security center. He pressed his palm into an electronic panel and the door opened. Over a dozen monitors were spread out over three of the walls. A desk covered with electronic buttons and levers stood before them.

Mr. Tambe made a move to leave, but Lynch stopped him. "No, you're staying here for the rest of the evening. Show me Miss Sansa's dressing room." Mr. Tambe swiftly tapped in the number.

Lynch clicked his tongue. "Yes. Perfect. They're talking." A feeling of smugness rose in him. They were a couple. His lure had worked.

Drex leaned in next to him, his voice hungry. "Let's get them both."

"Wait," Mr. Tambe protested. "Do what you want to the man, but I can't let you hurt the girl. She's my best dancer."

Lynch signaled to Drex. The man pulled two pairs of handcuffs out of his pocket. He placed one set on Mr. Tambe's hands, then used the other pair to fasten his legs together, winding the cuffs through the chair legs.

"I have nothing to keep him quiet," Drex said.

"I have a feeling the room is soundproofed." Lynch inspected the chair, suddenly very happy he'd not touched it. He wished he could rinse off his shoes.

"He's secure. Let's go," Drex said.

"No." Lynch watched the screen. Bryn opened the door of the dressing room. A bouncer rambled up the hallway and seized Zander. Lynch quickly shifted the camera's view to the hallway, then to the stairs as the bouncer dragged the kid down them. The bouncer threw Zander out of the exit on the first floor. The kid tried to get back in for a few minutes, then appeared to give up. Now the camera's only view was of Zander's back. He kept gesturing to the alleyway.

"Who's he talking to?" Lynch asked.

Drex shrugged. "Probably one of the couples here. The guy's trying to find a way back inside."

Lynch pulled his glove tight on his hand. "We should help him out."

He sighed, relishing the return of power. The mouse scurried here and there, so unaware. Yes, Lynch needed to get back home. Yes, he had orders. But he simply couldn't resist some playtime. The little bastard had given him a hell of a headache and he wanted some fun now. He'd have to be very good at camouflage since he didn't have the island's help here.

"He's going to escape. Let's go now," Drex said, his breathing labored. It was distracting.

Lynch held up a finger. "No." A moment of silence passed. "Zander will bring her to me."

Chapter 22

The door slammed, taking Bryn with it. Zander scrambled to open it and the security guard slugged him. Pain flooded his gut and he doubled over. The guard grabbed him and escorted him down the stairs to the first floor, then shoved him outside to the southwest corner of the building.

"Buddy, don't try to get back in, or you'll get a lot more than a punch to the gut," the guard called out.

The outer door shut and Zander banged on it. He tried a couple of other doors, but everything was locked. He peeked around the back, and there were fifteen-foot stucco walls shielding the pool. Bouncers at every entrance. They weren't allowing anyone to re-enter the club. There had to be a gate or something overlooked by security. If he could just talk to Bryn one more time, he knew he could convince her to leave with him.

There was a noise behind him in the alleyway. Someone kept hissing at him. A man dressed in black stood hidden around the corner, away from the cameras.

"What the hell, who—" he broke off. The GUT emblem rose up on the guy's jacket. The name stitched below it read "Manny."

"How'd you find me?" Zander asked.

Manny chuckled. He had the razor-thin military haircut and barrel chest like a lot of the GUT guys had. "Dr. Brecker's had this place watched for months now. I guess the girl's valuable like you." His tone was sarcastic, as if doubting that value. "We saw you walk in, then asked the bouncers to keep an eye out. The doctor's awful pissed at you, my friend."

"I know, I know. But someone's been threatening her," Zander said. "Can you get me back inside?"

Manny scoffed. "Hell, no. We have no pull with these guys. This is a crack security detail, the best money can buy. You're on your own with that."

"Give me an hour then. It'll take you that long to get a car and a flight home put together," Zander said.

Manny put his hands up. "Alright, I'm not good with this hero shit. Say your goodbyes and we'll find you later." He wiggled a finger in Zander's face. "Girl or no girl, you're coming back. Hale Brecker's orders."

He joined another GUT man farther down the alleyway and they left.

There was lots of noise—bottles rolling and clinking on the ground, chattering in the pool area. The alleyway stunk of piss and garbage. His legs jittered and he walked in a circle. Should he wait out here and hope someone exited? He groaned. It would only be the bouncers throwing more people out. His only choice was to go around to the front and hope they'd let him in. Maybe security hadn't radioed out his description. Zander started to head in that direction when a side door on the first level opened and Lynch Katlan stepped out, holding a beer and limping. The two men stared at each other in surprise.

"Shit, I can't believe it," Lynch yelled, a little too loudly.

"Hey," Zander froze. His feet stuck to the pavement and his mind raced. Why was Lynch here? The man looked relaxed in a leather jacket and jeans, but this couldn't be a coincidence.

"Seriously, what are you doing here?" he asked, ignoring the other man's good mood.

Lynch shook his head and let out a hoot. "Oh, man. I'm glad I ran into you before Damaris did."

"Damaris is here?" Chills went down his lower back, and Zander leaned against the brick wall, suddenly lightheaded.

"Yeah, that guy, um, the guy who took you? The doctor? He told Pete about this place." Lynch leaned to the right and hocked a wad of spit in the corner. "So Damaris and some guys came up here."

"Wait, why does Damaris even care?"

Lynch searched his face. "He's pissed. Do you remember the rumors about all the crazy experiments in the tunnels?" His eyes grew wide. "Damaris thinks you know something."

"Me? Why?"

"I don't know," he scoffed. "You know how crazy secretive they are." His voice went quiet and he studied Zander. "Do you? Know something?"

"I don't . . . I mean no."

Lynch frowned. "Hey, it's cool. You don't have to tell me."

"It's not that I don't trust you. I really don't know anything, I swear." He shook his head. "I can't figure out what Damaris wants with me."

"You and me both," Lynch snorted. He abruptly softened and touched Zander's shoulder, concern in his eyes. "We didn't know what to think. I mean, this old guy comes in and just steals you off the island. It went down huge; everyone was freaked. No one knew if you were dead or alive or what the hell happened." His fingers gripped Zander's shoulder a little too hard and Zander shrugged him off. A hurt look crossed the man's face. "I'm only trying to help."

"I know you are. I appreciate it, I really do. I just don't understand what's going on."

Lynch grinned and gave him a playful shove. "I can't believe I actually found you. Where did the old guy take you? Who was he?"

Zander felt hopelessly confused. He had that sick feeling again, but he couldn't figure out where it was coming from. Lynch sounded sincere. There had been a lot of rumors on Kadera about him, but they were all lies, just a bunch of fantasies by drugged-out kids. The man was his friend, a good person who cared about animals and had protected Zander from the truly violent bastards on the island. Like Damaris.

Damn Brecker. Zander shook his head, muttering to himself. "How could he have been so stupid to say something? And to Pete? I bet the kid spilled his guts as soon as he got back to the island."

"Oh, you have no idea," Lynch whispered.

"What did you say?"

"Nothing. So who is the doctor guy?"

"Bre—I mean, he's an old family friend. They needed me back home for something important." The name stuck on the tip of his tongue. Zander couldn't say why, but he decided to keep it to himself.

"Why are you here?" Lynch nudged him, grinning. "Oh, that's right. It's a girl. God, those dancers are gorgeous. Wish we could invite them back to the island." He looked up at the night sky and took a swig of beer. He choked on it, then shattered the bottle against the wall. "Not quite a Hypna, right?"

Zander stared at the door, heartsick. He kept picturing Damaris's fury. Why would the man travel halfway around the world just for him? At least they didn't know about Bryn.

"Wait, how did you guys know I'm here for a girl?"

Lynch opened his hands wide. "He knows you're here for a girl, that's all he told me. I'd really like to help you out, man, but Damaris is insane. Batshit and beyond." He twirled a finger around his head. "I've seen him hurt people, especially women. He likes it. No telling what he'll do to her."

He lowered his voice again. "He'll hurt her. Like he hurt me when he found out you were gone." He motioned to his leg. "Nearly tore off my kneecap."

"Oh, God, that's terrible. I'm so sorry," Zander replied. Lynch was a good guy. He didn't deserve to get mixed up in this. "You know, we should just split up. Thanks for the warning." He started to leave, but Lynch stayed still. He paused a second too long, studying Zander.

"You don't want my help?"

"You've done too much for me already."

Lynch's eyes flashed and he pointed. "Wait. You know, Damaris said something else." He snapped his fingers. "A name. He mentioned a name, something different. Bryn. Is that right? Bryn Sansa? No, that can't be right." His eyes hovered on Zander's reaction.

"Oh, my God." Zander bent over, his legs wobbly, no air left in his lungs. "We have to get her out of here."

Lynch groaned dramatically. "Damaris has guys all around us. Not sure what can be done."

"Can you get us through? Please? Just get us out of here and we won't bother you again, I promise. I'll owe you everything."

Lynch paused as if deep in thought, then gave a little smile. "Of course, Zander. We're friends." Just then the side door opened next to them. A group of patrons exited, laughing and cheering, and both men entered.

"You have no idea how much I appreciate this." Zander led him up the stairs to the third floor and down the hallway to Bryn's dressing room, then knocked on her door. "Hey, it's me. I know you're still angry, but I have someone here who can help us."

There was rustling behind the door. Zander muttered to himself. They might still have time. If they could get Bryn out of here with Lynch's help, they'd be safely in Colorado before morning. He closed his eyes and willed his heart to slow down. Then he heard it.

Whistling behind his head. Softly at first. A trill of notes in the air. Heavier footsteps on his other side. As each note made it to his ear, everything slowed. The melody took him back to the dampness of the tunnels. The rot, the stench of dead sealife and chemicals. Screams behind a door. Pleading. Blood underneath, leaking out from a much wider puddle. Oh God, he'd made a horrible mistake. He started to yell, to stop Bryn from opening the door, when an arm snaked around his neck and cut off his air. A gloved hand closed over his mouth as her face appeared in the doorway.

Brit Malorie

Chapter 23

Bryn Sansa stood inside her dressing room, her fingers gliding over her ring, rolling the bent silver back and forth. Joe had kicked that Zander guy out of the club. She remembered her dad giving her an oyster once and carrying the pearl around. He used to say stuff like that, about Bryn being made of the same stuff as stars, but Elder said a lot of things. Things that became hard to remember after his accident. She spread her bare toes and pressed them into the carpet, another nervous habit.

Zander Grace. She smiled as his face came to mind. Arrogant as hell, but she'd always been drawn to that in men. His eyes were this dark blue, and coppery hair curled around his face. It stuck up near his ears, giving him a mischievous look. And there was this sexy curve to his mouth, like he could tell exactly what she was thinking. Why had she kissed him during the dance? He was incredibly attractive, gorgeous really, but that wasn't it. She'd felt a sudden desire to be close to him.

She sat down and looked at herself in the mirror. Was his mission simply to take her back to Grace House? His bottom lip made this adorable pout when he'd begged her to leave, like he couldn't get enough of her. Bryn kept smiling, her mind dreamy as she pulled a pink camisole over her head, then slipped on denim shorts and ballet-flat shoes. She should leave for her apartment, but she delayed, her gaze returning to the door. What if he was still outside? She should just do one circle around out of curiosity.

Then a knock at the door. His voice. She rushed to it, wanting to apologize, to welcome him inside, to talk all night.

Bryn opened the door and her muscles tensed. It was that man from before, the one who'd threatened her. But now there was metal on his jawline.

"Hello, hello." She flinched as his gloved hand darted up her neck. "You caught my heart before but not my name. Lynch Katlan."

She tried to make her voice rough, but it came out as dry and weak. "What is this? I'm not in the mood."

"Get in it then." He gripped her head and pushed her into the dressing room, followed by two other guys. They held Zander but he slumped down, his face full of guilt and fury. Something was very wrong.

Lynch shut the door, then he moved a chair to the corner and made her sit in it. "I need you to be still for now. Oh, and let's get this out of the way." He strode over to the back wall panel and removed her gun, handing it to one of the guys holding Zander.

Lynch shook his arms and hands out. His facial muscles relaxed and he rolled his head in a circle. "Damn, why does the truth feel so good? Don't feel bad, Zander. Many people fall for that. It's natural. We're friends."

Zander looked nauseated. "The rumors, everything's true. It was never Damaris."

"Oh, Damaris is still quite the bastard. He wouldn't like you to forget that." Lynch walked up and curved his hand over Zander's neck. "And the rumors are *not* true. They can't even *begin* to describe what I am."

He lifted Zander up against the wall. Zander struggled to land punches against his large torso, but the man held him up easily.

"Did you think you could escape me?" Lynch screamed next to Zander's ear as he choked, his face growing red.

"Did you think you were safe?" he seethed, his voice heavy with bloodlust. His palms released, then squeezed again. "Not too fast now." Zander struggled, but his limbs finally went slack. Bryn looked away, tears sliding down her cheeks.

Lynch released him and he sank to the ground. Zander gulped in air, he couldn't seem to get enough.

He sputtered. "Just let her go. Please. You have me."

Lynch smiled. "You know, I've never understood why guys in the movies always say that. Let. Her. Go. Now why in the hell would I ever do that?"

Zander bent over as coughs wracked his body. "I'm willing to trade for her. I won't struggle."

"A hero now as well? The doctor does work miracles." Lynch made a noise of approval and studied him. "It's remarkable, you know. All this arrogance—a fierce new look. Where'd the emptiness go, Zander?" He chuckled, the sound echoing harshly in the dressing room. "You have purpose now. Like you're protecting something. Must be our lady."

Zander hesitated a second too long. "Yes."

"No. Something deeper." Lynch tapped the side of his own head. "Something, something. I think it lies wherever the doctor took you. How is the old man these days?"

Zander stood up and shook his head. "You'll never find him."

"Oh, I'll find him," Lynch sighed. "Only a physician can truly appreciate what I can do to him."

He paused. "You've inspired me. We're going to have some fun right now with Miss Sansa. Then she's going to Kadera and you're taking me to that wretched doctor." The glee in his voice was unmistakable.

"I'll never—"

"Oh yes, you will. I'll rip it out of you." Lynch's voice grew very cold.

He spread his hands wide, motioning for the two thugs to separate from Zander, then launched a series of hard punches to his sides. Zander's face contorted in severe pain as he collapsed. Lynch used his falling momentum to knee him, catching him in the head. Bryn cried out, but she couldn't run and there were no other weapons.

He walked over to her. She couldn't breathe, couldn't think, the fear was so bad. Her body hunched down, her arms close to her sides, trying to look as small as possible. Lynch knelt before her and lifted her leg up. He removed her shoes and caressed her left ankle, the leather of his gloves sliding along the arc of bone and ligament. He slid a switchblade out of his pocket.

"I should really concentrate on what I came here for. But you're such a delicious dis . . . trac . . . tion." He whispered the word, brushing his lips along her calf. Bryn shuddered, her body squirming against the wall. There was no place to go. Her eyes met Zander's, held them. His lips moved. *Hold on.*

Lynch tilted her face back to him. "Now, now, I think you should know the truth. That's fair. Zander led me to you. Zander is the reason you're about to go through what you are. If he'd been smarter, or if he really cared about you, you wouldn't be going through this right now."

He touched her chin. "You can stop this at any time. Simply tell me where he comes from. Tell me the doctor's name and where they live. That's it, sweetie. And remember, all this pain is his fault." He pointed the knife back at Zander.

Bryn tried to say it. Hale Brecker. Colorado. But nothing came out. Her father. An image rose in her head—he lay helpless in bed, impossibly old and very sick. She couldn't do it.

Lynch stroked her hair. "How to begin, how to begin? Do you believe in obstacles?" He kept his voice low, like the question was a secret. "Only obstacles give you strength in life. Zander left such a lovely gift for me, so I'll pass one onto you. Loss. I know, I know," he said, waving the knife in the air, "just a fleeting thought in your mind. That's why we have to make it solid. Real."

He tapped her big toe with the knife. "First, your dancing." He moved to the next toe. "Then your face, you really are quite the stunner." He moved to the middle toe. "Then your lying tongue. Three of your weapons gone. What will be left? What kind of person will you be? I'm excited to see."

Bryn forced herself to look clearly into his eyes. If she could just beg hard enough, he'd respond. He must be capable of sympathy, of real emotions. She started to say the words, to beg for their lives. But his eyes stopped her. They were reptilian. There was no mercy, no comfort in the green depths.

Her mind fluttered then. Everything became blurry and distant, like she watched from far away. She needed a safe place. She heard Zander's voice shouting about Maglia, shouting that he would tell Lynch everything if he'd just let her go. It all faded, her hearing muffled. Fear iced her spine, what was he doing, what—

The knife curved into her ankle. She screamed as her mind wrenched away. She tasted leather as he shoved his gloved fist in her mouth. Oh God, the pain, it coursed up her leg and radiated into her hips and her torso. Her other leg thrashed, slamming into the wall.

Bryn surrendered to the blackness, her eyes closing mercifully. Lynch slapped her and the sting shocked her awake. "Now, now. That's cheating. And so early in our date."

She fell out of the chair and sunk into the carpet, cradling herself. He got one of her scarves from the closet and wrapped her ankle tightly. "Can't have you bleeding out on me. Believe me, darling, a corpse is still fun but really a different kind of game."

The smell of blood overwhelmed her. There was something under it, something she recognized when he first came in—peppermint. Could that be it? She inhaled and coughed on the two smells as they collided. The pain ebbed away then returned. She felt limp inside and very cold.

He stood up. "I think I'll permit myself a celebratory cigarette. Bring him out to the balcony."

Lynch went out and the two other guys brought Zander to him. She was alone.

Bryn felt so tired. Pain ran down her leg like fire. There was this noise she couldn't get away from. Splat. Splat. Splat. She looked down, the floor spinning right below her. Red sprinkling on the carpet.

Thoughts bubbled up so fast. Never dance again. A psychopath. Where would he take her? A realization broke through—she wouldn't live through another encounter with that man. And if she did, she wouldn't want to. Bryn struggled for a thread of reason, anything to live for.

There were voices in the hallway just outside the door. She heard the word Lynch. Those were his men out there, waiting for him to give more orders. Her mind grasped for anything. She needed a place where they couldn't follow, where they couldn't find her. That trickling sensation distracted her as drops ran down her foot. Bryn gritted her teeth. Grabbing the ends of the scarf, she took a deep breath and pulled it tight. The ache burst out in fresh pain and black traveled across her vision. She stood on her other foot and braced against the wall, praying to stay conscious. Her gaze traveled upward, resting on the dusty panels. The ceiling. She paused a second, making sure it was real, understanding inch by inch. They didn't know. They really didn't know.

Chapter 24

The guys brought Zander to the balcony and pushed him forward. He looked over the railing. Guests chattered below him, colored lights dancing over their skin. Women in party dresses, men in suits—all oblivious to the horror happening above them. Rage rolled over him in great waves, a coat of brittle red blurring his sight and heating his skin. He gripped the metal of the railing until it sliced into his hands, every muscle in his body rigid. He couldn't think when he was like this. He had to force himself to relax somehow so he could think of a plan. He had to find a way out for Bryn.

"I can handle him. Back off," Lynch ordered the two men behind them. He took a cloth from his pocket and wiped the blade of the knife. He removed his gloves, then released them and the cloth over the railing. Specks of Bryn's blood floated off as they sailed down. He closed the switchblade and tucked it into his back pocket.

"Oh, don't be mad. Have you been working out?" he asked sweetly. "You look great. I really mean that. A bit different than the bone-thin wastrel that was kidnapped from my island."

Zander remained silent. He closed his eyes and pictured Lynch sailing through the air after his gloves, screaming. The fury was so powerful specks crossed his vision.

Lynch pulled a cigarette pack out of the front pocket of his jacket. "You know, Zander, I've figured out your problem. The normal world," he gestured in a circle, "it blunts people. Grinds you to a stub. You need to get back to Kadera." He flipped his lighter back. "Then you'll come to your senses."

Zander jerked his head. "What did you say?"

"It'll be fun. Your girl can dance there. Wait—maybe not," Lynch chuckled as he lit the cigarette. "My bad. But you can have her all to yourself. She'll love Seed."

Zander focused on the clue. The senses. His rage started to fade. His muscles relaxed and a cool breeze pulled the heat from his skin. He felt along his face; there were cuts and bruising from where Lynch kneed him. Severe pain along his sides—reminders of the man's punches—but he had to focus on the clue. "You don't know about the strangeness of the island, do you? The real reason for it," Zander whispered.

Lynch ignored him. He inhaled smoke, then looked at the cigarette with disgust. "Not even close."

"And why they want me back." The senses. Kadera amplified the senses. People read each other through the back of the neck. He'd always thought of it as a scam, just a bunch of silly kids that would believe anything. He closed his eyes and a memory rose in his mind. The chains. Human beings sitting in great chains, streams of emotion and sensation coursing through them.

"It can't be connected," he murmured. "It's impossible."

"I'm glad you've decided to help the girl. Finally." Lynch made a clucking noise. "What do you know about the experiments? Has Damaris ever made you participate in them?"

"Experiments?"

"Yes," Lynch said impatiently. "During your impassioned plea for the girl's life, you shouted out the names Maggie and Leah. Who are they?"

"Maglia," he murmured. Palms reading the back of the neck. Emotions exchanged. It couldn't be.

"What is Maglia?"

"It's a place."

Lynch smacked him in the chest. "Like what, like Mexico? Explain."

He steadied himself. "You have to let Bryn go."

"This again?" Lynch groaned. "Now where's the fun in that? Kadera's already destroyed you. Let the island sink her teeth into something fresh."

He tried one last effort. "The rituals and the readings are all bullshit. It's just drugs and mind suggestion." Zander lowered his voice and leaned forward. "But I know the truth. You'll never find out about Maglia unless you let Bryn go."

"Aren't you forgetting something?" Lynch turned his back, his head craned upward to gaze at the moon. He let out a plume of smoke and laughed, the rich sound welling up from his gut. "Perhaps you'd like a bit more play after all. Shall we try her eyes next?"

Zander heard a loud noise behind him, like a rusty lever turning. Beneath his feet, the platform dropped away. He grasped at the railing but fell too fast. His fingers slipped off the metal, and there was only open air around him.

Brit Malorie

Chapter 25

Bryn's hand let go of the lever. The panel slid back into place behind the table. Lynch's men were standing behind their boss and Zander, so when the balcony dropped open, they peered over and watched the two men fall into the pool below.

She crawled, keeping her ankle off the floor. She climbed her hands up the wall, leaning forward. Don't put weight on it, don't— She almost cried out as a spasm rocked her left leg. Her teeth bit down on her knuckles. With all her weight on her other leg, she moved the chair over.

Lynch's men were about eight feet away. One of them pointed down to the pool area and snickered. He nudged the other man. "Now they're gonna fight. Lynch'll kick his ass."

Bryn felt gingerly along the scarf. The tendons were loose, possibly the bones, too. Parts of her ankle ground together, jostling unnaturally. She closed her eyes, her head swaying. Using her knees, she eased herself up on the chair and felt along the ceiling. Where was it?

Her fingers wouldn't work. She couldn't find the ceiling panel. An edge, wait, wait—she pushed with all the force she could muster. The distinctive pop of the slat opening.

One of the guys startled at the sound and turned. He yelled at her to stop. Bryn gripped the sides of the opening and pulled herself up. Her hips caught. She jerked downward to dislodge herself. God, why wouldn't her hips move? She twisted again—the opening squeezed her and she couldn't breathe. She scrambled against the metal walls of the vent, nothing to grip onto. A hand caught her good foot and yanked. Her chin slammed down on the metal and stars flashed over her vision.

Flames surged through her. This was her life, dammit! She was so close. The slat crumbled a little. Bryn kicked outward and heard a yelp as her foot planted on something hard. She twisted her hips in a new angle and pulled them clear. Lifting herself up, she looked back as a hand reached for her. Moving fast, she crawled down the vent.

Where could she go? The man was coming after—no, wait. He couldn't fit, but he was still coming. Her thoughts jumbled. Just move, get as far as you can. Bryn felt nauseated. The smell of blood filled her nose and made her dizzy. It slickened the metal and caused her to slide too fast down the chute. Sirens penetrated the fog in her mind. There were police outside.

Taking a deep breath, she popped off the slat on the last exit vent and descended gently, bracing herself to let go, willing the floor to hit her good leg.

Her ankle smacked the carpet and she screamed, sparks of red and purple over her eyes. She covered her mouth, listening. Silence outside the door, but it could be a trick. They'd search every room. The ferociousness of Lynch's gaze; he wouldn't leave here without her.

Bryn forced herself to move past her paralysis. Creeping out into the hallway, she braced against the wall, then hobbled down the stairs to the back exit. She didn't know where the police were, but she could make it. The main street was just outside and she'd limp until they found her— please, God, anyone. The night air swallowed her and she felt exposed. A huge crowd milled outside. She backed down a smaller alley behind the Lolita, the brick grinding against her fingers. Her muscles wouldn't stop shaking. She had to get the police, but she waited, her trepidation building. He'd get her again. They were waiting just around the corner for her to come out.

Then a hand covered her mouth.

Chapter 26

Water plunged into his mouth and ears, knocking the breath out of him. Zander quickly rose to the surface of the pool, coughing forcefully. He climbed to the side and crawled out. Guests murmured around him and stepped back. Suddenly, he saw Lynch crawling out on the other side and adrenaline surged through his body. He heard Bryn's voice again, crying out in pain. And that bastard's smug smile. He'd kill him. Zander launched himself forward and hit Lynch's waist with his shoulders. Something metallic clattered to the ground. He threw punches deep into the man's sides. Lynch attempted to put him in a hold, but Zander slipped through. Their clothes were drenched. Lynch yelled and slammed Zander's head down on the patio surface. He reached out and gripped the back of Lynch's knees, then pulled forward. The man fell down on his ass, a stunned look on his face. Zander's hands flew around his neck. There were these deep growl noises. He wondered what they were, then realized they came from inside him. The rage filled him with so much strength that Lynch struggled to break apart his grip. He brought his knee up and cracked Lynch's head down on it. Blood blossomed on the man's nose, but Zander had to hop backward as pain ripped into his knee. Dammit. That metal implant. He wanted to rip it out of Lynch's skull. Zander stepped on something hard. He knelt down and felt along the patio. Lynch's knife.

He closed his hand over it and opened up the blade. Lynch crawled on all fours, pushing himself forward, his teeth bared. His body hit Zander's chest in a straight shot. Faces swam around them. The crowd had multiplied in size. There were cheers and boos as the two men grappled. Blue and red lights flickered in the corner of his vision. At first he thought it was the pain in his head, then realized it was something outside. Cops.

He had to do something now. Zander bent in close, his head pressing into Lynch's shoulder. The steel warmed in his hand, but where? A patch of skin shone in the neon lights, right above Lynch's collar. No. He realized the right spot, the best one. A sure thing. His hand was still wet and it slicked the handle. Don't think about it or it'll never happen. *Don't think about it.*

Zander launched an uppercut punch with the knife sticking upward. It penetrated Lynch's shirt but went in at a bad angle, colliding with one of his ribs. Zander twisted the blade and pushed it in farther. It was so damn slippery, blood and water everywhere. Lynch let out an embattled roar and his fist slammed into Zander's gut. Hands grasped Zander's collar and pulled back, but he fought them. Arms crossed his chest and pulled him away from Lynch.

"Let me kill him!" he screamed, not caring about the crowd.

A voice near his ear. "We have to get out of here." His vision cleared and he saw Lynch's men on the other side, pulling him away, too. Uniforms penetrated the crowd. Manny and the other GUT man pulled him through the crowd. A bellow of rage sounded behind Zander and he took one last look. His eyes met Lynch's and held them. A seething hatred washed over him again and he tried to fight off the two men, straining against their grip. He swore the deepest revenge in his heart and cursed himself for not killing that monster. He should've aimed for the neck.

They made it past the perimeter of the crowd where Zander finally pushed the two guys off him. "Wait, just wait a minute. I have to find Bryn."

Manny looked him over. "Our assignment was to get you. We'll come back—"

"It'll be too late. She'll be gone," he yelled. "Lynch will take her."

"We're just a surveillance team. We don't have the manpower to fight them. Besides, why would they take her?"

"Dammit, I don't have time to explain. Your orders are to protect her, right? You've never dealt with these animals. They'll kill her."

The men hesitated. The one motioned to Manny. "If we lose him, we're in deep."

"Give me a phone!" Zander ordered. "Let me do one sweep of the perimeter. If I can't find her in twenty minutes, I'll leave, no question." His body was in severe pain, but adrenaline gave him a steady surge of energy. Bryn wouldn't survive Kadera. His only chance was to find her now, while Lynch and his crew were distracted by the cops.

The GUT man handed him a cell. "A car will be waiting at the corner of Elm Street and El Dorado. Find her and be there. Otherwise, we'll take you by force."

Zander nodded. He had to find an entrance to the club but also stay out of Lynch's line of sight. He wound his way through the crowd, keeping his head down, which wasn't too hard considering how much everything hurt. It felt like he had a concussion, possible sprains, maybe a few broken ribs. He had to take tiny breaths and each one sent pain shooting up his sides. There must be a door left open. Someone must have been careless and in a rush to see the fight. He stopped and blinked rapidly. There was a shadow, a slender form leaning against the brick wall. The relief that filled him was like nothing he'd ever felt. A cop walked out to the perimeter of the crowd. Bryn made a move to signal him. Zander came up behind her and closed his hand over her mouth before she could say anything.

Her teeth clamped down on his skin and he yelped, fresh pain spreading. "Shhh," he whispered, peering around the corner. "Thank God I found you. We have to get out of here."

She watched him, the panic on her face not subsiding. "Why should I believe you? You're the reason they're here." Her jaw hardened. "I want to go to the police."

"He'll expect that. They'll bribe whoever they need to, then walk right in and take you," Zander muttered. "The only safe place is Grace House right now. You have to come with me."

She hesitated, then nodded. Leaning against him, she hobbled down the alley, careful not to jostle her leg. She buried her face in the warm pocket of his neck as the world swam around them.

"Do you know where the cross streets of Elm Street and El Dorado are?" he asked.

She nodded, pointing out the direction.

There was a black sedan idling at the cross streets. He opened the backdoor and let Bryn inside, then he slid in next to her. The car pulled forward, winding down the streets of lower Miami, taking rights and lefts.

Bryn watched through the back window. "Are they really gone?"

Zander took off his shirt, leaving himself in a white undershirt. It was still damp, but he draped it over her shoulders, covering her pink camisole. He could still smell the vanilla in her hair.

"Jesus, what a night," the driver muttered.

Zander silently agreed. He'd wanted her to leave with him, but this wasn't the persuasion he'd had in mind.

"Wait, how are we getting out of here?" she asked.

"There's a helicopter about twenty miles from here. We just have to drive awhile, make sure we've lost them," the driver replied. Their car wound through the streets.

"I can't ever go back, can I? They've been watching that place?"

"I don't understand how he found you. How he guessed you were the one. . . ." He sighed, perplexed. "We hadn't met before tonight."

His fingertips brushed her knee. "Let me take a look," he whispered. The car hit a bump and she winced.

"I don't want you to." Bryn shook her head, her hands pressing into her thighs.

"Okay." Zander cursed softly and a new tension entered his jaw. He called up to the driver, "Radio ahead and make sure Brecker has the exam room ready."

He put his arm around her and rested his lips on her temple. "I'm so sorry, Bryn. I didn't know he would do this to you."

"Oh, my God. I'll never dance again. The one thing I love more than my life, more than anything." The sobs overcame her, her breathing in ragged gulps. Her fingers moved to her ankle, then backed away. "I just want to save it. I want to put it back together."

Zander stayed quiet and simply held her, feeling utterly powerless. Yet being this close to her made him realize how incredible she was. Her quick thinking with the balcony drop had saved his life. Then she'd rescued herself, escaping two armed men despite barely being able to walk. He could see traces of her father, the courage and resilience ingrained in the Sansa's.

Bryn nestled her face into his neck again. His heart wouldn't stop fluttering. The streetlights flickered through the car window in quick succession, the moon full in the sky.

"My friends, my apartment, my job. My whole life was there," she murmured against his skin. "Who are you, and how do you have the power to change everything?"

***

Hours later, they arrived back at Grace House. Zander paced outside the exam room. The longer Brecker took, the more worried he got. What if she'd lost too much blood? What if she had trouble walking for the rest of her life?

Brecker left the exam room, his face already red.

"Before you start yelling, tell me how she is," Zander demanded.

The doctor removed his gloves. "Well, I stopped the bleeding and gave her an IV for the blood loss. Stabilized the ligaments and tendons.

She'll need surgery that's beyond my skill level. It's so specialized I'll have to check where they can do it."

Alarm flooded Zander. "Don't take her to a hospital. That's exactly what Lynch'll be looking for, a surgeon for that specific injury. Arrange for one to take a vacation, fly him in privately with GUT."

"Fine. Now, what the hell were you thinking?"

"Elder asked me to talk to her."

"You should have called a Pensare meeting. We discuss these things," Brecker said.

"You didn't know Lynch was watching the Lolita."

"But I could have had more security go with you."

"Yeah, they worked out great. Lynch hurt her. Dammit, Brecker, I led him to her." His fist grazed the wall. He wanted to smash something. "Don't you understand? He hurt Bryn!"

Brecker hesitated. "You barely know this girl, Zander. Why are you reacting like this?"

He leaned back against the wall and slid down, exhausted, the trauma from the night dragging him under. "I don't know. I feel like I do know her."

"Well, she's here. A new traveler."

"No! Leave her alone!" Zander cried out. Brecker raised his eyebrows.

Zander took a few deep breaths and rubbed his head. "Bryn needs time to heal." He paused. "Don't push her."

Brecker gave him an obnoxious grin.

"You know, you could hide your satisfaction," he muttered.

"Just think of the effort I could've saved. All it took was a beautiful girl to keep you here."

Zander grimaced. The dangers of traveling weren't lost on him. But now he wasn't sure Bryn should endure them either.

"It's a wonder Lynch hasn't tracked you back here yet," Brecker murmured.

Zander sighed. Why didn't he go for the neck? The world would be rid of that psychopath. He'd made a lot of mistakes in his life, but he had a feeling this one would be the worst.

"Lynch'll find us soon enough. And I don't know how you'll keep him out."

Brit Malorie

Chapter 27

Hundreds of tiny worms and insects squirmed just below the grotto walls, lighting the lab space up with phosphorescence. There were metal shelves filled with flasks of chemicals, trapped gases, and powders. A lab bench was built out of rock and hardened mud with the top smoothed flat. On it sat a microscope, a centrifuge, a distillation apparatus, and other basic lab equipment—everything powered by lithium batteries. Griffin twinkled on a small clay perch near the lab's entrance.

Elder Sansa used tweezers to gently spread the core sideways, then peered at the cells through the microscope. This morning he'd chanced upon a dead strand that had been torn apart by the pianta, a carnivorous plant species. The outer layers—the ones involved with thought, logic, and social skills—had already decayed, forming a gray, hardened shell. Only the innermost layers traveled onward to Afterlife—a sheath the color of pearl, a thin ring of crimson, and then the deepest piece, a solid circle of bluish-green, the same color as the highest level of miran, Settimo positive. Elder theorized the pearl sheath was the dream layer. It protected the crimson sheath, which may be the subconscious layer, responsible for all of a person's hidden desires and memories. But the central piece, the core that ran below all others? He wondered if the core was the source of our deepest emotions, the side of a person that almost no one else saw or touched. The barest bones of the soul. He was most fascinated by the trinity of mind and body and strand. How did the strand connect to the mind? Was there a connection between strand and body that the mind could not touch?

Elder exited the grotto and walked up to a ledge nearby. The Veil worked like a cloth that lay between Maglia and home, and there were places where the cloth bunched up. The Pensare had found one such pocket in southwestern Boulder, and they made small trips up there to deliver objects to Elder. If a metal or glass object's molecules were charged and moved through the pocket at the particular angle of 36.478 degrees, it could pass through the Veil. Using a metal cart, he and Jason had moved lab equipment from the crevice down to the grotto.

Equipment like this high-powered telescope, which let him observe regions around Maglia. Past the canyons and the mountain ranges, the lakes of vapor and the long fields of dust and static electricity, Elder spied. He spied on the Woods, a region just outside the great Viperian city of Dimora. The Vipera gathered there to spin in huge cyclones, building up negative charge. He spied on Chalice, a haven for the Lusha angels, which appeared as a massive fireball similar to the sun. At sunrise, in a series of sonic booms, great bursts of light and dark rocketed out from Chalice and Dimora, spreading far out into the mesh. Sunset went far more gentle as the two species streamed homeward in great twin rivers on opposite sides of the world. Night was for the Lerium, sleep creatures that penetrated the dream layer of the strands and infused miran during their slumber. Elder had to sleep here since his mind still needed rest, but he didn't like it. One of the Lerium was curious about travelers. He'd made threats, and Elder wondered if the creature might interfere with his mind while he dreamed.

The old scientist focused the telescope on the center of the mesh. Despite the high power, he could only make out shadows flickering across the walls of the great orb that hovered there, the Sorrelle. The origin of us all. The place where a strand was first woven, then flung out into the sky to grow with the rest of humanity during its lifetime. The orb also cut the strand at the moment of death. Elder shifted the telescope to the great darkness that swirled directly underneath the orb, and his back muscles tightened. The Calamata. The strands fell into the churning vortex for passage to the Afterlife. From this distance they looked like ribbons that fluttered down several miles to be sucked quickly into a whirlpool of black.

Elder let out a shiver. Soon his own strand would fall. He could only hope that he made it into the Calamata. So many dead strands were caught in thick bundles of live ones. They haunted the living as ghosts, although even that was preferable to landing on the cold Maglian ground to be fed upon by the creatures here.

He went out to harvest more ingredients for his serum. First he collected large sacks of nitore blossoms, which he would later spread out to dry. Then he captured glider bugs and placed them in a plastic box that he carried on a string. Picking up several dead strands off the ground, he collected them in a satchel that hung around his waist. He approached a small pianta nest. The carnivorous plants were able to lash out several feet with tiny spears on their leaves. They caught dead strands, then dragged them back to the nest to feed upon. Elder carried a small hatchet in his belt. He chopped at the nest and managed to rescue three ghosts without getting bit. Pianta venom was mildly irritating in small doses, but once he'd fallen into a large nest and almost died. His mind still reacted to the bites as his body would have at home. He'd had a brain fever for several days, which Jason had cured at Grace House.

He was heading back to the grotto when a strange noise came from his left. Crimson flashed above him. A mass of blood-red, sightless birds raced upward along his side. They nearly tore off his head before he hit the ground. He watched their formation rise high up in the sky. Those birds remained deep inside caverns far from daylight their entire lives. He'd only seen a couple of them come to the surface when injured and only at night. Something very deep must have scared them. He hurried back to the lab.

Elder laid the nitore petals out on the soil outside. Once they were dried, he'd distill the essential oils from the flower material. He pulled out each glider bug, holding the squirming thing by the head. Gently, he squeezed the head and released the serum sac located in the thorax.

Glistening drops of glider fluid appeared, which he collected in a glass vial, then he placed the glider bug into a separate box to be released.

He turned next to the dead strands. Very carefully, he pulled away the gray outermost layers, careful not to disturb the vibrant swirl of colors on the inner layers. He added the outer layers to a large bucket of organic solvents. He'd use cell fractionation later to remove the nutrient-dense cells. Elder hesitated. Sometimes, in his lonelier periods, he'd try to pick up sensations and images from home—a world he would never see again except through others. There were dead strands from many different centuries, like an Aztec warrior, or a wife from 1910, or a famous inventor. Elder still held hope that he'd stumble upon Jason's strand someday. What if he was out there, suffering in a wretched pianta nest or under a swarm of Vipera? Or worse, caught in the gray swirls of the Valley, the dust-filled ring that surrounded the black vortex of the Calamata. Souls caught there could lie in limbo for centuries.

Deeper in the lab, Elder checked on his bacterial collections. He'd swabbed the beneficial nesso bacteria off the strands, then transferred the swab to a luria broth, composed of salt, tryptone, and yeast extract. He picked up a flask and swirled the liquid, peering at it with a flashlight. The liquid was heavily clouded. Excellent.

He hoped that the combination of the beneficial bacteria, the nutrient mixture and the glider serum would form a potent healing serum. When he found a wounded strand, he first swabbed the wounded area with ethanol to kill the harmful bacteria, and then he applied the serum and monitored the healing process. He found the rates much higher than normal.

His thoughts turned to Zander. Would the boy have the courage for what needed to be done? It was an enormous responsibility for one so young and immature. Yet Elder saw what Brecker did: boldness and strength simmering just below the surface. There was so much of Jason's courage in the boy's eyes. Elder suspected that courage lay in his own daughter as well. Threads of American spirit—these children would fight forever. They didn't know how to give up.

He picked up the small flask that held his first batch and gently swished it, picturing the great wound it was intended for, the damage certainly greater than anything he'd seen in his ten years here. He felt this urgency each day to make more, always more. Failure would have drastic consequences for Maglia. The serum would have to be enough as there were no other answers. No time and no answers.

Brit Malorie

Chapter 28

Zander noticed he wasn't gasping during the steady climb like before. Weeks of solo hikes on the trails around Grace House had given him endurance. Weaving his way through the pine and aspen trees, he looked for a particular trail that ran alongside the Crystal River. He'd always loved this hike, spending his childhood chasing rabbits and muskrats through the montane shrub. He and Calvin used to steal Nora's pots and smash huckleberries in them, creating exotic potions to destroy the woodland trolls. They'd build forts out of rotting timber and paint signs to warn away intruders and girls. Zander's temper had been a force even then; the two boys would pound each other with small fists until Jason came out to stop them.

It had been a month since they'd returned from the Lolita, but it still felt like a nightmare. What bothered him was not that a monster like Lynch existed, but that he could fool Zander so completely. He'd ignored his gut and look what it had cost Bryn.

She seemed to be adjusting to Grace House, but she still got that startled look sometimes, as if wondering where her old life had gone. He'd find her asleep in her father's room sometimes, her hand folded in Elder's. Zander would carry her up to her bedroom and lay her down on the bed. She'd curl up, facing away from him. He wished it would go away, this desire to fix everything for her, to shield her in the safest life possible.

Small pebbles crunched under his boots as he came across an old riverbed, the water much lower than he remembered. It was dusk and the sweet, tangy smell of the pinyon trees made his nose buzzy. Zander picked up a handful of the dirt. Scissoring his hands, he let the grains fall downward in a mist. He'd taken a few more trips since returning home. It wouldn't be long now before everything would depend on him. He looked upward at Colorado's lie of free blue sky.

Time to turn back. He followed the water out a few yards then stopped short. A man stood in the center of the riverbed, the water up to his waist. His head was tilted upward, his hands suspended above the river. He looked Hispanic and in his late thirties. He wore a faded denim jacket and jeans. His black hair glistened in curls, his skin the color of damp earth. A tattoo descended over his right temple, a bundle of lines that angled down his forehead.

Zander leaned against a broad oak tree, his fingers digging into the bark. The air felt heavy and chilled with twilight. He wondered at the stillness, like Nature had stopped quiet to listen. A feeling of exhilaration came over him, but he wasn't sure why.

The man's hands lowered until they hovered just above the surface of the water. First his left ring finger dropped, then his right index, then his right thumb and left middle finger. Then all his fingers plunged, his hands speeding over the surface, playing the water like a piano. The fingers tapped and the drops fell, creating a series of tiny waterfalls, a rush of pearls returning home. The man spun around, letting more drops fly before others plunged in a natural jazz. His hands were clouds bursting over open water, vibrant and alive. Each bead of water held a different note. It should have been impossible, but Zander could actually hear music, a symphony raining down. The song crescendoed with the boom of cymbals, his palms crashing down, adding resonance to his ballad.

The man's hands slowed and the drops returned to the river. He spread his palms wide over the surface, breathing heavily. His eyes met Zander's.

"Thank you," he said.

"For what?"

"Your strand has a captivating melody. Very intense, powerful. A sense of protectiveness. I can see why Hadley likes it." A Spanish accent laced his speech.

"A melody?"

"The strand's core has tension. Vibrations help to stabilize it, like a delicate orchestra. That is why humans love music so much. The deepest harmony syncs with our strands and spirals down the core." The man stepped out of the water and held out his hand. "My name is Tomas." He pronounced it like Thomas.

"You must know who I am," Zander said, slipping his palm into Tomas's grasp. A cooling sensation sank into Zander's skin and the sweetest comfort enveloped him. It gave him the feeling of winding down a slow-moving river, cushioned and safe.

Tomas let out a hoarse cough, and a little zap passed through his hands, like a . . . tremor of despair? It was so unexpected Zander tore his hand away. The man smiled half-heartedly.

"So, what do you do?" Zander asked, not sure what to say. The man must be a sort of caregiver, like a social worker or a nurse. Maybe non-profit.

"I do construction in Denver." There was heavy dirt under his fingernails, and his denim jacket frayed at his neck and hung too large over his white T-shirt. Tomas's bare feet crunched down on the dry grass of summer, his clothes and hair drenched from the river music.

"I am sorry it took me so long," he said. "I meant to come sooner, but I have been with family in Peru for the summer. I needed something there."

"Ah, it's fine. No rush," Zander replied, a little bewildered.

"Tomas!" Both men turned at the sound of Hadley's voice. She pushed past Zander and leaped up, squeezing the guy in a hug.

He laughed. "My tiny power plant. I knew I felt better."

With the little girl stuck to his side, Tomas slid on his boots and walked a few yards. A strained look crossed his face, and he set her down but still held her hand as the trio headed up to the house. Hadley chattered about her police work and Maglia, her legs bouncing as they walked. Zander kept sneaking glances at the man.

Hadley plunged inside the side entrance and headed for the dining room. Smells of Nora's pot roast sailed through the open door and his stomach growled. Before they could follow her inside, Tomas touched Zander's elbow. "Can we speak in private? Please."

Zander paused. "Sure, um, how about the library?"

Tomas started to follow him in, then suddenly bent over as coughs rocked his chest. He waved Zander off and headed away from the house. Zander shrugged and joined everyone else in the dining room.

After dinner, the group moved to the library for the evening. Brecker, Isaac, and Liz took the main armchairs encircling the gas fireplace. Hadley took a smaller chair off to the side and Zander sat next to her. Tomas entered the room and gingerly sat down. He steadily gulped the water Nora brought him. The low lights bounced off the sweat on his skin.

Then Bryn walked slowly into the room, a white brace securing her ankle. Zander felt an involuntary sigh move through him.

Hadley grinned. "You know, I think Bryn is the last piece of our puzzle, and now everyone's strands can grow stronger and entangle." She grew whimsical. "I can almost hear the lullabies of the nitore flowers making us into a real home."

"That's nice, Hadders," he murmured. Grace House did feel like home with Bryn here. Isaac and Brecker teased her, then Liz whispered in her ear. She laughed at a joke Isaac made, then took the elderly man's hand and squeezed it, her smile warm. Her eyes attracted the firelight. Sable hair fell in loose curls around her shoulders, the light bringing out tones of amber and honey. Zander sighed again. He wished she would look at him.

Instead he caught another look from Tomas. The man's gaze was so open, so sincere, it was as if he could see inside Zander's heart and embrace every emotion he'd ever had. *I will go with him, wherever he leads.* He shook himself a little. Where did that come from?

"Who is that guy?" he whispered to Hadley.

"He's a Salire."

"He said he worked construction."

Hadley laughed. "He does. I meant he has a Salire strand."

Zander gave her a confused look.

"It's Italian. *Sa-lee-ray.*" She drew out the last syllable like he was stupid. "Okay, so Salire strands are really important to the mesh. They grow out of the ground, like really big oak trees. They—" She paused, her hands drawing pillars in the air. "—they hold up all the strands. Picture it like giant oak trees holding up a canopy of vines."

Zander paused. He did remember reading about Salire strands in his studies, but he hadn't actually seen one yet on his trips. "That's right. They act like beams, stabilizing the mesh. I guess I thought they'd just be regular people."

"Oh no, they're very special. Salires have thousands of connections at the very top, even to lots of people they never meet. They're also a big deal for energy transfer, like huge superconductors." Hadley nodded her head solemnly. "It's a pretty big responsibility."

"So what does Tomas do with these superpowers?" Zander asked, a little sarcastic.

"People come to him for help."

"Like a faith healer?"

"Kind of, but without all the flash. More like a spiritual counselor, I guess. You sensed it, right? He has a whole lot of positive miran."

"Yeah, but I felt something else, too," he hinted.

Her face crinkled up and her lip trembled. "It's cold over here." She left him and sat down cross-legged in front of the fire.

Zander watched her. Yet again, another Pensare secret. She'd tell him when she was ready. He refocused on the group, his gaze returning to Bryn as always. He'd cared about women before but never like this. He could watch her for hours, finding the tiniest details. The curves of her face, the swell of her bottom lip, her lashes fluttering against the heat of the fire as she listened to Liz, never turning away, never distracted. When you needed her, you were the only person in the room.

"So I'm curious about Zander's return home. He tells me he wasn't that bad," Bryn teased.

"Are you kidding? When he first woke up, I'd never heard a roar like that before. Raleigh was afraid to bring Asha to the house," Liz said, letting out a low chuckle.

"You should have seen his aura back then. Gray mixed with like, vomit green and chunks of gooey black," Hadley said, painting the air with her hands. She scooted over on the carpet until she sat in front of Liz's armchair. "If auras could kill, it was gonna rip my head off!"

Liz ran her fingers through the little girl's blond hair. Bumbles sauntered in between the chairs and circled three times in front of the fire before plopping down. The cat tried to groom himself, awkwardly reaching over his large belly for his hindpaws.

"I actually meant to dump Zander out on the streets of Denver with twenty dollars. Let him rot among his own kind," Brecker added.

"Ha ha, very funny," Zander turned to Bryn. "They're exaggerating. I was detoxing. Not a great place to be."

"You know, Miss Hadley, you weren't such a pretty sight yourself when Dr. Grace first brought you," Nora said. "I seem to remember someone eating all the food in the kitchen and leaving the packages strewn about. I thought we had a raccoon infestation."

"It was mostly Bumbles."

"I believe it. That animal is entirely too large, Hadley. Why do I suspect he's getting a bit more than cat food most days?" Brecker said. The cat paused in his grooming and his tiny head glared up at the doctor. "Like a pound of salmon that goes missing every week."

"You know, I just read an article about a new trend: liposuction for animals," Isaac inserted.

The room roared with laughter. Hadley reached out and scratched the cat's belly. "Not fair. Have you ever tried diet cat food? Gross. No way he'd survive."

Brecker looked stern. "Either he goes on a diet or he gets some exercise."

"Fine. I'll take him running. "

"How?" Zander asked.

Hadley shrugged. "I'll show him. He's very smart, you know."

"Yeah, right." His gaze returned to Tomas. During their conversation, the man's breathing had grown haggard and his skin tone turned a dull gray.

Everyone went quiet. Liz and Brecker exchanged worried glances. Tomas stood up. "You know, I should really go rest." He took a couple of steps to the door, then collapsed to his knees. Toppling over, he clutched his side and let out a painful moan. His body went into spasms.

"What the hell's wrong with him?" Zander asked. He knelt down and tried to brace the man's head as the spasms subsided, but then his body began shuddering with severe coughs. Drops of dark fluid appeared around his mouth.

Brecker checked his pulse. "Let's get him down to the traveling room. There's medical equipment down there." He and Zander carried Tomas to the elevator, then down to the basement.

They laid Tomas on the bed. With Nora's help, Brecker placed him on a respirator and an IV drip. The man's eyelids fluttered. He grasped Zander's hand and wouldn't let go.

"I feel like he wants something from me."

Brecker grimaced. "He's dying, Zander."

"Cancer?"

The doctor stared off, a little dazed. "In a strange way." He squeezed Zander's shoulder. "I thought his time in Peru would help, but as you can see, well, I need to run some tests to gauge how far the illness has progressed. Let's have a meeting tomorrow to discuss our options. You'll have all your questions answered then."

Zander released his hand from Tomas's feverish grip. According to Hadley, a Salire strand held up thousands of normal strands. What would happen to them if he died? How long could he hold on for?

Chapter 29

The Pensare met in the conference room the next afternoon. Gage connected the projector to his tablet and put up an illustration of a Salire strand. It showed a tall structure that looked like an oak tree, branching out at the top to connect with thousands of strands in the mesh.

"We're not sure how it happened," Brecker frowned, "but a few months ago, a crack formed at the base of Tomas's strand. At first, only a few Vipera were able to feed there, but over time, they've actually widened it." Gage flipped to a new illustration and received a few gasps; it revealed a crack about two feet wide. Black lines entered through the crack and ran up through the trunk, passing into the thousands of connections above. Zander couldn't believe this was happening to the same man he'd met just yesterday.

Brecker continued, "As we speak, Vipera are burrowing into Tomas's strand, gaining access to thousands of people through their most vulnerable connection. A Salire's bindings are the most sacred, most sensitive . . ." his voice wavered. He took off his glasses and wiped his eyes.

"Hadley mentioned something about energy transfer. The Salire strands work like huge superconductors?" Zander asked.

"This is only a theory," Gage said as he flipped to a new diagram. "But we believe that Salires have very deep roots that penetrate to the liquid core of Maglia. The roots pull positive miran up and push it up through the trunk and out to the strands, then move it further outward to the mesh. But," he took a deep breath, "this complex system is what the Vipera are taking advantage of now. They use it to move huge amounts of negative miran up through Tomas's Salire to the mesh. The negative miran is corrosive, damaging his system. It truly is cancer of the soul."

"My God, they're eating him alive," Raleigh whispered. She let out a choked sob and pressed her face into a tissue. Gage squeezed her shoulder.

"What's happening to the people? Everyone connected to him?" Bryn asked.

"Right now they're going through tremendous sorrow, heartache, depression. Many also have physical symptoms similar to cancer, but their doctors can't find the source. It's beyond medical knowledge."

Everyone went quiet. Zander didn't want to ask what he was thinking, but it was important to understand. "How much time does he have?"

Brecker shook his head. "Not much. He returned to Peru to say goodbye to his family and seek a special type of shaman healing. Elder has tried to determine the extent of the damage with his telescope, but the Vipera infestation is blocking his view."

"There is something we can do. We can bring in his bindings for a counseling session," Liz inserted. Both she and Hadley were softly crying, too.

"Bindings?" Zander asked.

"The thousands of people he holds up, love. All those strands suffering," Liz replied.

"But if they're suffering, do we really want them around Tomas?"

"Yes, strangely enough," Gage answered. "Meditating with them and counseling their problems will help the positive miran flow through Tomas. The Circle will help, too, with Hadley's energy."

"It's a good idea, but I'm afraid it will provide little relief," Brecker said. "Based on the tests I ran last night and this morning, his body is failing rapidly. I'll give him as much medical treatment as possible, and along with the counseling sessions, well," Brecker hesitated, "I give him no longer than a month, maybe six weeks."

"What happens when a Salire strand breaks?" Zander asked. He pictured one of those giant Sequoia trees in California. If it split at the base and fell, the weight would be so immense the momentum would pull everything to the ground.

"Obviously, it happens," Brecker answered him. "Salires die, sometimes from natural causes, sometimes from unnatural ones, like assassinations. Gandhi, Martin Luther King, Jr. It's incredibly traumatic. Elder has seen it happen a handful of times. When a Salire is about to die naturally, the Lusha transfer its bindings to stronger parts of the mesh before it falls, but they can't get near Tomas because of the Vipera swarm."

"So when the crack widens enough, the Salire will crash to the ground in Maglia and Tomas will die here."

"Yes. Most of his bindings will break off, and the Vipera will have a feeding frenzy. It'll take years for the Lusha to penetrate that nest," Brecker broke off, his voice frustrated.

"What about the Archlusha?" Zander asked. The Archlusha were the highest order of Lusha. Surely they could help.

"The Archlusha must stay in the Valley, the region surrounding the winds of the Calamata. They don't leave except under the most dire of circumstances. Unfortunately, a Salire's collapse isn't cause enough," Brecker replied.

Zander grabbed a notepad and began sketching out the strand and its base. "Do we know how Salire strands heal?"

"Elder's developing a serum for normal strands to help them heal. He's making a super-concentrated batch for Tomas's Salire," Brecker answered. "Unfortunately, we still have a couple of weeks until it's ready. We also can't apply the serum while the Vipera are feeding there. We need a distraction."

He sighed. "We really thought the rituals down in Peru would propel enough miran through the Salire to knock out the swarm. They did help quite a bit, but Tomas can't go through them forever. I'm afraid it's time for a traveler to interfere."

Zander stayed quiet. Now he knew why the Pensare had kept this from him. There were dozens of Vipera swarming at the Salire's base. Just being a few feet from one had paralyzed him with fear and depression, so how could he possibly apply the serum with those awful things around him? Elder would be too weak to help him. It seemed nearly impossible.

Brecker shook his head. "We'll break for now. Liz, can you help fly in the bindings for Tomas? We'll try to draw up some possible solutions on Zander's next trip."

Chapter 30

Bryn headed down to the meditation room after the meeting. She hesitated just outside the door. Raleigh and Liz were chatting with Hadley. Asha sat in the middle, fiddling with her toddler toes. It was a completely normal scene, but Bryn had to force herself to enter.

They quieted when they saw her. Liz smiled and motioned to an open spot in their circle. It was almost worse because they were all so nice about it. She sat down, her fingers already caressing her ring. They went through the breathing exercises, but instead of relaxing, Bryn felt her anxiety ratchet up.

Raleigh began to chant, but Liz held up a finger. "Darling, be honest with us. What's happening in your head?"

Bryn spoke, her throat dry. "There's a few things, I guess."

Liz stroked her hand. "Tomas's problems are on the forefront. Your mother and father—they're always in our sessions. And someone else. . . ." A little smile played on her lips. Bryn knew who she meant.

Zander. The only calm she felt in her life right now. Everyone had told her stories about his temper, his selfishness, his drug abuse. But she didn't see that in the man she spent her days with. He was always caught in his own reverie, dreaming, watching the sky. Waiting for a veil to lift.

Bryn felt uncomfortable as the women scrutinized her. She didn't like people pretending they could get inside her head. Her mother had been the worst, claiming to be psychic in order to con people out of money. Iris had always been a little odd, but she had a complete mental collapse after Dad's accident. Frail and scattered with frizzy blond hair fanned out around her head, she'd mutter around the trailer for hours, her velvet robe swishing. Tarot cards scattered in the cupboards, crystals in Bryn's backpack and lunchbox. Every math test or afterschool play was an omen, a sun crossing into a moon quadrant, an unbalanced aura.

She looked up at the other women in the Circle. Warmth entered her hands as she held onto theirs. They smoothed open a path for her. But shame rose up like a brick wall, forcing her back. *They'll find out you're a bad person. They'll tell Zander.* She released their hands.

Liz studied her. "Alright, that's enough for today. Just takes time, that's all. Baby steps, baby."

Bryn headed to the kitchen. She tried to make herself useful most nights by helping Nora cook. Outside in the garden, she picked a bag full of fresh Roma tomatoes and bell peppers. She plucked basil leaves, then buried her face in the tingly scent. After chopping up fresh bulbs of garlic, she added the pieces to a pan with oil. Sweet smell filled the kitchen, and she could feel the heat in the sizzle. Last night, she'd set dough out to rise; Bryn grabbed it now and added a little olive oil, chopped basil, garlic, and onion to it. After a few minutes, she dumped a rainbow of sliced peppers into the pan and stirred. She closed her eyes, her toes automatically bending up. In her mind, she soared, jumped and spun, seeking the release of her body. Instead, it remained full of lead and tied to the ground.

Bryn wished she could share the Circle's warmth. She loved helping people, the feeling of sharing another person's innermost emotions, finding solutions for their problems. As long as it was only their problems that were solved. She imagined the box. It was a rich cherry wood with embossed edges. Not large. Firm lock. It opened slightly. She pictured her pain as a charcoal gray, then shoved it inside. Missing her father, her anxiety about her mother, break-ups with old boyfriends, that horrible Lynch psychopath. Everything went into the box, never to see the light of day. She paused. Her dancing. That couldn't go into the box yet.

Someone came up behind her; she assumed it was Nora. "I'm just prepping the bread. You can chop up the tomatoes if you want," she called out, her palms flattening out the dough. Her hair was clipped back, but pieces tended to fall around her face no matter how tight she wound them. She tried to nudge a stray piece with her shoulder, then blew it away, exasperated.

A hand came over her side and tucked the stray piece behind her ear. Bryn froze. A voice whispered next to her. "What are you making?"

"I was just, uh, making pasta. A sauce for the pasta. And bread."

"Mmm . . . onions, garlic," Zander said. His fingertips lingered in her hair. He twisted another piece and tucked it in.

A shiver went down her back. "Thanks," she said, her bare hands burying themselves in the dough.

He rested his head on her shoulder. A sun-baked smell floated off him from being outside all day. It mixed with the scent of grass from lying on the lawn and sweet undertones of—

"Why does it smell like beer in here?" she teased.

He took a step back, his hands opened wide. "Hadley says I smell okay. She says I smell less like a vagrant every single day."

"She was being polite, cowboy." Bryn smirked and tipped an imaginary hat.

"That's the Colorado life, honey. Take me or leave me."

"Can I get a minute to decide?"

"Ouch. By the way, you smell like Bryn."

"I smell like what?" She playfully elbowed him. "Careful now."

Zander turned her around. She held her dough-streaked hands up in the air. He bent down to her waist level and sniffed her jeans, then up along her shirt. He unclipped her hair and brought the black curls forward. He took one last dramatic sniff.

"Very thorough," she murmured.

"Trust me." He tapped his chest. "I'm a scientist."

"Or a Rottweiler."

"You know, I can't really identify your scent," he said. "Little bit sudsy. Citrusy floral girlness. Streak of mean in there." She raised her eyebrows. "A whole lot of delicious. Very Bryn."

"Why are you such a dork?" She laughed a little.

His eyes softened. His thumb smudged a tiny bit of flour on her chin. He leaned in.

Bryn abruptly turned back to the dough. Why was he distracting her? Dinner needed to get done. She felt irritable all of a sudden, her skin flushed.

"Why so much food?" he asked.

"It's a lot of people to feed," she snapped.

"Can I help?"

"No, I've got it covered," she replied quickly. He leaned into her, his lips near her earlobe. His hands slid down her forearms and circled her wrists.

"Then why am I always left hungry?" he whispered.

The heat from the sizzling pan seemed to fill the kitchen with steam. Her insides felt liquidy, like her stomach and heart had melted into her feet.

"Not sure what you mean," she said slowly.

Zander hesitated, then pulled away. Grabbing a slice of pepper from the pan, he shook it out to cool it off and popped it in his mouth. He sat back against the counter and grinned, watching her. Bryn stood still. He'd just been teasing her the whole time. She slammed the dough in a breadpan and set it in the oven.

He stole another pepper. "I hear you left meditation early."

She steadied herself. "I guess. Maybe something's wrong with me."

"Nothing's wrong with you, Bryn." He gave her that brazen grin again, his eyes very blue against the coppery red in his hair. "Learning how to calm my brain took forever. But the Circle can really help."

"I know," Bryn said, her voice sounding tired. She washed her hands in the sink. "I wish I could get over it."

Zander studied her. "Can we try something? It'll be less intense than my first time. I'm not nearly as powerful as Hadley," he murmured. He took the frying pan off the heat and the sizzling sound died.

He moved behind her and leaned in close, his breath moist on her earlobe. He slipped his palm on the back of her neck. "Do you trust me?" he whispered.

A single "yes" escaped her lips before she knew it.

"If you stay long enough, you'll never want to leave." He took a deep breath and his palm grew warm.

Bryn felt the tension slowly drain from her neck, her shoulders, then from her legs and toes. Color burst across her vision, cream into yellow into gold. Gradually, it became orange, then red. She moved higher. Rich purples, indigo, royal blue. She wanted to stay in the blue, stay safe in his eyes. But it fled from her, draining away. She reached outward to stop it.

Her hand banged on something metallic. She looked down, surprised to see the white enamel of the stove. Zander leaned against the counter, catching his breath.

"That was incredible," she said.

"I know the Circle's tough for you. But you'll learn to trust them with your life someday," he murmured.

Bryn nodded as the realization hit her. *I'm falling for him.* She knew herself well enough to recognize it, but it was happening so fast this time, faster than ever before. How could she feel this close to him already?

"I have something for you," he said, a mischievous grin flickering across his face. It was so sexy it made her toes curl inward. Dammit. She had to stop herself. Sooner or later he'd find out what she'd done, what kind of person she was.

He studied her. "What are you thinking up there?" he whispered.

"Nothing. What? What is it?" she said. A plain brown package sat on the table. She sat down and opened the package along the seams.

She gasped. "Oh, Zander, they're wonderful." A pair of black ballet slippers sat nestled in the box. "My favorite brand. The most flexible, the best I've found. How did you know?"

"A tiny spy told me. Try them on." He knelt down before her.

"Wait, stop," she laughed as she tried to dodge his hands. He yanked off her sock.

"You have very strange toes." He pulled up her right foot as she protested. "They're hooked and twisted. Do all dancer toes look like this?"

She kicked out at him, but he held on and tickled her sole.

"Alright, Cinderella," he murmured, placing a slipper onto her good foot. Bryn wiggled her toes, reveling in the satin against her bare skin.

"There's something else." He pointed to the box.

She looked again and inhaled sharply. In the tissue paper lay a blush-pink calla lily. He gently tucked the flower behind her ear. "Now, that's perfect."

Chapter 31

"What are you thinking about?" Cye asked. She came up to the bed as he lay there, his arm twisted behind his head.

"Let's see," Lynch replied as he sighed deeply. "Two men that need to die. One that threatens my island, a problem that must be solved very soon. And the one that escaped." He needed to concentrate on Palefu, the new ringleader that grew bolder right in front of him. But his thoughts kept returning to Zander. Kadera was the problem. She made things easy with her special nature and he'd grown lazy. Plus, the kid had surprising new fighting skills and the ability to keep things from Lynch. His fist clenched. He wanted to break the little bastard in half. Zander normally would've confessed the doctor's name and about the security force that helped him escape, but he must have suspected something during their talk. Lynch's cloak of normalcy didn't conceal enough. Then there was the girl—he'd underestimated that darling bird, too. A hidden lever, a drop-away balcony. A tunnel system, a relic from the '80s. Of course, Lynch couldn't have foreseen something so rustic, like a silly plot from a spy novel. And they'd both slipped through.

His mind returned to the sweeter details. He thought of Bryn Sansa, the spirit rising in her eyes as she fought him. And the flicker as it abandoned her. The delicate spray of her blood, the spasming of her wing when he'd clipped it. The nightmares that would follow her for years, his actions blackening her life like great splashes of ink. She was foolish to believe she'd ever be safe.

Cye watched him expectantly. He asked her to prepare some food while he sat and thought, then he'd explain to her what he needed. She left and washed her hands. He stared at the ceiling and focused on Palefu.

Lynch encouraged clans to form on the island. They created a stabilizing force for the tourists, giving them a sense of belonging and providing distraction. There at least a dozen groups, including nature-meditatives, fantasy, costume play. Some were based around bloodlust, strange sex, vampiric rituals, acting out as animals. They fought amongst themselves, which kept the leaders occupied and prevented power from collecting in one group. But one clan had gone unchecked for too long. A Tongan man named Palefu had formed a bloodlust group, and Lynch had underestimated the man's appeal. He was even larger than Lynch, if that could be believed, nearly seven-feet-tall with 350 pounds of dense muscle and fat. Bald-headed with a pig-snout, the man had a baritone voice and an uncanny ability to pump up his followers, which had grown to over fifty.

He did not resent the man his own unique hunger. There had been hunters like Lynch on the island before, and he usually let them remain as long as they stayed quiet and preyed on only a few before leaving. He tolerated the petty thievery, the drunken rapes, even the occasional murder from a fight. Unfortunately, this man's hunger needed spectacle. Not only did Palefu's clan demand blood, but he'd added spiritual crap to the mix—worship the gods of war, the gods are alive on this island and they clamor for blood. He'd heard that the clan had recently sacrificed a man in the tourist area for godsakes. Lynch only killed in Marae and only to real criminals, like that doctor who stole Zander. Palefu's spectacles might exhilarate the anarchist kids, but the bread-and-butter tourists, the ones with real money, were scared and fleeing.

Then came the clincher. Now the man screamed about how Lynch would be the ultimate sacrifice. Lynch clawed the sides of the bed, the rage making his heart spasm. He could not bear such a loss of control. It was too late for a midnight sacrifice. Palefu's followers were expecting that and they'd riot upon the man's disappearance. No, he would have to assert dominance in an open and very specific way. Previous kills flickered through his mind, but nothing seemed to fit right. Cye came back into the bedroom.

"Dove, I told you that a man must die." He licked his lips. "Not simply." He explained that he needed her to spy on Palefu, to blend in with his followers, to find out what the man's plans may be. How did Palefu specifically want to kill him? Cye nodded, the corner of her mouth turned. She seemed pleased that he needed her.

***

A couple of nights later, Lynch rested in his beachhouse, waiting for the girl. She'd had ample time to survey Palefu and he expected a full report. Damaris had been distracted with the experiments in Marae, so he hadn't taken the time to punish Lynch for Miami, but it would come soon. No more projects, no more Cye, and Palefu's power increased by the hour. He'd gone through several cleaning rituals to reduce his anxiety.

Lynch drew his bath for the night. He'd started to remove his clothes when he heard footsteps on the verandah. The bathroom door opened, and Cye sagged against the doorway. Lynch was not surprised often, but he was surprised at that moment. She held her arm close to her chest like an injured bird. Great swaths of bruise covered her face and the left side of her naked body. Her legs shook and he caught her as she fell. He carried her to the tub and slid her into the water, allowing her a bath for the only time. Red smeared the inside of her legs and she cried out as he washed her gently.

She stared ahead, her eyes vacant. Her finger brushed his. Lynch stopped a moment, caught off guard. Pity. The feeling was so incredibly rare that he didn't recognize it at first. He'd only felt it one other time. For his mother.

"Do you feel angry?" he asked.

Her eyes finally met his. "No. I'd take much more for you."

He dried her off and made a cloth sling for her arm, then carried her to his bed.

"I need to see," Lynch paused, then lowered his voice. "Please."

Surprise formed on her face. She nodded. He slid his hand onto the back of her neck. Most readers simply got fleeting sensations, fragments of sounds, colors, tactile, tastes. Lots of emotion. But Lynch could not only see images, he could shuffle them into a narrative. Palefu shouting to his group. The gods of war demanding Lynch's sacrifice, his blood must rain down the volcanic slopes of Kadera. Then a whisper from one of his followers, pointing to Cye. "Hello, lovely. Bringing information back to your master? Yes, I know you're his. You can tell him I'm coming for him. I'm taking his island. More recruits every day now. But you won't be taking only information back with you, oh no." And they'd seized her.

Lynch sensed impassably what came next. He was disturbed only that Palefu knew. He knew that the girl was Lynch's and the man had still violated her in full spectacle. There could be no more delay. He gave the girl painkillers and let her sleep in his bed for the only time.

He sat outside on the verandah and leaned back in his chair. Watching the moonless Kadera sky, he welcomed the black to join what was already in his mind. He needed the right plan, just the right shade of death. He could say it was for Cye, but there was no need to lie. It was for Kadera. Petal had taught him to be careful and he was. But the island gave him a breathtaking freedom. He could be his true self. He could hunt as he pleased. And Kadera helped him, giving him access to his prey's private emotions, their weaknesses, their cravings.

Lynch lit a cigar, a Gurkha Beauty, one rolled from a tiny farm in Honduras. If one simply walked up and murdered a man, the crowd naturally rebelled as if the man were innocent. But if the killing were a natural result of some other violence, the crowd sometimes allowed for it. The sweet smoke filled his mouth like a sugary caramel, which was swiftly eclipsed by a buttery flavor.

There was an arrogance to Palefu. Perhaps it was just that, or perhaps it was more. Sometimes knowledge gave a man that kind of arrogance. Lynch pulled breath up from his lungs and released it, letting the delicious smoke sit on his skin. Knowledge of the island, hidden doorways, keys. The man had over fifty followers and it was possible they might have found some link to the experiments. He wanted Palefu's head, but what he really needed was inside that head.

Brit Malorie

Chapter 32

Zander surveyed his father's study. His official reason for going through his father's papers was to clean them out and find more information to help Tomas. But he was still curious about Kadera and the senses. Could there really be a connection between the island and Maglia? If there was any evidence, he wasn't sure how to find it. Jason Grace was a man who loved hidden places. Zander had just spent two hours searching the oak desk in the middle of the room. It held nineteen visible drawers and cubbyholes, plus seven secret ones. A leather armchair rotated behind the desk. The western wall was made up of bookshelves. Mixed in with the books on physics and spirituality were a surprising number of fairy-tale collections and detective stories. A grandfather clock chimed in the study's corner. The eastern wall had shelves with all kinds of puzzles and mind-benders, also picked up during Jason's travels. He'd always said that he could only find an answer to a puzzle when a different one had a hold over his mind.

Zander turned as Nora bustled in. She was carrying a large box full of papers and souvenirs. She set it down on the desk. "I was going to put this into storage, but I figured you might want to look through it first." Her voice was a little too business-like. "Can't have a tomb in here, you know. Must move on."

He knew the entire Pensare would love to keep this room frozen in time. He remembered the flush of excitement that ran from his toes to his hair when Jason would return from a trip, always with a pair of cool artifacts for him and his cousin. Heavy coins, masks from Venezuela. Cryptic inventions that now gathered dust. Riddles that kept Calvin deciphering for weeks.

Nora scrunched up her face. "I swear Dr. Grace just dropped random things in his pocket. He'd treat a piece of garbage sold to him from an orphan boy the same as a thousand-dollar piece of artwork."

"Hey, Nora, speaking of art, I've been meaning to ask you about that," Zander said, pointing to an outline of dust on the wall. Her mouth did a little judgmental downturn. Wait, it came to him. A rare piece of Chilean art used to hang there, something that Jason had spent weeks searching for in South America. Zander had a clear memory of trading it for pills in college, his hands wildly searching for anything not locked down. What a monster he'd been.

He pushed past the desk and hugged the woman. "I'm so sorry, Nora. I was such a bastard, lying to everyone, stealing things." His voice wavered. "What happened to me?"

"Oh, sweetheart, I forgave you a long time ago. I wasn't sure you'd stay when Dr. Brecker first brought you back, but I'm so glad you did. This is always your home." Nora wiped at her eyes then left the room, her hands in a flutter.

Zander sorted through the box she'd brought in. He unrolled a piece of thick ivory paper and revealed the painstaking scribbles of two young boys. It was a treasure map for the woods behind Grace House. There was also a tutorial on the precise way to trap goblins. Calvin's work.

The door to the study opened again and his uncle peered in.

"Alright if I join you? I'm trying to help Nora with the sorting," Seth said warmly, bracing himself in the doorway.

Zander motioned for the older man to come in, then showed him the map and Seth chuckled. "Ah, yes. The goblin project. I think it kept you boys busy for the better part of a season. Calvin measured everything out to the smallest detail. I miss him so much. I'm torn between asking him to come home or letting him finish his studies with the Vatican."

A short stack of photographs rested in the bottom of the box. Nora came back in. "I found those photos under a panel in Dr. Grace's desk. I swear we'll have to break that desk apart to get everything." She let out a snort. "Silly man. Why did he hide them? I'm going to make a nice display for the hallway."

Zander flipped through them as Nora looked over his shoulder. There was a great one of himself and Calvin when they were Hadley's age. "That sweet boy always liked his blond hair cut very short, never a hair out of place," she murmured, then looked at Zander disapprovingly. "But you had that red mop that stuck out all over the place. Always that wild look of trying to conquer something."

He grinned, remembering a pair of childhood best friends who fit together perfectly. He'd always been dramatic and in charge, while Calvin supported him and figured out the fine details. But the two boys had grown into two very different adults, one given to science, another to religion. And now Zander wondered what kind of man would be coming home from Italy.

Nora peered over his shoulder. "You were such a handsome child, but what a temper. All that red hair, full of fire, that's what we used to say. I think you got that from your Grandpa Joe. Jason and Cecilia were both so mild-mannered. You could be nice, too, once in a while." She frowned. "Usually when you wanted something."

"Sounds right," Zander laughed. There was a photograph of him and his parents. He stared up at his mother like she had radiance. Jason had his arm around them, looking uncomfortably away from the camera.

"I wish things could have been different for us," he said. He picked up the last photo and nearly dropped it. It was of a young Polynesian girl in her early twenties. She had dark eyes and her hair was braided down her back. She gave a teasing look to the camera, but there was hardness there, too.

What truly stunned Zander were the palm trees in the background and the shells around the girl's neck. He recognized them. This smudge in the corner, it looked almost like . . . it could be . . . a dome made of green glass.

Zander turned the photograph around. The words floated in his vision. Kadera, 1995. It couldn't be.

He shoved the photograph at Seth. "Did Dad ever mention Kadera? An island named Kadera?"

Seth studied it. "1995. Let's see, now that I think about it, he did spend some time there. The name sounded familiar when Brecker mentioned where you were."

"Can you remember anything?" he pleaded.

"Alright, let's see," Seth maneuvered his way into the leather armchair. He leaned his cane against the desk and rubbed his hand lovingly over the worn wood. "Around 1995, I was living here with Calvin after Karen abandoned us, trying to decide the direction my life should take. You were eight years old and you boys were always on some adventure in the woods. Jason was never really home. He flew around the world, looking into myths connected to Maglia. He'd heard rumors somewhere in New Zealand, I think, about a special drink that could move one through space. I warned him not to get too excited." Seth let out a chuckle and waved his hand in the air. "There are hundreds of native cultures with spiritual ascension and magic drinks. All empty myths."

Zander couldn't help smiling as he glanced at his uncle's cross shining brightly in the afternoon sun. "How long was he there?"

"Oh, back and forth for about a year. He brought you back those special shells. You were irritated. At that age you thought shell necklaces were for girls," he said. Zander's fingers found a slick surface buried down in the bottom of the box. He lifted out a string of shells, the same ones still found on the island today. A black opaque surface crisscrossed by white lines.

It felt like his head was spinning out of control. He sat down on the edge of the desk to steady himself. Dad had been on Kadera. He'd spent a year there doing God knows what. Of course, the island must have been a very different place in 1995, but still . . . what had he found? And how was it linked to Lynch and Damaris now? He tried to remember what Lynch had said, something about experiments?

"Every time your father would come back from the island, he'd be downstairs in the lab for weeks," Seth said. "He ordered hundreds of different chemicals, like he'd learned something new and needed to try it out. But you know, that I understand. That was typical Jason."

His uncle turned away and stared out the window, his eyes growing hazy. "It was how he'd act sometimes, almost like. . . ."

"What? Please, it's important."

"No, I must be mistaken. It's ridiculous," Seth murmured.

Zander gestured frantically.

"You're going to think I'm crazy," he shook his head, "but I knew my brother better than anyone. He was like that only one other time in his life. With Cecilia. He was in love again."

Zander's jaw dropped open. "With a woman?"

"I think so, yes. Jason was dreamy, bashful. Different than his scientist self," Seth shook his head. "Never age, my boy. I'm probably mistaken. Chalk it up to my addled brain."

"But, but," he sputtered, "Dad never brought anyone back." He waved the photo at Seth. "Whoever this woman is, we never met her."

"No, of course not. I remember the last time he returned from the island, oh that was," Seth took a deep breath, "very bad. He was furious, truly heartbroken. You shied away from him for weeks. That's when he really dove into the research and made some breakthroughs shortly after. He never spoke about Kadera again. Until your last night here."

Zander stared at the woman in the photo. She beckoned the camera, but her mouth turned down shyly. He jerked at Seth's last words. "What do you mean?"

"Surely you remember. You two shouted for over an hour." Seth stood up and studied the bookshelves. Nora brought in some more empty boxes and laid them on the floor.

Zander tried to remember. Too many drugs in too short a time, there were only fragments left. The girl's head in the photo was blurred, the paper worn from constant fingertip caresses.

"Dad sat here at this desk, touching this photo. He did that all the time and I was sick of it. Why was he so fascinated by this girl, this place? He tried to hide the photo, but I snatched it the moment he stood up."

"What did he say?" Seth asked.

Zander paused, the words flowing again after two years. "He said something like, 'I know you have to leave. There was a time once when I had to be anywhere but here. Wherever you go, don't go there. Kadera's not a place for the living anymore."

He tucked the photograph in his pocket. "The last conversation I had with my father on this earth and we fought. He was desperate to show me the discovery, but it was too late. I hated Grace House and everything it stood for. Then when I heard the name Kadera during my backpacking, nothing could stop my curiosity. I had to see the place." He swallowed, his throat dry. "I remember now."

Seth studied him, then stood and walked around the desk. He squeezed Zander's shoulder. "You just weren't ready before. But you've grown. The man I see now has more potential than Jason did. You have a chance to be more open-minded than he was."

"More open-minded?"

Seth smiled. "Well, I didn't want to bring this up yet, but I'm hoping you'll think about opening the research up to others outside of Grace House. Other organizations can make vital contributions to Maglia. The Church—"

"What the hell?" Zander interrupted.

Brecker popped his head into the room. "Are you both ready for our meeting?"

"What's he talking about, Brecker? The Catholic Church invited in?" Zander demanded. A few mornings ago, he'd come up from breakfast and noticed Seth and Brecker talking quietly at the top of the stairs. Brecker looked relieved, and Seth kept patting the man's shoulder. It looked like confession. At the time, Zander hadn't worried about it. He knew Brecker had been raised Catholic, but he'd assumed that the physician had long moved past his religious upbringing. But perhaps there was a deeper reason for Seth's inclusion in the Pensare.

"I'm pretty sure my father didn't want religion to have any part in his discovery."

"Zander, it doesn't matter if you believe," Brecker replied. "The majority of strands have some kind of religious faith. We have to understand that faith, not simply flick it away because we don't like it."

"I can't believe I'm hearing this."

"People wrap their lives in religion, and we're trying to help people. Even Jason realized this. Why did you think Seth was a member of the Pensare?" Brecker's voice rose in frustration.

"Dad's reckless affection for his own brother," Zander said. He knew it. Deep inside, no matter how nice he pretended to be, the old man was plotting.

"And Calvin?" Brecker asked. "He'll be a priest and a traveler, and he *will* be invited into the Pensare. This discovery's not a toy for you and your cousin to fight over. We're a team."

Zander glared at him. "You're really going to do it, aren't you? You'll just hand the dimension over to religious zealots?" He bent over, nauseated.

"Oh, and scientists should be in control?" Seth shouted. "Maglia is God's most immense creation."

"Maglia is a testament to the laws of science. Everything's circular—birth and waste, predator and prey. Human souls are a combination of chemicals and minerals. The strand itself looks like a damn DNA helix," Zander replied.

Seth winced at his profanity. "You choose blindness! The Lusha and Vipera are angels and demons. The Calamata is the path to Afterlife, the Sorrelle is the source of Creation."

Zander felt his temper go. His vision blurred, and he didn't recognize the words that flew out of his mouth. "There's no evidence of angels and demons, just positive and negative charges. Maglia is proof that religious nonsense can be explained by science." He moved closer to his uncle, his voice seething. "That means less God, not more."

"Zander!" Brecker yelled and moved in between the two men. "You need to cool off. Now."

Zander slammed his fist down on the desk. "Brecker might coddle your fantasies, but I don't trust you. Your brain will always be stamped as property of the Church. When I take over the Pensare, there's no access for anyone but scientists. That includes you." He swept out of the room.

***

Seth needed to sit down. All his effort over the last few months to guide his nephew onto the correct path, and it had been an enormous waste. The boy refused to see the truth.

The doctor ran his hand through his hair and sighed. "He didn't mean that. Zander's just young and immature. He'll come around."

"Is that true? What he said about taking over?"

Brecker shrugged. "It's part of Jason's will. Zander was always his first choice. I'm really just a placeholder, and when I retire, he's next in line."

Seth limped over to the window. His hands wouldn't stop trembling. How could he have been so blind? To believe that scientists could be reasonable, compassionate, cooperative? Well, he was blind no longer. His nephew would never admit the Church had earned her place in Maglia through sacrifice and grace.

Brecker continued. "He's Jason's only child and our primary traveler. What did you expect?"

"What about Calvin?" Seth croaked out. "You know he's the right choice."

"I hope he'll travel, too, but Zander will always have first priority. You three will have to learn to work together, I guess." Brecker headed out the door. "Don't worry, Father. We'll figure out a balance. Just give him time."

But Seth worried very much. He should have seen the lust gathering in the boy's heart, always dreaming of the dimension. It would only grow worse the more he traveled. Seth had watched his own brother grow possessive over it, secretive and defensive.

When he joined the priesthood, Seth was still young, with a disgust for his family's wealth. He'd sold his share of Grace House to Jason and donated every penny to the Church. So his brother had control over the house, the land and the laboratory. At the time, Jason's experiments had seemed like delirious ravings, but now there was no inheritance for Calvin and no claim on the research.

Brecker would be lucky if he made it to retirement. Zander would find a way to wrest control from him, from Calvin, perhaps even from the Pensare itself. There'd be no stopping the reckless boy. Fear moved through the priest's heart. He had to do something.

Brit Malorie

Chapter 33

Zander stared at the ceiling, willing himself to fall sleep. Why was he so restless? He sat up and turned on the lamp. It was guilt. His uncle had left for St. Sebastian before Zander could apologize. How could he have said those things? He'd just felt so off balance, all those memories, that new information about Dad and Kadera. Seth had caught him by surprise and his temper had just taken over. Words flew out of his mouth, things he didn't even mean. He really loved his uncle and hadn't meant to hurt his feelings. The man had devoted his life to the Church. Of course he wanted them to share in the discovery. There had to be a compromise they could work out, especially when Calvin returned.

His stomach rumbled. He got out of bed and pulled on a pair of sweatpants, leaving his chest bare. He headed down to the kitchen. Rustling through the fridge, he found some cheese and leftover turkey. After sitting at the counter, he made himself a series of tiny sandwiches with crackers and washed them down with milk.

The door to the kitchen opened and Bryn poked her head in. "Couldn't sleep either?" she asked. Her hair lay tangled on her shoulders, her skin blushed and puffy.

"What woke you up?" he asked.

"I had the strangest dream. It was the future, I guess. The discovery had been made public," she said. "It was a new age. People nourished their relationships, knowing their emotional connections with other people were physical. Meditation and counseling were ingrained in everyone's daily lives."

He smiled. "That's a lovely idea, but I doubt the public will ever know. We can't risk the government or a large organization marching in. We'll just have to do what little we can, like helping Tomas."

Her chin wobbled. "But should we interfere? I'm heartbroken for Tomas, but if we shift the balance too far in Maglia, we don't just destroy a beautiful place. We destroy ourselves."

"You've been talking to Isaac," he chuckled, "and you're making my head hurt now."

Bryn smiled and hugged herself. He shimmied his palms along her shoulders to calm her down. He loved that she cared so much. All this tremendous warmth inside her heart, aching for the world.

"Let's just focus on each problem as it comes." He traced the countertop. "I wish Calvin were here."

"I thought you were nervous about him coming home."

"I am. I don't know how much he's changed." Zander shrugged. "I still miss him. You'll understand when you meet him. Calvin's just different. The way he sees the world, like it's cut into a million puzzle pieces and he can fit those pieces into shapes no one has seen before. He'd take one look at Tomas's impossible problem and think of ten different solutions. That's why I don't understand. . . ."

"What?"

"I don't understand why he chose the Church. Everyone thought he'd go into medicine, but something happened when he turned eighteen, nobody knows what. And they got him. Brecker was absolutely crushed by his decision. He'd mentored Calvin for years." Bryn moved alongside him and rubbed his back tenderly.

He took a deep breath. "It hurt me, too. We grew up together. I was sixteen and I lost the only true friend in my life. I started partying pretty hard to forget about it and well, you know the rest."

Zander looked up, amazed that he'd just said all of that out loud. He'd never told anyone about those feelings. That's how it was with Bryn. You wanted to tell her every little thing you'd ever felt.

"You know what's strange though?" he said. "My dad predicted Calvin's choice. I guess he saw something nobody else did." He rinsed off his dishes and put them in the dishwasher.

Bryn looked around. "I'm glad we're alone. I've been meaning to show you something. I'm not quite sure what you'll make of it, but I hope you'll laugh." She turned around and unbuttoned the top buttons on her pajamas. She let the fabric fall down her back, revealing the skin between her shoulder blades.

He stared a few moments. "Alright, now I need to sit down." He moved to one of the dining room chairs. Bryn sat down next to him and scooted in close.

"Where did you see it? Why did you get it?" he asked.

"I was pretty wild at sixteen, too. Hated my mother, ran away from home, series of bad boyfriends. I went to a tattoo shop. My friends pressured me to get something crazy, but I froze. I could only think of the one my mother got right after Dad's accident."

The tattoo lay directly between her shoulders blades along her spine. It was a mesh of thick and thin lines spiraling out of the initials V. M. The lines twisted and spun around each other like strands, creating loops and knots.

"It makes so much sense. Maglia, the strands. All of our lives, connected," she murmured. "Like it's been there, shimmering beneath us, this whole time. I'm having emotions I've never had before. They feel deeper." Pink flushed her cheeks. "I'm sorry. It sounds ridiculous when I say it out loud."

She took his palm and placed it against hers. "Is this it?"

"What do you mean?"

"Our strands. The tendrils. Are they connecting in the mesh above us? Is this what it feels like?"

"Yes." Zander felt numb and chained to the floor, no air left inside him. Every morning his eyes searched for what made her his. The tiniest gap between her front teeth, the freckle on her earlobe, her mouth slightly too big. The sly smile when she teased him and the blush in her cheeks when he teased her back. The precious dimple in her chin that wobbled when she was upset. He loved her for what other men couldn't see.

She wiped her eyes. "I felt this connected to my father. I remember him being the only person in the world. Does that sound crazy?"

"No," he whispered. She laid her head down on his shoulder and the cotton of her pajamas rubbed on his bare chest. Vanilla drifted up and something underneath. Bryn. A scent that was so special, it was unlike anything else. He resisted a shiver.

"When I learned what happened to Dad, what I did." She took a deep breath. "When Mom told me I'd never see him again. . . ."

She closed her eyes. "I remember running to the beach. The sun, the sound of the birds, how hard the sand felt under my feet. Waves crashing down on me, they just kept crashing down, they wouldn't stop crushing me." She pressed her face into his neck.

He touched her hair, her skin, wanting to lift away the pain. Had she been keeping this inside the entire time? For years?

"Oh, Bryn," he whispered. "You have to know. Your dad loves you so much. I can see it in his eyes."

She stood abruptly, wiping her face with her sleeve.

"Why won't you travel? Please just tell me. Whatever the reason is, it's not worth it."

She refused to look at him. "I just, I. . . ." She shook her head.

He stood and hugged her tightly. "Okay, okay. It's all right. It doesn't matter."

Zander walked her upstairs to their rooms. Moonlight gathered in the hallway, leaked in by the far pane window. It reminded him of that first night, her body in red and lit up by candles on the stage.

"It's a full moon tonight," he smiled.

"Do you turn into a handsome werewolf now?"

He stroked the scruff on his jaw. "I might already be there."

Her body hugged the doorway as her fingertips stroked a soft patch next to his ear. "Not quite monster quality. You can do better."

Bryn. His eyes adored what his voice, his mouth, his hands could not—fastening her beauty in his mind the only way he knew how. Words caught in his throat. Why couldn't he just say something wonderful, something to make her love him suddenly and deeply?

She looked to the side, disappointment lingering in the curve of her mouth.

"Well, goodnight," she murmured, the door eclipsing her body. It closed and the noise jolted him.

Moonlight, instead of caressing her hair, now dimmed on the wood grain. He went into his room to lay down. Staring up at the ceiling, he imagined her pulling back the sheets, the ebony curls falling on the pillow.

Was she thinking about him? He could pretend she was. He returned to memories of her dance, tattered now through hours of use. Bryn was gravity and he was falling and there was nothing he could do to stop.

Brit Malorie

Chapter 34

Kadera had its own version of Ultimate Fighting. An octagonal cage measuring thirty feet in diameter had been set up on the beach at the southernmost tip of the island, mounted five feet above the sand. It stood on steel posts that embedded in the volcanic rock below. The cage walls were six feet tall and made of heavy vinyl-coated chain link. The wood flooring was specialty plywood sealed against rot and engineered not to bow too deep under the heaviest of fighters. A thick vinyl mat was anchored to the wood. The fights usually combined elements of mixed martial arts and common street fighting. There were no rounds, no points, and fighting only stopped when someone lost consciousness. There were two referees per match and they had powerful stun guns. The Kaderian flag rose high above the ring: seven concentric circles, all different widths, shimmering against the purple backdrop.

On this particular day, Palefu had already beaten four men and was on his fifth. There were only a few hours left of daylight, the unique swirl of colors already tingeing the Kaderian sky, readying it for sunset. Lynch had watched the man's fights for several days. He wore a dark green satin jacket over his upper body, always keeping the hood out long over his face, head down, shoulders hunched. Cye hid behind the thicker trees on the opposite side of the cage, her face also concealed in an identical green jacket.

Palefu was all brawn and no skill; he simply pounded his opponents into unconsciousness. But he was also great at takedown defense. The better fighters tried different combos to take him down, but he blocked every time. The man was just so damn solid, part Tongan, with nearly three inches of height and well over eighty pounds on Lynch.

Lynch had studied Muay Thai kickboxing for years in Thailand and incorporated several MMA and wrestling techniques during his first year on Kadera, but he hadn't been inside the ring since. He bounced a little on the balls of his feet. It disturbed him that he hadn't fought in so long. It would take months of repetition training to re-awaken the instinct in his muscles, and he didn't have that long.

Palefu did a particularly dramatic body slam, his massive torso crushing the poor moron beneath him. The man screamed, his head snapping back with a crunch. The referee put a hand out and Palefu acted like he could rip it off, but he held back, circling. He pounded his chest and screamed at his followers in the crowd. Lynch noted his weakness, a weakness that most men of power shared: when his excitement reached its peak, he grew careless, the bloodlust inflaming his senses and overwhelming logic. Lynch had learned to control this from his early days with Petal. Sweat and spittle flew over the ring and pooled on the mat. He shuddered. The pain he was about to experience didn't scare him nearly as much as all the pollution in that cage.

Palefu roared at the crowd and the people roared back, a mass of fists and rocking heads in the air. The referees dragged his victim outside of the ring and callously dumped the body in the sand. Palefu dried off his skin with a towel. He blew a kiss towards Kadera's flag and exited through the cage door. He pounded down the steel steps and the crowd parted for him.

Now was the moment. Lynch's stomach seized, but he forced it down. Coolness entered him. Each fight must be seen as a chess game, with the superior fighter thinking several moves ahead. This match would be about psychological play as much as physical prowess, and no man played like Lynch Katlan.

He entered the ring and stood motionless, the hood still shielding his eyes. The crowd quieted and Palefu turned. The stunned look on his face was quickly replaced by one of glee, his fists clenching.

"Finally! The coward faces me," he shouted as he bounded up the steps and entered the cage. He looked down on Lynch. It was rare that a man was able to do that. Lynch moved to the far side of the cage and pulled cotton wraps out of his jacket pocket. He placed his right thumb in the loop of the wrap and wrapped his knuckles five times, then his wrist three times. His thumb was wrapped twice again, then through the webbing off his fingers. Not too tight, not too loose. As he wrapped, Lynch closed his eyes, picturing the cloth winding around his hand, the routine hypnotizing him. He wrapped his left hand and pulled out a pair of worn MMA sparring gloves from the other jacket pocket. He slipped them on and welcomed the snug fit, the slick comfort of his striking fists cradled in soft leather. A different kind of killing glove.

He motioned for the referees to wipe down the mat's surface. Removing his jacket, Lynch revealed his bare chest and spread his toes on the vinyl, then slipped in his mouthguard. He wore specialty MMA shorts constructed from a spandex-microfiber blend for maximum kicks and knee moves. The referee did a quick check over his body for weapons then backed up slowly. A thin piece of white cloth encircled his bicep, a *praciat*. His master in Thailand had blessed the cloth as a protective charm. Lynch was not a superstitious man, but he needed all the help he could get.

Palefu made a big show of leaning forward against the cage wall and pissing through the chain-link, the crowd laughing. He wore only simple boardshorts and no gloves. The man tucked himself back in and faced Lynch, then he started wiggling his arms and rocking left to right, which sent tremors through the plywood beneath them. Despite the reinforcements, the cage floor might actually break.

Palefu's message was clear: he was much heavier, and that alone would cause tremendous damage. This was very serious. Lynch took a deep breath. It had been a long time since another man was the predator and he was the prey.

"What am I gonna take from you? What's left?" Palefu taunted him.

"I already took your girlfriend," he shouted and the crowd roared back. "I already took your people," and the crowd roared louder. "I guess all that's left is your throne." He leaned in, smacking Lynch with a hideous reek—several days of dense body odor and rotten seafood. Lynch wouldn't be surprised if the man smeared himself with it on purpose. "Your island. Ka. Der. Ah. Such a sweet girl, open for the plunder."

Lynch's hand quivered. The man threw his head back and laughed. "That's it. That's your spot." He cracked his hands. "Let's get this over with."

The referee gave them each a fearful look and exited the cage, locking it from the outside. No one was under the impression this was a simple fight. At the end of it, one man would be dead and the other the new leader of Kadera.

Lynch let the man have the first hit and absorbed it in his left ribcage. The shockwave traveled through his lung and gut. He reciprocated with a jab directly to Palefu's sternum, taking the man's breath and causing him to back up. His own breathing was measured—in through his nose, out through his mouth. Every time he threw a strike or absorbed one, he exhaled a quick, short burst of air.

He allowed the first few strikes then began slipping them. Every time the man missed, Lynch retaliated with a three-punch combo: a hook, an uppercut, followed by a right cross. Palefu looked surprised. Lynch felt the oil rise up on his skin. An old trick from Thailand: fighters rubbed seed oil into their flesh. It absorbed after being rubbed in, then beaded to the surface once the fighter began to sweat. Palefu's fists skidded over Lynch's bare chest with no force. Lynch used the opportunity for a rapid flurry of strikes and kicks, everything in combo for maximum damage. Palefu spent the next few minutes fiercely guarding his face.

He launched a fake hook towards Palefu's kidney. When the man moved to the side to block it, Lynch hit him with a right cross, then he spun his hips rapidly, balancing on the ball of his foot. He kicked his shin outward and hit a sensitive nerve on the outside of Palefu's left thigh. Then he dove in, delivering elegant Muay Thai kicks to the man's legs.

Palefu foolishly kept his arms raised high to protect his face, leaving his torso and legs exposed. Lynch ignored the trails of blubber wobbling under the man's gut and aimed for Palefu's solar plexus, collar bone, and temples—just enough for tremendous pain, but not hard enough to knock him out. That wouldn't work for what needed to come next.

Palefu finally backed up against the cage wall, letting out short exhales through his mouth. When he came back out, Lynch leaped up and bent his forearm downward, smashing his elbow down on the soft tissue right above Palefu's eyes. The man backed away, shaking his head wildly. But Lynch followed him, battering the man's face for a few seconds until Palefu turned and went into a crouched position to recover.

When the man came back out again, Lynch got excited and overthrew a right hook. Palefu seized his back. Digging his fingers in, he forced Lynch's head down near his waist and wrapped his arm around Lynch's neck in a guillotine hold. Panic filled him and momentarily froze his muscles. Palefu applied maximum pressure, cutting off his air supply and pressing against his carotid artery. Sweat poured out of the man's armpit and Lynch almost swallowed some. He threw his arm over Palefu's shoulder to relieve even more pressure from the choke. He lifted his leg and hooked it on the inside of the other man's leg, then shoved his hand into the choke, driving downward with his weight to break it open. It felt like his wrist was going to break instead, but finally Palefu's fists opened and he let go.

Lynch backed into a corner. Confidence was not usually a problem for him, but he had real doubts whether he could pull this off. He peered out through the cage wall. The crowd had tripled in size and now surrounded the entire cage, the noise deafening. At first, he'd been able to avoid the droplets and spray, but as he grew tired, the man's blood and sweat rained over him. His skin was contaminated by this man's filth, but he forced himself to rise above his own neuroses. He stood still a moment, slowing down his breathing, hypnotizing himself. The droplets were gone, the sweat gone. He pulled his mind from the pain. Kadera helped him. He imagined her placing a thin protective layer of air between his skin and the sludge and felt better. There was only air and force. The air molecules separated for his hand, moved apart for his shins. He opened his eyes and saw Palefu in slow motion, visualizing his moves before he made them. More important than his life was his dominance. He had to destroy this man.

Lynch exploded forward and hooked Palefu's right leg with both palms at the back of the knee. But he didn't stop there. As Palefu teetered, Lynch moved his arms up around the guy's blubbery torso. His foot swept out and caught Palefu's left leg. There was a second where it could go either way. The man's arms windmilled, and Lynch was actually surprised when Palefu fell with a thunderous boom on the mat. But that didn't stop him from driving all his weight down on top of the bigger man. Despite Lynch's weight, the man was able to brace himself up at an angle, then pushed Lynch off of him.

But he'd made his point. Palefu's confidence was shaken. He seemed embarrassed and this led to mistakes. He swung too hard with no accuracy; Lynch easily dodged his strikes and kicks. The great beast was tiring himself out, but he still had some surprises left. He snuck an overhand punch through Lynch's guarded fists, and the hit reverberated through his jaw. He shook his head, rattled. He unguarded himself for only a split second, but Palefu slipped through and got his hands around his throat. The man slammed Lynch's head down on his knee, then released him, laughing. Lynch spun in a circle, blood in his eyes and streaming out his nose. He leaned up against the cage wall, wiping furiously. He couldn't think, he couldn't breathe; everything was red and wet and inflamed. He felt a towel near his feet—Cye must have slipped it through the opening between the chain-link and the mat.

It was time to give Palefu what he wanted. A sacrifice. Lynch did another Muay Thai kick to Palefu's thigh, then let his leg pause for half a second too long. He had excellent balance, but still allowed the body slam. That was nothing compared to the pain when Palefu drove his entire weight down on him. It was so bad white lightning sank through his vision. This wasn't pretending anymore. His body lay still—he couldn't move.

Palefu stood up and raised his hands above his head. He had cuts all over his torso and abrasions on his arms and legs, but he was triumphant. This was necessary, yet fire coursed through Lynch's blood. Palefu and Zander escaping him, defying him, pretending victory. The rage was the only thing that could make Lynch's muscles twitch. He'd need every last ounce of strength for what would come next. It must be imprinted on every pair of eyes out there.

His gaze caught Cye's. She stood at the back of the cage in her dark green jacket, her head just tall enough to peek up over the mat, her eyes moist. Slowly, so as not to attract Palefu's attention as he bathed in the public cheers, Lynch's left hand removed the glove on his right, then unwrapped the cotton strips. Cye rested her palm near the opening between the chain-link and the mat. A flick of her wrist. Metal caught the fading sunlight as the object slid across the vinyl. All eyes were on Palefu. Lynch closed his right hand over the silver claw, then slid the ring end over his middle finger. He hid it underneath his side as he lay on the mat.

"How should he die?" Palefu screamed at the crowd, then knelt over Lynch. He pressed his palm to the back of Lynch's neck, the ultimate domination. Palefu searched the scar, then abruptly stood up, a confused look on his face. He faced the crowd and grinned again, pumping his fist in the air. Lynch gripped the claw and steadied himself. It would have to be very fast, with as much force as he could muster.

The metal traveled upward. Lynch pushed through the first layer of resistance, the rayon of the man's shorts, then through the flesh and the layers of muscle in the perineum. The razor edge punctured the flesh easily, but the muscle was sinewy and required every bit of strength left in his arm. With slicing movements, the claw bore through the perineum, then up into the pelvic cavity. Palefu's face formed an O in slow motion. A half second passed in absolute silence. Then the most horrific scream rose. Lynch gave one last push with the claw and broke through the prostate, then the bladder. Finally, the claw entered the man's colon. Still Palefu didn't move, just stayed on Lynch's arm like a grotesque puppet. The scream cut off and Palefu let out a low moan, his torso bending over.

Blood trickled down Lynch's arm and he took a deep breath. This was going to be bad. He hooked the claw deep into the squish of the intestines and pulled down with a tremendous jerk. A giant wave of gut and muscle and sheets of blood splashed down on the mat. Rolls of intestine fell like overstuffed sausages, along with a yellowish gland and part of the man's bladder. Lynch swiftly dodged the bulk of the splatter, but his arm and side were still grossly contaminated. Palefu's face was a dull gray, his mouth opening and closing. His legs gave out and he sank to his knees.

Lynch stood up. Despite what must be tremendous pain, Palefu's eyes took on a murderous rage. He swung his fist out loosely, but Lynch caught it, bending his arm back as he seized the bulging neck. He would take what was his. He pulled the images out of the man's mind, intending to savor them later. One in particular, a vision of tunnel walls opening, stayed with him. His instinct was correct. The man held the keys to Kadera this entire time.

Palefu fell. He sprawled backward on the cage floor, breathing heavily, blood pooling out of his lower half. Lynch's white praciat was now red. Things had been put right. He spoke the first and last words he'd ever say to the man. "I understand why you challenged me. You are a good fighter. This is what I am." His bare foot came down on Palefu's neck. Lynch pressed his weight into it, crushing the hyoid bone and windpipe. Palefu let out a gurgling sound and struggled under Lynch's weight, until he let out a final rattle and stilled.

The crowd stood silent and slack-jawed. He strode to the cage door. The referee quickly opened it and Lynch jumped down the steps. He landed near Cye where she waited with a large bucket. She stared at Palefu's body, her face emotionless. He grabbed the water and poured it over himself, the man's filth swirling away from him into the sand. But the bucket wasn't nearly enough. He felt an intense desire to rip his own skin off. He needed his beachhouse and a long-lasting ritual and a hell of a lot of antiseptic. He and Cye walked away from the cage, the silent crowd parting in great waves around them. They left Palefu's carcass to lie in the dwindling sun for the animals to feast upon. Not even the man's most devout followers cared for his husk now. The crowd dissipated, their thirst for violence satiated for months with such a spectacle. In fact, many would leave Kadera the next morning, searching for a palliative to soothe the monstrous image in their heads.

Later that night, after the deepest of ritual cleansings, Lynch sat outside under the island moon and sorted through the man's memories. Most were a meaningless succession of torture and rapes, but one returned to him. It was a hazy image, more blurred than the rest. That bothered him. Why should it be hazy? It looked like two distinct boulders, three feet between them. The two boulders were not distinct due to their size or shape, but due to the symbols carved on them. The boulders sparkled like limestone, with sea-green and ebony flecks. The first symbol was a carving of three spiral lines that formed an upside-down triangle. The second symbol was seven concentric circles, identical to the symbol on the Kaderian flag. Palefu's hands rested on the two rocks, and the man moved into the space between them. Then they appeared to move away from him. A cave appeared, but all four of the reddish-orange clay walls were solid. Palefu struggled at each wall, pushing with all his strength, attempting to scale it, feeling along the crevices. Finally, he had no choice but to crawl back to where he came from. And the memory ended. Lynch knew without a doubt that it was another entrance, similar to the one he and Damaris took to the underground tunnels. But he'd never seen those particular boulders on the island and certainly not a cave like that one.

Could he go to Damaris with this new insight and with what Zander had told him at the Lolita? Would it be enough for the man to finally share his knowledge about Kadera? Lynch didn't think so. He got the impression that Damaris and the other heads were waiting for Lynch to pass some kind of test. He'd have to find this cave on his own and discover what Palefu could not.

Chapter 35

Zander sat at the dining room table reading the newspaper. Birds chattered outside the window. A plate of whole-wheat toast, eggs, and turkey bacon lay before him, along with a glass of chocolate milk.

"Hey, guess what?" Hadley waltzed in from the kitchen, her legs a jumble of movement. She did a quick spin and knocked into the chair. "Bryn's teaching me some dance moves this afternoon." She did a little strut in a circle.

"Oh, yeah? What time? I'll come and watch."

"Don't. You'll make me nervous and I'll mess up."

"I'll watch from the mirror room. You won't know I'm there," he said. Now that her brace was off, Bryn liked to practice in the meditation room next to the wall-length mirror. The mirror had a two-way view; the other side was a small room meant for observing the Circle while they communicated with Elder.

Hadley poured herself a bowl of cereal, her smile dreamy. "Do you think I can be like Bryn someday? My hair will be black, and I'll be really beautiful and smart, and I can dance just like her." She did another quick spin, her arms flailing.

"You're already beautiful and smart. But her hair's not just black," he replied. "It has a little red, some amber. A lot of honey color. Depends on how it catches the light."

Hadley rolled her eyes. "Geez, weirdo. Sorry."

He smiled and plucked an apple from the fruit basket in the middle of the table. "What do you see?"

The little girl caressed it with her palm and grew dreamy again. "I see the shape of an apple," she said, "but I see it hanging from a tree, touched by breezes and sun and tossed around by wind. Rain. I see energy." She stroked the green skin. "It's touched by all the living things that made it, but there's a little spot." She pointed. "A creamy pink. That's from the person who picked it. From his life."

"That's kind of how I see Bryn."

"Why? You're not psychic."

"I know," he chuckled. "I've been meaning to ask you something." It was rare that he got Hadley alone.

"Yeah?" She poured herself some orange juice, spilling little puddles on the oak table.

"Have you built up a shield around Bryn yet? Do you know what she thinks about?"

"What do you mean?" A smirk appeared on the girl's face.

"You know what I mean. Stop it."

Hadley counted on her fingers. "What movies she likes, what clothes, what she thinks about Grace House, a certain blue-eyed boy."

"Yes, that's what I'd like to know."

"Oh, really? Why?" She made a kissy face.

"Stop it. This is embarrassing enough."

"Ewww. I smell a crush—wait, what would one smell like?" Hadley looked perplexed. "Well, you'll have to figure it out yourself."

He groaned. "Your shield's up."

"No, but a man should have to work for a woman's love. He'll appreciate it more."

He gave her a baffled look. "How would you know? You're ten."

"I heard it on Dr. Phil," she muttered, her mouth full of cereal.

"You don't watch TV."

She hesitated a second. "Bumbles does. He told me."

"The cat? The cat told you I have to work for Bryn's love? Alright, I'm done with this." Disgusted, he went back to his newspaper. Hadley erupted into giggles, milk dribbling down her chin.

Later that afternoon, Zander slipped into the basement and entered through a small door about ten feet from the door of the meditation room. The mirror room was very cramped, and he had to brush a quarter inch of dust off one of the chairs before sitting down. Unlike Jason, Brecker trusted the Circle to have worked out the kinks on its own.

He watched through the two-way mirror as Bryn and Hadley met in the meditation room. Bryn was dressed in stretch capri's and a tank top, Hadley in her bizarre striped leggings and an oversized T-shirt.

Bryn showed the little girl some stretches, then spun off a few twirls and leaps in a small dance sequence. Although clumsy at first, Hadley watched carefully and after a few minutes, began fully extending her arms and legs and balancing for each spin, her eyes following Bryn in worship.

After thirty minutes, the little girl's face turned red and puffy, her breathing labored. They stretched and Bryn told her how wonderful she did and that it was a good beginning for today. Hadley left and Bryn changed the song on the stereo. Piano notes rolled from the speakers, and a voice full of sultry heat and pain caressed the air. Bryn spun with the music, her moves more complicated as the song crescendoed. Bending back for a spin, her face winced in pain. She landed hard on the floor then rocked back and forth, squeezing her ankle. Taking a deep breath, she started again, pushing farther and spinning faster.

There was a light knock on the mirror room door and Brecker poked his head in. "Hadley said you might be in here." He saw Bryn through the mirror and frowned. "She should be taking it easy."

Zander traced the glass. "She can't help herself. She's in love," he replied softly.

The doctor turned to him and there was tension in his face. Dammit, a lecture was coming.

"Zander, you need to be careful. I'm not saying you can't have a personal life, but Bryn may not—"

"What if we're meant to love each other? To travel together?"

"I know it's tempting to think that way," he replied. "But Bryn's a cautious person, not a risktaker like you. Even if we could convince her, she won't travel much. She won't stay here."

Zander let his hands drop from the glass. It was something he couldn't put his finger on before, but Brecker was right. There were so many walls in Bryn. In order to strap-in for trip after trip, a traveler had to be willing to do whatever it took, to face whatever danger lay beyond the Veil.

"You have to make a choice between a normal life and one dedicated to the research," Brecker said. "You'll save everyone a lot of trouble if you decide now."

Zander groaned. "What are we doing all this for? What's the point of all this sacrifice if not love?"

"I'm only trying to help—"

"Bullshit. You want me to choose Vita Maglia. You're so much like Jason it's disgusting."

"Fine, it's true. You're good at running away, Zander, and I'm afraid that when Bryn inevitably runs, you'll go with her."

The older man pointed to himself. "I feel like my entire life has built up to this point, to this slim window of opportunity." He leaned in. "This window, it's what history is made of. You can't throw it away."

"I can try to have both."

"You'll fail." Brecker slapped his palm. "I tried to be married once, your father tried it. It's not fair to any family you might have. If you want Bryn to be happy—"

"What if I don't?"

"You don't want her to be happy?"

"Not without me," he murmured. Bryn spiraled for one last push, breathing fast, her skin flushed pink. "I want to be the one for her."

"Not only will you grow old and your body start to break down, but there's a strong chance you'll die on one of these trips. Do you really want to put her through the same thing her father did?"

That was it. The one thing he couldn't argue. Pain filled him, the heartbreak. It felt like Brecker had split him open.

"I'm truly sorry, Zander, but I think in time you'll see—"

"Just leave me alone." The voice sounded like the one he came here with—the punk kid who had to be dragged back to Grace House.

The doctor opened the door and left.

Bryn felt for her necklace and drew it out slowly. The ring pressed against her lips, then dropped back down inside her neckline. Zander traced her outline in the mirror. He felt the edges of the prison he'd fled two years ago.

Brit Malorie

248

Chapter 36

The wheel got stuck on an exposed root. Seth sighed, then backed up the motorized wheelchair and twisted hard to get around it. After a couple of tries, he was headed back down the path. His morning rides through the woods were routine now. The rides rejuvenated him, and the mountain air brought his color back—he could tell, since he looked in the mirror quite often these days, not out of vanity. To be honest, he still couldn't believe the sight of his own face.

Before his one disastrous trip, he'd looked young for his age. A little gray at the temples, some natural laugh lines around his eyes and mouth. He'd always attributed his youthful look to the serenity of God in his life. Now he wondered where the old man in the mirror had come from. He still didn't understand how Jason had escaped aging despite all of his traveling. Then again, he guessed trauma had snuck up on his older brother. Dead at fifty-five. Jason would spout off about Maglia, her potential, how she proved Einstein's theories, and then he'd stop and grow pale, his mind caught somewhere else. Their father, Joe Hickock Grace, had been the same way close to his end. One minute he was boisterous and screeching about some adventure in 1939, the next he'd be silent and staring off into space. Just a feeling, he'd say, like a spider had crawled up into his brain and hid there. Objects and people blurring, fading. Seth now knew his father's strand was thinning rapidly in places, preparing for the break.

The air grew thick with tangy scents of pine and evergreen. Lilacs bloomed on either side of him. But Seth didn't pay attention, his hands gripping the armrests of his chair. Just remembering made the rage surge through his veins.

He could see now that he had been desperate to believe his nephew had changed, that the discovery would open his mind. He'd believed the boy would see Maglia and experience a profoundly spiritual awakening.

But his nephew had no reverence for anything greater than himself, for things he'd never understand. Yet Seth could tolerate that. What he couldn't tolerate was the pity in the boy's eyes. As if Seth were the poor wayward child that needed a few lessons in how the world worked.

The wheelchair caught on torn branches and small mounds of dirt, but he was patient. He took a morning ride through the woods near St. Sebastian nearly every day. But on special days, he took a different path, a deeper one on a trail that forked around the west side of Glenwood Springs and went past a rustic convenience store. Hanging on this store's back wall was a half-broken payphone.

Cell phones were tracked, of course, so most were surrendered at Grace House. Even St. Sebastian was monitored periodically by GUT security. Seth drove his chair to the very back of the store near the restrooms. The store's owner didn't look up from his newspaper. Many times Seth couldn't even get a dial tone. Whacking the handset against the main unit, he was rewarded with a loud metal clang. A rat scurried across the linoleum floor and under the wheelchair. He banged the handset again, and a scratchy dial tone could be heard.

Seth punched in a collect call to a number he'd memorized months ago, ever since he'd discovered the truth about his brother's seemingly insane tales. The line rang a couple of times, then a recorded voice asked if they'd like to accept the call.

"Caelitus Mihi Vires." The syllables cut through the scratchy phone line like blunt hailstones.

"Di Meliora," Seth answered softly. "Zander has traveled more since we last spoke."

"Excellent. He's making good progress. Soon you'll have new evidence for His Holiness."

"The boy is completely beyond God's influence. He'll never travel for the Church."

"We knew that. He's like his father, a scientist who ignores his own heart."

"He's much worse. Zander's already possessive over the dimension. He'd rather destroy all hope of others traveling than give up power," Seth cried out. He looked around quickly, but the phone was so far back in the hallway no one could hear him. Still, he should lower his voice.

The voice grew pensive. "Are you sure? Well, your son's education is almost complete here. I hate to send such a gifted pupil away, but perhaps he's needed more at home."

"Calvin will not have a chance to travel if his cousin can help it," Seth said. If pressed, he'd admit that he strayed from the truth, but his instincts were correct. Zander might not be able to stop Calvin from traveling initially, but sabotage was not beyond his nephew. He'd spoken in depth with Gage Madison about Zander's psychological profile and it was clear the neurologist had grave suspicions that Brecker ignored.

"That changes things completely," the voice said with an edge of panic.

All scientific proof of the dimension lay in energy and radiation measurements, meaningless to most people. There were the photographs and X-rays, but these could be easily falsified. Unfortunately, the only way to prove the dimension was real was to quickly fade someone with the Recipe. The fade for a normal person only lasted about thirty seconds, but that might be enough. Seth sighed, wishing he could take His Holiness to Maglia himself and let the small man witness God's most glorious creation.

"We must maintain access. From what you've told me, any reckless action could shut off the route completely," the voice said. Both men went quiet, imagining the horror of first discovering direct access to the human soul, then losing it forever. "I see now that we must install your son as the primary traveler as soon as possible. If we control the traveler, we control the experiments, and they'll have no choice—"

"I forgot to tell you. Zander brought that girl back, Elder's daughter. I don't know if she'll travel."

"The girl worries me less. There are ways to remove her if necessary."

"What?" Seth asked, his throat dry. There was a window at the far end of the hallway. A cloud passed over the sun for a moment, and his eyes closed in the dimmed light. "I never agreed to that."

The voice chuckled. It sounded like gravel crunching on the bad connection. "I meant with money. It's your nephew's hunger we must defuse. You could—" The line went dead. Seth shook the handset.

The next words out of the phone left him stunned. For just a moment, he wondered if he was confiding in the right person. But the voice belonged to a man of the cloth. The cloud moved past the window and let sunlight back in.

"I can't do that. The boy's an irritation, but once Calvin comes home—"

"Do you want His Holiness to step in? He's more likely to take over if the primary traveler is a student of the priesthood, a pious and mature young man."

Seth interrupted. "The line's going dead. I'll contact you once I've found a better one."

"What? I hear you just fine—"

Seth hung up. He hadn't meant for any of this to happen. He'd just been ranting; he did that when upset. Naturally, he put the souls of the world before any personal relationships, but he was a deeply moral man.

Seth exited the store, deep in thought. The Lord had designed the dimension and all that lay within it as a complement to home, a unique gift for His greatest creation, man. It gave human beings the ability to love and care for each other in reverence to Him. Seth returned to his daydream. The research placed squarely under the dominion of the Holy See. A billion Catholics comprehending the magnitude of their faith, with millions more joining every year. Calvin working side by side with His

Holiness, saving hundreds of souls, introducing light and grace into their lives.

But his vision would never take place as long as Zander blocked the Church's entry. Seth paused, then shook his head. He wouldn't technically be hurting the boy, but no. It was impossible. If the Lord willed that future for Zander, then so be it, but Seth would not interfere. He would have to absorb power slowly until the Church could be invited in.

He sucked in breath noisily, his mind in turmoil. He'd have to fight every day. His bones ached just thinking about it. And if trauma had its way and he died, Calvin would be alone. Alone to battle his cousin and the scientists for a lifetime.

Brit Malorie

Chapter 37

Maglian breezes rippled through Zander's form as he stood next to Elder. "Is Tomas's strand far?" he asked.

"Yes, but I wasn't planning on walking. Let's take the Lusha streamways."

Zander raised his eyebrows. "We're flying?"

"I wouldn't call it flying. More like paragliding. The Lusha ride on this network of jetstream currents through the air." Elder pointed to a small cluster of lights gathered on a cliff about forty feet above them. "There's an entry point there. Since we don't weigh much, we can join them."

Zander followed the older man slowly up a steep incline to the top. The lights floated near the edge of the cliff, then one by one tipped over the side. Instead of falling, the Lusha rose even higher as they were catapulted through the air, creating sparkling bands in the sky.

"Brace yourself," Elder said. They stepped off the side in unison and he felt a falling sensation. Then a billow of air caught his form and Zander was flung up into the sky. The winds caught him and he glided alongside Elder.

Zander pointed to the orb levitating in the center of the mesh, pulsing like a giant heartbeat. The vibrations knocked around the particles in his form. With each beat, the orb sent out newborn strands to join the mesh. "Is that the Sorrelle?"

"Yes. At the beginning of life, a strand is flung out from the orb. It enters the mesh and connects with other strands, then grows thicker and longer with age. At the end of life, the strand is cut."

Zander thought a moment. "Sorrelle means 'sisters' in Italian. Why call it that?"

Elder smiled. "Do you remember your Greek mythology? The three Moirae sisters: Clothos, Lachesis and Atropos. Clothos weaves the thread of life, Lachesis measures the length of the thread, and Atropos cuts the end with her shears. It sure seems like their work."

"Does the Sorrelle have anything to do with the Masterfade?" Zander had come across the term in his studies, but no one could tell him much about it. "It's a device that allows the user to fade past the Veil?"

"In his travels, Jason heard rumblings about the Masterfade, a relic that's been hidden for hundreds of years. It allows the user to travel between dimensions," Elder chuckled. "I'm sure the legend also included werewolves, aliens, mermaids. Jesus probably drank out of it, too. Jason never found out what the relic actually was or where it's been for the last few centuries."

He pointed to a section of strands that grew so heavy it looked like a forest. "We're about to land. Stay flexible, let the air toss you down, don't fight it."

Zander toppled to the ground and rolled into a somersault. Standing up, he gazed around. The strands hung down like vines, encircling what looked like massive oak trees. As they walked closer, he realized the oaks were really thick strands, several feet in circumference. Their bases spread out over widely on the ground, surrounded by a sea of nitore flowers.

Elder made a grand gesture. "Salire strands. Essential to the stability of the mesh."

"They're holding it up, like a giant canopy," he murmured. The tops of the Salire strands rose hundreds of feet above them. There the branches flowed upward, connecting to the mesh above it.

They passed a few Salire strands that were broken and lying sideways on the ground. "Salire strands stay here when they die?"

"Eventually, the Lusha will transport them onward into death, but it takes decades. That is their sacrifice. The soul of a Salire stays in Maglia long after the souls he's carried pass on."

Elder motioned to a broad Salire about fifty feet in front of them. "That's Tomas's strand. You can see why we can't get close."

Zander covered his ears though he knew it wouldn't stop the hundreds of shrieks and screeches, the wails and howls. A solid wall of cacophonous noise. A black tumor rippled on one side of the strand's trunk. It was actually dozens of Vipera burrowing into the side. The smell, like a mixture of gasoline and acrid burning, invaded his form. The air felt drenched with hate. He had to look away from the sprawling black mass of writhing, squiggling creatures feeding on Tomas.

"We have to ask ourselves, what will attract the Vipera more than a Salire's inner chemicals?" Elder said. "What can we distract them with?"

Zander searched the ground for materials. "What's that?" He pointed to a small geyser several yards from the Salire strand, spraying a plume of yellowish liquid into the air. The liquid hit the ground, then gathered in pools.

He approached the geyser and sniffed the air. "Smells like ammonia?"

"I think so."

"I thought ammonia gas was supposed to be deadly."

"I'm not sure if it is in Maglia or not. But either way it wouldn't be deadly to us," Elder laughed.

Zander felt sheepish. "That's right. I keep forgetting this isn't my real body." He had to reach way back into his memory of high school chemistry. "Ammonia. We could add a piece of sodium metal."

Elder nodded. "Each sodium atom would lose an electron. The ammonium molecules would surround the electron and keep it stable."

"A powerful reducing mixture," Zander added. He grinned at the older man. "A luxurious pool of negative ions for these beasts to drown themselves in. How many of these geysers are around?" He trailed off as he surveyed the area. He counted at least ten surrounding the Salire grove. The pools might distract the Vipera initially, but he'd need at least an hour to clean the wound and apply the serum.

Elder paused. "I have another idea. I'll ask the Archlusha for their help."

"I thought they already refused."

"They've refused to help us themselves. But they might direct a large number of regular Lusha to form a barricade."

"Really? They'll do that for us?"

"I have some pull," Elder winked. "As long as the Vipera have already left the wound, the Lusha can easily form a line of defense surrounding Tomas's strand."

He looked up at the sky. "It would only happen at dusk, right before the Lusha return to Chalice for the night. The timing will have to be perfect."

Zander felt hopeful. These new ideas might give Tomas a chance. But they still had to figure out how to block the Vipera afterwards so the wound could heal.

"Look out!" Elder yelled. Something crawled along Zander's side. The strangest sensation hit him, almost like a sting. One of the smaller Vipera must have escaped from the nest and lunged at him.

It was only a split second of contact, but the pain was like thousands of sharp needles in his brain. Images swirled through him. *His dad tortured and dying in a cage. Bryn's body slashed in long red cuts, her voice rising in horrific screams through the air. Himself failing, full of drugs, everyone at Grace House staring at him in disgust. Maglia burning, charred like a region of hell, the Lusha squealing as they were captured and eaten.*

The pressure built up in his chest and exploded like shrapnel in his head. His legs spun out from under him and he thrashed on the ground. And he heard it. The feeding. Being ripped apart with tiny teeth that cut like knives, his insides torn out. A negative chill spread through his core, pulling him down into the deepest pit of depression. There was no way out, no way—

Elder shouted to the Circle to pull him out now. He woke up in the training room seizing. Brecker swiftly put an oxygen mask over his face, and Zander gulped in sweet air. The details wouldn't leave him, the agony, the raw torture and pain, the lingering smell of charred flesh. Liz ran inside the room and placed her bare skin against his to pull the negative miran out.

After a few minutes the images faded and he calmed. He removed the oxygen mask and drank some water.

Gage and Hadley came inside the room. Hadley took his hand.

"What happened?" Brecker asked.

"One of the Vipera . . . bit me, I guess. If that's what they do. I had no idea they were like that." As Zander closed his eyes, all his hope for Tomas's healing dissipated. How could he go near those things again? There were dozens of them there, a shrieking, monstrous horde.

He stared off, his fears growing rapidly even as he felt Hadley's warm energy enter his palm. He kept his eyes averted from hers but couldn't stop the trepidation.

The little girl shook her head. "Stop it. It was only one time," she cried out.

"I know, Hadders, but you don't know—"

"You have to do it. You have to help him."

"It's a huge risk. Do you realize that? None of our ideas will work. Wait!" Hadley ran out of the room. Liz gave him a sad look then followed her.

"Come on!" Gage yelled.

"There are dozens of them," Zander insisted. "It only takes one to destroy me. My mind, my life. It won't work anyway."

"Can you believe this?" Gage tossed his hands up in the air. He turned to Brecker. "Surprise, surprise. Your great hero won't do it."

"It'll only work *if* the Vipera leave the wound, *if* the Lusha barrier keeps them out, *if* the serum does anything. Then on top of it all, those evil things will just swarm the wound again when we leave. It'll never heal. Elder's too weak to help me. He can't save me again if something goes wrong. I'm supposed to go ahead with this?"

"You're supposed to grow a pair, yes. You have to take risks!" Gage demanded.

"Your ass isn't going in there," Zander yelled back. "Don't lecture me on risks. Risks are fine. This is suicide!"

Brecker leaned in and squeezed his shoulder. "Listen to me, okay? This healing isn't just for Tomas. It's for the people connected to him. He's passing sorrow into all these people who can't endure it. Children, like Hadley."

"Maybe the Lusha will help more than we think. Maybe they can save these people," Zander whispered.

Brecker continued as if he hadn't heard him. "And if Tomas dies, it'll be terrible. Some of his bindings will experience devastating depression for years, possibly suicide. It's the way the mesh works. This isn't a decision you can make lightly."

Zander rubbed his eyes. They were making it worse. He wasn't Hadley or Liz or Tomas. He couldn't handle the weight of all these lives.

Gage groaned loudly and slammed his hand against the wall. "Your father would do it."

He left and Brecker looked a bit dazed. "Alright, alright. We have a week or so until the serum's ready. We'll figure something out."

Zander tilted his head, fighting back tears. Gage was right. He was a coward. He'd never be like Dad, he couldn't fix anything in Maglia, this discovery was wasted on him. The Vipera were just too powerful. How could he battle an entire nest when the smallest touch nearly killed him?

Chapter 38

After Zander was pulled out by the Circle, Elder left the Salire grove and headed back to the lab, deep in thought. Griffin swept up beside him, then zipped off. Elder followed at a much slower pace, but as he approached the lab, he figured out why the Lusha was so excited. A metallic ball about the size of a fist rolled along the ground. It spun in a tight circle and the light chased it. The ball rose up and ricocheted off the grotto wall. It swooped back and rolled down the side. The Lusha twinkled and knocked it back. A giggle floated through the air.

"Hello, Hadley dear," Elder called out. "Is Zander okay?"

Yeah, but he's shaken up. We're worried he won't do the healing now.

Elder grimaced. He remembered his first brush with the Vipera. It was something the boy would have to endure if he wished to travel.

"He does not have a choice," he called out grimly.

I know. I wish I could help him be brave.

Elder paused. Everything was changing so fast. The Vipera appeared larger and more aggressive. The cyclones in the Woods were much bigger now with great smoke clouds and hideous, heart-wrenching sounds rising from Dimora. The Vipera had always released negative miran when they ripped minerals out of the strands, but now they poured great amounts of depression and rage into the mesh even when they weren't feeding. Where did that insatiable evil come from?

He sighed and the little girl sensed his thoughts. *The Vipera grow more powerful.*

"Not just the Vipera. It's the Archvipera. I don't know why they're gaining strength over the Archlusha, but I can smell it here, taste it in the air. Feel it in the strands."

The Circle feels it, too. Do you think Tomas will turn the Great War?

"The Archvipera are already turning the Great War for their side. We must turn it back. You and Tomas and the travelers. All human souls are at stake," he replied. "We'll need all of the Salire before this is done. And Tomas is a very special Salire. The most important."

If he falls. . . .

". . . we all are lost," Elder murmured. He didn't like to dwell on these things. Hadley was called back by the Circle.

Griffin lingered beside him and morphed into a broad golden sheet. Images from the last few weeks flickered across the surface. Bryn appeared, dancing deep in the woods, aching for the spins and leaps she used to perform flawlessly. Such beauty. She reminded him of her mother, Iris, when they'd first met. He placed a hand against the edge of the rippling sheet and emotions trickled through. His child had worked so painfully hard for many years—all the hours of practice and training now erased because of a psychopath. She felt worthless. Her heart refused to let it go. What would her life be now?

A new image appeared on the golden sheet. Bryn stood near a small waterfall in the woods. Zander climbed on the rocks above her, his bare chest and auburn waves caressed by sunlight. Her eyes lingered on the muscled lines of his body, his broad shoulders and the curve of his lower back. He called to her. She smiled slyly. He jumped down to a lower rock and reached for her hand. She let his fingertips brush hers, then pulled away. He chased her and they fell on the grass. They talked, comforting each other, the rhythm of their voices making its own melody. The flush in her cheeks, the tingling nerves running through her body. She touched her lips and imagined the taste of Zander's skin.

Elder startled—the children were falling in love. Looking upward at the mesh, he stood in awe at the vastness of Maglian connection yet the power of her inside his own life. He and Jason had shared a wonderful friendship for years and now their children would create something truly beautiful, a love that would last the rest of their lives.

***

Later that evening, Hadley Porter sat with Tomas on the riverbank. She watched the water swirl around their bare feet as the moon ascended. They'd just finished the counseling session with his bindings, and she could already see the flush of positive miran in his skin.

"I wish there was more time," she said softly. She pictured something she saw in a book once called a spindle. She imagined it as a magic spindle that could stop time from running away. Catch it, trap it, make more of it. Threads of time, sheets of time, great blankets of it that one could just sit and play under, keeping her secure and safe and warm like the down comforter on her bed. She liked to bury herself under the covers and pretend the world outside had stopped.

Tomas pointed to her bracelet. "Beautiful."

Hadley touched it, her fingers running over the interlocking metal clasps. Tourmaline stones appeared to float inside the segments. She loved spinning the stones in different kinds of light—the stones shone gray then green, then pitch black.

"My brother made it for me. He put a lot of love into it, that's why it's lasted as long as it has." She sighed. "But he's almost gone from it."

"Do you think of him still?"

"Sometimes," she murmured. "He's blurry now." She used to search for Adam's strand, hoping that he was still caught in the mesh somewhere, haunting other people. Then she could visit him. But several months of searching had given her nothing. There were just too many places he could be. He could be lying on the Maglian cloud surface or trapped in the Valley. Or perhaps his strand has passed into the peace of Afterlife, and she wouldn't see him for many years. That was the best place for him, yet it gave her the most sorrow.

"I never asked you how he died," Tomas murmured.

"There was a bridge by our house in Savannah. He drowned in the river. No one knows what really happened," she said. Back then her abilities were barely developed, just these intense feelings that seem to come from everywhere. If she could just find Adam's strand, maybe she could finally understand what happened that night.

"He was very sad at the end, yes?"

Hadley nodded. "He was different than other boys. He didn't like himself."

"You wonder if you could have saved him."

She stared hard at the water as she willed the tears away, but the corners of her eyes still burned. She did wonder that every single day. Her guilt rose up before her, a small ebony bird with white flecks along its sides.

"You could not," Tomas said slowly. His words stilled the air around them. The ebony bird flew upward, blending into the night sky until it disappeared. Her neck and shoulders relaxed.

"I have heard the more trauma a strand endures, the thicker it becomes. It does not break. I believe that because of you," he said.

"I'm almost eleven," she said, her voice solemn.

Tomas chuckled. "A new era of responsibility." He studied her. "I shouldn't joke. You're wondering what will happen as you grow. Will your abilities stay the same? Diminish? Explode?"

Hadley nodded.

"I only know another year is coming. A year of Maglia, of whispering strands, of Bumbles and school and grownups making very silly mistakes all around you."

Her mouth twisted. "Too many of those." She studied him in the moonlight. His color was much better and he looked peaceful. They'd bought a little time, but soon even a bindings session wouldn't be able to help.

Chapter 39

Zander lay asleep in the backyard, his body stretched out on the long grass with one sandal hanging off his big toe. Bryn crawled up to him. She hesitated, then slid her head onto his chest. She rubbed her face in the soft cotton of his shirt, craving Zander smell underneath the tingling scent of his aftershave. A week ago, he'd abruptly told Brecker he needed more privacy, then moved into one of the bungalow cottages behind the house. He found excuses to leave a room after she entered and spent all of his time with the other scientists. At first she just wondered, then she began to realize what was happening. Why couldn't she see it before? He was trying to let her down easy. The research was his great passion, not her.

He yawned suddenly and Bryn darted back. His eyes found her.

"Hi."

"Hi."

His hand crept up her shoulder and combed through her hair. He held up a leaf. "Your hair's this wonderful leaf catcher. They can't help but get sucked right in."

"Yeah. Summer hazard," she replied quietly. Her hand instinctively covered the pink birthmark under her right ear.

Zander pushed her hand away. "Stop," he murmured. "I want to see all of you."

An uncomfortable pause passed. "You know, your birthday's coming up," he continued. "What do you want? You can have anything."

"Anything?" She raised her eyebrows.

He spread his hands wide. "Anything. I'm a spoiled rich kid, remember?"

"How could I ever forget?"

He grinned and tapped his chest. "And she strikes at the heart. Merciless."

Bryn looked around. There was rustling in the house, people walking around the grounds. She wanted to be alone with him. Not that anything would happen, but. . . .

"A hike," she said, resolute.

He frowned. "Are you sure? What about your ankle?"

"I need to test it out."

"Uh, okay." Zander sat up, then ran his hands through his hair and shook out the grass pieces. "We'll go when Hadley's done with meditation."

"No. Let's go now."

"Just us?" A tense look crossed his face, but he quickly covered it with a smile.

Bryn nodded. "That's the only gift I want."

***

Golden waves of aspen trees flooded the trail and the burnished orange of scrub oak fluttered in the summer breeze. Bryn breathed in the sweet fragrance. She watched Zander's back as they hiked, their feet crunching on sticks and through weeds. Inside the deep stone crevices teemed wildlife in their natural roosting areas—falcon nests, swallows, rabbits with long ears.

She wore a white tanktop, denim shorts, and a thin jacket. Her feet slipped a little in her hiking boots. The air was damp and swollen with late afternoon thunderstorm, but there was the smell of campfire, too. Tiny shots of electricity tingled her body, and the smoke seemed to cling to her lust, mixing deep in her blood. A fire inside her.

He stopped suddenly and she collided with him. She looked up over his shoulder. A coyote pup sprawled lazily across the path panting, the edges of his fur baked in bronze. He stared them down, then skitted off with a yelp. She gingerly stepped up the path, but Zander remained motionless, staring at the pup as it ran into the bushes.

"I wish I could be that," he murmured.

"A coyote?"

"Free." He looked over to her. "Let's just get out of here."

She started to laugh, then stopped. He looked serious. "We can't just leave, Zander. People depend on us."

He grimaced and turned away. "I was just kidding anyway."

Bryn called out to him. "Hey, talk to me."

He kept walking. She yelled after him, her voice turned bitter. "Hey, you can leave anytime you want. Just go."

He turned around and his eyes searched her. "No," he finally said. "There's too much I love here."

They lapsed into silence. A snow-white falcon tracked them carefully, black spots spattered down its breast. Plumes of thundercloud materialized in the distance, the sky bruised with patches of indigo and pewter.

She wracked her head for something clever or flirty to say. Zander startled as drops pattered down on his jacket. "Damn, the storm started sooner than they said it would." His voice was low and hard.

Water slid down her skin. "I guess this was a bad idea."

"We'll have to take shelter in that cave up there until the storm moves on."

He motioned for her to pass him. Bryn jogged lightly up the trail, then hit a pile of mud and fell. Pain tipped through her ankle and she cried out.

"Are you okay?" he asked. She nodded, furious at herself.

He helped her up. She tried to limp a few feet but whimpered.

Zander lifted her up. "Hey, no damsel in distress here," she protested.

"It's only a few yards."

The cave was inside an outstretched rock formation. "What if there are bats?" she whispered in a spooky voice.

"Don't scare me like that," Zander joked, peering deeper into the darkness.

He put her down and she leaned against the wall, her ankle throbbing. He leaned against the other wall, as far away as possible. The ring on her necklace caught the light and reflected it.

"I've been meaning to ask you about that. You never take it off," he asked, pointing to the ring. "You don't have to tell me if it's too personal." He dragged his fingers through his hair. The auburn locks appeared as a mess of dark on his head. It was getting too long already. She resisted the urge to reach out and straighten it. Touch.

"No, it's not a secret. My mom didn't do much right, but she did enroll me in a dance class. When I turned sixteen and we were fighting all the time, she threatened to take it away, the one thing I truly loved. So I dropped out of high school and left."

"You haven't seen your mom in seven years?"

"I visit once in a while. A girl always needs her mom." She caressed the twisted metal. It made her feel more stable just to hold it. "Right before I left, there was this flash of silver in a back corner of the dance studio. The ring was just lying there. I guess I think of it as a promise to myself to always put dancing first in my heart."

"Nothing else gets to be first?" he teased. "No special someone?"

She gave him a sly smile. "I might feel differently if my ankle doesn't heal completely. And if I stay at Grace House."

"If you stay," Zander muttered. He looked outside.

She bit her lip, her chest tightening. Thunder cracked loudly outside the cave and gave her goosebumps. It sounded far away, but she wasn't sure.

"Hey, you're cut." He closed the space between them and knelt down. Spitting on the corner of his sleeve, he patted at the light scrape on her shin.

"Um, thanks, Dr. House. I think I'll survive," Bryn laughed. The cave felt very damp and the rain sizzled outside. Her hair lay tangled at the base of her neck and leaked drops of muddy water. She tried to comb her fingers through it. "I guess this is living wild."

Zander grew somber. He lifted her foot and touched her ankle, his fingers lingering on the scar tissue. "I wish you'd never met me."

Her hands fell down to stroke his hair, to comfort. "Don't say that."

He stood up quickly and placed a hand on the wall. Her heart seized—he was too close.

"I don't want you to hurt like that again," he murmured. "If it wasn't for our lives here, I'd go straight to that island and kill him, I swear, Bryn. I'd kill him for what he did to you." He choked a little. "I can barely stand it."

She pulled him close and caressed the side of his face. "Listen to me. I feel safe with you." He leaned into her hand and his lips brushed her inner wrist. The air grew very warm despite the chill of the cave. The ache in her heart, the heat down below. Why couldn't they be together, just this once? She closed her eyes and leaned forward. *Just give me this.* Her mouth searched for his.

A breeze met her. Cold air.

There was nothing there. Zander stood near the cave's opening, his back to her. She walked up behind him and pressed her face into the space between his shoulder blades, his nook. She wanted to hold him, to heal everything between them. Her fingertips touched his and he jerked away.

He muttered to himself. "Brecker . . . Maglia."

She stepped backward, stunned. He was thinking about the research.

Zander turned and gave her a troubled smile. "It's clearing up. Should we head down?"

"Sure." She tested her ankle and it seemed to be all right. Her cheeks burned. Why had she opened herself up like that?

They headed down the muddy slide. She braced her feet and moved slower. Dammit, she should have worn better hiking shoes. She slipped a little and he caught her arm.

"Whoa there," he said warmly.

She pushed him away. "Let's go. I have meditation."

He stopped and studied her. "You don't want to stay longer? The sunset should be amazing." The thread of sweetness in his voice only increased her nausea. Now he felt sorry for her too.

"Nope. We're done here." Her legs walked fast to the car.

He followed her to the trailhead and they drove back to Grace House. Lapsing into tense silence, Bryn hugged herself tightly. She kept her eyes straight ahead at the darkening sky. How could she have been so wrong?

Chapter 40

Towers of Kyre burned on the outskirts of a giant pit. The people danced and flung themselves against each other, a mass of hearts and lungs and limbs in unison. Music pulsed from giant speakers, rocking the sand. Dreadlocks and bikini tops and Hypna bottles moved in wide circles. Women touched each other's skin, clasping palms together, slick tongues moving out of mouths. Sweat and scent coated every inch, a wilderness of bodies.

Along the periphery of this orchestrated madness, a lone predator searched. He crept in the dark, trails of Kyre flickering along his jawline. He was not like them. He did not feel what they felt. And the same thing that made his victims feel close to each other also gave them warning when he drew near. So he had to match his rhythms just right to theirs.

Lynch took in the oily heat of the Kyre. Cye stood beside the inferno and shadows crisscrossed her wired body. Their eyes met. She turned her head, sufficiently warned by Damaris. He spotted a teen near the outskirts of the rave, her hair twisted into rainbow dreadlocks, her face a shallow oval with thick lips. He moved in close, searching for her scent above the others. She tried to move forward, seeking personal space, but other bodies blocked her. He'd been developing his skills lately. He could gather glimpses from the air around someone. She turned and he felt a name. *Perla.*

The crowd flung her into him. He slipped a hand behind her neck and relished her, catching a fresh wave of emotions and memories. Careful to shield his own thoughts, he leaned in and whispered her own daydreams back to her. The girl had dramatic visions of singing stardom. She'd stolen a moderate amount of money from her parents and ran here, believing Kadera somehow held her destiny. She was right. Saliva gathered in his mouth. His table waited.

He gave her the answers she'd been looking for her entire life. Her eyes opened wide, lips parted, her head tilting towards him at that special angle. "You understand me," she murmured. She was his.

A shock rippled through him and he jerked backward. The girl winced and shook her head. Damaris slid in beside him, then turned and walked away. Lynch's feet followed him while his mind shuffled itself back together. The man rarely interrupted Lynch's hunt, so this must be important. The girl returned to her friends, unaware of her brief glance into a possible future.

They came to a clearing twenty yards from the rave scene. The water lapped and trickled onto the sand, the moonlight stretching it to their feet.

"We discussed this. No more projects."

"They keep me at my best," he replied.

"You could use a little hunger. You've grown a bit too relaxed."

"Palefu felt the brunt of my skills," Lynch said smugly. He'd been reveling in his memories of the man's last moments.

"Sure he did," Damaris said, his voice irritated. "On Kadera. It's not like Grace will simply waltz back here."

"You haven't left the island in ten years. You'd be surprised at how heavy the outside world can be."

Damaris ignored him. "I think this next experiment might be it. Success is very close. If I could only break through these damn psychological walls."

"You can always visit my table. It's excellent therapy," Lynch chuckled. He automatically rested his arm against his left side. Over his fresh scar.

Damaris grimaced. "I bet you'd enjoy that. I'll work on it myself, thank you. No need to hide that either." He motioned to Lynch's side. "Grace slipped you."

"I twisted. It's just a scratch."

"I doubt that. He's an escape artist like his father." Damaris made a clicking noise with his tongue. "The Grace men have skill."

"Pure luck." Lynch's crew had been searching the island since Palefu's death, but there was no sign of those boulders anywhere. Yet he felt emboldened. "I'm ready to know more."

Damaris laughed. "After your colossal failure in Miami? Are you joking?"

His gut seized. "Zander told me things in Miami. He let information slip. I know there's more to this island." He hesitated, wondering if he should gamble. "I know about Maglia."

Damaris studied him. "You know nothing. Leave it alone." He started to walk away. "Don't get comfortable. I'll have more information on Grace's location soon."

He left and Lynch stood motionless, hypnotized by the water, watching the Kyrelight cascade on the waves. They were never going to tell him, not without a push. The waves. Water. It reverberated in his mind. Something about how the water looked—it had a cloudy look. His men had searched every nook and cranny of the island but only the land. He remembered the image, the haziness of it. The boulders would appear hazy if they were viewed underwater. That pressure he'd felt in his chest—it was from Palefu holding his breath.

Lynch hurried back to the beachhouse. There was old snorkeling equipment in the storage left by the previous tenet, a life-long surf bum. He sifted through the gear until he spied it: an LED headlamp for underwater use. He took a pair of goggles, a mask, snorkel, and fins. He'd gambled his hand away earlier with the mention of Maglia. Damaris must have appeared confident because he figured Lynch would never find the entrance, but the man might take precautions just in case. This had to be done tonight.

There were miles of coastline around the circumference of the island, but he had a hunch. His men had been surveying Palefu for the last couple of months, and there was this one small lagoon where he liked to relax and snorkel. The lagoon was located on the northernmost tip of Kadera, near the grand tree and Damaris's private beach. He used a four-wheeler and drove up to it. There were a few groups on the dirt roads, but almost everyone was up at the rave or camping on one of the beaches.

Rain fell from the night sky. The boom of the combers crashing against the coral was thunderous. He slipped the headlamp and goggles over his head, then slipped noiselessly into the water. Turning the light on, his gaze met sand and shallow coral formations. He used the diffuse lowlight for the broadest vision and to conserve battery power. Small crabs escaped his view by scuttling under the ledges. Damselfish and parrot fish scattered in tiny spurts. He took deep breaths from the surface and ducked his head back under. His eyes searched the rock formations just under the water, but nothing matched. The memory had been so hazy that he wondered if he had the colors of the boulders right or if he'd ever be able to see the symbols at night.

He searched for three hours until he exhausted every rock in the damn lagoon. There were literally hundreds of sinkholes, coves, depressions, and caves Palefu might have visited. What if it was on Damaris's private beach, a place so secure even Lynch couldn't enter without an invitation? A chill entered him as he stood in the water. He looked upward; there was a coral ledge to his right. He decided to sit in the enclave underneath it for a moment and try to think. The rock walls seemed to hug Lynch from all sides—he couldn't even stand up. The water came to his waist. His muscles trembled from exhaustion. No wonder Damaris had been so arrogant. There must be thousands of rocks along Kadera's shoreline. Not to mention all the small lagoons and waterfalls inland.

Dawn seeped slowly into the Kaderian sky. He rested his head back against the rock wall, feeling like he could fall asleep—almost. He startled. The ceiling. He could just barely make out the color of the rock in the new sunlight. He flipped on his headlamp. Of course. The enclave was tight for men like Lynch and Palefu but roomy for a small man like Damaris. He felt along the ceiling with his hands, his body still in an uncomfortable crouch. Seaweed naturally stretched across the rock crevices, but there was this one strange spot where it looked like seaweed had been crammed in on purpose. Lynch pulled it out quickly. His fingers traced the symbols carved in the two boulders. They hung down from the enclave's ceiling.

But the boulders had been hazy in the memory. The tide must have been in, and Palefu must have explored this place while snorkeling. But if the boulders hung from above, would the entrance be in the ceiling as well? Lynch tried in vain to remember the image details. Like waking from a dream, collected memories were blurry to begin with and soon lost all detail, until you were only left with an idea of what happened.

Lynch thought Palefu had moved in between the two boulders, but the man had dropped through, not climbed up. He searched for an opening around the boulders, but it was all solid rock. Could there be a panel, a switch? He searched along the ceiling when his foot suddenly pushed through into open space. He knelt down as far as he could and almost laughed. It was an optical illusion. From above the rock wall appeared solid, but there was actually a horizontal ledge along the wall's bottom that hid the opening. It only measured two feet by two feet. How in the world had Palefu found it, and how had such a large man fit through it? Lynch's hand slipped through, then his arms. He took one last deep breath, then dipped his head and torso below the water line. The rock scraped his sides, and he realized it was expanding and stretching around him. He pushed harder, feeling terribly claustrophobic. This was it. Lynch was about to find out what the hell was happening on this island.

Brit Malorie

Chapter 41

Zander sat alone in the darkened meditation room. No one knew he was in here. His back slumped against the eastern wall, his head bowed down. It had been a week since his encounter with the Vipera, but the pressure kept building. He couldn't think, couldn't feel, couldn't even move anymore. He'd stopped eating and sleeping, stopped talking to anyone. He used to have the cushion of time, but that was gone now. Containers of sodium metal surrounded the Salire grove, ready to create the chemical pools. Elder had a flask of the serum ready. The healing had to be done this afternoon.

Driving around Glenwood Springs yesterday, he'd run into an old dealer from his college days. On impulse he'd purchased a bottle of Oxycontin and hid it in a false panel in the back of his dresser. He hadn't taken one, but it made him feel better to know they were there. He just wanted to lay in dreamland, oblivious to Brecker's hope, Gage's judgment. Little white pills to erase it all.

As if all this pressure wasn't enough, he was consumed every moment by Bryn. He'd think he was fine, that he could live just fine without her. But the damn thing grew, a love that fed upon his stomach and brain and heart. Nothing quenched the fever, not reason or facts or cold water. It just burned until the air was gone from his lungs, and he was left so delirious it felt like he was dying.

Zander pressed his forehead into his hands and rocked back and forth. Fear washed over him in great waves, separating him from everything he loved. The weight of Tomas's life, of all the lives connected to the man. He'd fail. His brain couldn't concentrate on simple tasks, much less a responsibility of this magnitude. He couldn't do it. But Tomas would die if he didn't— Oh God, he needed help.

Sunlight peeked in through the basement windows, settling the room in a dusky gray hue. Zander startled as the door opened. A figure passed through the shadows and sat down across from him. Dried mud flaked off his toes and black curls fanned out over his head.

"Tell me," Tomas murmured.

Zander hesitated. The man touched his hands. "Tell me what you need."

Surprised, he felt tears down his face. Raw truth poured out of him, the one thing he truly needed above everything else. Words escaped his lips before he knew what he was saying. "Dad. I need Dad. I need his mind, his courage, his heart. I need him here with me."

"I knew your father well. He would tell you that everything will be okay."

Tomas embraced him as the sobs shook his body. "I can't do this alone."

"Your deep wound is believing that your father never loved you. This prevents you from being whole." Tomas traced the side of his face. "You must know different now, Zander. Know that he loves you deeply. He spoke of you many times, what he wished for your life, what kind of man he thought you would be."

"I didn't believe him. I ran away. I failed him."

"It does not matter. He understands."

"I'll never see him again."

"Yes, you will. There is much that lies beyond the Calamata. He waits for you there. You must release your guilt."

Zander shook his head.

"You must. He knows and he understands. You are free." Tomas touched his forehead.

"I can't do the healing without him. It's too much."

"What is too much?"

"All these people. The weight of it."

"Do not carry them."

"But—"

"They are mine."

"But you'll die—"

"Then I must die." Tomas smiled as if to lighten his words. "I am not afraid. I will live in my true home forever."

He touched Zander's forehead again. "Leave the dust behind," he said. "Let the world fall away."

Zander closed his eyes as his head fell into the man's hands. Tomas kept murmuring. "Let me carry this burden. I will carry myself and all others. Think only of the problem. It lies out there, unsolved. You want to conquer it. I know you will solve it simply for that reason."

He opened his eyes as the realization hit him. Tomas was right. Zander didn't want to do the healing for all these people he'd never meet. Just let him solve the damn problem. "Do you think I'm terrible?"

The man chuckled. "No. Never. It is who you are. It is where your courage comes from."

Morning filled the room. Along with the warm sunlight came a relief so immense Zander struggled to stand. He felt solid, whole.

Tomas touched his hands again. "I am humbled that you have chosen to save my life. Do what you can. Nothing more."

Brit Malorie

Chapter 42

Bryn stood knee-deep in the stream, her toes digging into the silt. She bent down and cupped her palms in the cool water, then sprinkled it on her face and arms. She left the stream and put on her sandals, then slowly walked the path back up to Grace House, a place that didn't feel like home anymore. Zander had made it clear that he didn't love her, and she couldn't keep following him around, heartsick and unwanted. She couldn't stay here.

She'd visit her mother first then, build a new life somewhere. Brecker had mentioned they'd support her if she wanted to attend college. There might be other ways she could help the research besides traveling. Maybe she could study counseling. Her sessions with Gage had really helped. Instead of suppressing her problems, she wanted to work through them and help other people work through theirs.

She took the path that wound around the cottages. When Grace House came into view, she stopped. Zander sat cross-legged on the grass in the backyard. He was talking to someone sitting across from him.

Bryn crept closer. It was a young woman about her age. White-blond hair swept straight down her back. Intelligent, quick eyes. She looked like a model in a French perfume ad, her body long and very thin, a twig figure in tight jeans. Zander spotted Bryn and motioned for her to join them. She walked up grudgingly.

"Hey, I wanted you to meet Phina," he said. "She's a psychic that used to work with the Circle. She flew in from Paris to help with Tomas's healing."

Phina let out a giggle, a tinkle of a sound. Her hand rubbed his back. "Oui. Zander and I were reminiscing." Her voice was light, airy.

Probably like her brain, Bryn thought.

"I can't believe it. The last time I saw you, you were this stupid punk kid. Now you're all grown up. Maglia suits you." Phina appraised him, her eyes playful.

"How long are you staying?" Bryn asked. The woman's perfume was potent, full of lavender.

Yet another giggle. "Not sure. I came to help out the Circle, but I forgot how fun Grace House is. I should really stay longer. Do you remember. . . ." She purred something in Zander's ear and his eyes grew wide, then he threw his head back and laughed.

Bryn turned away. She'd known plenty of women like Phina at the club. Aggressive, sneaky girls that she couldn't compete with. The woman even had a traditional dancer's body, that ethereal, straight-hipped wispiness.

Bryn sighed and looked down at her body, too many curves, not tall enough. She didn't want to fight anymore. Zander looked lighter, more relaxed than she'd seen him in weeks. He must be relieved that a sexy, uncomplicated woman had finally entered his life. Phina kept touching him, rubbing his back, whispering in his ear.

Bryn stepped aside quickly, needing to get as far away as possible. He called out to her, but she kept running.

She made it to the far side of the last cottage, blood pounding in her ears. Sitting down on the grass, she rested her back against the wall and felt lightheaded. There were footsteps around the side. *Don't let him find me, don't let him*—a hand touched her shoulder.

Zander knelt down next to her. "What's going on?"

She shrugged him off and stood up, quickly wiping her face. "Nothing. Just needed some space."

"Wait, Bryn, you're really upset, you're crying." He turned her around and hugged her. She tensed up. "Relax," he whispered. She let herself sink into his arms, his smell tingling her nose and making her heart rise. He still had that soapy scent from his morning shower. She rubbed her face against his skin.

He stroked her hair. "What's the matter?"

An image of Phina rose up in her mind, that woman putting her damn hands all over him. Anger moved through her and the words tumbled out of her mouth. "She can't touch you anymore. I don't want any woman touching you like that."

Stunned, she realized what she said. His lips kissed the sensitive skin on her inner wrist. He hesitated, looking regretfully towards Grace House. "They're waiting for me, but we'll talk after the healing, okay? I'll explain everything, I promise." He looked like he wanted to say more, but instead turned away.

A sudden fear came over her. He couldn't leave. Bryn came up behind him and slid her arms over his chest, resting her face in the nook between his shoulder blades. "Stop. Just wait a minute," she murmured against his back. "I need you."

Zander took a sharp breath. He turned and pushed her up against the cottage wall, pressing his body full against hers. He kissed her hungrily, his fingers in her hair as his tongue slid into her mouth. He tasted along the opening of her blouse and lingered on her neck. The hot breath made her dizzy.

"Feel it between us." He let out a short moan. "The connection. Feel it."

She drew back for air and he forced another kiss, knocking the breath out of her. Her hands fumbled around his waist and lifted his shirt, needing to touch him. Skin against skin. Her nails dug into his sides and he gasped. He lifted her hips and rocked her body against his. "Damn clothes," he growled. She laughed and kissed his lips, his nose, his chin, wanting every part of him.

He knelt down and lifted her blouse. Licking the bare skin at her waist, he teased her belly button, then lowered. His tongue moved along her inner thigh and her legs quivered. Bryn let out a deep moan, so deep she didn't recognize the sound. "I want more, more, *more*."

There was rustling along the sidepath. Someone was coming. Zander stood up and braced himself against the cottage wall. She pulled him to her. Her face nestled in his neck, craving Zander smell just one more time. He trailed kisses on her face, over her eyelids, finally resting his lips on her temple. He tried to break from her, but she held tight. That same feeling of apprehension rose in her. Something was wrong.

***

The late summer rains had left deep mud pits on these paths. Seth's cane kept sinking into them, and he had to jostle it free several times. He stopped and watched the young couple. From a distance, it appeared like any boy consoling his love. Zander leaned into her, as if he could absorb her sadness into himself. Seth looked up at the blue sky above, so deeply perplexed he remained motionless. Bittersweet, yes, but what was a simple love story compared to the movement of the great world?

He finally rustled forward, making enough noise to alert the pair. "It's time."

Zander tilted her face up to his. "I have to go."

He kissed her deeply, then finally released her. He joined Seth and they walked down the curve of the path, the boy's face strangely grief-stricken.

Zander put out his arm. "Stop."

"They're waiting for us."

"I know. I just, I've been meaning to apologize, Uncle Seth. I do respect your beliefs and I know you're only trying to help the Pensare and Grace House. I shouldn't have lost my temper. I didn't mean the things I said."

Seth patted the boy's shoulder. His hand shook a little and he pulled it back. "Of course, of course. You're passionate like your father. Like myself. Everything will be okay."

He repeated the phrase quietly to himself. "Everything will be okay."

Brit Malorie

Chapter 43

The two men went down to the hallway outside the traveling room. Zander waited until his uncle left him, then braced himself against the wall, so overwhelmed he couldn't breathe. Her lips flashed in his mind, the fierceness of her eyes, the scent of her hair that lingered on his hands. This was more.

Bryn. There was no one else for him. A simple fact, yet his entire life tilted. What other women came his way, the discoveries he made, the evil he faced, Zander knew this one thing in the deepest quiet of himself. He wished he could see their strands intertwining in the mesh. If he could just get through this healing they could start their lives together.

He entered the traveling room and Brecker called out to him, "You'll be over there much longer than the previous trips." The doctor was setting up equipment on the far side of the room. "It'll take a few hours to do the healing, then we'll have to re-group to bring you back."

Hadley poked her head into the room.

"Hey, can I talk to you?" Her chin trembled a little, and her eyes were rimmed pink.

Brecker let out a loud groan. "Hadley, you're supposed to be in with the Circle."

Zander knelt down before her. "What's going on?"

The girl glanced over at Brecker and hesitated. She cupped her hand over Zander's ear and whispered, "Don't go. Don't travel today."

He drew back, startled. "I thought you wanted me to help Tomas. You know how important this trip is."

"I know, I know." She looked down. "I thought that before, but I don't like it now." Her voice went even lower. "I'll get in trouble if I feel underneath my shield, but I can't help it. Something's wrong."

Zander hugged her. "I'll be alright. It's just like my other trips, okay? You can protect me through the Circle."

She shook her head vigorously. "No, it's not over there. You don't know—"

Brecker interrupted them. "Hadley, please go next door and get prepared. There's a slim window when the Lusha can help us."

There was a moment when her pale green eyes caught his and a thread of fear passed through Zander. What if she was right? What if there was something wrong? Maybe they should delay the healing. He looked up and she gave him one last smile. Then the door shut between them and his fear evaporated. She was a sweet kid but just a kid. Everything would be fine.

"You okay?" Brecker looked concerned. "What did Hadley want?"

"Nothing." Zander shook it off. "She's nervous, that's all." He lay back on the bed and remained still as Brecker checked his vitals. He winced as the IV was inserted, then witnessed the purple fluid enter his veins. The Recipe.

"Where did Dad find the Recipe?" he asked.

Brecker looked up sharply. "Oh, experimentation. Years of it. Many different combinations of chemicals."

Zander closed his eyes now during the fading process. It unnerved him to watch the colors leak out of people. His thoughts returned to the softness of Bryn's hair around his fingers, the heat of her mouth. If he could only make her happy, if he could. . . .

A few minutes later, his eyes opened to sparkle and light and shadow. He and Elder took the streamways to the Salire grove. The older man stayed on a small ridge along the periphery of the grove, several yards from the swarm. The violet sunrays gave a beautiful glow to the trees as the sun fell lower.

Zander picked up the sodium metal—silver-colored squares with a soft, clay-like texture that had to be stored in containers of mineral oil. Using tongs and a pair of flexible aluminum gloves, he walked around the grove and placed several squares into each ammonia pool. Hydrogen gas bubbled up and a vibrant indigo swirled through the yellowish liquid. He rejoined Elder and studied the bustling swarm. Every last one had to be distracted from the wound, and it needed to happen soon. It was dusk and the lights were pulling away from their places in the mesh. They'd return to Chalice soon and stay there for the night.

"Come on, come on. A delicious meal right there," he whispered. He could scarcely believe it, but one by one, the Vipera moved away from Tomas's strand. Some flew up into the sky to return to Dimora for the night. The others crept to the chemical pools, creating a dark ring around the perimeter of the grove. The last demon lingered, then finally disappeared into the sky.

"Now," he whispered.

Elder closed his eyes and let out series of short whistles, like a bird call. "Look up. You won't want to miss this," he said.

Zander held his breath as the sky filled with dozens of falling stars. The lights glowed against the violet dusk, swaying in the breeze. They came closer and he could feel their gentle warmth.

"The Lusha Descent. I've only seen it one other time, when a Salire had to be carried into the Calamata," Elder said.

The lights floated into a line formation, then weaved into a ring around Tomas's strand. A golden barrier of protection.

Elder motioned to the Lusha. "Now it's your turn. You have about an hour. Good luck." He handed Zander the flask of serum.

Zander nodded, anxiety clenching his stomach. Vipera kept shooting upward to head home for the night, and the remaining ones were still quite distracted by the pools. He stepped through the barrier and examined the Salire's base in the golden light of the Lusha. He couldn't believe his eyes. The fissure looked like it was drenched in rot. A heavy grey slime coated most of the inside. Zander started digging it out and carried it a few yards away. Underneath the grey was an even deeper rot, black pus. The smell was awful. Months of pain, suffering, and depression. He dug it all out and deposited it on the pile, then examined what was left. The damage was so deep it was tough to believe the serum would really do anything. The crack extended across the Salire's entire right side, then it went deep, past the six layers all the way to its core. Those monsters would continue to feed on the man, attracted to his pain, like predators stalking a wounded animal. The despair was so immense, it washed over Zander and pushed him back a few steps.

Then his fingertips caressed the Salire's core. The vibrations of Tomas's breathing. The sepia color in his eyes, the overwhelming sincerity. The gentle power of the man who had held him while he'd cried for his father. Zander uncapped the flask and poured serum along the edges of the fissure, then let the rest of it pool inside.

A sound he didn't recognize came from above. Seconds passed and he began to realize what was happening. It was a cracking sound. The Salire was structured like a massive oak. All that rot and slime had been holding its right side in place. But he'd dug it all out, and there was nothing there to hold the base together.

The bindings snapped above him. It was collapsing! Terror ran through him like a shockwave. Zander shoved his feet into the dirt and rammed his shoulder into the trunk. It was so heavy—he couldn't brace it for very long. He could feel the Circle: Hadley and Raleigh and Liz and Phina, all pressing upward with him. Zander felt a little give and he looked up. The top of the Salire had been hooked by one of the thicker bindings. The tree hovered in the air, the strand's loop around the top the only thing holding it up. The loop looked very strained. It could break at any moment.

There had to be something, dammit! He needed something to brace it. He wished fervently he'd brought wooden rods to pin the trunk in place, or some kind of sling. He shook as panic overwhelmed him. The loop will break and the Salire will crash and Tomas will die and he couldn't think, *dammit*. His heart was beating so fast and he couldn't think!

He closed his eyes. Everything disappeared, all the noise, all the animal life around him. One breeze passed through and he focused on its ripple through his form. Tomas's words came to him. The problem. There was only problem and solution. He opened his eyes and searched the grove. The simplest solution. It would have to be heavy and solid and . . . the dead Salire. One lay before him like a fallen oak tree covered in nitore flowers. Zander ran over and pulled up its end. It took all his strength to drag it over to Tomas. He lifted the end up as high as he could, then walked his hands downward to keep it hovering in the air. A final snap above him as the last binding broke. A loud cracking sound echoed through the grove, and the Lusha barrier shuddered. The top of the Salire fell about six inches and landed on the dead one. It held. Zander couldn't believe it. The dead Salire was shoved about two feet into the ground, but it held, bracing up Tomas.

It wouldn't be enough. He had to tie them together somehow so their weights balanced each other. Dead strands lay around him. They looked like broken vines. He quickly grabbed one and wrapped it around the bases of both Salires, then continued the process with another dozen. He layered the dead strands strategically over Tomas's wound so they worked like a bandage, shielding it.

He finished just as the first Lusha shot up into the sky. In a series of sparks, the rest of the angels followed. Zander hurried out to the periphery of the grove and joined Elder.

"Will it hold?" he murmured. After the last light was gone, the Vipera drifted back over to the wound, pouring over the trunk like a wave of oil. But they couldn't break through the bandage.

Elder looked at him with gratitude. "I can't believe I witnessed all that. I wish I could have helped you."

"We had no idea of how bad the damage was. It was stupid. We should have brought more tools, like rods or—"

The older man placed a hand on his shoulder. "You were amazing. Such courage. Jason couldn't have done a better job."

Zander turned back to the grove, pride rising in his heart. He looked upon the giant triangle—the two Salires bracing each other up and the dead strands forming a bandage across the bottom.

"But what will actually heal Tomas?"

"Now that it's covered, the Salire will heal from the inside, just like the human body. The serum and the beneficial nesso bacteria will help."

"I can't believe I had an impact on all those lives," Zander said. He looked at the top of Tomas's strand, all the coils pouring out and linking into the mesh. "All those people and everyone they're connected to."

He thought of Bryn and warmth rushed his heart. He could have it all—heal in Maglia and give her a wonderful life.

***

Seth limped down to the basement. He waited just inside the laboratory until he saw the nurse, Caroline, leave the traveling room. Moving slowly with his cane, he braced himself against the wall, then entered.

He watched Zander dream quietly in bed. Slow, deep breaths. Seth flipped the alarm off on the EKG. He stood rigid as precious seconds went by. The research required great decisions. Heartbreaking ones. He'd prayed for weeks now and received no answer.

His nephew slept, peaceful, his eyelids fluttering. Zander appeared to love Maglia above all else. He'd be grateful for a chance to stay there permanently, living in the Lord's beauty, appreciating His creation. It would be sad, the Pensare would grieve, but there would be some wonderful benefits. The boy would live among the strands for years in a place very close to heaven. The big decisions would be left to the remaining members, like who obtained ultimate control over the research.

And which organizations were invited in. His nephew's words resonated in his mind: "That means less God, not more." And that glance of pity.

Sweat formed around his neck. Had this room always felt so small? There had to be another way. Maybe he should just talk with the boy more and change his heart gradually. Yes, that was the answer. Seth headed to the doorway. The Lord would help him to slowly open up the boy's mind.

He paused by the door. But what if this was the right path for Zander? Out of the boy's greatest pain would rise his greatest triumph. His life could truly mean something, like Elder's. He could do so much more if he were permanently in Maglia. When Calvin traveled, instead of competing, the two cousins would help and support each other, one in Maglia, one at home.

It made so much sense in his head that Seth ignored his heart just this once. He picked up a small pillow from the end of the bed. It would only take a minute.

As he dragged one foot forward, then the other, he didn't think of his own son. He didn't think of God or the Church. He thought of his brother. *Forgive me, Jason.*

Brit Malorie

Chapter 44

Lynch popped his head out from the tunnel and surveyed the same reddish-orange clay walls from Palefu's memory. And just like in the memory, the walls appeared impenetrable. They were concave, rounding into each other and into the floor and ceiling, creating the feeling that one was inside an enormous bubble. Palefu must have thought it was another optical illusion; that's why he'd felt down every inch, but there were no crevices or cracks.

Lynch separated the room into small squares and stepped on each one, then shined the headlamp and blew air on the clay. The door mechanism might be activated by light, smell, air flow. Searching the great expanse of clay, he worried he would miss the mechanism because it all looked the same. He stepped back—wait. The tiniest sound. It wasn't as loud as a click, more like a shift in the air. Had he imagined it? He stepped forward, then back again. No click. He waited a few moments, then tried again on the same spot. Nothing. Aggravated, he did another turn around the room, trying to remember the exact order. It must be weight distribution. And due to Damaris's small stature, it would be the slightest shift. A man of Palefu's size and strength stepped without finesse, stomping his way around. His large weight would depress the mechanism too far, resulting in an unsolvable puzzle.

Lynch studied the floor very carefully. The mechanism was so subtle, the floor must curve at almost imperceptible degrees. And it wouldn't be a simple floor mechanism; it would probably be a sequence of specific weight shifts on the floor and against the wall. After another hour of studying the floor and walls minutely, he could see how the junction between the eastern-most wall and the floor had this one place, yes. The section dipped about twenty degrees lower than it should when compared with the rest of the room. Lynch moved his foot to the edge of the space and dragged it gently over the floor, while simultaneously brushing his hand over the wall right above it. Nothing happened. He sighed. It would take hours, but he'd have to repeat the process over every inch of the room. And he didn't know if it might be a much more complex combination of steps and brushes in sequence. He tried it again, this time placing slightly more weight on the indent, then pressed harder with his hand.

His hand grasped something different this time—a lever? The smallest panel of rock, only a quarter of an inch thick, blended seamlessly into the wall, another optical illusion. Lynch felt around it, then slowly rotated the lever. The rock slid away from the surrounding walls. He slid through and found himself in another rock cavern. He followed it to the end and discovered a basket, similar to one for a hot-air balloon. He climbed into the basket and it rose.

Quickly, he calculated his location on the island. He'd pushed himself down into the clay room, about ten feet, then horizontally walked about two hundred feet until he came to the basket. Now he was rising several feet per second. But he could see through the walls, so he couldn't be inside a cliff. There were no buildings this height on Kadera. The cracks grew wider, and there were flashes of green and brown, and the sound of birds. Sunlight and warm air passed over his skin.

The basket came to rest and Lynch climbed out. He entered a large room shaped like an octagon. Each of the eight walls had a small porthole window in the center. The ceiling was made of several layers of clear glass. It was mid-morning, and the sky spread wide-open above him, no clouds, just a great stretch of fresh blue. Lynch made it to the closest window. Of course! The grand tree in the center of Kadera. The trunk was over fifty feet in diameter and rose two thousand feet above sea level to jut out above the forest canopy. From the outside, one could only see the thick vines that spiraled up the trunk diagonally and thousands of branches, nests, and great palm leaves. The grand tree had always been a mystery, but now he knew it wasn't a tree at all. At some point in history, the tree had been hollowed out, and this room at the top oversaw the entire island.

Most of the room was taken up by an enormous stone basin. Lynch touched the oily liquid inside it. A heavy fragrance emanated from the basin—flowers and herbs cascaded along the bottom. On each of its sides a marble column rose and connected to the glass ceiling.

Curtains surrounded a doorway on the southern wall. Lynch tried the door and it was locked, but next to it was a square panel. He opened the panel and revealed two horizontal switches. He flipped the first switch. Nothing happened. Then he looked closer at the glass ceiling. There were threads of metal woven into the glass and they were flashing with subtle sparks. He flipped the second switch. The oily liquid traveled up from the basin into each column, then up into miniscule grooves cut through the glass above. The liquid met the electrical current.

Lynch stared upward, straining. It took several minutes, but the blue of the sky faded away, replaced by something so strange . . . it was impossible. He couldn't understand what he saw next.

Brit Malorie

Chapter 45

Anxiety entered the Circle. Hadley first sensed it as a gray thread looping around and around. The thread expanded and washed out the color. They'd have to release soon; the energy was no longer pure. Hadley sent a thought to Liz. *I can't find him. Can you look?* A few minutes passed, and she felt Liz's grip on her hand tighten. Three taps in her palm—the signal to release. She descended to Prima positive, the upper levels still heavy on her mind.

Dr. Brecker stood near them, his hands flailing. "I don't understand what happened. That stupid nurse left him alone."

"We can't pull him out. We can't even find him," Liz said, her mouth twisted in concern.

"According to the EKG, he stopped breathing for about a minute. Now you're telling me his mind is trapped over there?" He slammed the table and Hadley winced. She was always left raw after the release, sensitive to light and sound. How had she lost Zander? She'd been focused on the brittle red spot—he was right there. Then the spot simply flickered out. Was she too distracted with the healing?

"You can't find him?" Hadley asked, her voice wavering.

Liz stroked her hair. "We'll find him, honey. We have to think of him like Elder now and not try to pull him out, just communicate. Rest a few minutes. We'll need your full strength."

Hadley laid her head on the oak table. He must be so scared. She should have refused to do the Circle until they listened to her.

***

Zander brushed off his face. A glimmer of heat passed close to him then faded. Then it drew close again. He opened his eyes. The last thing he remembered was talking to Elder, then everything went dark.

Griffin fluttered next to him. "Can't you be something else?" he asked grimly.

The point of light expanded into a ball. The ball morphed four stout legs, floppy ears, and a long snout. The thing let out a hoarse bark.

"You're the strangest looking dog I've ever seen, but it fits," he chuckled. Shadows and lights buzzed in the mesh high above him, but it felt empty, like sitting silent in a crowd of people.

"Do you know why the Circle hasn't lifted me out of here yet?" he asked.

Griffin shook his head and long strings of drool flew from his mouth. "Where's Elder?"

To his thinking place, Halo, to be alone.

"Where's his thinking place?"

The Lusha whined and scratched his dangling ear with his hindleg. Zander groaned. This felt ridiculous, like arguing with a real dog.

"Come on. I refuse to hang out in the Lost & Found," he demanded.

Griffin let out a loud bark and Zander winced. The dog took off on a sprint across the cloud cover. He tried to keep up, but he felt strangely exhausted.

The dog stopped near a circular opening under a ledge. Zander crawled inside, the vapor pulling at him like taffy. He entered an enclosure with a dense cloud over it. A nitrogen pool trickled softly in the center. He realized that for the first time in Maglia, he felt still. No whirling vortexes, no scattered Lusha or engorging Vipera. No whispering strands. Quiet.

Dad had documented Halo's in his notebooks; they were secluded places where a traveler could feel anxious or worried without fear of attracting the Vipera. Elder sat silent in a meditation pose.

Zander?

"Hadley? What happened?"

Are you okay? We couldn't find you.

"I think I'm alright. I'm moving pretty slow since the healing. What's Elder doing?"

He's communicating with some of the higher Lusha. There's a. . . problem.

"Can you pull me out now? I'll talk to Elder later about his obnoxious pet." Griffin perked up.

Should I tell him? How do I—

"Tell me what? Hadley!" he shouted. What the hell was going on? Anxiety trickled through his gut. This was more than just the healing.

Something happened to your body here. We're not sure how, but you stopped breathing and slipped into a coma.

"Is this a joke, Hadley? I know you're upset, but it's not funny or cute."

No, it's real. Elder's asking the Archlusha how to get you home.

Revelation seared through him. Zander fell to his knees, sinking deeply into the cloud cover. He was really trapped here. Oh, dear God. Had this happened because of the healing? Were the Archlusha angry that he interfered?

"I can't be trapped here, Hadley," he called out in a panicked voice. They'd figure it out, they had to. The little girl's warning played again in his head. He'd been too distracted, he'd just written her fears off as childish. What was going to happen to him?

Elder finally shook himself out of his meditation. He startled when he saw Zander.

"Follow me," he said. They left the Halo and walked back up to the streamways. "You have three days, then the forces will hold you here permanently."

"Three days for what?"

"You need a dose of Settimo positive on this side."

"The highest energy level? The one we've never achieved back home?" Zander asked. "Where the hell do we get it?"

"Only the Archlusha can infuse you with Settimo positive. The highest order of Lusha."

"Okay, great, let's have Griffin call one of them."

They found the dog lying on his belly, panting happily. He sat up and tried to lick Zander's face. It was a slobbery mess of gas and light until Zander pushed him off.

"You must remember," Elder said softly. "The Archlusha can't travel out here. They're so powerful they'd damage large sections of the mesh." The man's jawline had this tension in it that Zander really didn't like. "I was hoping I wouldn't have to show you this yet."

They floated on the streamways until Elder directed them to the steepest cliff and they landed. "We have to be very careful up here!" he shouted.

The great length of the mesh rose above Zander, spanning as far as he could see. Billions of strands curled and weaved through the canopy. A whirling sound surrounded them, like a hurricane.

Far below the Sorrelle and the mesh, a massive vortex spun. Zander had seen photographs of black holes from deep space, but this seemed darker because of the movement, like an inky whirlpool. The Calamata.

"That's where we go when we die?" He shivered violently. As they stood there, hundreds of strands broke free of the mesh and plunged into the vortex. The vivid colors of each strand faded into the darkness as they spun into oblivion.

"Yes, the Calamata. It is Afterlife," Elder said, his voice low and full of reverence. "The immense gravity is designed to pull the strand towards its center. Can you feel the force from here?" he asked. Zander watched gas particles from his form float away from him. He took a step back.

"But the strands have to make it past the two rings first." Elder pointed to a line of fiery red that encircled the darkness. "The Crimson Ring is the boundary of the Calamata, the point of no return. It's very thin, only a couple of feet across. Once a soul crosses that, there's no going back. It's released into death."

"How do all the creatures and the strands resist getting sucked into the vortex?" Zander asked. It was on the tip of his memory.

"The answer is the Valley," Elder replied, pointing to a much wider ring the color of slate gray that surrounded the crimson line.

"That's right. The Valley is a deep well full of ash and dust, built up over time. It acts as a buffer, insulating the gravitational pull of the vortex," Zander said. "It makes me think of 'Ye though I walk through the Valley of the Shadow of Death' and all that."

"Yes. Jason believed some of the Biblical authors were travelers and near-deaths."

Zander could make out slight gradations amid the whirling circles. The rim traveled downward. *The damn thing pulls you in.* His eyelids were strangely heavy, but he couldn't close them. *The Calamata.*

"Don't look too long." A hand passed in front of his vision. "The Calamata is meant to attract the strands after they're cut, but it works on us as well."

Zander shook himself out of it. He could have fallen right off the edge; the Calamata was that hypnotizing.

Elder paused. He seemed to be avoiding Zander's gaze.

"Why are you showing me this now?" he asked quietly.

The older man took a deep breath. "You have to see this because that's where you have to go. The Archlusha stay in the Valley. It's the only way to get home."

"And if I fall into the Calamata?" he asked.

"You won't make it back. Your mind's gone forever."

Zander resisted one last glance towards the beckoning dark. The two men made it to the streamways and floated back up, heading as close to the center of the mesh as possible. Elder told him some strategies to survive. "Your toughest problem will be keeping your form intact despite the strong Valley winds, so you'll have to bury yourself deep into the layers of ash and dust at the bottom."

"Bury myself," he muttered. He thought about his studies, what he'd learned about the Valley. He tried to envision the place. Hurricane-like winds, the gray mountains of dust that drenched everything. The enormous gravity of the vortex just inside in the Valley's center. Death. Strands couldn't even resist its tremendous pull. He tried to understand what he might have to do.

He lowered his voice, looking out to their destination. "The Valley's very dangerous, right? I could be pulled apart by the winds. I could fall into the vortex. I could die."

Elder listened quietly.

Zander swallowed hard. "If I manage to make it out alive, I could still wake up at home with my mind damaged, like I've had a stroke." He shook his head, murmuring. "I'm afraid."

The older man smiled gently. "Of course you are. You have a choice. Maglia is full of wondrous life. You could always stay and help me here. But I must be honest with you, Zander. I miss people. It's like a knife deep in my heart every single day. If you have a chance, you must take it."

Zander nodded. He wanted to believe that he had the courage to get home, but deep inside he wondered. Would he be able to step into the gray winds when the time came?

On the second day, close to dusk, they climbed the nearest ledge to mark their progress. Elder pointed to the gray patch in the distance. "You'll make it, just barely. I know you're exhausted, but we have to keep going."

Zander looked down and caught motion from below the ridge. He leaned over the edge.

"Hey, there's someone here," he shouted. "There's someone here!" A young man, dressed in a ripped t-shirt and shorts, paced about twenty yards below them. Elder studied the figure.

"Should we talk to him?" Zander asked excitedly. Another traveler?

"It doesn't look like he heard you," Elder said in relief. "Stay away from him. You must stay away from anything in human form."

"Why? How long has he been here? Maybe he can help us."

Elder's face turned sad. "He only crossed a few minutes ago. And he won't be able to help anyone." Griffin floated near them.

"Why?" Zander was confused. The guy wandered in a daze, calling out for help, obviously upset. Upset. Pockets of dark hovered over him, spiraling down the mesh.

"Hey! Over here," he stood up and yelled. The man turned.

"What are you doing? Get down!" Elder hissed.

"They're coming." He sped along the cliff's edge. He had to warn him. Maybe if he could just touch the guy, pass some positive into him.

"Stay away from him!" Elder shouted.

Zander ran down the incline but couldn't stop at the bottom. He tumbled, flailing as he tried to catch himself. The man came up too fast, it was all a blur, he was going to hit him—

They collided. The loud smack of air hitting air, then images surged through him. *The beach, he's on the beach, the smell of fire, kids chattering, birds swooping down. He's being dragged somewhere, underground, the tunnels stretched long and black, volcanic rock. His muscles won't stop shivering. Green glass everywhere, mud on his body, pain like needles through his skin, he can hear screaming. Someone hovers over him, muttering. Thin. A thin place. . . .*

Zander startled as the man pulled away and the images stopped.

"Where am I?" the man pleaded. "I just want to go back."

"You have to let go of the fear," he said, utterly bewildered. Were those his memories somehow?

The ebony streaks formed a funnel shape above them. The Vipera were coming. It was too late.

The man trembled, his eyes searching Zander's. "How do I get back to the island?"

305

"The island?" His stomach seized. *Don't say it*, he thought. *Don't say*—

"Kadera. I don't understand how I got here," the guy looked up at the sky. His teeth chattered and he clawed at his own skin, dragging through the particles. "They mentioned something about a road. Another road to here. To whatever this place is."

Then the man looked above and shrieked, but the sound masked was by an ominous growling, like thunder roaring down.

It was too late. Shadows snaked down from the funnel and burrowed into the man's ears, his eyes, his gut. His form exploded in shards of black and gray. Darkness everywhere, chilled, sucking the positive miran out of Zander's form. He couldn't escape.

"Griffin!" he screamed. Elder pulled him backward and cowered. Dozens of lights darted in to form a shield above them. Vipera smashed into the barrier. Zander covered his ears, the noise tearing him apart.

Chapter 46

It was so impossible, like nothing he'd ever seen. He couldn't understand. They crisscrossed above Lynch, creating tangles and connections. The blue had disappeared, the sky swarmed by these strange vines. It was filled with light and radiance, too bright for his eyes.

He heard a sound near the doorway. Damaris stood there, watching him. "I'm impressed. Obviously, we need to up our security measures. Grace didn't know about the enclave. How did you discover it?"

"Palefu. He stumbled on it in his lagoon." Lynch motioned his head upward. He spoke slowly. "What is it?"

"It's called Vita Maglia," Damaris replied. "It's a newly discovered layer to the planet, a sort of ecosystem that protects human souls."

"Those lines you see," he pointed to a cluster of vines, "they're called strands. Each strand is a person's emotional life enclosed in chemicals and a solid fibrous core. Kadera is very close to this layer, the closest to it on earth in fact. It's why we can transfer emotion fluidly through the skin, why our senses are mixed up, why the island's physics are altered."

"We send people to Maglia, but they're torn apart." Damaris pointed to a dark patch in the mesh. "Torn apart by those things. A half-animal, half-demon creature called a Vipera. They're attracted to the negative energy. Anxiety, depression, anguish. In fact, I just left a particularly brutal shredding." He paused. "I could see Zander through the man's eyes as he died."

"Zander?"

"He goes there. Or his mind does anyway. His father could as well." Damaris grimaced. "Even if our guys manage to avoid these creatures, within a few minutes their bodies give out."

The strands faded away, along with the lights and the dark patches. Lynch was actually disappointed to see simple blue sky again.

"It heals itself so quickly," Damaris murmured. "The Veil."

"You said that before."

"Yes. With the glass panel."

"What happened then? Was it this place?"

"It's Maglia, but a different region. What you saw on the glass panel, all the shades of black? Dozens of Vipera, swirling in great cyclones on the outskirts of Dimora, the Viperian city. Sometimes one even has the strength to reach through the glass. There are different methods to penetrate the dimension. We use gamma radiation sometimes. Also electrical surges and herbs."

"Did you discover this? Did Zander?"

"No, no," Damaris chuckled. "The Polynesian natives on this island discovered Maglia over two hundred years ago. They traveled by ingesting the island's minerals but could only see the dimension for a few seconds at a time. Fleeting glimpses of the mesh. Never enough time, never enough protection from the demons."

He sighed. "Then Zander's father arrived. He worked with some of our people here, people you will meet very soon." His eyes moved to the doorway. "They made great strides with him and nearly opened a permanent route."

Damaris knelt down by the oily liquid in the basin. He tapped his fingertips on the surface and it rippled outward. "Then the man betrayed us, setting us back for decades. Stealing our ingredients and ideas." He clenched his fist and his jaw tightened. "And for the final straw, Jason Grace strengthened the barrier between Kadera and Maglia. It's taken us seventeen damn years to wear it down again."

Lynch smiled. "Sounds like quite the bastard."

"Oh, we took revenge." Damaris gave a little smile of his own. "But we need his son. Zander holds his father's secrets."

He stepped towards the door. "I'm glad you passed this test. The experiments will be much easier with your help. Come. I'll show you everything we've discovered up to this point. And there's someone you should meet. She's just returned from long travels abroad."

Brit Malorie

Chapter 47

When everything finally quieted, he opened his eyes. The Vipera and Lusha were gone. "I can't believe that just happened."

Elder steadied his breathing. "You have so much to learn."

Zander softened. "I'm really sorry. I thought we could save him."

"I know. The human condition. It hurts, but you can't do anything. The Vipera swarm so quickly."

"Who was he?"

"I'm sure the Pensare mentioned there are routes we haven't discovered yet. Zombie travelers are people that accidentally travel. They cross over from accidental energy surges and thin places in the Veil."

"Thin places. Where are they?" Zander asked slowly.

Elder shrugged. "I don't know, there's only a handful over the earth. They're usually surrounded by lots of rumor, migration, sacred rituals. The Bermuda Triangle might have been a thin place once. That would explain the missing ships and planes, the loss of time reported by pilots. Stonehenge as well, back in prehistoric times."

"Yes," Zander said. He remained on his knees, discovery rushing his mind. "It explains everything. Kadera's a thin place in the Veil. The twisted senses, the crazy sunsets, the feeling you know someone deeply. The invisible creatures that claw and scratch. And if the Veil's thin, that means—"

Elder finished his thought. "People can cross there. Accidentally . . . or on purpose."

"My father went to Kadera seventeen years ago. He must have heard rumors about traveling, about movement through dimensions. He must have discovered the Recipe there."

Elder's eyes grew wide. "Are you sure—"

Zander didn't hear him. "They're sending these poor kids over, but they're destroyed by the Vipera as soon as they cross. Somehow they learned who I am, that Jason was my father. That's the reason for the protective order. That's why they sent Lynch after me."

Elder paused. "If the Veil's thin, this place should also be thin between people. Between living things. The slippage of emotions. People might appear psychic."

"Yes, boundaries disappear on the island. I can't believe I didn't see it. I lived there for a year and it's like this fog descended over me."

"Zander," Elder got his attention, his eyes urgent. "You know these people. If they're able to create a stable doorway, what will they do to Maglia?"

He took a deep breath. "You can't imagine. I have to get home and tell the Pensare. We can't let them through."

The two men walked all the next day, stopping just before dusk. Elder stood silent, peering into the haze. Gray walls rose in the distance.

"I'm afraid I have to leave you now," Elder said. "I'm too weak to go any closer to the Valley. I also have to alert the Archlusha to this new threat."

Zander nodded. He'd noticed that every time the man moved, particles scattered from his form like he was shaking out dust.

Elder smiled half-heartedly. "I wish I could reassure you." He paused. "I sensed your feelings for Bryn a long time ago. Perhaps I can give you a reason to go on?" He reached out and brushed Zander's chest with his hand. Zander closed his eyes as images and emotions flooded him.

He can smell, hear: *tiny fingers, freckles scattered over her button nose, her hands in fists on toddler hips. Defiant, bold. "No, that's mine, Daddy."*

Sun. Bryn splashes him on a California beach, her tanned ten-year-old legs pouncing on small waves. She glares at him, a look that rivals sunlight, orders him to stay, not just in the water, Daddy. Stay forever. Don't leave again, for stupid science again. Ferocious sobs shake her small body. Who is this forceful child? She demands a normal father, to be rid of this imposter. He stays very near, returning her splashes until her eyes grow heavy. He wraps her in a beach towel and carries her home to her pink Barbie bed. But don't you know, Brynsie? You're my heart, walking away from me. Her bottom lip trembles and he doesn't want to go. Now she's thirteen, her face simmering in anger. Nothing he does, nothing he says is ever right. She yells at him for always leaving, always being gone. He finds her before his flight to Japan, her fist clutching something to her chest, a secret that will haunt her forever. On the beach in Japan, when his heart is collapsing, he opens the bottle and knows. She flushed his heart medication, his pills. . . .

Zander fell to his knees on the cloud cover. He missed all the Bryn's: toddler, child, woman. Everything was clear now—why she refused to travel, why she wouldn't see her father. Ten years later, the guilt still ate her alive. Guilt over a rash decision made when she was a petulant teenage girl.

Griffin whined softly next to him.

He stood up, then teetered forward on weakened legs. He had to get home.

Brit Malorie

Chapter 48

As the Valley edged closer, depression sunk into Zander so deeply he wasn't sure he could go on. When he came up to that wall, would he be able to cross it? Was he about to lose everything he'd found since returning home? A real family, a new purpose for his life. Falling in love for the first time . . . just to lose her forever?

The night grew very dark. He must be close to the Valley, but he couldn't see anything. Even Griffin's light dimmed. The poor Lusha needed rest in Chalice, but he stayed with Zander, ever loyal.

Silence. But Zander heard something. It sounded like whispers. That name again . . . Adriel.

The dog's body went rigid. He erupted into a flurry of barks.

Zander startled as a form solidified in the dark. A man walked towards them. His pants were held up by suspenders and he wore a white cotton shirt. His face was utterly smooth, his hair slicked back under a fedora hat.

The man moved his fingers in a circle. The Lusha's barks diminished, then stopped as the dog became drowsy. He rested his head down in slumber. Wasn't there a warning from Elder? Yes, something about humans in Maglia. The man motioned for Zander to sit down on a nearby embankment, then joined him.

He found it difficult to speak. "Did you hurt Griffin?"

The man smiled. "I don't like being barked at like a common intruder."

"I'm not supposed to talk to you."

"Yes, well, Mr. Sansa and I, we never could come to an understanding. The elderly are so resistant to change. The young are a bit more malleable."

The man studied him. "I bet your mentor tells you almost nothing. Ten years isn't a long time here. Look at me, I've been around longer than the human brain can comprehend." He shook his head. "You're all so temporary."

Low whispers filled the back of Zander's mind. He shook himself, but they remained.

"Adriel," Zander said uneasily.

"Yes, that is what you may call me." The man smiled again, and Zander felt warmth bubble up inside. "So, what do you think of her? The great and wondrous Vita Maglia."

"It's beyond belief."

"Mag's a special girl but a little boring with the years, like a long marriage. Now, your dimension, Home, as you call it—that's real progress."

"Are you a Vipera?"

Adriel leaned back and clutched his gut, roaring with laughter. Zander blushed. "No, I am Lerium. We don't take sides."

"Lerium?"

"A strand has seven layers. The Lerium are sleep creatures that work through the dream layer. We care for the strands at night while the Lusha and the Vipera rest."

The two men were bathed in Griffin's light as he slept at their feet, snarling and whining in his dreams. Zander looked down. His legs felt far away as they swung back and forth, his form rocked to sleep, his mind wrapped in lullaby. A presence crawled heavy in his head. Something alive pulled at strings of information, searching for just the right one.

"Ah, someone's attempting a connection. Trying to save your life, I imagine. And the other one . . . so that's what they're up to. Maybe they need a little help," Adriel murmured.

Zander reached out to connect with the other man's mind but was only allowed on the periphery. *Damn Jason, almost had that one. Still have to figure out how he died, but his son is better, Elder and his silly deal with the Lusha.*

"What deal?" Zander asked.

"Tsk tsk. You shouldn't intrude in the minds of others. It's rude." Adriel wiggled a finger at him. "Then again, it's not like there's a skull around your thoughts here." He laughed again, his mouth opening far too wide. Zander joined in and rolled on the waves of laughter, like he was having a beer with friends. Why didn't Elder like this guy? Why— His thought evaporated. Couldn't he just curl up right here? Rest his head. . . .

Adriel waved his hand in front of Zander's fluttering eyelids. "You should stay awake for this part. Annoying side effect, I know."

"What deal did Elder make with the Lusha?" he asked.

"The same deal your friends will make with the Vipera."

"My friends?" Zander searched for who the man could mean. "Kadera?"

"You knew all along, of course. Just needed a spark to light up all those clues."

Adriel looked around. "There's been rumblings for a few years. The poor kids they send over are destroyed here and left brain-dead at home. Mag's natural resistance to intruders. You are the bacteria in the system."

His voice lowered as if telling a secret. "But if they get ahold of Masterfade, different story, yes."

"Wait," Zander stiffened. "What do you mean?"

Adriel smirked. "The Great Masterfade. Well, some use it as a term for death. Or it could be—"

"The device. It's real?"

"It's just a myth." Adriel winked. "A device that lets the user travel between dimensions, regardless of genes or tricks or open roads. If it were real, it'd be quite powerful. Your friends would have unlimited access." He leaned in.

The light created such strange illusions on the man's face, like he was changing, morphing into new people. The smooth skin rippled outward, like liquid silver. His voice also changed subtly, like he was trying on different accents, ages. "By the way, your friends are already searching for it. Any day now."

"What will they do to Maglia?"

Adriel smirked. "Oh, you know that better than anyone. Cause havoc, misery, suffering. Blacken entire sections of the mesh. The Vipera could use a few travelers on their side. Devastating weapons you all can be." He nodded. "Of course, you can run and hide and leave the fight to the Lusha, and that may work—but at the cost of strands." He sighed loudly and inspected his hands. "So many souls torn to shreds."

"What can I do?" Zander asked.

"If Masterfade exists, it's remained hidden for hundreds of years. Last I heard, a little European town—Well, perhaps I shouldn't say. Not sure I can trust you." Adriel wiggled a finger at him. "Although I'd hate for someone else to get *her* hands on it."

"Please."

Adriel relayed fragments, a couple of names. "Don't worry about holding onto those. You'll remember if the time comes."

"If?"

"If you make it home. Tick Tock."

A short clicking noise sounded behind them. Adriel peered into the darkness. "Mmm . . . I must be going. Traveling, traveling. We'll meet again."

He stood up and brushed Griffin's light off his pants in swift, irritated motions.

The clicking sound grew louder. The man tilted his head at a strange angle. "We're friends then, you and I?"

"Yes." Zander's throat felt parched.

"Excellent." Adriel tipped his hat and moved his left hand in a circle. Zander wondered if it was a dream and closed his eyes.

The next morning, he awoke and recoiled in shock. A wall of pewter gray stood before him, climbing in all directions forever. He was about to ask Griffin if there were some way to cross it when the wall moved. Only then did he realize it was spinning so fast it appeared solid. Above him were powerful clashes of lightning. Peals of thunder shook the cloud cover beneath his feet. A perpetual thunderstorm, one that rooted him to the ground. Griffin barked to pull his attention away.

Don't look too long. It's the Great War.

"That's a war?"

The war between the Archlusha and the Archvipera for control of Maglia. It rages on in eternity under the Sorrelle.

Zander's eyes could just make out the great orb floating above the flashes.

"What now?" he asked.

We go through the wall.

"You'll call out to the Archlusha once we cross?"

Yes. I hope she's in a good mood. I'll need help getting out too.

"Do you really think she'll help us?"

The Lusha looked away. That sinking feeling again. Once he entered the Valley, he'd have no protection from Griffin and he couldn't make it back out if the Archlusha abandoned him.

How could he have been so reckless before? Getting so deep into drugs, breaking his father's heart. Now he was about to lose everything he loved—Bryn, Hadley, Grace House. His life.

The Lusha's golden body flattened into a vertical disc. *Now.*

His desire to live, his courage, everything diminished. His feet failed him. He couldn't move.

"You have to." His teeth clenched down. "You have to. There's no choice. You have to get home. You're the only one that can stop them."

Fear paralyzed Zander, but a greater fear made him move again. An alliance between the Vipera and the evil on Kadera would work unfathomable destruction here. A madman like Lynch was only the beginning. Millions of souls would be lost. He had to protect Maglia.

Zander willed his foot forward. One step, then another. The golden disc wrapped around his body, coating him in a sphere. For the first time in three days, he felt safe. Safe inside his guardian angel.

Chapter 49

Gray swirls pummeled the outside of the sphere. They penetrated the wall in seconds, and the gleam grew distant as Griffin left to search for the Archlusha. It was surprisingly warm. His ears and nose and mouth were buried in heaps of dust. The winds toppled him over and Zander crawled. He dug himself deeper into the heavy dirt layer on the Valley floor.

His hand caught on a strand and foreign emotions spiked through him. There were probably thousands of them in this place, caught here in the bizarre limbo between life and death. But he couldn't stay still. The winds kept pushing him forward. He kept crawling for what seemed like hours. Where was Griffin? How much time had passed?

Silence. Zander looked up, startled by the loss of sound. The winds were gone. Somehow he'd passed into an inner region of the Valley. There were no strands here. Shivers went down his back. The stillness was eerie. He stayed here, waiting, until he noticed his hand. It moved in slow motion. Something was very wrong. His foot. He tried to step with his foot but it moved too slowly. The quiet felt heavy and deep and impenetrable, as if he were standing on the darkened ocean floor with miles of water on every side. Then the realization came to him. His feet, dear God, his feet were moving backward. On their own. Something pulled him against his will. He didn't understand what was happening. Then he turned around. Red floated before him. He was too close. He screamed but no sound came. His strength was nothing compared to the immense gravity as the Crimson Ring dragged him forward.

Zander screamed again, his mouth open as he clawed at the muck on the Valley floor. The blood-red ribbon loomed closer—the Point of No Return. The red was so thin he could see the ebony behind it, a solid black. The Calamata. Death. His legs crossed into the vortex, then his hips, then his chest. His mind broke apart. He'd never make it home.

Brit Malorie

Chapter 50

It was midnight at Grace House. Bryn woke up, her body painful with exhaustion. She took the elevator to the basement. It had been three days since Zander's accident and she hadn't allowed herself to cry. She felt that if she could just hold her tears inside, she could still lie and dream and hope a little longer. The lights were dimmed in the traveling room. Brecker lay asleep in the chair, his head resting at an uncomfortable angle.

Zander looked peaceful, but something had happened. She could feel his strand through hers. He was dying and there was nothing she could do. Her knees hit the floor. She understood her mother's grief now. How she could bury herself in a man, how a love could run that deep.

She crawled up onto the bed and fit her body alongside his, searching for his scent. All that met her was antiseptic sting. Fury blinded her, her muscles trembling. Why should they have to lose their lives for this? The damn research that consumed everything around it. Promises crossed her lips. If he'd just wake up, she'd go far away with him. They'd leave Grace House and build a life together. He'd never go through this again.

Bryn rested her face in the hollow of his neck. Her body curved into his like a vine climbing a tree, reaching for the sun. Her lips moved with no sound. *I need you.*

Brit Malorie

Chapter 51

Light pierced the interminable gray. Dust shimmered with specks of dove pearl and honey flax. Sunrise loomed, the most spectacular he'd ever see. Griffin's twinkle warmed him on his right side, but the light above was purer, thinner somehow. This was death. He'd never see anyone he loved ever again. A voice trickled down his consciousness like water, free-flowing and pooling in the broken places.

"First of all, sorry. They'll tell you I'm not a quick sort of chick. Griffin's a shy and reluctant boy but still my fave." Sweet laughter rolled from the light. "Damn, why am I awake at this hour? Zander love, always trying to find his way back home. Even when he is home."

If he focused, he could make out blond hair, the cool weight of it edging out a face. Lips moving fast, not waiting for him to catch up.

"Anyway, hi! They call me Aron Alyce. Twill be interesting to see your new chance play out. The Chosen One brings balance to the Force and all that." Zander's heart inflated in his chest until he thought he'd burst apart. Lungs and legs and wonderful, whole brain. She was infusing him with Settimo positive. "Hey kid, relax this time. Bounce the weight of the world off. Listen to danceables. Explore all the countryness you can handle. I've eaten lots of tasties I should not tell you about—ox stomach, pigs' feet, chicken feet, fish skin. Dried seaweed. Saturate the sensicals. Yep. What you've done is never enough."

The Archlusha's light waned. He reached for it. "The trick is not to capture the flame, nada. Settle yourself in, warm your hands. Let go."

"Yay for rebellious punk sons and clutchety old men, for golden puppies and sunshine in the chill of spring. Yay for delicate girls that aren't fixable. Mamacita and Dadders are waiting for you in the next, but not yet. Not yet." The voice drifted away, and Zander found himself sending thanks out to the great void as he closed his eyes.

Brit Malorie

Chapter 52

The first thing he felt was pure exhaustion beyond even his heaviest drug-filled days on Kadera. Zander ran his fingers up and down his arms, then sat up and reached for his feet. He was all here. He sat back in bed, exhilarated. Hadley lay asleep against the side of the bed, and there were two pink fingerprint indentations on his palm. She must have been passing positive miran through him for hours.

He patted her head. The sweet relief on her face was more than he could bear. He let out a groan as she hugged him.

"I think that was my eighth life," he said.

"Bumbles will let you borrow some of his. He loves you too," Hadley whispered. The cat sprawled on the corner of the bed. His paws felt the blanket until he found feet underneath. His fangs hovered over the big toe, then chomped down. Zander jerked his foot away.

"Why is he always attacking my toes?"

"Perfect snack size." Hadley grinned.

"Sorry, Bumbles, I'm not lunch just yet," he laughed. "Everyone else okay?"

"Yeah. Phina left. Errands in Paris." She crinkled her nose.

"You didn't like her? I sure did."

"There's something mean about her, something only other girls can see. Besides, there's enough blondes around here." She laughed at her own joke.

"Agreed." Zander hesitated. His memory itched with the remnants of a dream. Something about Masterfade and a sleepy country town in Europe.

He patted her head again. "I want to see everyone, but could you get Bryn first?" Hadley grinned and headed out.

A minute later, Bryn rushed inside. She hugged him tightly, her hands touching his face, his shoulders, his body. "I can't believe you're here, you're alive," she murmured. He kissed her deeply and laced her fingers with his. "Hi."

"Hi," he murmured. She gave him a weak smile, her eyes puffy and bloodshot but still achingly beautiful. Heaven. He touched her face and she leaned into his hand.

"Hey, there's something I want to tell you." His thumb caressed her bottom lip.

"Oh, yeah?"

"Elder showed me his accident. He showed me what happened."

A tense look crossed her face and color rose up in her cheeks. She pushed his hand away.

"Hey, you can't blame yourself for what you did at thirteen. Just like I can't keep reliving all the terrible things in my past. Look at me, Bryn." He tilted her face back to him. "You don't have to feel bad anymore. Your dad loves you. Think about it, okay?"

She nodded. There were shouts outside in the hallway and the door opened. Everyone piled into the room and he got several hugs. Warmth flooded him and he grew breathless. His family.

"I hope I didn't cause too much trouble," he said, his voice creaking.

"Oh, you've been nothing but trouble from the beginning," Brecker laughed. "You know I'm not a praying man, but thank God you made it back home."

They chatted for a few minutes until Brecker asked everyone to let him rest. The doctor squeezed his shoulder before leaving, his eyes full of relief.

***

That afternoon, Bryn lay stretched out on the grass in the backyard. She thought about her father, about the last ten years. Every time she'd imagine traveling, she'd see Dad's face crushed in disappointment and anger, a man filled with wretched hate. But he'd forgiven her a long time ago. Why had it taken her so long to see that the past didn't matter? She felt this incredible release inside her. Everything would be okay.

Bryn sighed deeply. Except everything wasn't okay. Despite touching him and talking with him, she couldn't believe Zander was actually alive. There was a new edge, a feeling that she could lose everything she loved at any moment. It was all catching up with her—Lynch and the trauma in Miami, her father's frail body here, and now Zander.

She made her way through Grace House up to his room. Nora was inside, gathering the bedsheets. "Oh, Zander's down in Dr. Brecker's office, dear. Moving a bit slower, but that boy's head never leaves the research," she clucked.

Bryn took the elevator down, needing to be near him for a while, even if she had to hear scientific chatter. She stopped just outside the office door.

"Why didn't I see it?" Brecker said, his voice incredulous. "I was there. It felt strangely familiar, but—"

"Hell, I lived on Kadera for a year and I couldn't see it. I think the island's been twisted somehow. There were years of experimentation there," Zander replied. "Who knows what they did to it? What Dad did to it."

"What are we going to do? If that monster Lynch penetrates the Veil, he and the Vipera will be impossible to stop."

"I know," Zander said grimly. "The Masterfade will give them permanent access."

"I thought it was just a myth. Jason never found anything."

"I think I may know where it is. If the device exists, we can't let Lynch get his hands on it," he groaned. "I'll have to leave again."

Bryn rested her head against the wall. It's what she didn't hear. The hesitation, the underlying need to escape. Both absent from his voice. Zander was committed. A full traveler and scientist, just like his father. Maglia above all else.

Vita Maglia

329

Something inside her crumbled. She couldn't go through it again. Waiting by his bedside, next to his body while he was dying far away. She startled as Nora came up behind her. The woman clasped a slim journal in her hands, the thick pages frayed and secured with a rubberband, her face looking wistful.

"Isn't it wonderful?" she whispered to Bryn. "He's growing into the man Jason envisioned, dedicating his life to the research. I think he's finally ready for this." Nora caressed the shiny surface of the journal, then pressed it to her chest.

"He'll leave," Bryn whispered.

"Yes. And we'll wait for him here, like always."

"I won't."

Surprise clouded Nora's face as Bryn pushed past her down the hall. She ran outside and up the path to the woods, the space where she could dance and think and be alone. A shudder ran through her. She couldn't keep losing what she loved. Every time Zander took a trip, she'd wonder if he'd wake up. The only way they could be together was far from Grace House. Far from this damn discovery that would destroy their lives without a second thought. She remembered the coyote pup on their hike, the way Zander had stared at it, craving his freedom so badly. He just needed a way out. If she asked him to go with her, he would. Love pulsed up through her heart and fluttered outward. He'd choose her.

Chapter 53

Zander wiped his sweaty hands on the side of his jeans. Bryn had asked him to meet out here at dusk, but she looked a little wild as she paced inside a patch of trees. The air hinted of smoke—a distant fire? Branches broke above and something howled, calling out the first of the stars.

Gathering his courage, he walked out. A blush-pink cotton dress wrapped her body and brushed the tops of her knees. She let out a little shiver. It was cool for late summer and she only wore a light denim jacket over her dress.

"Hey." He hugged her tightly, his hands lingering around her waist. "What are you doing out here? I looked for you all day and couldn't find you."

"Just thinking," she murmured.

"Hmm . . . sounds like ominous female code," he joked. Her eyes flickered to the driveway.

There was so much to say, but his mouth went dry. "Bryn," he tilted her chin forward. "Look at me, okay? What's the matter? Are you still upset about your dad?"

She shook her head. "No, that's not it."

Zander leaned in, his voice husky. "I came back for you. So we could be together."

"But for how long?" Her words sliced the air.

He drew back. She kept looking at the driveway. He turned to see what had her attention. A black truck sat there, its engine humming in the night. "Why is there—" He tilted her head up, but she refused to look at him. "Wait. You're leaving? Why?"

There was urgency in her voice. "Come with me. You have your inheritance now, we can go anywhere."

He stood still, completely bewildered. "That money's for the research. It wouldn't be ours."

Her lip trembled. "Why should I stay, Zander? So I can wait around this place," she gestured widely, "for you not to come home?"

"What's that supposed to mean?" he groaned. "You're afraid, I know. But you have to face those fears. You can't just run from them. We can build a life together."

He softened and leaned into her. "Please stay. You'll be safe here."

"But you won't be. I can't go through what I just did, again and again."

Zander paused, considering. He hadn't realized how much the last few days had affected her. But Maglia was worth the risk. Why couldn't she see that? He touched her face and felt tears. "Hey, listen to me. I'm sorry about everything that happened, but it'll be okay. We'll be okay."

Bryn crossed her arms and looked away. Anxiety rose up in him—she didn't understand. He had to convince her.

"I'm not doing this right." Zander unbuttoned the top of his shirt. He took her hand and slid it inside the fabric, moving it over his bare chest to his scar.

"I want you to feel my heart as I say this," he murmured. "You make me believe in Maglia, more than anything I've seen or felt there." He raised her wrist and pressed it to his lips. "Our strands are connected above us, but that's nothing compared to how they'll be in twenty years. Our love will mean so much more. Please stay."

Bryn looked at him clearly, her chin defiant. "Could you stand by and watch while I died in a faraway place? With no way to save me?" She shook her head. "You can't ask me to go through that again."

"You won't have to."

"Stop." Her voice shook and she wiped at her eyes. "Oh God, Zander, I have to go."

He pulled her close, then trailed soft kisses up her neck, her chin, the tip of her nose. His lips rested on her temple as he whispered against her skin. "You're inside me."

It must have been residue from Aron Alyce, but he could make out the edges of Bryn's aura—the deepest emerald color lined her hair, her face, her eyes. Glints of spring green and aquamarine.

Tiny shoots of gray vapor curled out from her aura, webbing through the emerald like smoke. Ache flared inside him.

"I'm hurting you," he said. "I can feel it too. I'll stop, Bryn. I'll leave you alone. Of course, you have the right—"

She stopped him with her mouth. Her tongue slipped gently inside and met his, then flicked along his lips, the heat making him crazy. His hands moved over her dress like they could melt into the fabric. Sparks raced in his blood and he tried to breathe, so dizzy with her scent.

The van's engine shut off. The stillness intruded and she startled. Backing away, she increased the distance between them until only their fingers touched.

"Come with me, Zander. I can't stay here. I'm not ready for all this sacrifice."

He looked up at Grace House. His home, his family. He closed his eyes, thinking of the breeze that swept through his form during the healing. Tomas's words. Stepping forward into the Valley. Forgiving himself. An impulse greater than anything he'd ever felt, coming from a place he'd never see.

Zander pulled her forward and kissed her deeply, holding her, breathing her in. His voice cracked. He didn't recognize his own words. "I am ready for that sacrifice. I can't go with you."

Bryn stared at him with stunned amazement. Rocking backward, she turned and ran to the driveway.

"Wait. It'll get better!" he shouted, reaching for her. The blur of her legs, she was too damn fast. Still, he almost caught her. The truck door banged shut right as his hands slammed the metal. "Stop the truck," he shouted. "Stop it!"

Her voice called from inside, "No. Drive. Just keep driving."

Brit Malorie

Chapter 54

Gradually, he began to recognize sounds—the breeze rippling the surface of the pond, shuffling in the treetops. His heart finally slowed. His mind could not grasp what just happened. Bryn was gone. He had to force air into his lungs; it wouldn't come on its own. How could she just leave? He meant nothing to her.

Zander wanted to go home now. He walked into Grace House and up to his old room. Heartache ripped through him and crushed every muscle, every inch of skin. He curled his body into a tight ball and shoved his face into the pillow. He was split in half, a knife searing through his organs, hollowing him out. Drugs. The craving rocked his mind. He had to get her out of him somehow.

He slid the panel out of his dresser, then sat down on his bed, caressing the bottle. Wait. He gritted his teeth and punched the pillow. Where was that strength, that same resilience that made him enter the Valley? He thought of his gift from the Vipera—the vision of him failing, everyone hating him, a coward with no willpower, Maglia burning—all the beauty and sparkle and light extinguished forever. Waves of ache flooded his heart. He couldn't do it.

He'd already given up Bryn for the discovery. The choice was made, and now there was nothing left but to live with it. He went into the bathroom and flushed the pills.

The next morning, he didn't recognize himself in the mirror. His eyes were empty and bloodshot, his skin stretched and haggard. Like a zombie. He'd barely slept an hour last night. But he awoke with these words on his mind: "A device that allows the user to travel, regardless of genes or tricks or open roads. They'd have unlimited access." Where had that come from? Details swiftly came back to him. Masterfade. A distraction from his anguish, a new obsession. An image of Lynch came to him, the man reaching for the device, a look of triumph on his face. If he got ahold of the Masterfade, it was all over. And the man was already looking for it.

After packing his suitcase, Zander choked down a quick breakfast. He stopped by Brecker's office and surveyed the stacks of files and papers. It felt like years had passed since that stupid junkie had rolled his wheelchair in here, searching for dirt on the Pensare.

He told Brecker his new plan. The doctor nodded. "I hate for you to leave with so little information, but if you think they're close to the device, you have to go. Should I send GUT with you?"

"I'll let you know when I need them."

"You'll have all the money you require." Brecker embraced him. "I've always felt like you were my own son, Zander. You've made me prouder than I ever thought I could be. I'm sorry about Bryn. She told me last night."

Zander held himself still and took a shallow breath. "I can't think about that now."

"There's something else. I'm not sure how to say this, but your uncle—" Brecker balled up his fist. "The nurse mentioned that she saw Seth leaving your room. I mean, well, he was alone in there. . . ."

"What is it?" Zander stole a peek at his watch. He had to visit someone important before his flight left.

Brecker smiled uneasily. "Nevermind. You have enough to deal with."

***

Hadley paced in the entryway. Everything was falling apart. Bryn left without saying goodbye. Zander looked horrible, his eyes sunken in, restless. What was going on? Her legs and arms wiggled, full of pins and needles. Bumbles crouched next to her, the olive green eyes tracking her movements. He let out a squeak.

"I don't know, I don't know," she said. She wanted to break apart her shield more than ever.

The elevator door opened and Zander came out with a suitcase in his hand. Startled, Hadley felt tears in her eyes.

"Where are you going?"

"I have to leave for a while. It'll be okay." He lifted her up and gave her a hug.

"This is stupid. You're so stupid," she shouted. Things couldn't be that bad. How could he just go after everything they'd been through?

He set her down and kissed the top of her head. She grabbed his legs and pulled backward ferociously. Zander gently removed her arms then got down on his knees. "Hadders, I have to do this. Look at me. *Look at me.*"

She shook her head in jerky motions. "No, no, no."

"You have to trust me. If I don't go, we'll lose everything."

"You can't go! You can't." The tears streamed down her face, all the emotions jumbled inside her. This felt very, very bad.

"But, but," she sputtered. "You'll be alone out there. I can't protect you."

He touched her face gently. "I'm gonna miss you. Keep things running around here. Keep Bumbles on his diet, okay? No matter how much he complains."

Someone walked up behind her. Hands clamped down on her shoulders. "Let him go, Hadley," Dr. Brecker said.

"She didn't mean it," Hadley called out, struggling under his grip. "Whatever Bryn said, she didn't mean it. She'll come back!"

He hesitated, then shut the front door after him. The truck door slammed outside. Dr. Brecker's hands let go and Hadley ran out.

"Zander!" she yelled. She sprinted after the black truck, but it was going too fast and her legs were too small. She swerved up one of the hilly inclines. The truck curved around the road. Hopping over bushes and large branches on the trail, her sneakers slid in the dirt. If she could just make it to the top, she could almost see him. Hadley pumped her legs but didn't see the stupid rock. She crashed hard, skidding across the ground, her lungs burning. Pain shot up her shins and elbows. Rocking back and forth, she tried to catch an inch of air. By the time she stood up, the black speck had disappeared.

Chapter 55

Lynch walked farther down into the tunnels until he entered a new cavern. Screeches and wails echoed off the volcanic rock. Damaris shouted at a group of men in the corner. A dark creature, the source of the noise, quivered there. That alone would not have been strange, but the thing was shimmer and shadow.

"Add more lead dust. We have to weigh it down. Whatever it is," Damaris said. A pan of lead powder dropped from overhead. The thing shrieked, the cries penetrating Lynch's eardrums. It streaked the air and spewed black dust on the cavern floor.

"It's not made of anything," Lynch said, entranced.

"Yes. Control is impossible without adding matter to it," Damaris replied. "These are the damn things that destroy anyone we send. We have to figure out some kind of shield." He paused, his face thoughtful. "Or a truce."

Lynch studied the man. He'd learned so much over the last few days. Damaris had studied physics at several universities in Europe. Ten years ago, he came here to study the remnants of a meteor that landed roughly two million years ago. The meteor was embedded in the ocean floor just off the coast of the island and carried minerals found nowhere else on earth. About fifty thousand years ago, two underwater volcanoes erupted nearly simultaneously, creating damage similar to the Krakatoa eruption in Indonesia in 1883, the force equivalent to one million hydrogen bombs. The lava flows had lasted decades, creating the broad network of lava tubes under the island's surface. This massive explosion caused most of the meteor to vaporize and enter the sky along with clouds of superheated gas.

The combination of this immense energy blast and the meteoric minerals destroyed five layers of the Veil permanently. High energy surges or gamma radiation could be used to disrupt the sixth, but the last layer was the strongest. There were only certain times of the season they could even try as the Veil's strength waxed and waned during the year.

Besides strengthening the last two layers of the Veil, Jason Grace also stole a large portion of the meteoric minerals for whatever concoction Zander must be using to travel. Then he created a small explosion on Kadera's western rim, burying the last remnants of the meteor under the ocean floor.

The two men watched the Vipera as it struggled against the extra weight of the lead powder. It turned the demon into a great cluster of inky ribbons, furling out in spools. It didn't know what it wanted to be. One moment its tentacles unlocked, hitting the ground with smacks like a giant squid, then it had pincers, then claws that dragged on the cavern floor. Human faces appeared grotesquely on its surface only to cry out in pain and gush open. A black tentacle jetted out and tore off one of the worker's arms. The flesh burst apart and blood splashed on the rock floor. Screams climbed the cavern walls. Neither man noticed.

"Try the cage," Damaris shouted out.

"A simple cage won't work," Lynch said.

A steel cage lowered over the shadow. The Vipera let out a howl, lashing out through the bars, but remained trapped. It shrunk in on itself rather than touch the steel.

Damaris smiled. "You're right. But a cage with electrified aluminum plates? The thing seems to be repelled by positive charge."

He called out to the men. "Bring some bodies down. I want to see it destroy. The living and the dead."

"A charged cage. Brilliant. Her idea?" Lynch said.

"Of course," Damaris replied, a thread of reverence in his voice.

"So this Vipera creature crossed through the glass panel?" Lynch asked.

"Yes. It was a particularly strong hour for a crossing, or so these Polynesian priests tell me. Full of sun symbols and seasonal omens and boogedy-boo," Damaris scoffed. They'd been going back to the old native rituals in the hopes of breaking apart the seventh Veil layer permanently.

He spit on the floor. "Fucking herbs. Fucking ritual bullshit. It all pales in comparison to those damn minerals. Jason Grace cost me years."

He smiled. "But there's another solution on the horizon. We know where his son is going next. And we're going to need the device he's searching for."

Excitement pooled in Lynch's gut. "How?"

"We have an ally on the other side. He wants Grace distracted. It should work to our mutual benefit."

His eyes held Lynch's. "Listen to me now. You must follow Grace. Wait—" Damaris raised a finger. "—wait until the kid has what we need. Only then do you capture him. Grace must be alive."

Lynch nodded. He had no problem with alive. Alive meant the most fun. Alive did not mean intact.

The older man studied him. "Can I trust you to complete this mission? You know Grace, his strategies, his flaws. The soft places he'll retreat for. Yet for some reason unknown to me, you haven't remained objective. I cannot protect you with another failure."

"It's done," Lynch replied. He moved over to the cage to lay down on his side, his face close to the creature. Amazingly, the Vipera calmed. It spread along the bars, hovering near the steel. Damaris was wrong. It wasn't an animal. Lynch closed his eyes. It was an abyss and it matched the one inside him.

His past and his great future flowed before him. Petal, all of his kills, his victories. A tingling in his center—the creature was searching for his strand to connect with. An alliance. He'd be given strength in order to defeat Zander and those light creatures that aided him.

Kadera wasn't enough for him anymore. What was earthly suffering compared to the eternal? Why be content with a man's surface when one could devour his soul? Lynch shivered, imagining the sheer volume of pain he could inflict with all his limitations gone.

A great new hatred entered his heart. He would capture Zander Grace. He would take all that the man loved, including this new world, and when his mind broke, Lynch would watch with the greatest satisfaction of his life.

He must return to his true love. For others that love was money or drugs or women. For Lynch Katlan it was to plan, to let time build walls around his prey. Until the precise moment to put things right.

Chapter 56

The truck traveled into Aspen and approached Red Butte Cemetery. "I'll only be a couple of minutes," Zander said.

"Just a few. There's a flight to catch," the driver replied.

The sun shone low in the sky. He walked up the path, searching the rows, until he finally spied a small enclosure kept apart from the rest of the cemetery. He bent down in front of the two headstones and picked up a handful of dirt, feeling the grit on his skin. His hands scissored, letting the grains fall on stone.

His voice wavered. "I'm glad I came home, Dad. I haven't changed much, I mean," He choked a little. "I wish I could be brave."

His first memory darted across his mind of his mother rocking him to sleep. He kept falling in her arms, gently falling with no end. "No matter the world, we'll have each other. My love will protect you forever."

He bowed his head and caressed the granite headstones. "I'm not sure what lies beyond the Calamata, but I know you can feel me," he murmured, his fingertips digging into the stone, wishing it to be so.

He headed back to the waiting vehicle and slid inside, careful to keep his face tilted away.

They drove down to the entrance and took a right. They passed the houses and stores that lined Aspen. Zander ran his fingers down the hard surface of the journal Nora gave him as he packed his suitcase. She told him: "Jason gave me this before he died. It's about his time in Kadera. He made me promise to only give it to you when you were ready."

There were ridges left from ripped-out pages. He tipped the journal back until he found the last page and the sharp lines of his father's writing. "Zander sleeps now, only eight years old, but I see the man he will become. What kind of sacrifices will he have to make? How can I leave this burden for him?"

He tucked the photo of the Polynesian girl into the page. The barest hint of a smile troubled her lips, an otherworldly light in her eyes. What had she meant to his father? Had they been in love?

Love. He looked up at the trees. The streams, the woods. His home.

"Stop," he said. The driver looked at him in the rearview and pulled over to the shoulder. "Go back."

"Are you sure?" The man asked, his fingers lightly tapping the wheel.

Zander sat silent, not knowing the answer. Everything he loved was back there. He closed his eyes. Not everything. He could almost hear her breathe, the delicate pressure of her head curled into his neck.

He couldn't stay here. Not without her.

"Tick tock."

Zander startled and glanced up at the driver. Where had that come from? His heart felt hard in his chest, the string of Kadera shells rolling between his fingers. There were other mysteries to solve.

He looked out the window, already missing his life. "Nevermind. Let's go." The words stayed on his lips. *Let go.*

The driver whistled and slowly pulled back onto the road.

Chapter 57

Seth Grace leaned on his cane while he waited outside on the stone walkway. He rested in the shadow of the great house his family built and the research it would become famous for. After Zander's unfortunate accident, he'd quickly left for St. Sebastian, where eventually Brecker confronted him. Seth had simply replied that the boy was fine, perfectly fine when he'd left him. When that explanation failed to satisfy, Seth said he'd felt dizzy at the time and had needed his medication upstairs in his room. Brecker turned from him then, a mixture of confusion and anger on his face. Perhaps this was not the first time the doctor had suspected him. No matter.

There might be a few more unsavory acts before all was done but they were justified now. The Lord had shown that He was firmly on Seth's side by saving the boy's life and clearing the path for Calvin to take over.

Seth tapped his cane on the natural stone. He'd actually felt a bit relieved when his nephew woke up. Obviously Zander was meant to play a part here. The boy also couldn't have picked a better time to run away again. Everything was about to change.

An Escalade pulled around the corner and stopped. The truck's sidedoor opened and a threadbare suitcase toppled to the pavement. A man stepped out, his skin still pale despite years in the Italian sun, the lines of his body sharp against the sky. Loose blond curls floated around his face, his hazel eyes covered by amber sunglasses. Heavy gold flashed just under the neckline of his linen shirt.

The young man stepped forward and made the sign of the cross. Dropping down to one knee, he kissed Seth's hand.

"Hello Papa."

Brit Malorie

Acknowledgements

I'd like to thank all of my friends and family who have given me advice and support during the creation of this work, including my second family at SMRTL.

I'd like to thank my mentor and great friend, Mary Phillips, for taking two years of her life to spend on a sad little writer who drifted in from the rain. You may be a "mean, vicious, downright cold-hearted old woman," but the book is a thousand times better because of it.

My beta-readers provided valuable insight during this process. Thank you to Kathy Weber, Danielle Clifford, Kayla Blonquist, Margene Fox, Kim Weber, Will Kenyon, and David Payne.

I'd like to thank Evan Mark, who showed me a wonderful new way to see the world and opened up my life forever.

I'd like to send a special thanks out to Judy Field, the poor soul who was forced to endure endless cat stories and tidal waves of artist angst yet never turned me away.

Lastly, I must send love to my mercury, a true angel and the inspiration for Aron Alyce.

10211958R10212

Made in the USA
San Bernardino, CA
09 April 2014